L. C Aaron

Rev. Samuel Aaron

His Life, Sermons, Correspondence, etc.

L. C Aaron

Rev. Samuel Aaron
His Life, Sermons, Correspondence, etc.

ISBN/EAN: 9783744746779

Printed in Europe, USA, Canada, Australia, Japan

Cover: Foto ©Raphael Reischuk / pixelio.de

More available books at **www.hansebooks.com**

HIS LIFE,
SERMONS, CORRESPONDENCE, ETC.

PUBLISHED BY REQUEST.

NORRISTOWN, PA.:
1890.

INTRODUCTION.

At the request of a number of the friends of the late Rev. Samuel Aaron this volume has been prepared. I regret exceedingly that so few of his sermons, lectures, speeches, etc., have been preserved. A number of the sermons are largely notes of sermons, just as Mr. Aaron prepared them for his own use. That the work may prove a source of pleasure, as well as of profit, to those who read it, is my earnest wish.

L. C. Aaron.

CONTENTS.

CONTENTS.

REV. SAMUEL AARON.

Samuel Aaron was born in New Britain township, Bucks county, Pa., October 19, 1800; and the old house where he was born is still standing, but has undergone numerous alterations and repairs, so that there are now but few traces of the original building left. He was of Welsh-Irish extraction; his father being of Welsh and his mother of Irish descent. The offspring of a second marriage of his father, he was the youngest but one of four brothers; the family consisting also of three sisters.

His father, Moses Aaron, a farmer in respectable circumstances, was a member of the Baptist church, and a man of sincere and humble piety, who endeavored, both by precept and example, to train up his children in the nurture and admonition of the Lord. His son Samuel always cherished the highest esteem for his character, and most filial respect for his memory, and was accustomed to speak of him in simple but expressive and comprehensive language as emphatically "a good man."

The second wife of Moses Aaron was Miss Hannah Kelly, a native of Hilltown, Bucks county, Pa. She was also a consistent member of the Baptist church; a woman of piety and social worth. She died when the subject of our sketch was but three years of age, and at the age of six he had the misfortune to lose his father also.

Left an orphan at this tender age, he was placed under the care and control of an uncle, a kind-hearted man by nature, but unfortunately addicted to habits of intemperance. The little boy was frequently obliged to trudge bare-footed to the village store and back with the jug of liquor, and often felt tempted to break it against the stones along the road. He was compelled also to carry it to the men in the harvest field, and hated to do it. His uncle was very cruel when intoxicated, and his little nephew would frequently hide in the barn to escape undeserved punishment, and wish that he could die. The sad condition of his guardian's family and business affairs, and the neglectful treatment he received then, made him in after life the terrible enemy he was of every form of intemperance.

Samuel, with his brothers and sisters, attended school at New Britain, and the former learned rapidly, and was noted for his intellectual ability when a mere boy. At school he read aloud in "Sanford and Merton"; and his voice was so clear, and he spoke so distinctly, that he presented a great contrast to the other boys. He was kind and polite to the girls, and a favorite with them. An old lady (who is still living) who went to school with him when he was a small boy, said lately, that on cold winter mornings he would keep at a distance from the fire in the school-room, and say to the other boys, "stand back, boys, and let the girls have the warm seats." As he set the example, the boys could not refuse to receive his advice and do as he did. He was fond of wrestling, playing ball, skating, and other athletic sports, and entered into them with all his heart; but he had at the same time an equally active brain; composed verses, rhymes, etc. He had a quick and violent temper, but brought it completely under control after he became a Christian. He worked upon his uncle's farm for several years, attending school during the winter months, and there imbibing that taste for reading and study which afterwards, in connection with his great natural endowments, enabled him to become such an accomplished scholar and well-informed man.

After leaving his uncle he went to live with 'Squire Roberts, and attended school at Montgomery Square, Pa. His teacher, Mr. Collom, an excellent, mild-tempered man and a capable scholar, was exceedingly kind to his youthful pupil, and encouraged him to cultivate the talents he possessed. This kindness was never forgotten, and was often referred to in after years by Mr. Aaron, who cherished the memory of his former teacher, and always spoke of him in the highest terms of admiration, respect and affection.

At sixteen years of age, obtaining a small patrimony inherited from his father, Samuel entered the Academy of Rev. U. Du Bois, at Doylestown, Pa. In referring to that event years afterwards, he says:

"In the Spring of 1817, I was first introduced to the knowledge and notice of the Rev. U. Du Bois. I had not unfrequently seen him in public, and heard him from the pulpit; but at that time it was decided by my guardian, a respectable old farmer, that I should receive from him some lessons in the ancient classics. I was dispatched alone to negotiate my admittance into his school; and with not a little bashful reluctance, greedy as I was for that sort of knowledge, I presented myself and my purpose to Mr. Du Bois. I have the most vivid remembrance of the interview; of my own rustic dress and appearance contrasted with his perfectly genteel form and bearing; how he fixed at first his black eyes upon me, sparkling through his spectacles; how he smiled hope and encouragement upon me when he heard I had come to woo the Muses; how eloquent was every look and word in praise of learning and the learned; how he spoke of bright men who had risen from what is called humble life, and amongst others of Mr. ——, then far advanced in years and intellectual honors, though in early life the teacher of a common school. In a few minutes he put me at my ease; made me feel I was more than a clumsy cipher in the human series, and strengthening the determination in my soul to be useful, virtuous and intelligent. From that hour until his death, his kindness beamed upon me without variation or eclipse; in spite of all that was weak and all that was wrong in my course, his affection was that of a father and a friend. He had no peculiar, far-fetched modes of thinking or of teaching. He seems to me now to have adapted, with sound common sense, his workmanship to such tools and materials as he had. He succeeded well, I think, in educating, that is, drawing out, the powers of almost all who had anything in them; whether he toiled enough to fill up empty or leaky skulls, I dare not undertake to say."

The boys at the Academy looked upon the new pupil with great admiration, when they heard that "that boy has been through the arithmetic."

At twenty he connected himself with the Classical and Mathematical School of John Gummere, at Burlington, N. J., as both a student and assistant teacher. While there he became a favorite with teachers and pupils, corresponded with many of them for years, and retained them as friends through life.

While at school in Burlington he decided not to remain a teacher very long, as he thought he was not fitted for the work, and shrank from the responsibility. His friends thought he underrated his abilities, and it is probable he did so.

In the Spring of 1821, having completed his education, he returned to Doylestown, Pa., to assist Rev. Du Bois in the Academy, and remained there for some months. Before leaving Burlington he received the following testimonial of respect from some of his friends:

"BURLINGTON, N. J., February 1, 1821.

We, the undersigned, have agreed, as a testimonial of respect for Mr. Samuel Aaron, that we will give him a supper at Wilde's Tavern, on the evening previous to his leaving Burlington, and we appoint Mr. Valentine and Mr. Bennett to order it at such time, and to notify us. Wm. Kimber, John L. Newbold, Wm. R. Richardson, James H. Bennett, G. Black, C. Holmes, J. Elkinton, Esq., Samuel S. Grubb, John M. Brown, B. B. Pittman, Wm. Valentine."

In March, 1821, one of his Burlington school friends wrote him as follows:

"I saw a letter from a young man in Doylestown, who spoke very much in thy praise; said thou wast considered fully competent to teach the Latin and Greek languages, and gave his opinion that thou wouldst make out very well in the Academy. It is a frequent fault with mankind to overvalue their abilities, but I think thee underrates thine. I can assure thee thou art regarded as a paragon by the students of this school, and I believe thou art by our teachers also. The young man who wrote the letter I have just referred to, observed that 'the learned feared yet loved thee.' I have not mentioned these circumstances to flatter thee, but I want thou shouldst duly appreciate thy abilities."

Some time after a friend wrote:

"Guess what I have heard about you since I have been in this place. Why, that you have the name of being the best reader in the United States. Don't let it make you vain."

In 1822, at the earnest solicitation of John Gummere, Mr. Aaron returned to Burlington, and again taught for Mr. G——. He was there until 1824, when he married Emilia, eldest daughter of his old friend and preceptor, Rev. U. Du Bois, and not long after that event he left Burlington and opened a day school at Bridge Point, about two miles from Doylestown.

Remaining there but a short time, he next became principal of Doylestown Academy, and was there for a year or two.

Upon his return to Burlington he was offered an excellent position in Philadelphia, but declined, because he was too independent to be under the control of others. He now decided to study law, and many of his friends were willing to aid him, as they were desirous that he should make the law his profession. One of his intimate friends in Philadelphia, who was deeply interested in the matter, sent him the following letter:

"PHILADELPHIA, December 3, 1826.

Dear Samuel.—Your letter of the 31st ult. came to-day. I rejoice in the adoption of your present resolution. It has always appeared to me, and I hope my views were correct, that the frame of your mind was better adapted to law, and that law would be more in unison with your taste than the drudgery of disciplining youth, and I exhort you to go on with the law. Let me not hear of your mind's repenting after you begin. Think not, until you have given the law a full experiment, of returning to teaching. You know your own powers. When you have deliberately determined, destroy the bridge that you cannot recross. * * * It makes my heart sick, such is my interest in you, to think of your longer delaying. The time passed in teaching has grounded you well in science, and where that is, the superstructure may be lofty. * * * If you are in haste to become a lawyer, you can study a year in Burlington, another here, and gain admission to Common Pleas. * * * I believe I have answered all your questions. Should you embrace the law as a profession, you shall receive the most strenuous aid of your friend; and think not this will be a one-sided connection. If you avail yourself of my books and office, I want you to become my preceptor, and give me instruction in the Greek language, one hour each week. I can advise you in legal pursuits, and after you have passed two years in the novitiate, Mr. Chauncey will introduce you to the court.

Yours sincerely,   J. R. W."

Previous to the receipt of the letter quoted above, Mr. Aaron wrote to a friend, as follows:

"There is much truth and force in the views you offer with respect to our —— scheme, and I will consider them well. Perhaps after all it may be impracticable for me ever to change my avocation as a teacher. If so, my opportunities here for acquiring information are superior to what they could be there; and I trust that with the industry I am now using, and which I do most seriously mean to continue, I will be able after a while to engage in something better than my present business with a fairer prospect of success. It is a question worth considering whether I am really fitted for conducting the education of youth. I speak of it in its widest sense. Those parents, whose children I should prefer, would hardly think so. It is not my own pecuniary interest I am to consider; it behooves me to regard seriously the circumstances of those placed under my care as affected by that relation with me."

Always a youth of pure morals and exemplary habits, Mr. Aaron, in the year 1826, made a profession of religion, and became a member of the Baptist church, at Burlington, N. J. Some months after that he gave up the idea of becoming a lawyer; was ordained as a minister, and in 1828 became pastor of the church at New Britain, Pa.

He retained the position but a year, when he felt obliged to resign on account of his arduous duties as a teacher, being at that time principal of the Doylestown Academy. He feared that he could not go as well prepared as he wished to the pulpit; but the church was unwilling to give him up. An aged Baptist minister wrote for his encouragement:

"I do know, or think I know, that the friends at New Britain have always been satisfied and more than satisfied with thy sermons; they have been edified and often enraptured. Don't relinquish preaching, my brother; the Lord is always ready to direct and assist by his spirit and influence. He hath said: Lo, I am with you always," etc.

In February, 1830, Mr. Aaron's wife died, and three years after, in April, 1833, he married Eliza G., daughter of Samuel Currie, a farmer of New Britain Township. Immediately after his marriage he started on a tour, extending through several of the Western states, with the intention of settling there if he found a place to suit him. But just after leaving home he was met by John Gummere and Charles Atherton, who persuaded him to give up his plan of finding a home in the West, and settle in Burlington, N. J., when he returned from his trip.

In connection with Charles Atherton, he took charge of the Burlington High School, formerly kept by John Gummere. In a year or two Mr. Aaron became sole principal, and the school attained a very flourishing condition. In addition to conducting this large school, he was for five years pastor of the Burlington Baptist church. At this time he wrote to a friend:

"I am likely to have my hands full of labors and my mind of cares of the most weighty kind; for, in addition to the school, the little church here needs the service of somebody that will work for nothing and find himself. The morality of a great many in Burlington is more unexceptionable than common; and that the religion of the place might become more animated and more general is my fervent desire."

His school was highly recommended by the New Jersey Baptist Association as one likely to afford candidates for the ministry; the best preparations in the shortest time. This institution was under the direction of the Central Education Board, appointed by a convention formed out of the Baptist churches in the middle states. "In December, 1834," so the

minutes of the Association stated, "Rev. Samuel Aaron and
Rev. H. K. Green were engaged as professors in the Burlington Seminary. Theological students were received at seventy-
five dollars per annum, which included board and tuition."
In 1836 there was a minute again commending the Burlington Institute.

In 1837 Mr. Aaron was asked to take charge of Had-
dington College, but declined the proposition in the following
words:

"Having reflected on the subject pretty fully since I saw you, I beg leave
to say that no inducement of which I am at all aware would move me to leave my
present situation for a similar employment. Here I am not under the control of
others; elsewhere it might be different; as I am, merit or demerit is awarded as
it deserves; the caprice of individuals might modify that result in a public school.
Besides, I have now a fine school of about seventy scholars, which should not, I
think, be rashly left for an uncertainty."

At another time he says:

"As to the bestowal of gratuitous education upon young men, very few, in
my opinion, possessing good talents and noble principles, would accept of it. I
hardly dare speak my views of academic education in this age of splendid theories
and multiplied experiments. The judicious and conscientious instructor of a human
creature will certainly regard him as a moral, rational and corporeal being, and bestow upon his heart, mind and body respectively a due proportion of attention.
The first of these departments of his labor will receive his greatest and most constant care. As the mother minds her tottering babe not to punish its missteps but
to prevent its fall, so will the good teacher incessantly watch over his youthful
charge not to detect and chastise but to prevent obliquity of principle. He will use
his utmost exertions to preserve them from vicious associations, knowing that the
heart of youth, like the heated wax, receives and long retains the likeness of what
impresses it. Above all, the most important part of an academic education is to
have a teacher who lives as one that expects to bear a scrutiny that regards moral
principles only, and not the rational or physical powers except as the used or abused
instruments of the soul. Truth and frankness on the part of pupils towards their
preceptor will follow the use of such means, and he may with reason expect their
manhood to be crowned with virtue and their immortality with happiness. To a
young American the most important mental acquirement is, in my humble opinion,
a thorough knowledge of our own strong and beautiful language, to which all other
early studies, classical and scientific, should be regarded as merely subsidiary. For
the master spirits of the world are not those whose skill in science has made earth,
sea and air pay tribute to the intellectual and corporeal wants of man, but those
whose tongues and pens have thrown light and heat upon his soul, and thus enabled it to know and enjoy the rights, the virtues and the glorious hopes which its
author has bestowed."

While living in Burlington Mr. Aaron frequently delivered
public addresses upon questions of reform and lectures upon
scientific subjects, thus manifesting that capacity for varied and
exacting labor and that disposition for extended usefulness
which so eminently distinguished him during his entire career.

In 1836 he was presented with a handsome silver plate,
bearing this inscription, "To the Rev. Samuel Aaron, from a
few friends, who have derived much profit and pleasure from
his lectures in Natural Philosophy, before the Burlington Lyceum, 1836."

In April, 1841, Mr. Aaron was called to take charge of
the Norristown Baptist Church, at the same time re-opening
a select school for boys formerly kept by Wm. M. Hough.
The Burlington Gazette, May, 1841, says:

"On the last evening of Mr. Aaron's residence in Burlington, he took his
leave of the community at a temperance meeting held in the hall of the Lyceum,
which was crowded to such an extent that many were unable to obtain seats. Of
his remarks on that occasion, I shall say nothing. The impression made was too
deep to be embodied here, and will long be remembered by those who heard
him. His removal from Burlington is felt by many to be a loss not easily to be
repaired," &c.

Soon after moving to Norristown, Mr. Aaron was asked
to take charge of the Academy there, and he removed his
school to that time-honored building. While teaching here
he was violently set upon in his school-room by two ruffians,
of whom one stood with a cane uplifted to prevent rescue,
while the other brutally beat him for some pretended personal
offense contained in a recent temperance address. Mr. Aaron
at the time holding non-resistant views, with wonderful self-
control, like his Master, stood silent before his assailants.
For this offence they were arrested, convicted, and condemned
to pay a fine and short imprisonment.

February 10, 1842, Mr. Aaron, in connection with Rev.
I. N. Hobart, started a newspaper, "The Truth." In that we
find these words:

"We intend then to plead for the dumb, because he is dumb, and maintain
in our humble sphere the rights of the oppressed of every class; to rebuke sins by
their right names," etc.

Mr. Aaron's popularity at this time as a champion of temperance and anti-slavery, and also as a teacher, was such that the way was prepared for the erection of "Treemount Seminary," which was effected in 1844, and in December the school was opened.

Having resigned the pastorate of the church, he now devoted himself with all the energy of his nature to the establishment of a school for young men, which became famous throughout Eastern Pennsylvania and New Jersey, not only for the number of its pupils, but for the scholarship, skill and ability of its principal, and the thoroughness of the instruction afforded to its students.

From this time, for a period of twelve or fourteen years, this school often contained during a session one hundred and twenty boarders, and as many as sixty day scholars. During this period, many of the most eminent soldiers, civilians and scholars of the country were partly or fully trained within its classic walls. Mr. Aaron's motto was "Let us be true"; and the only things he would not tolerate in his pupils was deceit and plain falsehood. His last words to an intimate friend, when leaving Burlington, were, "Let us be true"; and his friend wrote him long afterwards, that he often thought of those words, and tried to live by them. Many of his pupils, years after they had left his school, wrote to him, expressing their sincere gratitude for his kindness to them, and spoke of their school days, while under his care, as the happiest years of their life. One of them, who became a soldier in the Union army, said to a friend, "I did not like Mr. Aaron when I first entered his school; but before leaving there, I became so attached to him, that I would have fought for him." Another wrote to Mr. Aaron: "I can never forget the first words that fell from your lips at family worship the morning after I arrived at Treemount,—'The fear of the Lord is the beginning of wisdom.'" Still another: "Permit me to assure you of my highest regard and affection. I have ever traced my anti-slavery convictions to your influence upon me in boyhood; and in later years, have often longed to see you face to face, and enjoy your friendship and·counsel. When I have witnessed the general defection in the ranks of the professedly

Christian ministry from practical Christianity and human brotherhood, your life and example have often seemed to me green oases amid the Sahara of profession. Your reward is sure."

Many of his pupils, through his influence and example, became earnest and useful ministers of the Gospel. One, who is now an Episcopal clergyman, in writing to a friend not long since, says, "What a world of memories crowd upon my mind, as I think of 'Treemount,' and the happy days there. I have been in Mount Holly at —— church several times since Mr. Aaron's death, and have nearly always visited his grave. I feel much indebted to him for his goodness to me."

A former pupil now living in New Jersey said lately that when he was a school boy at Norristown he had seen Mr. Aaron give what he felt sure was all the money he had about him to a poor fugitive slave, and then forward him to the next station, on the under-ground railroad. Some time after Mr. Aaron moved to Norristown, he with several other lecturers was asked to deliver an address on temperance in Philadelphia. He accepted the invitation, and accompanied by a number of friends went to the meeting. A handsome carriage had been provided for those who were to speak, and Mr. Aaron was asked to ride with the others. He replied: "No, I will walk with the delegation from Norristown." So the carriage passed on with the vacant seat, and he walked after it. He would not fare better than his friends: if they were obliged to walk, he would go with them. The relator of this little incident, by the way, said that the speech delivered that day by Mr. Aaron was the best address on temperance he ever heard. Many persons can no doubt remember his devotion to the temperance cause; his words of earnest entreaty; his scathing denunciation of the sin of intemperance; his tears of pity for the fallen. At the time when social drinking was universal and popular, he boldly branded it as a burning sin. His invectives against rumsellers were unsparing, and yet many of them sent their sons to his school, and some remained during the vacation, that they might be under his influence.

Becoming involved in the financial crisis of 1857, through endorsements for a friend who failed for a large amount, Mr. Aaron gave up Treemount to his creditors, abandoned the pleasant home which his taste and enterprise had beautified and adorned and where he had anticipated passing the remainder of his days, and in May, 1859, accepted a call to the pastorship of the Baptist church at Mount Holly, N. J. The best years of his life had been spent at Norristown, and it was a bitter trial to him to leave there, seek a new home, and begin life anew. He gave freely of his time and money to advance the interests of the people there, and he left behind him a number of sincere friends.

A warm welcome awaited him at Mount Holly, and he found himself among kind friends. A letter written by him on May 28, 1859, to friends at home, says:

"Everything looks as bright and promising just now [as to this Mount Holly enterprise] as the face of earth and sky this beautiful morning; and yet, perhaps, both are equally uncertain. A church meeting so unanimous and hearty as that which has called me hither all agree that they never before witnessed, and prospects for a school brighten every day."

Later he writes:

"My heart yearns to see you all, and I feel hardly able to endure another week of absence. I am loved and honored here too much; crowds flock to my ministry, and every heart and home seem open and glad to entertain me. A new world is spread out before me, and nothing seems wanting to my felicity but the presence of my dear ones, the payment of my debts, and the conversion of souls. I am reminded of the first of my ministry at New Britain, and can hardly help feeling that I am young again. Next Sabbath morning I hope to address a discourse to all persons under afflictions and trials. My late sermons have aimed to explain the relations and duties of pastors and people. Everything has been received with enthusiasm."

In a letter of June 28th he says:

"I am still too well used, too much flattered, and too much admired. It makes me feel humble and ashamed."

In September, 1859, Mr. Aaron's family removed to Mount Holly, and the Mount Holly Institute was opened for the reception of students, Mr. Aaron and his son being the principals, and the school obtained a liberal patronage. As an instructor of youth, Mr. Aaron was equalled by few in the energy of his devotion to the work and in his success in inspiring his pupils with his own enthusiasm in the pursuit of knowledge. Among the three thousand, and upwards, who sat, from first to last, under his instructions, it is believed that not one could point to an act of injustice on his part. His pupils never failed to love and respect him, and many of them sorrowed over the tidings of his death, much after the manner and depth of children over the loss of a parent. As a minister of the Gospel, he had little regard for human creeds, and never allowed himself to be governed by the conventionalities and technicalities of the "divinity schools." He excelled as an expository preacher. He unfolded the meaning of the sacred writers with master skill, and impressed the sacred lessons taught by happy illustrations, which fastened them upon the memory and heart. It was his custom on Sunday mornings to take up a topic, and often finish it in the evening. Toward the last, he had taken the incidents in the life of our Saviour in their order of time, following him step by step to the end of life. On Sunday evenings he delivered a course of lectures on the prophecies that relate to the nations surrounding the Hebrews, which were intensely interesting and impressive and full of valuable information. On Wednesday evenings the Psalms were taken up in their order, the sixty-ninth being the last that was explained. His last sermon had for its text the words, "By love serve one another." He took fearless hold of the slavery question, and drew multitudes of both friends and enemies to hear him in advocacy of human rights.

During his residence in Mount Holly, his time was fully occupied in teaching, preaching, visiting the members of his church and congregation; also, the sick and dying. To the latter class he was always welcome, as he never spoke harshly to them of their sins, but would talk kindly to them and pray for them, and entreat them to come to Christ. He was a man of the tenderest sympathy; very fond of children, and enjoyed talking to them and drawing out their ideas upon different subjects.

Mr. Aaron received numerous calls to churches in New England, the Western and Middle states. He was warmly attached to the people of Mount Holly, and refused to leave them when offered a larger salary elsewhere. The last winter of his life was peaceful and happy; nothing occurred to trouble or grieve him. He was preparing a work on mathematics, which he hoped would meet with favor, but it was not completed. He frequently spoke of writing his life for his children, but could not spare the time from other duties to carry out his intentions. During his last illness he took an interest in all that was taking place at home and abroad, and insisted upon having the daily newspapers read to him, that he might know the latest war news. To those who took charge of him through the night he would explain verses in the Bible, if permitted to do so. Not long before his death he requested that one of the windows in his room might be opened wide so that he could look out "at the glory of the heavens." It was a lovely morning in the Spring, his favorite season; the sun was just rising, and after looking earnestly at the sky, his eyes turned towards the trees and grass which looked so fresh and green, he said, "How beautiful are all of God's works." Upon hearing that Richmond had fallen and Lee surrendered, he exclaimed, "Thank God! I rejoice in the salvation of my country." His last words were addressed to the Divine Being to whom he had committed the keeping of his soul in his youth,—"Thy grace is sufficient for me." On the evening of April 11, 1865, surrounded by his sorrowing family and a few friends, "he fell asleep." Upon his face there rested an expression of perfect peace; and all who looked upon him, felt that his long struggle with error and sin was at last ended; the battle had been fought, and he had won the victory.

His funeral services were attended on the Saturday following in the Baptist church at Mount Holly. The house was crowded, and many were unable to obtain admittance. The funeral sermon was preached by Rev. Wm. S. Hall, of Philadelphia, from the text, Job vii, 16: "I would not live always." A marble monument, erected by the Baptist church of Mount Holly, marks his last resting place in Mount Holly

Cemetery, and a memorial window has been placed in the church where he labored so faithfully the last six years of his life.   .

> "And as a bird each fond endearment tries
> To tempt its new-fledged offspring to the skies,
> He tried each art, reproved each dull delay,
> Allured to brighter worlds, and led the way."

SERMONS.

1 Cor. xi: 26.—"As often as ye eat this bread, and drink this cup, ye do shew the Lord's death until he come."

I. The design of the institution of the Lord's Supper.

II. The qualifications necessary for attendance.

1. The institution of this ordinance most strongly proves that our Lord Jesus Christ was what he professed to be : that he was endued with prophetic power, because he clearly discerned, and in instituting this ordinance set forth, his death ; to which he *voluntarily* submitted, in order to procure that salvation for his people, which he promises through the shedding of his blood for the remission of sins ; *voluntarily*, because there was nothing to hinder his escaping from the hands of his enemies. Our Lord Jesus Christ was, therefore, what he professed to be, and not a most wicked and shameless impostor (as many of his pretended admirers would make him, without seeming to intend it, by robbing him of his Divine attributes), for no such shameless impostor, however much he may love sin, is disposed also to court infamy, and seek by a public and ignominious death to render himself the abomination of mankind.

2. This celebration is a standing memorial of the awful but, to saints, delightful truth, that our Lord Jesus Christ will come to judge the world, as says the text, "till he come." To unbelievers it speaks a loud memento. That same Jesus declares, by the perpetuation of this ordinance, that you shall see him, even every

eye; and they that pierced him; and they and you shall wail because of him, and your hearts, and spirits, and daring and courage, shall be broken as was his sacred body; your souls and
theirs shall be poured out in vain agony, as was his holy soul,
when he cried out in agony, with your sins upon him, "My God,
my God, why hast thou forsaken me." It is true, that should
this celebration cease; should Christians become unfaithful to
their loving, and expiring Lord; should they misunderstand (as
we fear many do) or neglect their duty, and lose their glorious
privilege, and this heaven-ordained remembrance no more bear
testimony to the word of God—still, God that cannot lie, and
Jesus Christ, the amen, faithful and true, would be found unfailing, for he has not made his coming to depend upon his
people's celebration of his death; still, the trumpet would
sound—the dead be raised—the living changed—the great
white throne descend—the Judge would sit—and heaven,
earth, and hell, await his final and omnipotent award. But,
unbelievers, though this grand event is infinitely more certain
than the perpetuation of this dying feast of our Jesus, suppose you consider it only as parallel in probability with that
circumstance, and can you, dear dying friends, can you be indifferent to your fate depending? Is it at all probable that the
followers of Jesus, think you, will neglect this ordinance? Are
you not greatly shocked, when you behold any one approach,
and eat or drink at this table unworthily, in the midst of careless, notorious sins, appealing to the searcher of hearts, and
publicly saying by such participation, "I am a sincere believer
in the Lord Jesus Christ, so help me God?" Does this in
another shock you? And will you not view this oft-repeated
celebration as a beacon to warn, to direct, and to save yourselves? O, mistaken charity, that frets over faithless Christians,
and leaves its own work undone! its best interests and hopes
forgotten! But, believers, true friends of Jesus, the design of
this institution is, in relation to this coming of your Lord
and Master, to afford you ineffable, and glorious consolation.
Are you pious enough, hearers, to look for this event with
joy? Can you, with the first followers of Jesus (while devils
believe, and tremble, and with all their past agonies still deem
this last day of time the first moment of their fall), can you

lift up your heads with joy, that the coming of your Lord
draweth nigh? In view of a dissolving universe, the great
apostle said at the hour of his departure, " I know in whom I
have believed, and am persuaded that he will keep that which
I have committed to him until that DAY." Alas, Christian
hearers, do you sometimes wish, and almost pray, that there
might be substituted a day less awful, and a judge less severe?
O, repent, repent; and seek faith enough to reply to him that
says " Behold, I come quickly; amen; even so; come,
Lord Jesus."

3. This ordinance is an affecting, visible pledge of Christ's
love to his followers. Those were words of distinguished and
distinguishing mercy that Jehovah spake by the prophet Isaiah,
" I am the Lord thy God, the Holy one of Israel, thy Saviour;
I gave Egypt for thy ransom ; Ethiopia and Seba for thee." " I
have loved thee ; therefore will I give men for thee, and people
for thy life." Yes, murmur, you that debate and dispute with
God, that he gave idolatrous Egypt, polluted Canaan, and proud
Babylon, for his humble and injured people; then turn to the
communion table and behold his people commemorating the
gift of his *own son*, the immaculate Lamb of God, and what will
you object? He gave his enemies for his friends ; and that you
said was cruel ! He gives his friend, the darling of his bosom,
for his enemies; awakes his sword against his fellow, and the
man that is his equal; and will you but gaze, wonder a moment,
and then perish forever ? Say what you will, it is a visible and
most affecting pledge of love divine, of love that none but God
could feel; that none but God in human form could display.
Will any man dare decide that Jehovah was mistaken in de-
termining that nothing but the everlasting death of sinners, or
the temporary sufferings and death of his equal son, was sufficient to satisfy the claims of his law ? And if he should, will he
deny that it was matchless love, that induced our Lord and Saviour of his own accord, cheerfully, to lay down his life for his perishing enemies? He that dares this, can hazard anything !
Souls with him are playthings ; immortality a bauble ; eternity
and omnipotence, a mockery. But is that man here ? If he
is, let him bear me witness, that he is warned once more. But
if none such, then why, oh why, do you fail and heedlessly

neglect to eat of this bread, and drink of this cup, and shew the Lord's death until he come ; and openly acknowledge and subscribe, this visible, affecting pledge, of the love of our dying Lord ?

4.   But another design of the Lord's Supper, *is to improve and strengthen Christians in the Divine life, and cause them to grow in grace.* This conclusion is very palpable, from the natural and scriptural interpretation of the symbols, that is from the meaning indicated, by the use of bread and wine.   Our Lord says to his followers, " Labor not for the meat, that perisheth," &c.—John vi: 27, 48.   Now, there is no public, Christian ordinance, so solemn, and so important to believers, as this visible indication of their faith in the Lord Jesus Christ, this confidence in his body and blood as the food of their souls. It is incontrovertibly manifest, from what has been read, that men only live forever by faith, in the Son of God.   " He that eateth my flesh, and drinketh my blood, dwelleth in me, and I in him.   As the living Father hath sent me, and I live by the Father, so he that eateth me, shall live by me."   As sure as God exists, Christ exists ; and there is the same certainty of immortality and glory to every persevering believer.   And as he that eateth and drinketh unworthily, eateth and drinketh judgment or damnation to himself, not discerning the Lord's body, and so profaning holy things ; so, certainly, he that being prepared to discern the Lord's body, eats of this bread and drinks of this cup, feeds on that bread that has come down from heaven.   As respects man, then, it seems to be the principal design of the Lord's Supper, to promote his growth in grace, and constantly to renew his spiritual strength.   Behold, then, believer, and admire the precious provision made for thee, in the person (prepared like bread) of the Lord Jesus Christ. The cup, which you with right preparation participate, is the communion, or participation of the blood of Christ ; and the bread that is broken, is the communion of the body of Christ. And that your soul has life and health from such participation, is as sure as that a child has growth and strength from needful food and drink ; nor is the one more or less mysterious than the other.   A person may partake of the most wholesome food and drink, and yet his digestive powers be so

impaired as to fail entirely to separate from it the essential nutriment, and appropriate it to its proper use, for the support and comfort of his natural body, so that disease and death may be the consequence; and in like manner may one partake unfitly of the emblems at the communion table, his soul not discerning the Lord's body; that is, not assimilating to itself that spiritual, heavenly, immortal nutriment that Jesus prepared by the sacrifice of himself. If all this be true (and surely the half has not been told), then does it become of vast moment that every communicant should have the essential qualification, which come therefore in the second and last place to be considered.

1. It is believed by most judicious and learned divines that Scripture baptism is essential to a proper participation in this ordinance, inasmuch as no countenance is afforded in the New Testament, nor in the early practice of the churches, of a contrary conclusion. But some good men deem the initiatory rite of baptism immaterial, at least unimportant. As it does not so materially affect the practical objects at present in view, I shall waive the further consideration of these points on this occasion.

2. But in the second place, surely an open, credible profession of faith in the Lord Jesus Christ is essential to communion at this table. I do not say a positive assurance of faith, and a hope eminently confirmed by experience, for this would preclude the very first approach of every mortal ; but a reasonable persuasion in the person's own mind, as well as in the minds of others of unmixed faith, and humble confidence in the Lord Jesus Christ ; such as is the result of much fervent prayer for Divine aid and illumination ; and of impartial, laborious self examination.

3. Christ in this ordinance is to be regarded with admiration and awe. These emotions of the soul cannot but be roused in every thoughtful person by every attribute pertaining to the character of our glorious Lord. "Beside the incomprehensible mysteries of his original character," says Dr. Dwight, " his incarnation, his life, his death, his love for mankind, his propitiatory sacrifice of himself, his resurrection, his exaltation, his intercession, are all marvelous beyond measure, and are investigated

by angels with astonishment and rapture." Hence his character is declared by the prophet Isaiah and summed up by himself, when he appeared to Manoah and his wife, in the title " won-derful." This extraordinary character, combined of all that is great and good, is exhibited in the most touching manner at the communion table, and demands of us the highest exercise of religious admiration. This exercise of the Christian spirit is formed by the union of wonder, reverence and delight; wonder excited by the greatness of the things which are done; rever-ence for the exalted character displayed in doing them; and de-light in the manifestations which they contain of mercy and goodness and in the benefits flowing from them, to the count-less multitude of the children of God. At this table the whole character of Christ is brought before our eyes. We behold him here, in the act of giving his life a ransom for many. Again his body is broken; again his blood is poured out for the sins of men. His compassion for this sinful world is presented to us in living colors. We cannot fail to remember who it was that thus loved us, and gave himself for us. We cannot but remember that he who was the Brightness of the Father's Glory, and the express image of his person, and upheld all things by the word of his power, by himself purged our sins, and then sat down on the right hand of the Majesty on high. We cannot but call to mind that by him whom we here follow to the cross, all things were created that are in heaven, and that are in earth, visible and invisible ; whether they be thrones or dominions, principalities or powers; that all things were created by him, and for him ; that he is before all things, and by him all things consist. We cannot fail to recollect that he is now head over all things to the Church ; having a name above every name in this world, or in the world to come, reigning in a kingdom which is an everlasting kingdom, and ruling with a dominion which shall know no end. We can-not fail to realize that the day is approaching, in which he will come in the clouds of Heaven, with power and great glory ; with the voice of the Archangel, and with the trump of God will summon the dead from their graves ; will sit on the throne of judgment and pronounce the final doom of angels and of men ; while from his face the Heavens and the earth will

flee away; and no place be found for them any more. This
is the "Wonderful" person whose sacrifice of himself is sym-
bolized, or set forth by figures on the altar of Christians;
whom we there behold bleeding, broken, dying and consigned
to the grave. This condescension was exercised, this humiliation undergone, for the love wherewith he loved the church,
and gave himself for it. Who that has any share of the heavenly spirit, can fail to exclaim in union with the heavenly host,
"Worthy is the Lamb that was slain, to receive power and
riches, and wisdom and strength, and honor and glory, and
blessing; for he hath redeemed us to God by his blood; out
of every kindred and tongue, and people and nation; and hath
made us kings and priests unto God, even *his* Father. To
him be Glory and Dominion forever and ever, Amen."

4. We should approach this table with feelings of PROFOUND-
EST GRATITUDE. In every nation, and in every clime, the feeling of gratitude has been manifested with universal approbation towards those who have been considered promoters of the
common weal, or benefactors of mankind. Even many that merely illustrated and adorned humanity with their wit and genius;
and not a few who with bloody ambition became the whole-
sale butchers of our race, and destroyers of nations, have been
held up to the grateful remembrance of future generations.
Painting and sculpture, and immortal poetry, have borne their
names and honors on to distant ages, and invoked and secured
for them the gratitude and homage of mankind. Yet few of
these admired children of Fame, were free from the grossest
vices; such as would render their influence and presence bane-
ful in private domestic life. Their career of public glory and
benevolence, nothing but selfishness, promoted and ennobled
by commanding talents and fortunate circumstances. Compared as to their motives, their persons, or their achievements,
with the Lord Jesus Christ, they appear like a rush-light in
presence of the sun. The benevolence that they really possessed flowed from his infinite fullness into their hearts, as all
the real benefactors of mankind have testified; the beneficence
they practised he empowered them to perform. But his benevolence was infinitely free and disinterested; and his beneficence wide as the universe. The scattered rays of boundless

love and mercy were concentrated and clustered round his
sacred person on the cross; presenting a scene of intense and
infinite splendor; claiming (and yet to receive) from heaven,
earth and hell, their chief and their eternal admiration, and
from his own redeemed their boundless gratitude.   Towards
this absorbing gratitude our souls are led when we approach
the sacramental table.   We stood on perdition's crumb-
ling verge; we infinitely needed the deliverance, by such a
sacrifice.   We believed it not.   We wished not; much less
asked for a deliverer.   There was no eye to pity, no arm to
save.   At that awful period, unsolicited, undesired, unwel-
comed ; to be rejected, insulted, mocked, outraged and. murdered; this benefactor came, threw himself into the breach
between us and hell.   In infinite madness we rushed upon
him, as if to push him into it and follow ; but he was too
strong and too kind ; he snatched us from its blazing jaws,
and has brought us to his house and to his table this day, to
commemorate his love and our deliverance.   When he did so
God said concerning us, " Deliver them from going down to
the pit, for I have found a ransom."   The guilt of our sins
was washed away in the blood of Jesus.   The gates of hell,
to all his humble followers he closed forever.   The door of
heaven he opened with his own hand ; plucked out the sting
of death ; and destroyed the victory of the grave, and from
that gloomy mansion opened in his own person, a safe and
cheerful path to the world of immortal glory; whither he hath
ascended to prepare a place for each of his sons and daughters.   There on a throne of majesty and mercy, high and lifted
up, he intercedes for them, and to them he calls from that
happy world.   Listen to his comforting words, " He that over-
cometh shall inherit all things ; and I will be his God and he
shall be my son."   " And God shall wipe away all tears from
their eyes, and there shall be no more death, neither sorrow,
nor crying, neither shall there be any more pain ; for the
former things are passed away."   " And there shall be no
night there and they need no candle, neither light of the sun,
for the Lord God giveth them light, and they shall reign for
ever and ever."

Mark xii. 34: "Thou art not far from the Kingdom of God."

An address to the thoughtful is my object on the present
occasion ; and I know not how such may be more appropri-
ately addressed, than by saying to each one of them, " Thou
art not far from the kingdom of God." These were the terms
in which Jesus Christ accosted a man, who showed in a conversation between them, the character of thoughtfulness.
Who, having heard the memorable reply of Christ to the question of the Pharisees and Herodians, " Shall we give tribute
to Cæsar ?" and having witnessed his confutation of the infidel
Sadducees concerning the resurrection, accosted Jesus saying,
" Which is the first commandment of all ?" Meaning undoubtedly " What is the substance of the Divine law ?" Upon the
declaration of Christ, " Thou shalt love the Lord thy God,
with all thy heart, and with all thy soul, and with all thy mind,
and with all thy strength—and thou shalt love thy neighbor as
thyself;" the scribe fully and thoughtfully—if we may judge
from his language—assented, and added this weighty com-
ment, drawn from an intelligent and thoughtful perusal of the
scriptures ; such love " is more than all whole burnt offerings
and sacrifices." Now it was believed, or at least pretended by
some of the Jews, that the offering of sacrifices, especially of
whole burnt sacrifices, was Jehovah's chief command, and of
course, the most meritorious act that his worshipers could
perform. But this *scribe* had *read* and *understood* the stern
rebuke of the prophet Samuel to Saul, the disobedient and
wayward King of Israel. " Hath the Lord as great delight in
burnt offerings and sacrifices as in *obeying the voice of the Lord.*
Behold, to *obey* is *better* than sacrifice, and to *hearken* than the
fat of rams. For *rebellion* is as the sin of witchcraft and stub-
bornness is as iniquity and idolatry. Because thou hast rejected the word of the Lord, he hath also rejected thee from
being King." Which rebuke was given when Saul had pre-

served a few of Amalek's chief things, contrary to the Lord's
command to make a splendid sacrifice to the Lord God. This
scribe had understood the word of the Lord by Hosea, "I desired mercy and not sacrifice, and the knowledge of God more
than burnt offerings." He remembered the awful, heart-search-
ing, heartrending questions of the penitent soul in Micah's book,
" Wherewith shall I come before the Lord, and bow myself
before the high God? Shall I come before him with burnt
offerings, with calves of a year old? Will the Lord be pleased
with thousands of rams, or with ten thousands of rivers of
oil? Shall I give my first-born for my transgression, the fruit
of my body for the sin of my soul?" He remembered the
divine direction also, " He hath shewed thee, O man, what is
good; and what doth the Lord require of thee, but to do
justly, and to love mercy, and to walk humbly with thy God?"
I say this scribe knew and seemed to feel the force of these
and many other scriptures that might be cited, as appears from
his remarks to Jesus, and this together with Christ's words to
him, " Thou art not far from the Kingdom of God," shows
that he was a serious, thoughtful man, and therefore warrants
my appeal to my fellow mortals from this interesting passage,
upon a state of mind which we either have now, or *must have*
before we exist much longer.

I. Let me solemnly direct your minds to some of the
encouragements that connect themselves with a seriously and
religiously thoughtful state of the soul. 1. " Thou art not far
from the Kingdom of God." So said Jesus to the scribe, and
so trembling mortal he says to you. As the sea-tossed, storm-
driven sailor, when the compass and the stars inform him that
some safe shore is near, safe when reached, though guarded by
furious breakers and threatening rocks, indulges the fearful
hope that he shall reach it with life, though on a single plank,
and makes a renewed and desperate effort at the pumps to keep
his crazy ship afloat a little longer. So may the sin-sick wanderer from God, with trembling, listen to the son of God, who
says to him, " Thou art not far from the kingdom of God."

2. To be particular, and, if possible, pointedly instructive. One encouragement is to be derived from your respect,

like the Scribe, for the divine law. If you can say, "the law is holy, and the commandment holy, and just and good," it is an encouragement; some slight encouragement at least; for the time has been, hearer, if it is not now, when nothing was more indifferent to your feelings than the divine law; and faithful preachers know, by bitter experience, that if they want the friendship of this world, they must not bring Jehovah's holy law too near the consciences and the practices of their fellow men. But they know, too, as you feel, ye thoughtful, that heaven and earth shall pass away, sooner than one jot or one tittle of the law shall fail. And when you perceive that the Almighty and everlasting God has placed his life and his law side by side, as co-existent, and one to support and to sustain the other, as you who are thoughtful do feel, then your interest in this awful truth, your tremendous perception of responsibility, forms some encouragement, that if there be any help for any soul, it may be vouchsafed to you. For it is written: "To him will I look," &c.

3. Your deep interest in the Holy Scriptures; your sense of your own depravity; your perfect self-hatred as a polluted wretch (not a hatred that leads you to desire your own ruin, but to wish yourself better than you are; holier, I mean; more like the holy God of the Scriptures); this is another feature of encouragement in your case; your full conviction that you ought to go to perdition; your wonder that the all-wise and all-just God could have spared you so long; all constitute some faint encouragement at least; that if a ransom may be had for any one, perhaps it may be paid for you. No man is so likely to try so much to prepare for trial before the God of mercy, as he who knows that he is guilty, and the law inflexible.

4. Your belief that Jesus Christ is the Almighty Redeemer, the only Saviour, able to save to the uttermost, given to save, and solemnly pledged to save the chief of believing sinners, your knowledge and belief of this, though far from giving you any assurance of a happy interest in Christ, may, nevertheless, afford a gleam of encouragement to your almost despairing soul. For, why should that Saviour forbid to approach him; one who feels that God is holy, just and true;

that feels himself most justly and most necessarily condemned to eternal death, and who fully appreciates the sole merit of the Son of God, to redeem from even the curse of Jehovah's law? You feel, indeed, that he has power to do it, to reject; for God hath given him the power; that he has law to do it; for he is the administrator of the law; that he has justice to warrant it; but you may tremblingly hope that he has mercy to prevent it. I dare not state any encouragement too strongly at the peril of all our souls, but there is more encouragement to hope that a man fully conscious of laboring under a deadly disease, and knowing well of a near and compassionate and most skillful and unfailing physician, may be visited and cured by him, than one who rejects the physician as an impostor, or feels that he needs him not. "The whole have no need of a physician, but they that are sick."

5. The possibility that, how many lying spirits soever there may be, and certainly are, ready to deceive all they can, it is the Spirit of God that has moved you; that has alarmed and convinced you; that has shown you what man must be; that would be righteous with his maker; that has disclosed to you without disguise the realities of the state to come; that has uncovered that perdition and revealed the adamantine chains and penal fire, and the wailing and gnashing of teeth; that are just one single step outside of death's door, to which all are rapidly hastening; the possibility that the Holy Ghost has taught you all this, as his first stern lesson, that must be imparted to the redeemed on earth, and to all men in either time or eternity, affords some slight encouragement; as, that being his work, it shall be perfected in your eternal salvation.

6. I was going, as the last ground of encouragement that occurred to my mind, to speak of the precious promises of scripture. But I dare not. Unconditional submission; yes, more; pure practical love to Jesus Christ are essentially necessary to ensure an interest in the promises of heaven. "If any man love not the Lord Jesus Christ, let him be Anathema Maranatha, accursed when the Lord cometh." And how dare I, or any man, bless whom the Lord hath cursed? And has then all been said that can be said to encourage the thought-

ful? I speak in regard to their present state—their hopes and expectations in their present circumstances. I believe, before the Lord, that nothing more encouraging ought to be said. I am only fearful, though not conscious, of having said too much.

II. It remains then to say some serious things concerning the discouragements of the thoughtful. Here the preacher will be censured. Why discourage some beginning to think, some that we hope may think about their souls, by presenting the difficulties as insurmountable, and the aspect of religion as so gloomy and so forbidding, that the gay and the thoughtless, and indeed all, must turn away from it in disgust? Some even of our brethren may slightly censure, to say no more ; and the world—this big, proud world, did they hear the preacher, and think him worth noticing at all—would rail. But, censure and rebuke, Christian brethren ; rail, thoughtless world,—Jesus Christ regarded neither one nor the other, swallowed none of his hard sayings, when the world said he had a devil, and the disciples, with few exceptions, determined to leave him. I believe that for one who is discouraged by the severest Bible truths from coming to Jesus Christ, that whole multitudes are induced, as professors or non-professors by unscriptural encouragements, to cry peace when there is no peace, and walk with calm minds and lulled consciences down to the gates of death. "Follow me, with not where to lay my head ; take up your cross and follow me ; I send you forth as sheep in the midst of wolves ; they shall persecute you from city to city," were the words of Jesus Christ to his most distinguished and, shall I not say, favorite followers. I will, therefore, under the awful sanction of his name and example, freely speak unto you, my dying fellow-men, of the discouragements to which as thoughtful persons you are subject.

1. The first discouragement is coincident with the first mentioned grounds of encouragement: the danger that all your apparent regard for Jehovah and his law may arise from slavish fear; that you regard his might rather than his right, and tremble at his power more than you reverence his justice. Such were the necessary conclusions of Pharaoh, Nebuchadnezzar and others who acknowledged his power. In going

thus far you are only even with the fallen spirits. And it stands to reason that no man ever loved his father because he beat him.

2. You are to be discouraged lest you look upon yourselves as rather unfortunate than guilty, and mourn with bitterness over the hapless lot that has consigned you against your will to the cruel tyranny of an Almighty despot. "I know thee, that thou art an austere man," etc. As nothing on earth can be more miserable than a state of helpless, hopeless, interminable bondage; so with regard to God, to view him as an implacable and Almighty oppressor.

3. Be discouraged lest you cherish the lingering hope of being saved for your tears, your convictions, and your penitence. Many a man is willing to make an agreement with God, to fast and pray, and punish himself. This is the religion of many benighted heathen, and of many self-called Christians; but most better informed people are in danger of deceiving themselves with their past experience.

4. The fact is discouraging that you are apt to wrest the Scriptures, which are become an interesting book to you, and you will be liable to speculate upon the mysteries of the divine oracles. There is likely to be much of this sort of instruction.

5. The fact is discouraging that many Christians, and so-called Christian ministers, will do much to lull your wholesome fears. They talk of the consent of millions. Oh! the doom of such!

6. The most discouraging fact of all is the sad, sickening sight of back-slidden seekers after Christ. The blossoms—the leaves—the fruit. The sad sight of apparent penitence, declined, cast off forever!

In conclusion, I will say that I have addressed myself to the thoughtful. If there are none such before me to-night, there ought to be.

NOTE.—The latter part of this sermon was not written out fully; there were only scant notes, and the publisher gives them just as they were written by Mr. Aaron.

REFUTATION OF THE SERMON OF REV. H. J. VANDYKE, DELIV-
ERED IN BROOKLYN IN DECEMBER, 1860.

" Do thyself no harm."—Acts xvi, 28.
" Love thy neighbor as thyself."—Matt. xix, 19.
" He that is greatest among you shall be your servant."
Matt. xxiii, 11.

" He hath shewed thee, O man, what is good; and what
doth the Lord require of thee but to do justly, and to love
mercy, and to walk humbly with thy God."—Micah vi, 8.

" Ye shall hallow the fiftieth year, and ye shall proclaim
liberty throughout all the land to all the inhabitants thereof."
Lev. xxv, 10.

" Let the oppressed go free, and break every yoke."—Isa.
lviii, 6.

" He that stealeth a man and selleth him, or if he be found
in his hands, he shall surely be put to death."—Ex. xxi, 16.

" Thou shalt not deliver unto his master the servant who
is escaped from his master unto thee. He shall dwell with
thee, even among you, in that place which he shall choose in
one of thy gates where it liketh him best ; thou shalt not op-
press him."—Deut. xxiii, 15, 16.

I have quoted these words of Scripture in reply to the
legion of pro-slavery preachers who mustered on the President's fast day to torture that Divine Book into the defence of
stealing men, scourging nude women, and selling infants by
the pound, torn from their mothers' bosoms. These men and
their admirers, beholding on every hand the nation's treasured
millions wasted by public robbery, the nation itself bankrupt
in money and running down in morals, have ever denounced
all sermons against oppression and every national "organic"
villainy as not fit to be uttered, as "political preaching," "a
desecration of the sacred desk and holy day." But as soon as
one-fourth of the nation's power had fallen into reformatory

hands by a legal and constitutional vote; as soon as traitors
in arms had begun to insult the nation's flag, to seize its treasures by force, and capture its forts and arsenals and men; to
torture and gibbet blameless Northern men; to shave the
heads and daub with tar and cotton the necks and bosoms of
polished Northern women, the teachers of their children; and
when the slow indignation of the North began to kindle at
this, then politics became a holy cause, and the Vandykes and
Vintons and Palmers and Thornwells, and all the herd, began
straightway to preach and pray against the men and measures
that stirred the ruffian traitors up, and to prove that reason,
and scripture, and Christ, and God, were on the traitors' side.

And now the men who could not bear that temperance,
or politics, or any practical religion, should disturb the pulpit,
have all turned sermon readers and tract distributors, and
many of them totter about through town and country under
the burden of Mr. Vandyke's sermon and something heavier,
imploring all to study its divine, unanswerable truth.   Like
priest, like people.   I feared they were hypocrites before; 'tis
hard to doubt it longer.   But I thank them for tearing off the
vail themselves, and so confessing by act their past hypocrisy.

I stand here, then, to-day to refute the so-called sermon
of Rev. Henry J. Vandyke; and the task is already done, in
substance, by the words I have quoted from prophets and
apostles, and the Son of God.   "God is love," says John the
apostle.   "Man's love to man" fulfills both law and prophets,
was the teaching of Jesus Christ; and the disregarded oppression of the poor and the crying of the needy are oftener threatened with the vengeance of God than all other sins together.
So when Henry J. Vandyke, or any other man, entangles
Scripture to make Jehovah a tormenting devil towards his
weaker children, and to make him use the stronger portion of
mankind as the agents of his bloody malice,—such teacher is
blinded by ignorance, interest or prejudice; for Scripture can
not contradict itself.   The daring, perhaps unconscious, blasphemy which sets God to mocking his own Ten Commandments, is substantially refuted by the whole tenor of his word;
still the habits of the world require that man should contend
with man, even in vindicating heavenly truth.   I attack, there-

fore, in form, this vaunted champion of slavery, ancient and modern, who sees the prophets of God inaugurating a harsher system than that of Carolina, and Christ and his apostles approving and enforcing the slavery of the Roman Empire, whose laws gave the master power to torture, cut to pieces, burn or crucify the innocent slave at will, and feed him to his fishes.

The effort of Mr. Vandyke is honestly reduced to the following proposition : " American slavery is sanctioned by the Almighty, because he established and enforced a harsher system of slavery among the Hebrews ; and because his son, Jesus Christ, and his apostles, saw and approved a far more cruel system among the heathen of their time. Therefore, to oppose American slavery tends to utter infidelity."

I am sure that I present his position fairly, and any sober man that hears me to-day shall have an opportunity to put me right at some suitable time if I have erred. To substantiate this horrid dogma is the aim of Henry J. Vandyke ; of his success he boasts, and writes to a Southern secession Doctor of Divinity of the "amazing sensation" created by his sermon. To promote this end the thing has been multiplied by millions in papers and pamphlets in order to flood the land ; and it is said that in many places, and even in Mount Holly, industrious and willing colporteurs, drunk and sober, religious and profane, hawk it about as God's own voice sanctioning the traffic in human bodies and in human souls. This doctrine, therefore, I assail as false and blasphemous, tending to make the God of the Bible appear as a monster to every noble and thoughtful mind.

"God sanctions American slavery," is the teaching of Henry J. Vandyke. What is American slavery? He does not tell us. Why? Because he dares not tell, either falsely or truly. Not falsely, for American law books would prove him a liar ; not truly, for his very colporteurs would shrink from such blasphemy. Therefore he dodged the issue and set up a man of straw. But without definitions of the subject and the principles there can be neither reasonings nor proofs ; and so our champion has no arguments and reaches no conclusion.

"God sanctions American slavery." What, then, is American slavery? I will tell you ; not in my own arbitrary forms of speech, but in the words and thoughts of Christians, patriots and sages, and in the enactments and administration of the law.   Mark the descriptions and definitions well. "American slavery is the sum of all villainies," said John Wesley, a Christian and a sage.   " God has no attribute that can take part in its favor," taught Jefferson, our brightest and most suggestive statesman.   Washington regarded it as the greatest blight upon his country, freed his slaves as soon as he could, and pledged his vote for the universal abolition of slavery in Virginia if such question could come up.   And the illustrious Lafayette exclaimed in his riper years, "I never would have drawn my sword for America had I foreseen her continuance of slavery."

" Slaves shall be deemed sold, taken, reputed and adjudged in law to be chattels personal " (that is, equivalent to beasts and movables) "in the hands of their owners, and their executors and administrators, to all intents, construction and purposes whatever."—Law of South Carolina.

The marriage of slaves "cannot produce any civil effect, because slaves are deprived of all civil rights."—Louisiana Courts.   So slaves can be no more married than brute beasts can.

" Slaves are generally considered not as persons but as things ; they are held to be *pro nullis, pro mortuis.*"—Law of South Carolina.   That is, "as ciphers, as dead creatures," personally.

" It is not competent for any court of chancery to enforce a contract between a master and a slave, though the slave should have kept the contract fully."—Leigh's Reports.

" The slave has no legal right to worship God, and is often scourged almost or quite to death for doing so."—Judge William Jay.

" The slave can be no party to a suit."—Wheeler on Law of Slavery.

The slave can give no evidence against a white in any case whatever ; and should a slave, male or female, resist any outrage of a white, even by the lifting of the hand to turn aside a blow or attempt to escape from any torture, such slave may be struck dead with impunity and in strict accordance with the law.

The law forbids a slave to learn the alphabet; and in some States inflicts the most terrible penalties, even that of death, on any one who attempts to teach him.

An absconding slave—that is, one who hides in the woods or swamps—is outlawed in the following terms: "We do hereby declare, by virtue of an act of Assembly of this state, that if the said slaves, Ben and Rigdon, do not return home immediately after the publication of these presents, that any person may kill and destroy said slaves by such means as he or they may think fit, without incurring any penalty or forfeiture thereby. Given under our hands and seals this 12th November, 1836. B. Coleman, Justice of the Peace. James Jones, Justice of the Peace. Newbern, N. C."

The owner of Ben and Rigdon advertised them thus: "I will give the reward of $100 for each of the above negroes, to be delivered to me or confined in the jail of Lenoir or Jones county, or for the killing of them so that I can see them. W. D. Cobb."

This was twenty-four years ago, before Lincoln was nominated, and I believe there are hundreds of such advertisements. Slaves in Virginia are or were punishable with death for about seventy crimes more than white men are; and in other slave States the same rule is followed, though not to the same murderous extreme. Thus the slave is prevented by cruel penalties from knowing or reading the laws, and then made the victim of his enforced ignorance. Draco and Caligula were lambs to these slave-holding legislators.

The law of Louisiana makes provision for only two and a half hours rest for the slave in twenty-four; and the law requires fifteen hours labor in South Carolina. The legal allowance of food for a full-grown slave for a week is one peck of corn unground. They crush and cook it themselves.

No law protects or enforces chastity among the slaves. In that respect they are treated and held as brutes. Fornication, adultery and rape among slaves, or against the poor slave woman, is no legal crime. If she or any slave man lifts a hand to repel the white ruffian who assails her virtue, she or her defender may be stricken dead with perfect impunity. Thus the American slave, in point of rights of soul and body, is treated

by law like a brute, and worse; in point of duties and obligations, more is exacted of him than man can render.   Such is
a feeble sketch of American slavery according to law.   I am
ashamed of its weakness.   The facts are beyond description.

But according to Vandyke, "God sanctions American
slavery," and all his retainers say "Amen!"   Does our loving
Father in heaven, and did the gentle, tender-hearted Jesus,
sanction such legal relations, facts and statutes as I have faithfully though too feebly portrayed?   Press them on Mr. Vandyke and his pragmatical converts, and they would think that
the divine administration had changed hands; that Pharaoh
had caught them instead of Moses; and that the apostles ought
to have said, "Let as many niggers as are under the yoke,"
reverence their masters, instead of addressing white slaves.   I
am almost sure that these politicians who run about this town
loaded with the piety of Mr. Vandyke, would, under the lawful crack of American slavery's whip, like my sermon better
than his.   I may be mistaken, for the Southern masters have
metaphorically spit and trodden on them this many a day as
the "mud-sills of society," and they have been elated by the
compliment; but in the poor negro's place the witness, as
Friends say, might be reached through the skin and muscles,
though the brain and heart were torpid still.   Mr. Vandyke
should have argued, like Calhoun, that the negro is not a human being; then he would have been half consistent, for a
brute of course is entitled to no human rights, though it is
surely absurd and cruel to exact from a beast all human obligations.   But this hypothesis would have taken Mr. Vandyke
out of the Bible, and he is a preacher, and sure of meeting
Drs. Palmer and Thornwell in the slaveholders' heaven.

But as this hypothesis of the non-humanity of the negro
is put forward seriously, I will turn aside to notice it.   "The
negro is not human."   How do we determine who is a human
being?   Given that some are human beings.   They can do
things.   Then those that can do the same things are human,
too.   White humans can sing.   But Elizabeth Greenfield, who
is as black as soot, and called the Black Swan, is the best natural and native singer in America.   White humans can make
poetry; and Washington wrote to the young black girl, Phil-

lis Wheatly, that her poetry was "elegant." Some human whites are eloquent orators, and all our Federal Senators and Representatives are counted men, I think; but Frederick Douglas, Samuel Ward, and several other men, as black as jet, are superior in eloquence to nine-tenths of them. Skill in mathematics is considered a fair proof of human faculties; and Thomas Jefferson wrote a letter to the negro Benjamin Bannister praising in the highest terms the skill and accuracy displayed by the latter in the almanac which he had calculated and sent to Jefferson. Courage, military talent, generosity, and patriotism, are mostly reckoned among the finest traits of human nature; if so, a negro, Crispus Attucks, was the first man to give his life for our American independence,—and Washington and Jackson, most able and impartial judges, have eulogized the courage and excellent conduct of the negro troops who fought under their command against British foes for their white American oppressors.　　　•

Toussaint L'Ouverture, of San Domingo, a full-blooded African negro, and a slave till fifty years of age, having, with Christian generosity, saved his master and all his family from the vindictive rage of the insurgent negroes, then took the control of the bloody insurrection and turned it, with unprecedented skill, into a lawful warfare for human rights; coped successfully for ten years with the best military talent that Spain, France or England sent against him; baffled forty thousand of Napoleon's veterans commanded by Le Clerc, his brother-in-law, and left his country free. Twelve years after our revolution, with one-sixth of our number, and they all negro slaves, Toussaint struggled against a nation more numerous than Britain and equally as brave, ruled by Bonaparte, the greatest warrior of history, and won liberty and independence for his people, which have till this day remained unquestioned. And, mark it well, as the most remarkable fact on human record, the negroes of San Domingo are the only people under heaven who ever disenthralled themselves from slavery by their own right arms. And that negro Republic is this day in a far happier and safer condition than South Carolina.

Philanthropy and Christian charity are God's highest tests of human attributes; and a negro woman in New York was one of the very first to establish a Sunday school in that city, and fed and clothed some forty white orphans at her own expense.

I have now shown that some negroes have the highest mental and moral traits, as proof of their humanity; and I leave it for others to show that black skin and woolly hair cannot cover a human soul. This is a digression. I return to Mr. Vandyke.

"God sanctions American slavery," so teaches the Bible; and "the tribunal of reason and humanity" has nothing to do with testing revelation—revelation as expressed in the English language. "Take, eat, this is my body," says the English New Testament. A reverend, sleek-looking man takes a crumb of bread and says a Latin prayer over it, and tells me it is bona fide flesh and blood, the real body of the Son of God. I say "No; my human senses tell me it is bread." He replies, "What are your senses against a miracle and the word of God?" I answer, "When Jesus and his apostles worked miracles, healed the sick and raised the dead, they appealed to the human senses of the witnesses, asking them to believe what their senses perceived and us to credit the veracity of impartial persons. The senses came before miracles, and are their only tests, and much superior to them. Therefore, 'This is my body,' is not the meaning; but, 'This *represents* my body.' "

I see that Moses said, nearly four thousand years ago, that God first made plants and trees; then, monsters of the deep, fishes, and, strange to say, fowls of the air; next, the dry land brutes; and, last of all, man. Within fifty years the geologists have examined the rocky strata of the earth, and find these orders of creation laid up on those strong shelves exactly in the order in which they were placed by the unscientific prophet of God. So the geologists, without intending it, confirm my intellectual faith in Moses through the powers of my reason. Had they found man next to the primitive granite, and plants only among the surface clay and alluvion, I should have doubted—at least, been puzzled.

There is no heathen in China or Japan, except an idiot, who does not see and approve the outline principles of natural justice; condemn intellectually falsehood, fraud and murder, and admire truth, courage, temperance and generosity. These perceptions and intuitions of the human soul were made by the same hand as revelation; they were before revelation; they are the hooks on which revelation hangs, the things which revelation was made to fit; and that revelation which contradicts the senses, the reason and the conscience, is from the devil and not from God. All human jurists in Christendom, of any name, assume in man—at least, in enlightened man—the clear intuition of natural justice, and base all righteous laws upon that intuition. They make, however, one concession, namely: "If any competent law-giver violates natural justice, the unjust law must be so plain that it cannot be construed by any ingenuity in favor of right and justice." Is it wrong to apply this principle to the word of God, and to examine carefully whether some seeming support of injustice and oppression may not be so construed as to clear the meaning of all cruelty?

Mr. Vandyke ignores this principle. He finds in the Bible some dozen words—master, servant, bondman, bondmaid, rod, smite, yoke, money, buy, sell—and, presto, "God sanctions American slavery." Again, suppose that the Almighty did establish and enforce among the Jews a system of cruel servitude, even slavery (which I deny), does that make it a rule for other nations in an enlightened age? Did he not ordain the bloody rite of circumcision? Mr. Vandyke, being a Presbyterian, thinks that sanguinary ecclesiastical torture is superseded by the gentle falling of a drop of water on an infant's head. Did not God ordain that a man should be stoned to death for a blasphemous word against Jehovah, or a curse against a parent, and the same punishment for gathering sticks on a certain day? Did he not send fiery serpents to destroy a weary, fretful people, and cause the fire from heaven to devour and the earth to open its jaws and swallow up thousands of mistaken people who followed a few pragmatical leaders that envied Moses and Aaron? Did he not direct the Jews to wage exterminating wars upon their neighbors, sparing neither sex nor age, the hoary head nor the lisping babe?

Mr. Vandyke's retainers here cry out on my impetuous, sweeping rashness. No; blame your champion, who has set me on. If you and he claim the support of one wrong and outrage from the example of the Jewish law, you shall sustain the code or own your folly. The Jews were and are an oracular people, selected by heaven from among the nations, declared in the Bible to be an exceptional people, delivered from bondage, led by miracles, taught by prophets, and preserved for now four thousand years against all the efforts so often used to destroy them. And was any peculiar license which was conferred on them intended as a general privilege for cotton planters, priests and politicians? Was South Carolina authorized to secede and steal the nation's treasures by the ten plagues of Egypt wrought in her favor? I admit that we have been plagued on her account these many times for more than eighty years. But the plagues she caused us were more like Sodom vexing Lot than like righteous heaven trying Pharaoh. Did a power divine wall up the sea to make a path for Howell Cobb to lead his Georgians through to fetch and carry slaves and cotton? Did the mountains blaze and the earth stagger to give Alabama a newer and more binding law than the Constitution? Is Jefferson Davis a greater and more heavenly sign than the fiery pillar and the sheltering cloud, that he should lead Mississippi through "the wilderness of sin" to the Sodom of slavery? Is little, starving Florida, that has cost us fifty millions to buy her swamps and alligators and drive away her Indians, and that is not worth to-day as much as Burlington county,—has she been fed with manna from on high to prove her right to break up this fair Republic for the promotion of slavery?

Let Mr. Vandyke show these or such like signs from heaven, and it will place his favorite institution in the same field of view as Jewish servitude; only that their servants were mostly whiter than their masters, whereas Mr. Vandyke claims Scripture only for holding negro slaves,—while the only persons mentioned in the Bible who could have been negroes were, first, the wife of Moses, the most illustrious prophet of the Hebrews and the interpreter of God's first works; and, secondly, the Prince baptized by Philip (Acts v, 3), the Prime

Minister of the Queen of Ethiopia, who had charge of all her treasures, and kept them better, I doubt not, than our modern Baptist, Howell Cobb. These persons, if negroes, were certainly not slaves.

But, "the Bible sanctions American slavery"; for, according to Mr. Vandyke, there is no sin but what the Bible forbids, and it does not forbid the enslavement of negroes. Therefore that is no sin. If the Bible did not forbid polygamy that were no sin, says this reverend gentleman. Here Mr. Vandyke is out again. Sin is the transgression of the divine law; and when that law is clear, however learned, it is just as obligatory as the ten commandments. When Dr. Beaumont looked into St. Martin's stomach, and saw the inflammation and blisters caused therein by alcoholic drinks, no angel from heaven could have given better evidence that the supplying and drinking of such poisons is sin. God leaves us to find out most of our sins in a similar way. The Bible mentions but a very few. Did it descant on all, its letters would cover the surface of the earth and the face of New Jersey could not contain the introduction. In fact, the Bible is not a sin book, but a salvation book, blessed be God; it is given, not to specify all possible transgressions and moral diseases, but to point out and assure us of one glorious and perfect remedy. Our divine Redeemer scarcely mentions any outward sin except hypocrisy, fraud and oppression.

I am now ready for verbal criticism. I have already shown that American slavery is *per se* an infernal system, and cannot therefore have the sanction of God; that if Hebrew servitude were even a system of oppression, it gives no necessary sanction to oppression elsewhere; that a people following Hebrew patterns of domestic policy in enforcing radical and arbitrary distinctions among men, must have like authority with Hebrews. But do the words of Scripture, even of the English Bible, warrant the idea of chattel slavery? The word "slavery" is never used at all; and the word "slaves" but once, and that in the eighteenth chapter of Revelation, where Babylon is represented as sinking into hell at the cry of a mighty angel coming down from heaven and at the call of another voice from on high, which bids God's people to come out from her and have no union with her but let her secede, that they be not partakers of her plagues,—while those who sympathize with her, and have been enriched by her products, are standing afar off (perhaps as far as New York from Charleston) and bitterly wailing as she goes down, reciting the list of her splendors and her wealth, and closing one strain with those Southern articles of merchandise, "slaves and souls of men." Slaves and souls of men! Babylon going down to hell, having trafficked in "slaves and souls of men." This is the only use of the word "slaves"; and the scene reminds us forcibly of a city not nearly so big as Babylon and daily growing less, moving in the same direction, the good folks running away from her, and Mr. Vandyke and his cotton congregation weeping and wailing over her, crying Alas! alas! that great city, wherein were made rich all that had ships in the sea; for in one hour is she made desolate.

The truth is that the Hebrew language has no word for "slave." This is plain, because the slave trade was in full blast when King James' translators gave us our English Bible; and they would have rendered the Hebrew "evedh" "slave," if they had dared; but neither then nor since have any sect or body of Christians dared to put slave into the Mosaic law. And they never will, for the simple reason that it is not there. And the "Republic of Letters" is a free community, and no body of learned men can afford to make traitors of themselves to the truth of literature. Perhaps, however, the Southern traitors to their country and to common sense may bring out a new Bible with their new constitution. The word "evedh" is rendered both servant and bondman in a very loose and careless manner. It means simply and solely "one who labors for another either with body or with mind," under covenant or contract to do so. This the word "bondman," or boundman, clearly implies; as bound or bonded by contract to render service, precisely as a mechanic is bound by contract to build a house for another man. The word may also represent a youth, boy or girl bound out to service, as an apprentice or otherwise, by a parent or guardian on payment or promise of money or the worth of money for such service, which could not last more than six years unless the person himself at the end of the six years chose on his own account to renew the contract.

And no contract, service or obligation ever lasted, or could last, under Jewish law, beyond the year of jubilee, which was to that nation the ever-recurring type of that eternal and heavenly rest and freedom which their Shiloh or Messiah, the "desire of nations," should bring in. The phrase "forever," which cotton divines press into the service of eternal slavery, only carried forward the mind of a Jew to that epoch which their prophets had made known as the limit of a dispensation or institution connected with that. In regard to servitude and the enthrallment of debts we have the following beautiful, heart-cheering words (Lev. xxv, 8–13): "Thou shalt number seven Sabbaths of years unto thee, seven times seven years; and the space of the seven Sabbaths of years shall be unto thee forty and nine years. Then shalt thou cause the trumpet of the jubilee to sound on the tenth day of the seventh month, in the day of atonement shall ye make the trumpet sound throughout all your land. And ye shall hallow the fiftieth year, and proclaim liberty throughout all the land to all the inhabitants thereof: it shall be a jubilee unto you; and ye shall return every man unto his possession, and ye shall return every man unto his family. A jubilee shall that fiftieth year be unto you: ye shall not sow, neither reap that which groweth of itself in it, neither gather the grapes in it of thy vine undressed. For it is the jubilee; it shall be holy unto you: ye shall eat the increase thereof out of the field. In the year of this jubilee ye shall return every man unto his possession."

This language settles, if language can, the question of unending servitude. "All the inhabitants shall be free"; every human being shall return to his own possession. Why does not Mr. Vandyke urge the carrying out of this Hebrew statute, so benevolent, so sublime, so firmly established, so clearly defined by Almighty God? Because it would not please his cotton lords nor bring him so large a salary. The word "buy" is harped on as a certain defence of slavery. What does "buy" mean? Let us test some other words. David says, "I prevented the dawn of the morning." Does that mean that he hindered the dawn from coming on? or that he rose for prayer before it came? I anticipated the dawn? Paul told his friends that he had purposed to visit them for a long time, but had been "let hitherto." Does that mean that Paul had been "permitted" (as "let" now means) to visit them? or that he had been "hindered"? This play upon words to promote villainous oppression is base on the part of those who know better, and contemptibly stupid on the part of those who blindly follow them. The Hebrew for "buy" means to get or procure for a proper consideration. Boaz, the grandfather of King David, bought Ruth, the lovely and virtuous young widow of Moab, to be his wife. And the prophet Hosea bought his wife for silver and grain. Were these women chattels? Our worthy and useful fellow-citizen, William Risdon, has built some forty houses here, and he has, for money or money's worth, "got" mechanics and laborers to build them; "got" them precisely in the sense of the Hebrew for "bought." And indeed it is very often said that our legislators are bought up here in New Jersey, to betray their constituents, by means of a riotous feast or a purse of money. The Hebrew word would apply here also; though it was seldom used for so base a purpose. These wives, mechanics and laborers are certainly not slaves; nor is the bought Senator, in the meaning of Vandyke, though he is a far more degraded man than the poor negro that cringes beneath the lash.

The word "sell" is another term to conjure with; it is the co-relative of "buy"; and always, in the Mosaic law, when used in reference to a man or woman, means to dispose of one's self, in service or employ, for a valuable consideration. Levit. xxv, 39 and 47, illustrates this: "If thy brother near thee be waxen poor, and be sold unto thee," etc.; and in 47, "If a sojourner or stranger near thee wax rich, and thy brother near him wax poor, and sell himself to the stranger or sojourner, or to the stock of the stranger's family," etc. "Be sold" and "sell himself" is the self-same word in Hebrew; and you never find in this divine law a third man or woman standing by as a chattel, a horse or cow, while two other persons bargain and dispose of him. Never! Never! Two persons, and two only, make such bargains for themselves; and buy and sell mean get and hire. Nothing, however, is so necessary to slavery as some language of Moses, implicating him and his people in some diabolical cruelty; hence its pious advocates gloat with peculiar rapture over Exodus xxi, where having spoken of the death penalty for man-slaying, it says in the 20th and 21st verses: "If a man smite his servant or his maid (literally his boy or girl) with a rod, and he die under his hand, he shall surely be punished. But if he continue a day or two, he shall not be punished, for he is his money." "Continue a day or two." And what then? Die? No; continue a day or two, uncomfortable from the flagellation, and then get well. Herein it is enacted positively that a man for whipping his boy or girl to death must suffer death himself. It is implied that great severity involved punishment of some sort; but that a whipping, whose effects continue for a day or two, required no notice of the magistrate, as the master suffered loss of time and consequently money. If "continued" here means "survived," the translators would have said so; for they wrote in a cruel age and under a tyrant king. The meaning I give is the meaning of common sense and common humanity; and both these attributes come from God; while the allowance to whip a child so that he must agonize for twenty-four hours and then expire, comes entirely from another quarter, and agrees with that expressive Southern law, which imposes punishment on a master for killing a slave, "unless he dies under moderate correction." I quote the exact words of North Carolina law. What representatives are such teachers and teachings of the person and precepts of Jesus Christ!

Some find slavery in the ten commandments. Let us see. First commandment, "Thou shalt have no other gods before me." Slaveholder, "Thou shalt obey me alone, and not know that there is a God, nor read a word He says at all, unless I choose." Fourth commandment, "Remember the Sabbath to keep it holy." Slaveholder, "You shall work every day from day-dawn to bed-time, if I please." Fifth commandment, "Honor thy father and thy mother." Slaveholder, "Your father and mother are my 'niggers,' and so are you; if you prefer obedience or regard to them instead of me, I will whip you to death." Sixth commandment, "Thou shalt not kill." Slaveholder, "I will kill whenever I please, by shortening life by hard work or short food or flogging for idleness." Seventh commandment, "Thou shalt not commit adultery." Slave-holder, "There is no such crime from a white man towards a slave." Eighth commandment, "Thou shalt not steal "; that is, take another's possession. Slaveholder, "I will take every-thing that my slave produces, also his offspring, and every-thing most dear to him as my right; I will deprive him of all means of mental improvement, and leave him nothing but a bare existence." Ninth commandment, "Thou shalt not bear false witness." Slaveholder, "My slave shall not bear witness at all against a white man; and when I please, I will torture, scourge and burn him, to extort such witness as I want." Tenth commandment, "Thou shalt not covet"; that is, claim more than thy just and equitable share. Slaveholder, "I will have all, as regards my slave; and no contract shall exist as between him and me, binding me to what justice and equity require."

Although there is no word for slavery in the Hebrew language, yet the most exact definition of its nature, and the most fearful denunciation of its wickedness, is contained in Exod. xxi, 16. In the midst of the list of capital crimes, murders, blasphemies, etc., there are these words: He that stealeth a man or selleth him, or if he be found in his hand, he shall surely be put to death. Here we have getting, part-ing with, and holding; each a capital crime. Observe; not stealing a slave, but stealing a man—a human being; selling a man, and holding a man. Again, the fugitive law, Deut. xxiii, 15, 16: All kindness to the servant. Had he been property they must have given him up. The rests and recreations of masters and servants. The religious rights and privileges of servants and those of masters. Next to idolatry, oppression was the burden of the prophet's denunciations.

God then did not institute, etc. For a few moments I turn to the new argument of silence. Oppression denounced in Old Testament. Christ saw none in Judea. Christ did not rebuke slavery, nor idolatry, and mentioned few sins. So the Apostle's Epistle to Philemon v, 16, seems for the very purpose of answering these cruel cavils.

Vandyke's text:—No rights imply no obligations.

Christianity goes ahead of this.

NOTE.—The conclusion of this sermon, it will be observed, are simply Mr. Aaron's notes, which are given, however, just as the author wrote them.

Ecc. xii, 1: "REMEMBER NOW THY CREATOR IN THE DAYS
OF THY YOUTH."

I. The subject proposed for our consideration this day is
"The importance of early Christian education." About six
months have elapsed since I called your attention to the same
matter, and several remarkable facts that have since transpired
have inclined my heart to feel, my mind to think, and my tongue
to try to speak to my fellow-mortals—my dear Christian brethren, my respected and respectful but too thoughtless hearers
all—upon a subject concerning which God speaks not only in
his word most pointedly but has to us dealt out some striking
lessons in his providence, which last I will in the first place
try to show.

Three months ago it pleased Divine Providence, after repeated, long-continued and agonizing sufferings, to remove
from this life a child of two beloved members of this church—
a sprightly, thoughtless boy, just at that age, that critical and
interesting point, when every Christian parent trembles with
the anxious but vain desire to know whether the time of ac-
countability has begun and God has doomed the creature to
appear and answer for himself. Yes, my brother and sister,
when you bent with aching hearts over your expiring offspring,
did not these questions press upon your souls: Whether Christ
had redeemed him without a faith and knowledge of his own?
Whether, if a sinner, you too must answer for his sins and bear
a portion of his guilt? Still more to our present purpose,
Whether you had done all you could to lead and to devote
him to the Lord? Whether your prayers for him in faith had
moved and opened heaven for his departing soul, and your
persuasion, precept and example had led him to Jesus, who
said "Suffer them to come and forbid them not"? Ah! when
you were assured that death had set his mark upon him, and
when in those last hours you heard him call on that Saviour
whom his father's prayers, his mother's hymns and his Sunday
school lessons had revealed to him; when you heard him lift

his dying voice in prayer for himself and his young sister, you
needed not man to prove, for God by his providence did show
you, as he has also shown us, the value of early Christian education.

But again, a more striking, if possible, and more painful
instance, has within a few weeks called on us to hear him that
speaks from heaven. A blooming child of nearly equal age
and similar character with the other is hurried without the
slightest warning, in one instant, from perfect health into a
state of laceration and suffering beyond the physician's skill,
whence he speedily passes insensible to the grave. He too
had parents that, in a judgment of charity, feared God. They
had not hated their boy by sparing the rod; they had warned
him, and watched him, and prayed with him and for him in relation to the very thing that caused his death. They had taken
pains themselves, and sought the aid of others, to impress his
mind, upon the holy Sabbath, with divine truth. And what
was there, now that he lay bleeding, mangled, delirious, dying
before their eyes, to comfort them but the fact that they had
endeavored to do their duty? They then felt, what may the
Lord move you all to feel this day, the vast importance of early
Christian education.

Now, Christians fully awake to duty feel the truths just
urged. And shall not those mortals who are unprepared either
to live or die, feel them also? How merciful to this community are these particular circumstances. The fact is alarming
and most wonderful that they seem to feel it not. O, my hearers, are you still unwarned, still heedless?

II. But let us now observe, in the second place, that the
word of God is very explicit and pointed on the subject of
early Christian education. This is denied by many; insomuch
that many persons profess to be justified in neglecting the religious culture of their children on account of the silence of
the Scriptures in relation to Sunday schools, catechisms, and
early religious lessons. They insist that if this were a cardi-
nal duty, as the Sunday School Union and some preachers
represent it, the Bible itself would be full of it in plain and
pointed terms. Now, it must in candor be admitted that there
is not a vast mass of Scripture language devoted to this single

point exclusive of all others. But let us examine the Scriptures fairly, and we shall find the meaning and authority explicity—clear as light. Remember, hearers, I speak to you as believing Scriptural duties to be most important and fully obligatory upon us all, and admitting that nothing but the knowledge and the favor of God can make us truly happy. Now, with this admission, look at the law of love to man. "Thou shalt love thy neighbor as thyself"; and, "Whatsoever ye would that men should do to you, do ye even so to them: for this is the law and the prophets." But, again. The command is to all the friends of Christ (and the duty of all is to be so) to make known the gospel to every creature. Look, then, at this precept. Shall we carry it or send it to distant heathen lands?

But the great argument as to pointed Scriptural requirement on this subject appears to me to be this: While God enforces social duties, commonly in general terms, he mentions expressly in many places the youthful portion of mankind as a class of his moral subjects. I say, my friends, while the Lord requires repentance, faith and loving obedience from all mankind, he mentions the young as the special objects of his love and the subjects of his kingdom. Now, if I am not greatly mistaken, the young of the human race are far more distinguished, as a class, by the divine word than any other portion of mankind. Neither the noble nor the ignoble, the rich nor the poor, the wise nor the ignorant, are designated as so hopefully the subjects of divine influence and blessing as those in very early life. These assertions are proved by the history of very many distinguished saints. They are proved by the precepts delivered to youth, or concerning them. They are proved by the promises and encouragements expressed in relation to them.

III. Now to whom can all this authority and all this encouragement apply more properly than to parents? Your love for your children prompts you to do or suffer anything for them—except to bring them to Christ. To satisfy their wants, kind parents will deny themselves the very bread they crave in hunger; to deliver, if possible, their little ones from sickness and pain, they would gladly suffer in their stead—at least

some tender parents would; to rescue them from death, a father or mother would rush through flood or fire. What, then,
ought your love to prompt you to, in relation to the dearest
interests of your dear children?   What wretch would feast,
heedless, while his child was starving in his sight? Who would
stand unmoved and behold his helpless offspring dragged into
hopeless, endless servitude to the most cruel and tyrannical
master? Who would remain unpitying and uncaring while
monsters and serpents were devouring his child?   The power
of parents involves them in high responsibility.   If there is a
miscreant on earth pre-eminently hell-governed and hell-pos-
sessed, it must be he who strives to pervert the heart and pollute the soul of his offspring.   And Jehovah sears with his
hottest wrath and loads with heaviest curses those rulers, having supreme power, that made Israel to sin, and those parents
that made their sons and daughters to pass through fire to
dumb idols (Levit. xvii, 21; xx, 2–5).

Do you object to my assertion of your having power?
You know you have supreme and perfect power over their
persons; natural influence over their minds.   But the Lord
bestows upon those who seek it the highest influence over their
minds and principles. His direct and positive promise is to
this effect. Patience and perseverance are necessary. A parent may inflict hard blows or use harsh and angry words,—
the child will weep and tremble; but only fear, as he would a
wild beast. No food will force your child to a full growth of
body in a moment, nor a day, nor a year. Your labor should
be directed to render your child obedient, as soon as possible;
obedient, on grounds of reason. Then that reason should be
exalted and that obedience improved in relation to his heavenly father. To accomplish your ends much private discipline
should be used, as the divine spirit speaks privately to yourself; "not provoking to wrath." But you still plead want of
power and, more especially, want of time. Time you should
take. And what is in reality your greatest difficulty?   The
want of the power of religion in your own hearts!

Shall I here call your minds to the Sunday school as a
means not of excusing you from the performance of your great
duties but of assisting you in your labor? You will allow me

to speak freely, hearers, and commend for some special reasons our Sunday school to your notice. It is taught by persons mostly, if not entirely, of serious character, and many of them far beyond the bounds of capricious youth, and who have long persevered in their efforts to do good. It has pained my very soul to see the neglect with which our school is treated, and I am strongly inclined, in addition to my many arduous duties, to become one of its teachers. Sunday schools began among Baptists as a mere matter of tolerance. The leading and established members of each church looked with suspicion upon the movement. Hence Sunday schools became independent. There should be much wisdom and great forbearance in bringing about a different state of things. I have seen unhappy results of the separation of the Sunday school from the control of the pastor and church. I feel it very important to have a pretty strong grasp on my Sunday school.

———

.

Amos iv, 12: "PREPARE TO MEET THY GOD."

(*Funeral Discourse delivered July 16, 1851.*)

These words are an express command of the Most High God, and are connected, as you have heard, with judgments which he had brought in terrific form upon the people addressed, and with the threat of more awful judgments about to come. They are, indeed, according to the mind of God himself, a necessary inference from his work of executive judgment; for he says, "Thus will I do unto thee, O Israel; and because I will do thus unto thee, prepare to meet thy God, O Israel." And, my friends, this is the conclusion which we are to draw this day, for the heaviest stroke of the arm of God that is felt short of the eternal world has fallen upon a fellow-citizen, a townsman, a near neighbor; to some present a kinsman, a husband, a father. I am not mistaken when I say the heaviest stroke. For however in the coloring of fine language we

may paint sufferings worse than death; however a mawkish
sensibility may moan over the insufferable anguish of wounded
honor, the wreck of a broken constitution in which the fact
of life is only ascertained by ceaseless agony, the pittance of
an alms-house that remains to him whose extravagance has
drained a hoard of wealth, yet the light of reason, and still
more the light of Scripture, bid a man survive all such things,
and far prefer life with all its sure and nameless ills to death
with its uncertainty. An arrow of the Almighty, therefore,
has been discharged—yea, two of them—into our little community, and the old man and the babe, the ripe fruit and the
blossom, have fallen and, as regards this life, perished forever.
The irreparable breach, the voice of the mourners, the nearer
approach of our own similar fate, and, above all, the word of
Jehovah, say to every one of us, "Prepare to meet thy God."

But to apply the words particularly, I shall, first, address
them to those whose only hope is in living, not in dying; who
act towards God as if their only meeting with him were to be
a contest for the present life—as if they were determined, in
spite of their landlord, to keep possession of the tenement occupied on his sufferance. You, my dear friends, to speak plainly
(which is the especial business of ministers), are found in greater
numbers at a funeral than at almost any other place where men
dare preach. Many come then to a place of worship, out of
respect to their fellow-creatures, who are seldom found there
from a regard for the word of the Almighty. Well, now, my
friends, prepare to meet your God. As to making peace with
him through the Lord Jesus Christ, you have no intention of
that sort; then you must either beat him off when he comes
to remove you from being tenants at will, or you must buy an
inheritance beyond the stars with the treasures of good works
you are now laying up.

Let us look at the hope of the present life. The Eternal
says by his prophet, "I will take vengeance, and will not meet
thee as a man." When a man is about to meet his fellow for
purposes of vengeance, or in self defence, what precautions he
takes to be thoroughly prepared, what well proved implements
of death he carries, what friends he summons to his side, what
firm determination to his heart. But when Jehovah challenges

man goes not forth to meet with his fellow. This adversary
sits invisible above the heavens. He sends his apoplexy; it
comes, and the vital stream that warms man's heart forsakes
its channels and rushes in a torrent to overwhelm the regions of
mind and sensation, where, like a stagnant sea, it settles down
and buries deep the throne of reason and the powers of life.
He commissions fever, and the lamp of life, like Nebuchadnezzar's furnace, burns with a sevenfold heat, till its support is
wasted and it goes out forever. He speaks to dysentery, and
the numberless tubes that carry nutriment to flesh and blood
are closed; corruption's channel opens wide, and strength and
life flow rapidly away. Friends gather around and weep; perhaps they pray. Science appears and marshals all her powers,
her instruments of cunning workmanship, her opiates, her
stimulants, her drugs. But in vain are his own strength and
human aid, for man has met his God; the silver chord is loosed,
the golden bowl is broken, and man must go to his long home.

You see, then, careless soul, the unequal contest. Indeed, the departed generations among whose tombs we wan-
der, the few sad relics of their fate, forewarn you and imperi-
ously urge you to prepare to meet your God. Those who lift
up their eyes in torment find it the next desire to that of their
own deliverance, that their kinsmen and friends might not
come into that place of anguish. And those in Abraham's bosom would feel new thrills of joy to welcome their survivors
to the seats prepared for them.

But to return. If you cannot stand it out with God in
mortal combat, then, like the king who thinks he cannot engage with ten thousand an adversary who approaches with
twenty thousand, you ought to seek conditions of peace. We
have already agreed, however, that you cannot do this by submission to the Lord Jesus Christ, but must effect it by giving
such things as you have. And as the Eternal is a moral being, you must present to him a moral offering. Well, what
will you bring? Will you attempt to exhibit a perfect example of moral rectitude? This no man of sense dares think of,
for he knows that he has often departed from the straight path,
that he has often given way to causeless anger, that he has
often coveted, that he has often given way to vain imagination

and thrown the reins to pride and envy. But do you not propose to balance accounts with God, to make it an affair of debt
and credit, assured that you have done right in a majority of instances; at any rate, that you have meant well? And even if
you have generally failed, you attribute to him so much generosity that you verily believe he will frankly forgive you.
Now, we will suppose the best of the case; for instance, that
you have a hundred credits for a single debt. Will the balance of ninety-nine in your favor buy you a mansion in heaven?
Here a thought strikes me. If it will, it must be some one that
Christ has not prepared for; for he went, as he says, to prepare
a place only for them that believe in him, and love him, and
follow him. And, again, your mansion must be in some part
of heaven in which Christ does not dwell; because he said to
some of the most self-righteous men that the world has ever
seen, such as fasted twice a week, gave tithes and alms of all
that they possessed, and prayed much, "Where I am ye can
not come." Now, to find a mansion in heaven which Christ
has not prepared, who made all things of himself and for himself, and to inhabit a place there where he is not present, of
whom it is said that he is the very light of that city—the New
Jerusalem—must be extremely difficult.

But to return to the ninety-nine credits in your favor. Let
the prisoner plead before the judge. "I have saved one hundred lives, and have willfully murdered but this one individual.
I can prove that I have acted honestly—yea, even with honor
and generosity—in one hundred instances, whereas I have
stolen or defrauded but this once." Would the law therefore
acquit him? Or would it say to him, You have done no more
than your duty, by which no man can purchase a license to
perpetrate a single crime? Well, does human equity surpass
in strictness that of God? Examine the latter. "Thou shalt
love the Lord thy God with all thy heart," etc. And, again,
"He that keeps the whole law, and yet offends in one point, is
guilty of all." What clause of reservation is here left to encourage impenitent sinners to insult the Almighty with their
claims to merit. O, hearer, argument fails, illustration fails,
and I can only repeat the text in thy ears, perhaps for the last

time, thoughtless mortal, mortal hastening to the judgment, "Prepare to meet thy God." Prepare to meet thy God!

But I come, secondly, to speak to a different class. You that are stated attendants on the sanctuary. Prepare to meet your God there with more sincerity and desire. Prepare to meet him in your closets. Prepare to meet him as one that seeks your hearts. "My son, give me thy heart." Prepare to meet him in his providences. Prepare to meet him on the throne of eternal judgment. Prepare to dwell with him in heaven.

Thirdly, the mourners. I shall never meet you all together again. I must therefore be faithful. Be not presumptuous because of mature age. O, seek to redeem the time. "The Lord gave, and the Lord hath taken away; blessed be the name of the Lord. For whom the Lord loveth he chasteneth, and scourgeth every son whom he receiveth. Now no chastening for the present seemeth to be joyous, but grievous; nevertheless, afterward it yieldeth the peaceable fruit of righteousness unto them which are exercised thereby."

THE DESCRIPTION OF SINNERS.

1. Those that are in the way—the wicked or transgressors.

2. Those that are making their calculations—the unrighteous or lawless.

The first act without much thought; the second are philosophers, ungodly upon principle. The world is full of such. The first are the hands and feet, the second are the eyes and heads, in the service of the devil. The first are like Jeroboam, the son of Nebat, that made Israel to sin; the second are like foolish Israel, that obeyed to do iniquitously. The first are like the sellers and manufacturers of spirits; the second like those that drink them. The first are like kings and rulers that plan wars and intrigues; the others like the subjects that fight or execute. The first are like the citizen of the far country that had the swine to feed; the second like the poor prodigal that was almost starved in feeding them. The first are rather the rich, the polished, the gay, the honored—those that must have religion, if it is absolutely indispensable, in a coach, a fine house, a fine equipage, or high office; the others go their pilgrimage on foot, and sweat and groan as they trudge along the road to ruin. The first seem to be the more hopeless, because the devil gives them better wages, better fare. And yet we might suppose it would matter little whether a man were carried in a coach to the gallows or dragged thither by the hair of his head; whether he were suspended on a towering gibbet like Haman or hung up like a dog; whether he were strangled with a silken cord or a hempen rope. But the gay world think differently.

The apostle Paul thought his case peculiar that he should be pardoned, because he was a ringleader. And it is certain that the fate of a campaign depends mainly on the prowess and honor of the leaders. Many of these plotters of sin are not so accessible as the poor and undistinguished. They contribute, many of them, to the support of the gospel ministry; and it is thought sufficiently bold in the preacher even to hint at the possibility of their errors from the pulpit, not to censure personally their sins and charge them to their faces. The poor, thoughtless man, that lies expiring without attendants or the necessaries of life, is glad to hear the prayers or the teachings of piety; is willing to hear of his errors and acknowledge them. But he whose superior mind has collected money and purchased friends is not approachable by the humble follower of Christ, who can only bid him weep over his sins and flee for refuge to the poor, the humble, the forsaken Jesus of Nazareth, who had neither money nor friends.

Whatever may be said of the unfaithfulness of the ministers, those are still wanting who have a talent for convincing and convicting the sinners of a speculative and philosophical character; and whether he be rich in purse or rich in self-estimation, that man will find it hard to enter into the kingdom of

God. Even Christ himself kept aloof from those who thought they had no need of mercy, who thought that they were righteous and despised others, and his gospel was preached rather to the poor; not merely to the poor in pocket, but to the poor in arguments, and poor in self-righteousness and self-esteem.

———

Rom. xii, 1. The motive to action is "The mercies of God." God is merciful, plenteous in mercy, rich in mercy, abundant in mercy. We hear of the multitude of his mercies. How thankless, hard-hearted children sometimes reason. They say, my parents brought me into the world, etc. But a poor penitent does not see it so. A good Christian does not see it so. He sees that everything he has is of God's mercy, which fails not. How he blesses that mercy that provides for all his wants. Is he rich? Is he poor? Is he absolutely suffering? Is his reputation assailed? How wonderful appears that forbearance that spared him; that did not suffer execution to issue, and cut him off in his impenitence. How still greater that mercy, that not only spared him from death, but gave him life; that constrained him to come and taste the sweet things of redeeming love. How, above all, that great adorable mercy that pitied dying men and gave the life of the just for the unjust. Oh, hard-hearted man, that hearest this and does not feel it; canst thou feel anything? Present your bodies a living sacrifice. This is figurative; and like all Paul's illustrations, apt and forcible. To offer in sacrifice any beast that had died by accident or disease was an abomination. But the sacrifice was to be brought living to the priests without spot or blemish. Now this is used by Paul as an illustration of what the Lord expects of us. The beast offered was to be the best of the flock. So should the Christian; so must the Christian be the best among men. Holy—that is, set apart, probably—and acceptable unto God, according to the description given by the Lord. But as Christians, you are to present yourselves as sacrifices before the Lord. Now this is your reasonable service. Now, brethren, if these things be so, you are doubtless presenting yourselves as living sacrifices unto the Lord. But oh! the fact is far otherwise. In the phrase, to present your bodies, there is probably allusion to attendance on public worship, and the table of the Lord. Did you not solemnly, most solemnly promise, in the presence of God and many witnesses, to keep your places in the sanctuary? If a man were to neglect all these things for the purpose of more ardent, private devotion, he could not be excused because of the deleterious example. But a man never omits one duty to God for the purpose of performing another better.

Matt. xxv, 46: "AND THESE SHALL GO AWAY INTO EVER-LASTING PUNISHMENT."

I. Punishment a part or principle of the divine government. Does every prudent teacher punish? Does a father? Does a law-giver? The punishment brought on our world by the sin of our first parents. Sin possessed all; the woman especially. Reversed by Jesus. The punishment of man; of devils.

II. That punishment is everlasting. A tremendous word; and therefore many determined to explain it away. According to the word of God, everlasting punishment is just as certain to some as everlasting felicity is to others. Why so?

First. In contrast.

David.—"Men of the world, which have their portion in this life." "I shall be satisfied when I awake in thy likeness."

Solomon.—"The hope of the righteous shall be gladness, but the expectation of the wicked shall perish." "The wicked shall be driven away in his wickedness, but the righteous hath hope in his death."

Daniel.—"And many of them that sleep in the dust of the earth shall awake; some to everlasting life, and some to shame and everlasting contempt."

Matthew.—"He will gather his wheat into the garner," etc. "Wide is the gate that leadeth to destruction," etc. "Many shall come from the east and from the west," etc.

"Gather ye first the tares, and bind them in bundles to burn them." "The Son of Man shall send forth his angels, and they shall gather out of his kingdom all things that offend, and those that do iniquity; and shall cast them into a furnace of fire: there shall be wailing and gnashing of teeth. Then shall the righteous shine forth as the sun in the kingdom of their father." "The kingdom of heaven is like unto a net that gathered fish of every kind; which, when it was full, they drew to the shore, and sat down, and gathered the good into vessels, but cast the bad away. So shall it be at the end of the world; the angels shall come forth, and sever the wicked from among the just, and shall cast them into a furnace of fire: there shall be wailing and gnashing of teeth." "Blessed is that servant, whom his lord when he cometh shall find so do-ing. * * But and if that evil servant shall say in his heart, My lord delayeth his coming; and shall begin to smite his fellow servants, and to eat and drink with the drunken; the lord of that servant shall come in a day when he looketh not for him, and shall cut him asunder, and appoint him his portion with the hypocrites: there shall be weeping and gnashing of teeth." "Well done, good and faithful servant, * * enter thou into the joy of thy lord. * * And cast ye the unprofitable serv-ant into outer darkness," etc. "Then shall the King say unto them on his right hand, Come, ye blessed of my Father, in-herit the kingdom prepared for you from the foundation of the world. * * Then shall he say also unto them on his left hand, Depart from me, ye cursed, into everlasting fire, prepared for the devil and his angels. * *. And these shall go away into everlasting punishment: but the righteous into life eter-nal." "He that believeth on me hath life," etc. "Blessed are ye when men shall hate you for the Son of Man's sake." "Re-joice ye in that day, and leap for joy; for, behold, your reward is great in heaven." "But woe unto you that are rich, for ye have received your consolation." "God so loved the world that he gave his only begotten Son, that whosoever believeth in him might not perish but have everlasting life." "All that are in the grave shall come forth; they that have done good unto the resurrection of life," etc.

Paul.—Hath not the potter power over the clay of the same lump to make one vessel unto honor and another unto dishonor? What if God, willing to shew his wrath and to make his power known, endured with much long suffering the vessels of wrath fitted for destruction; and that he might make known the riches of his glory on the vessels of mercy which he had afore prepared unto glory. "Be not deceived; God is not mocked; for whatsoever a man soweth, that shall he also reap. For he that soweth to the flesh, shall of the flesh reap corruption; but he that soweth to the spirit, shall of the spirit reap life everlasting." "That which beareth thorns and briers is rejected, and is nigh unto cursing, whose end is to be burned." "But, beloved, we are persuaded better things of you, and things which accompany salvation."

This is a contrast in a variety of forms.

Second. The words of Christ. This doctrine is clearly implied. Jesus.—"I pray for them; I pray not for the world." "The blasphemy against the Holy Ghost shall not be forgiven unto men," etc. "He hath never forgiveness, but is in danger of eternal damnation." "If we sin willfully after we have received the knowledge of the truth, there remaineth no more sacrifice for sins." "What is a man profited, if he shall gain the whole world and lose his own soul." "Their worm dieth not," etc. "Betwixt us and you there is a great gulf fixed," etc. "He that believeth not the Son, shall not see life," etc. "I go my way, and ye shall seek me, and shall die in your sins," etc. "Whose end is destruction."

Third. Preparedness in this life is necessary. "Seek ye the Lord while he may be found; call on him while he is near," etc. "Behold, now is the accepted time; now is the day of salvation." "To-day, if ye will hear his voice, harden not your hearts."

John.—"He that is unjust, let him be unjust still," etc.

The word everlasting is applied to the Supreme. In the next place the nature of the punishment. Whatever suffering is most intense and acute in this life is used as a figure of that to come. I cannot see that the Almighty uses any particular agency in tormenting. They hated God and loved sin. They shall go to the capital city of sin's dominions. How

much more a refined and high-spirited person suffers, with an
angel's intellect and a devil's heart. Do you not think you
deserve some punishment? Are you quite sure of exemption?
If you avoid to do harm, and are quite sure you would not
have used Christ ill, would not some of you be very much
offended at reproof? And are not Christians afraid of it?

But lastly. Who are those that are to go away into
everlasting punishment? Are they murderers, robbers and
adulterers, etc., alone? They, doubtless; but our Saviour
speaks not of such here, but of those who have omitted to
perform some of the least imposing obligations apparently.
He speaks not of those who had done any harm—according
to the best codes of merely human morals—but of those who
have neglected to do any good.

Analogy as to future punishments in nature with Revelation. 1. We bring many punishments knowingly upon ourselves. 2. They come in consequence of actions the most
pleasurable and temptations the most overwhelming. 3.
These punishments are often delayed a great while, and then
come suddenly and unlooked for. 4. Even "innocent youth,"
as we call it, is no excuse for rashness and folly. 5. The neglect of proper seasons brings great disadvantages; certain
bounds being passed, irretrievable losses follow. 6. These are
not occasional consequences but fixed laws. These then are
awful analogies; and nothing but a complete demonstration of
infidelity should make any impenitent man easy. Many live
as if only to show the horrors of vice and folly. Though men
wish God, they do not wish earthly magistrates to compel them
to be holy and happy. The Scripture authority, I am sure,
was found overwhelming. Now another truth is as sure; that
every one in this house unwilling to confess Christ is exposed
to endless death. Be not diverted by Satan's devises, nor
deceived by the coldness of Christians. "Examine your own
selves, whether ye be in the faith; prove your ownselves."

OMNISCIENCE OF THE LORD.

His knowledge is perfect. He planted the ear; formed the eye; teaches man knowledge; darkness and light the same; all things naked and open; knoweth the heart and the thoughts afar off. He is infinite; cannot be searched out; looketh to the ends of the earth and seeth under the whole heaven; known are all his works; declares the end from the beginning. Times are not hidden from the Almighty. All time with Him; one indivisible eternal now. Our knowledge; but for the present moment, and confined to narrow bounds of space and material objects, you known not my thoughts nor I yours; hence we do not conceive of the intense power of omniscient vision. More especially does he view us now. But if we are sincere in our worship, we may invite with joy the unerring scrutiny of heaven; and great is our consolation that the Lord is greater than our hearts. For "a book of remembrance was written before him for them that feared the Lord and that thought upon his name."

How are we grieved at having our best motives misrepresented and misunderstood by men. But the Lord makes no mistakes nor does unjustly. He knows and he appreciates our charity and faith and patience. He loves the man that loves him. His eye is upon them that fear him; upon them that hope in his mercy; upon them that trust in him. "A meek and quiet spirit is in the sight of God of great price." He sees our true humility; our contritions and repentance; he counts unto us for righteousness, our faith in Jesus. He enters with you into your closets; he knoweth what things we need. He knoweth your adversities. He inclineth his ear from heaven to the groaning of the prisoner. He beholdeth and requiteth mischief and spite. He knows your reproach and shame. Be this then our prayer: "Let the meditation of my heart be acceptable in thy sight, O Lord. Teach me, O God, and know my heart; try me, and know my reins."

Very different is the case with the impenitent. They put far away the day, and either think God does not know, or forget that he does. As they wish not to be in sight now, so hereafter, and loudly will they call on the rocks to fall on them and hide them from the wrath of the Lamb. He knoweth vain men; he forgetteth not their forgetfulness of him; he knows all their pretexts for self indulgence. But dull as we are now of sight and knowledge, the day shall come when the scales shall fall from mortal vision, and we shall know as we are known.

How Jesus Spent His Sabbath.

" He entered into the synagogue," etc. He had no welcome there. If the rulers rejoiced to see him, it was that they might accuse him; entrap him; destroy him. He scans the silent workings of their hearts; mildly and effectually refutes their mental reasonings; disregards their bitter, causeless opposition, and heals the poor obedient sufferers. With fortitude and self possession unknown to human nature, with all the talent and learning of the land arrayed against him, at the peril of his life he entered their synagogue, because the name and word of the true God were there, and more especially because poor sinners were collected there, and taught and truly spake as man never spake. He proved it right to do well on the Sabbath day, and sealed his arguments with a deed of mercy demonstrative of God-like pity and Almighty power. Ye Sabbath-day sleepers, dreamers, loungers, visitors; ye that press your beds, and indulge your appetites, and read your novels, and crack your jests, behold the example of your Master. In works of mercy, disinterested and unintermitted, he spent his Sabbath. "Is the disciple above his master? the servant greater than his lord?" If the Master worked so much, is it proper therefore for the servant to do nothing?

The power of Christ and the duty of obedience. The same being whose voice resounded through the void and formless infinite, " Let there be light"; said in the accents of

mercy to the paralytic, whose arm hung useless at his side,
"Stretch forth thy hand!" Quicker than the word the
withered skin expanded, the shrunk muscles filled, the vital
blood rushed through the dry, cold channels long forsaken,
and the man extended it whole as the other. He was obedient; he did not stay in the obstinacy of sinful human nature
and pride of human reason, to argue the impossibility and
absurdity of attempting to use a limb over which his volition
had no control. He obeyed and witnessed that "Where the
word of a king is, there is power."

"LET THE WICKED FORSAKE HIS WAY AND THE UNRIGHT-
EOUS MAN HIS THOUGHTS."

But here an objection is made by some that they cannot.
If you mean that you cannot save yourself from perdition, and
make your way to the heavenly paradise, then I agree with
you perfectly; but if you mean that you cannot give attention
to your soul's affairs, that you cannot leave off sinful habits,
such as drunkenness, profane swearing, lying, fraud, bad company, and even impure and sinful thoughts, then I differ with
you. And I wish to convince you that you are permitting the
devil to lead you captive at his will. The common understanding of mankind, the just laws of all civilized nations, are
at variance with such a sentiment. When a man has been the
means of his neighbor's death by the accidental discharge of a
musket, or has unwittingly pushed a beam or wall upon his
head, who thinks of punishing him as a murderer? But where,
having planned and compassed his death, he attempts to excuse himself by pleading extreme hatred, or a bloodthirsty
disposition, or overruling destiny, who does not know that it
aggravates the crime? Who believes the most confirmed
drunkard when he says that he cannot quit drinking, any more
than he believes the seller, who says he could not but give the
liquor because the money was offered? Who believes the
robber that says he has no other way to get a living, or that

he cannot quit the practice because he has been so long accustomed to it? Men, in the accursed indulgence of their lusts, try to persuade themselves that it is fate, an overruling destiny, that has compelled them to sin, thus charging upon the Almighty all the causes and consequences of depravity, and making him, instead of the friend and benefactor, the foe and the destroyer of the human race.

But it is the depraved heart and not the rational head of man that reasons thus. Thus Adam reasoned when he said, "The woman whom thou gavest to be with me caused me to eat." And when Adam spoke thus he was depraved Adam; righteous Adam no more. When a man is dragged to the dram shop, tied hand and foot, a tube thrust down his throat, and ardent spirits poured through it into his stomach, the act is not his; he could not help it. But many sins that men freely indulge, they could not possibly commit by any agency but their own. No power in heaven, earth or hell, compels a man to give entertainment to sinful desires. They are children of his own; or they become his guests by his own consent or welcome. "Let the wicked forsake his way, and the unrighteous man his thoughts, and let him return unto the Lord, and he will have mercy upon him, and to our God, for he will abundantly pardon," is the command and promise of God. And what prevents the instant obedience of every individual present? Is it want of benevolence in the Lord? He does not lie. It is the resistence of the human will, loaded with the weight of original sin, buried in a mass of practical transgressions, all arched and coated over with an impenetrable crust of pride and carnal policy, and polished well by witty cavils. "The wicked shall be driven away in his wickedness; but the righteous shall have hope in his death."

My Friends, What Think Ye of Christ?

Have you ever made him as much the subject of your thoughts as you have your own temporal concerns? You have thought the story of the virgin, the manger, the miracles, the cross, the resurrection, and all the recorded wonders that attended and followed the ministry of Jesus; a curious tale, but not extremely interesting; in short, rather dry. Many a volume, pretending neither to truth nor probability, unfitted either "to raise the genius or to mend the heart," has rivetted your attention for hours, while scarcely more minutes have left you yawning over the history of the Redeemer. Now what is the reason of this distaste? Almost all of us, perhaps, quite, that compose this assembly, are considered by ourselves, and many of our neighbors, as a decent, good sort of people; and much complacency no doubt is felt by many of the company, that they are not as other men are.

But I will specify a means by which each one of us may determine pretty accurately the extent of our goodness and worthiness in the sight of our Creator and sovereign, disposer of our everlasting fate. If we had made and could preserve both ourselves and ours, our felicity might reasonably consist in our own good opinion of ourselves and our performances; but as another Being formed us, and lent us for a short period all that we possess, it behooves us carefully to conciliate his regard. Now that Being has given us a book containing a brief history of his dealings with men, and stating distinctly the duties we should perform with all our heart and mind and strength; and we are truly good when we delight in the statutes and fully keep the commandments registered in that volume. Now a heart-felt interest in this book, an unwearied perusal of it, a decided preference for it over every other, will prove us good; the contrary will prove us not so. The Bible is admitted by all of us to be a good book; by many of us the best of books. Why then do not all of us good people have a greater relish for this good book? The fact is the book is far more excellent than we esteem it, and we much less so than we imagine ourselves. Its standard of goodness is what the Being, in finitely good, uses for his measure, and our imaginary excellence it treats with neglect and silence. It says very little about beautiful women and brave men, ladies of accomplishments and quality, and gentlemen of spirit and high breeding; and nothing in their praise. It pardons no amiable weakness; palliates no fashionable vice; and aggravates with affected sensibility no imaginary crime. It puts little distinction, in point of worthiness, before God, between the self-complacent moralist and the notorious sinner; between the amiable, unbelieving lady and the woman of abandoned character. And while thus it places all on equal footing, it declares the probability that publicans and harlots shall go into the kingdom of heaven before the esteemed and honorable among men.

Now these are not as agreeable things to the best sort of worldly people, nor to any sort, as the praise and flattery bestowed on patriotism, courage, genius, philosophy, splendor and beauty. Have we a novel, a history of any description, a review, a newspaper, a jest book, a ballad, or even a dream book? Ten pages of any of them shall be read by many of us before one of the Bible. Are we not ashamed of this? Alas! no one blushes, because he knows his neighbor is as culpable as he.

Now the fact is, my friends, many of you do not make it your meat and your drink to do the will of your Heavenly Father as recorded in that book. You dislike the book and him that made it, and those that praise it and tell you the plain meaning of its contents. You profess great respect for it, but you do not take it for your guide to heaven. "All scripture is given by inspiration of God, and is profitable for doctrine, for reproof, for correction and instruction in righteousness; that the man of God may be perfect, thoroughly furnished with all good works. The Holy Scriptures are able to make wise unto salvation, through faith in Christ Jesus. These are written that ye might believe that Jesus is the Christ, the Son of God."

What are your ideas of God? I believe that God is a being, having an unchangeable existence from everlasting to everlasting—a spiritual being, of whose mode of existence we have no adequate idea; as invisible to our eyes and as impalpable to our touch as our own souls are. An almighty being; the source and author of all other existence, spiritual, animal and material, and upholding all things by the word of his power. A being perfect in knowledge; having infinite duration with all its events present to his mind, and infinite space with all its objects, like a point before his eye; that his understanding is infinite, discerning and ordaining the best possible ends from the best possible means; that he is absolutely just, benevolent and holy. "He reigneth, the omnipotent Lord God." "In the beginning He created the heaven and the earth." "He made the heaven of heavens with all their hosts." "There is no unrighteousness in the Lord." "He is glorious in holiness." "He is of purer eyes than to behold evil, and cannot look on iniquity." "The Lord God is merciful and gracious, long suffering, and abundant in goodness and truth." "The earth is full of his mercy." "The Lord God is full of compassion." "Yet God is angry with the wicked every day."

He has revealed himself to us in scripture as the Father, the Son and the Holy Ghost. He says in Isaiah: "I am God, and there is none like me; declaring the end from the beginning, and from ancient times the things that are not yet done; saying, my counsel shall stand, and I will do all my pleasure." "He worketh all things after the counsel of his own will." "Neither is there any creature that is not manifest in his sight; but all things are naked and open unto the eyes of him with whom we have to do."

————

Men have many motives to fear and to love the Lord their God. He is infinitely powerful; he made all things; he is God, and none else; has us and all things in his hand, our life and our breath; has commanded love and obedience; is kind in the gift of nature; when he takes away he only takes his own; he has every perfection—the only perfect being, wise, just, holy, unchangeable, eternal; will be our judge and our rewarder or punisher. But powerful as these motives are, they are outdone by one—his mercy through Jesus Christ. " In thy seed shall all the nations of the earth be blessed," was the most glorious communication made to the ancients. And Moses looked with deepest interest to that prophet, etc. The tuneful harp of the son of Jesse sounds most harmonious in the celebration of that glorious Prince, the only begotten Son of God, the King of Glory, at whose coming the gates were to be lifted up and the everlasting doors opened. The lips of the son of Amos dwelt on no theme so grand as that of the child that should be, etc. The devout soul of Daniel prophesied of the stone cut out without hands, which was to break the kingdom of earth and set up another kingdom which shall never be destroyed. In short, the most noble theme of Holy Writ, of prophets, apostles, saints and angels, is that Lamb that was slain, that Jesus who lived and was dead and lives again, and reigns for evermore. He endured the cross, he despised the shame, and is now set down at the right hand of the throne of God. When we view the most merciful Son of God, poor and persecuted, unfatigued in doing good, teaching patiently the dullest and most perverse minds, and consider that it was for us he lived a perfect life, for us he died an ignominious death, for us he arose and ascended in triumph and now stands pleading, showing the scars in his hands and feet—oh! when our eyes are opened to see these things as they are, we do not feel unconcerned; we wonder, as rational beings, why his wrath did not destroy those murderers suddenly.

But as Christians we rejoice with joy unspeakable and full of glory. We are ashamed of our coldness when we remember how our Saviour wept over Jerusalem, for sorrow that they would not come unto him and receive the gift of eternal life. It is worthy of note that our greatest consolation makes us seem ridiculous in the eyes of an unbelieving world. Glorious, figurative, beautiful, certain distinction between him that serveth God and him that serveth him not. Induce a man to believe in God, in his power and wisdom, and that he will strictly and severely judge, and the man will do anything. This is the way of some alarmed sinners; they would give thousands of rams, etc., their first-born, make their children pass through the fire, make pilgrimages barefooted, fast and groan. When a man sees that all these fail, when he understands the perfect obedience required by the law, he becomes rebellious and calls his Maker cruel. Now, the heathen gods were represented only a little better than men, though much more powerful; it was easy to be reconciled to them.

But you say, Is there no way of making up this matter? If I say to a generous fellow-creature, I am sorry for what I have done, he will forgive me. Will not my Maker do the same? He will not. But I will never do it again, is not that enough? No. But that Christian, or David, or Noah, or Peter, or Paul, did worse, and were they not pardoned? They were. And shall not I be pardoned for a less crime? You shall not, unless you seek and obtain forgiveness through the blood of Jesus Christ; he is the one mediator between God and man, who gave himself a ransom for all.

THE GARDEN OF GETHSEMANE.

This subject is of a deeply pathetic nature, from the character of the sufferer and the cause and extent of his sufferings. To see a parent with hard, incessant drudgery, and patient self-denial, strive from year to year to support his helpless family, is to my mind a moving spectacle. But he has the smiles of his companion and the caresses of his children to soothe his toil, and the hope that they will support his future helplessness. Men's feelings are touched by the recollections of the father of his country still adhering to his hopeless duty and leading his few and feeble ranks to battle, to the struggle for the rights of man, while they tracked their way with the blood that oozed from their unprotected feet and marked the frozen earth. Men are moved by the resolution of such heroes, and look upon them with admiration. Let a man give all praise and gratitude to patriots. They left obscurity and ease for toil and honor. Christ left the throne of supreme dominion for the lowest place on earth. He had no country, no friends, no rights.

There is ground for strong consolation to all those that flee for refuge to the suffering Redeemer. These awful sufferings were not designed to be thrown away; they were too great for that. The Lord had often and long before declared that he had no pleasure in the death of a sinner; and now, to stop all unbelieving mouths, he confirms by dreadful deeds what he had sworn to before in solemn words. The God that made the heavens and the earth drinks himself the cup of wrath prepared for guilty men. It does not pass by him. O, thanks be to his adorable mercy, it does not pass one drop of its bitter contents to the penitent sinner; but Jesus drinks it all. Therefore, my thoughtful, anxious friend, let me press you, in the name of the Lord my God, not to be faithless, but believing. Let me urge you by all that is interesting to you as man, all that is honoring to your Maker; all that is sweet and cheering in hope, all that is black and dismal in despair; by all that is pure and lovely in the just made perfect and the holy angels, all that is blasphemous and abhorred in devils and lost men; by all that is blessed and glorious in heaven, all that is accursed and tremendous in hell; by all the terrors of the law, and all the promises and encouragements of the gospel; by the stern justice of Jehovah, and the tender mercies of Immanuel,—that you rest not till you have given yourself up to Jesus Christ. Defer not till to-morrow what may be done to-day. Many a human being before to-morrow will be in another world. You may be one of the number. I saw a man dying yesterday, who had put off for many years, had put off till the very last, what ought to have been done at first, and it was an affecting sight. He called on Jesus at times, but had little or no assurance of hope to alleviate the agony of death. If the great being, who shed forth the glory and riches of the universe, who kindled the lustre of the stars and effused the dazzling splendor of the sun; if he from such exaltation became so lowly; if the sins of his enemies were imputed to him of his own consent; if he became a reproach and by-word and the song of the drunkard; if the infinite God did indeed submit to dwell for thirty-three years in human flesh, to live in abject poverty, subsist on charity, and die a pauper, then there is surely encouragement for every humble soul.

The shocking case of those that despise the grace of God! My friend, if God the Son, the second person in the glorious, equal trinity of God-head, did indeed suffer in that garden of Gethsemane such agony as caused him to sweat blood, such agony as made the first impulse of his will—his human will— a strong desire, a fervent prayer, to shun the conflict, do you think that sin can be in the estimation of the Almighty a trifling matter? When Immanuel agonized and shuddered thus in the endurance of its punishment, think you it can fall lightly on the sinner's head? When Junius Brutus condemned his guilty son to death, the Romans thought it an astonishing exhibition of his love of justice and hatred of transgression. What, then, when the Almighty Father condemns his innocent, his spotless, his well beloved, equal son to a most abject life and painful death for the crimes of others? Christ had told those who came to see and hear him, "And I, if I be lifted up from the earth, will draw all men unto me." "I am come a light into the world, that whosoever believeth on me should not abide in darkness." "He that rejecteth me, and receiveth not my words, hath one that judgeth him: the word that I have spoken, the same shall judge him in the last day."

"BEHOLD THE LAMB OF GOD, THAT TAKETH AWAY THE SIN OF THE WORLD."

I.   It is most shocking to reflect upon the sin of the world. Sin made man flee from his Maker. Sin drove him from his happy home. Sin blotted and deformed the whole face of creation. Sin brought suffering upon the very brutes. Sin brought groans and tears and death upon mankind. Sin has let loose ungovernable appetites and passions. Sin brought death and all its horrors upon the race of man. Sin took away all peace in life and all hope in death. Sin destroyed all claim to heaven, and made sure and certain an inheritance in hell. Sin made us enemies of God, the only good and our only friend; and servants of Satan, the adversary of God and man. Sin resisted, abused, insulted all messengers of mercy from

God to man; then murdered the Son of God. But does all this apply to us? What was the beginning of all this? The eating of an apple. Did you never do anything so bad? O, how shall I paint your dreadful state? Our way through life is like a path on the brink of dangerous steeps, over slippery rocks; we may fall sooner or later. O, if you lose your soul, what suffering is before you through eternity!

II. It is most delightful to hear that sin can be taken away. A great controversy as to the meaning of taking away the sin of the world! The virtue of the blood of Christ is certainly sufficient for all that apply. Takes away all kinds of sin: David's adultery and murder; the thief's public crimes; Mary Magdalen's sin; Zaccheus' dishonesty; everything but final unbelief.

III. How affecting to consider the means used for the removal or cure of sin! Incense smoked upon the altar; blood of lambs and fat of rams offered; Abel himself bled in defence of truth; the deluge came upon a sinful world, but did not wash away sin; fire came upon Sodom and Gomorrah; war, pestilence and famine were sent; blood of children shed; blood of saints and martyrs; death universal and eternal; the Lamb of God alone can take away sin. See John's account of him and self-abasement before him: Unfit to baptize him; unfit to bear or unloose the latchet of his shoe; Jesus' sacrifice compared to a lamb; offered daily; paschal lamb. See then and believe that the whole world lieth in wickedness—gross darkness. But a message goes forth. The Baptist in the wilderness first proclaims it most plainly. John is like the morning star; he brings the light—its first streaks. And when the Sun appears, he cries aloud, "Behold the Lamb of God!"

Ecc. xi, 9: "REJOICE, O YOUNG MAN, IN THY YOUTH; AND LET
THY HEART CHEER THEE IN THE DAYS OF THY YOUTH, AND
WALK IN THE WAYS OF THY HEART, AND IN THE SIGHT OF
THINE EYES: BUT KNOW THOU, THAT FOR ALL THESE THINGS
GOD WILL BRING THEE INTO JUDGMENT."

From fourteen to twenty-one years is the age of action,
of passion, of self-will, of needful toil, of disappointment, and
of deep religious impressions. The character is finished. You
have lost faith and confidence in others, even in your parents.
But young people ought not to seek exemption from paternal
restraint. Your state is like the trees in bloom, like the face
of nature in spring. As we walk abroad in the season of
spring, among the inimitable works of Nature's God, our senses
are indulged and our imaginations delighted with the smiling
beauty and the rich promise of the scene. The genial bosom
of the air that embraces us is perfumed with mingled fragrance
by the soft sighing of the western breeze, and thrills with the
melody of nature's music; while the green mantle of earth, our
fruitful mother, is spangled with all her blossoms; painted by
the sunbeams, God's own pencil, which, as if dipped in the
rainbow, imparts all its hues combined and simple to the garments of spring. Nor is all this profusion of fragrance, of
melody and beauty, to be thrown away. Health, peace and
plenty are to follow from it. These flowers are to bring forth
fruits to satisfy the wants of every living thing. Such is a faint
picture of material, irrational nature. You will readily see that
this picture is emblematic of the reality that is about to claim
our attention. I am on this occasion to address the flower, the
early growth of God's intelligent and accountable creation.

In you, my youthful friends, is the moral hope of the community, the religious expectation of the church, and to you are
held out the best promises of heaven. You are by far the
most interesting objects among all visible things; your welfare, the most important consideration that can possibly occupy
the human mind. Your entrance into the world, the protec-

tion of your helpless infancy, and the guardianship of your juvenile age, are the cause of more pain, more expense and more
anxiety than anything else that Providence has ordained. Im-
mense is the price that the world pays for you, my friends,
whether we reckon the mother's tremblings, pains and agonizing throes; the father's sweat and toil; or the mutual yearn-
ings and watchings of both, which God has made a parent's
instinct as a security for the welfare of the offspring. How
striking an illustration of a part of what I say is found among
the people called the Shakers. Do we wonder why those societies directly become so wealthy? The answer is plain. They
are comparatively free from the expense of raising children. I
repeat it, my young friends, you cost the world immensely.
And what is the inference? You ought to repay it by your
industry, your virtue, your piety. From you, as our vernal
blossoms, we must have our summer harvests and our autumnal
fruit. Let us not be disappointed. When the late frosts nip
the early buds, and the half-formed fruit drops blasted from
the tree, we are filled with regret; how much more when the
moral growth of the soul is destroyed or corrupted, and the
tree of immortality brings forth fruit unto death.

I have pointed out resemblances between you and the products of nature. It is proper now to state a most important
difference. When the fruit of the earth fails, neither the tree
nor the plant can be made to answer for the consequences;
but when you fail to produce the fruits of virtue and piety, the
blame rests upon you. "The fruit of the Spirit is love, joy,
peace, long-suffering, gentleness, goodness, faith, meekness,
temperance: against such there is no law." Young persons
are more susceptible both of good and evil, and they suppose
that when old age comes they will be equally open to religious impressions and free from worldly embarrassments. But
the most affecting thought of all is the neglect of our heavenly
Father till folly and vice have wasted our frames and consumed
our youthful fire. Death may claim us at any time. To remember our Creator is true religion, is salvation; to do it now,
true wisdom. Dear young friends, you become negligent of
parents; you are not apt to think whom your best friends are.
You like to be flattered, conciliated. You are the source of

intense anxiety to your connections and all lovers of mankind.
You are soon to occupy the stage of action and take the places
of your seniors, who will before long occupy their graves.
You possess almost boundless moral power. The text asserts
that man is a free agent; he is no machine. Gives the
reins to man! Is that wrong? It is delightful news to the
carnal heart, and you have then pleasures in life and in sin.
You have troubles also, as you suppose, and what are they?
Restraint and disappointments. But you have many pleasures
of sin for a season, and you roll it as a sweet morsel. What
are some of your joys? The thought of youth, the flow of
spirits? You are full of passions and ardent emotions. Let
thy heart cheer thee now. You are walking in the ways of
the heart, enjoying youthful friendship and affection, the voice
of flattery, and the glance of beauty. Disappointed, the heart
still tries other pleasures. You tread the mazy dance. You
indulge, or desire to, the impulse of every appetite. Revel or
desire to revel in all you think can gratify. The sight of the
eyes directs you only for some selfish purpose. "But know
thou, that for all these things God will bring thee into judgment."

Now, young man, I address you. You have had your
way. What now? Remember this, "God is not mocked: for
whatsoever a man soweth, that shall he also reap. For he
that soweth to his flesh, shall of the flesh reap corruption."
And again, if ye have sown the wind, ye shall reap the whirl-
wind. Young woman, young women, you have had your joys,
and your time is nearly over. Remember that! God is, calling you. He says, "Remember now thy Creator in the days
of thy youth, while the evil days come not, nor the years draw
nigh, when thou shalt say, I have no pleasure in them." When
mature years come, my young friends, they bring judgment
with them, often pain, poverty, and shame. You now feel,
generally, a cold indifference towards God. But do not forget
the last judgment of God—that awful day, when darling sins
that we have so eagerly embraced shall become a dead car-
cass. The judgment of God, who can fathom? Some dreadful earthly specimens we have seen around us. I wish I could
comfort you all. There are very many precious promises in

the Scriptures for you. I beseech you to accept the offers of mercy and to make your peace with God. "For God shall bring every work into judgment, with every secret thing, whether it be good, or whether it be evil."

—— ·—·· —

Isa. xliii, 10: "YE ARE MY WITNESSES."

By precept you must testify for the Lord. "I am with you to the end of the world." Are we willing to do this? Then God is with us, however humble, if we are only faithful. Human agents—women, faithful, pious women. One woman preached the gospel to me; I have never forgotten it. Precepts are less forcible than example. You must continue to be upright and sincere. Angels cannot do it, for we have no particular sympathy with them. Christ as a man showed this. It is impossible for human nature not to be affected by a good example. We must continue to exert this. Great obligations are resting upon Christians. In what manner are we to testify for Christ? As if we believed the soul to be immortal—act as if we believe it. You say that is true; but what particular thing can we do to show it? Live before the world to show that we believe the soul is immortal. If we believe that with the heart, we will act it out. A man who lives right will convince the world that he is in earnest. Live as if sense and time are vanity. Take the Christians here. Do they act as if they believed earth were a vanity merely for display? While they lived thus, could they preach against extravagance in dress, equipage, jewelry? They want to secure the admiration of the ungodly by endeavoring to lower themselves as far as possible to the standard of the world. Let me dress well, keep good company, and make no sacrifices. The world will say, What a contemptible man! professing Christ in the church, yet taking his glass of wine with us. They despise such Christians in their hearts, yet they praise them to their faces. We should testify, in the proof we give, of the blessedness of Christianity.

First, possess it. All love that is true makes no outside show; married people who really love make no outside show. We should show our sense of the danger and guilt of the im·penitent—a nice point to settle. Have you a friend you love? Let him know your concern for his welfare. Show your anxiety for the erring—be tender and affectionate, being moved by Christ's love. Have a high standard of holiness, rather than that of great knowledge. We should seek to be perfect in our sphere as God is perfect in his sphere. Aim at perfection—very high. We must practice self-denial. What good will it do a man to wear a long face or look holy? Nature tells us to indulge ourselves. God tells us to deny self, to give up what pleases us, and do good to others. Those who deny themselves most are the happiest. Some say, I cannot do this or that; I have no gift. Sabbath-school teachers get no pay, but pay the children for coming. Selfishness says it is Sunday. I will hire a horse and carriage and drive out and look at the beauties of nature, or enjoy myself reading. Here are children perishing in America. You must take them very young; show them you love them. You cannot force or drive people into good behaviour. Young woman, give up your party and go to the home of the poor drunkard; take some gifts with you to comfort and soothe those who are suffering or in sorrow, and God will meet you there. Visit the widow and fatherless in their affliction, and keep yourself unspotted from the world. You Christian men, who have your thousands, help your poor neighbor. He is a noble soul, but poor; can only pay you five per cent. interest; do not ask him to give you seven and three-tenths. Jesus Christ says help him. Throw off the two and three ·tenths; that will be self-denial, and it will prove you have got the right standard. By loving our brother we prove we love God. If you are wealthy, have a tender regard for all the suffering; help them to buy homes. Spread the table-cloth of God's great table and hand out of your abundance to the needy; it would prove that you are in earnest and a follower of him who went about doing good. You know what God said: "He that hath pity upon the poor, lendeth unto the Lord, and that which he hath given will he pay him again." "If riches increase, set not your heart upon them." "It is easier for a camel to go through the eye of a needle than for a rich man to enter into the kingdom of God."

Men of ability, lay off hope of honor. Suppose you are appointed a legislator. Make laws for the widows and the fatherless; strive to promote virtue in public life—this would be self-denial. Be all that is noble. The true Christian has courage, patriotism, love of the human race. Self-denial we must practice if we follow Christ. Election is coming. We show our religion by the way we vote—pray three hundred and sixty-four days and vote for the devil on the three hundred and sixty-fifth. Our voting is a prayer, and when I vote for a drunken, unprincipled man, it is equivalent to a prayer to the Almighty. I'll vote for no unprincipled man; no, never. If good men would scratch out the names of those unworthy to fill public offices, there are enough to prevent their nomination. All Christian men have integrity; they sell goods for one price; there is no deceit, no guile about them, and they will be sustained.

My friends, you have professed to be followers of Christ. Remember that "we are witnesses," and the thoughtless read men rather than their Bibles. Live up to that high standard which has been held up before you; take Christ for your model, and God will help you and bless you.

———————

John i: 9.—"THAT WAS THE TRUE LIGHT WHICH LIGHT-ETH EVERY MAN THAT COMETH INTO THE WORLD."

I. I shall endeavor to prove, my beloved hearers, that divine revelation is the only source of light that man has ever had to direct him in moral and religious duties.

II. And that this source of light has more or less shed its beams on Adam and all his posterity.

I shall blend together the arguments for the support of these two conclusions, and then try to apply the subject to our own particular use. Permit me to notice some erroneous

opinions, which it is hoped my general arguments will refute.
For instance, many believe, or say they believe, that we have
an inborn sense or perception of the moral fitness of things;
that is, that we are perfect judges of right and wrong as we
are formed by nature, without any revelation from God or instruction from man. Others believe that our Creator pours
the light of his own spirit into the heart and understanding of
every human being, and distinctly reveals to him the rule of
life and the hopes of immortality. These two classes, therefore, of misbelievers (if we dare not call them unbelievers)
maintain, or are bound to maintain, that if a child were born
in a wilderness, and nourished and brought up by wolves, he
would as infallibly know his moral duties and his immortal
hopes as Moses, the man of God, or Paul, the apostle of Jesus.
I shall notice none of the particular species of misbelief, but
proceed to state most solemnly the reasons why I think the
aforesaid doctrines, and all derived from them, are far from
true, and that the Word of God alone is the true light, and
that it does directly or indirectly enlighten every man that
cometh into the world. For what law-giver, what poet, what
philosopher, of very ancient times, ever pretended to discover
by his own reasoning the existence of God, or the doctrine of
future rewards and punishments?

Two of the wisest of the ancient heathen declare that "no
mortal can make laws to purpose," and that "laws are the gift
of God"; and that it would have been impossible for the different and numerous nations of the earth to have fallen upon
the same general principles of moral rectitude which their laws
express, had not these principles proceeded at first from the gods
and been handed down from father to son. All heathen nations also speak of an ancient flood, of the origin of nations,
and of the divine institution of religion. The part of the world,
too, where Moses wrote is that agreed upon by all other ancient authors as the earliest seat of learning and civilization,
and the point whence all knowledge first arose. In the bewil-
dering superstitions of all nations we discover traces of the first
principles of our religious faith—that is, the rite of sacrifice,
which has ever existed among all tribes of the earth. Now,
this universal custom cannot well be attributed to human rea-

son. It has been a costly practice, when it has required the choice of the flocks and herds; it has been a most painful requisition, when it demanded a darling child to pass through fire to Moloch.

GENERAL REMARKS ON SCRIPTURE.

Bible on Wine and Strong Drink.—1. Passages that seem neutral as to wine and strong drinks.—Prove the practice of drinking: In Esther the banquet of wine is repeatedly spoken of. Job i, 13: "And there was a day when his sons and his daughters were eating and drinking wine in their eldest brother's house." Proves fermentation: Job xxxii, 19, "Behold, my body is as wine that hath no vent; it is ready to burst like new bottles." Ecc. ii, 3, "I sought in my heart to give myself to wine." Ecc. x, 19, "A feast is made for laughter, and wine maketh merry." I have purposely omitted Canticles. Isa. xxiv, 11, "There is a crying for wine in the streets."

Passages seeming to approve of wine.—Gen. xiv, 18, "And Melchizedek, king of Salem, brought forth bread and wine; and he was the priest of the most high God." The great abundance and common use: Gen. xlix, 11, 12, "Binding his foal to the vine, and his ass's colt to the choice vine, he washed his garments in wine and his clothes in the blood of grapes. His eyes shall be red with wine, and his teeth white with milk." The temple service: Ex. xxix, 40. An offering: Lev. xxiii, 13; Num. xv, 5; Deut. xiv, 26, "Thou shalt bestow that money for whatever thy soul lusteth after: for oxen, or for sheep, or for wine, or for strong drink, or for whatsoever thy soul desireth," etc. Proverbially good: Judges ix, 13, "And the vine said to them, Should I leave my wine which cheereth God and man and go to be promoted over the trees?" So common as to be taken on journeys: Judges xix, 19, "There is both straw and provender for our asses, and there is bread and wine also for me, and for thy hand-maid, and for the young man," etc. To cheer and nourish: II Sam. xvi, 2, "The wine that such as are faint in the wilderness may drink."

Passages seeming to approve of wine.—Neh. v, 15-18, speaks of bread and wine in connection as tribute. Taxed. Mentioned with harvests: "In those days saw I in Judah some treading wine-presses on the Sabbath, and bringing in sheaves, and leading asses; as also wine, grapes and figs." Used to strengthen and enliven: Ps. lxxviii, 65, "Then the Lord awaked as one out of sleep, and like a mighty man that shouteth by reason of wine." Ps. civ, 15, "Wine that maketh glad the heart of man, and oil to make his face to shine, and bread which strengtheneth man's heart." Emblematic of heavenly feasting and enjoyment: Prov. ix, 2, "She hath killed her beasts, she hath mingled her wine, she hath also furnished her table." To medicate and cheer: Prov. xxxi, 6, 7, "Give strong drink to him that is ready to perish, and wine to those that be of heavy hearts. Let him drink and forget his poverty, and remember his misery no more."

Passages favorable to wine.—Isa. i, 22, "Thy silver is become dross, thy wine mixed with water." Extreme of want shown by mixture: Isa. xxv, 6, "A feast of fat things, a feast of wines on the lees; a feast of fat things full of marrow, of wines on the lees well refined." Isa. lv, 1, "Ho! every one that thirsteth, come ye," etc. Evangelical figure: Jer. xl, 12, "And gathered wine and summer fruits very much." Jer. xlviii, 33, "And joy and gladness is taken from the plentiful field; and I have caused wine to fail from the wine-presses." Dan. x, 3, "I ate no pleasant bread, neither came flesh nor wine in my mouth," etc. Hos. ii, 9, "Therefore will I return, and take away my corn in the time thereof, and my wine in the season thereof," etc. Zech. x, 7, "The restored shall rejoice as through wine." Luke vii, 33, 34, "John the Baptist came neither eating bread nor drinking wine," etc. John ii, 3, 9, 10, "When they wanted wine, the mother of Jesus saith to him, They have no wine"; "When the ruler of the feast had tasted the water that was made wine," etc.; "Every man at the beginning doth set forth good wine," etc. I Tim. v, 23, "Drink no longer water, but use a little wine," etc.

Passages unfavorable to the use of such drinks.—The drunkenness and denunciation: Gen. ix, 20, "And Noah planted a vineyard. And he drank of the wine, and was drunken." Gen. xix, 32. Num. vi, 3, of the Nazarite, "He shall separate himself from wine and strong drink, and shall drink no vinegar of wine, nor vinegar of strong drink; neither shall he drink any liquor of grapes," etc. A good definition of modern wines: Deut. xxxii, 32, 33, "For their vine is of the vine of Sodom, and of the fields of Gomorrah: their grapes are grapes of gall, their clusters are bitter: their wine is the poison of dragons, and the cruel venom of asps."

Passages against wine.—I Sam. i, 14, "And Eli said to her, How long wilt thou be drunken? Put away thy wine from thee." A good description of being drunk and getting sober: I Sam. xxv, 36, 37, "Nabal's heart was merry within him, for he was very drunken: and it came to pass in the morning, when the wine was gone out of Nabal, and his wife had told him these things, that his heart died within him, and he became as a stone." The stimulus to sin: II Sam. xiii, 28, "Now Absalom had commanded his servants, saying, Mark ye now when Amnon's heart is merry with wine, and when I say unto you, Smite Amnon; then kill him, fear not: have not I commanded you? be courageous; fear not." A family quarrel: Esther i, 10, "On the seventh day, when the heart of the king was merry with wine, he commanded to bring Vashti the queen before the king, to show the people and the princes her beauty." Emblem of Jehovah's wrath: Ps. lxxv, 8, "For in the hand of the Lord there is a cup, and the wine is red; it is full of mixture; and he poureth out of the same: but the dregs thereof, all the wicked shall wring them out, and drink them." Prov. xx, i, "Wine is a mocker, strong drink is raging; and whosoever is deceived thereby is not wise." Prov. xxiii, 29–32, "Who hath woe? who hath sorrow? who hath contentions? who hath babblings? who hath wounds without cause? who hath redness of eyes? They that tarry long at the wine. * * Look not thou upon the wine when it is red. * * At the last it biteth like a serpent, and stingeth like an adder." Fashionable and respectable drinking: Prov. xxxi, 4, 5, "It is not for kings, O Lemuel, it is not for kings to drink wine, nor for princes strong drink: lest they drink, and forget the law, and pervert the judgment of any of the afflicted." Isa. v, 11, 12, "Woe unto them that rise up early in the morn-

ing, that they may follow strong drink; that continue until
night, till wine inflame them! And the harp and the viol, and
the tabret and pipe, and wine, are in their feasts," etc. Isa. v,
22, "Woe unto them that are mighty to drink wine," etc.

Clerical and priestly drinking: Isa. xxviii, 1, 7, "Woe to
the crown of pride, to the drunkards," etc. "They also have
erred through wine, and through strong drink are out of the
way; the priest and the prophet have erred through strong
drink, they are swallowed up of wine, they are out of the way
through strong drink," etc. Isa. lvi, 10–12, "His watchmen
are blind: *   *   they are all ignorant, they are all
dumb dogs.   *   *   Yea, they are greedy dogs which
can never have enough.   *   *   Come ye, say they, I
will fetch wine, and we will fill ourselves with strong drink."
Jer. xxiii, 9, "Mine heart within me is broken because of the
prophets; all my bones shake: I am like a drunken man, and
like a man whom wine hath overcome." Emblem of the wrath
of God: Jer. xxv, 15, "For thus saith the Lord God of Israel:
Take the wine cup of this fury at my hand, and cause all the
nations, to whom I send thee, to drink it." Jer. xxxv, the
Rechabites; blessing of God. Curse of God: Jer. li, 7, "Babylon hath been a golden cup in the Lord's hand, that made all
the earth drunken: the nations have drunken of her wine;
therefore the nations are mad." Daniel's scruple: Dan. i, 8,
"Daniel purposed in his heart that he would not defile himself
with the portion of the king's meat, nor with the wine which
he drank."

Fashionable, genteel drinking: Dan. v, Belshazzar's fatal
feast. Joel i, v, "Awake, ye drunkards, and weep; and howl,
all ye drinkers of wine, because of the new wine; for it is cut
off from your mouth." Joel iii, 3, "And they have cast lots
for my people; and have given a boy for a harlot, and sold a
girl for wine, that they may drink." Amos vi, 4, 6, "Lie upon
beds of ivory, and stretch themselves upon their couches, and
eat the lambs out of the flock," etc. "That drink wine in
bowls," etc. Micah ii, 11, "If a man walking in the spirit and
falsehood do lie, saying, I will prophesy unto thee of wine and
of strong drink; he shall even be the prophet of this people."

The traffic. Adverse to strong drink: Hab. ii, 15, "Woe unto him that giveth his neighbor drink, that puttest thy bottle to him, and makest him drunken," etc. Eph. v, 18, "And be not drunk with wine, wherein is excess," etc. I Tim. iii, 3, 8, "A bishop must not be given to wine." "A deacon not given to much wine." Titus i, 7, "A bishop not given to wine." Titus ii, 3, "The aged women must not be given to much wine." I Pet. iv, 3, "For the time past of our life may suffice us to have wrought the will of the Gentiles, when we walked in lusts, excess of wine," etc. Tremendous curse of God: Rev. xvi, 19, "The cup of the wine of the fierceness of his wrath." Rev. xvii, 2, "The wine of Babylon," etc. Rev. xiv, 10, "The worshipper of the beast shall drink of the wine of the wrath of God, which is poured out without mixture into the cup of his indignation." I Cor. x, 21, "Ye cannot drink the cup of the Lord, and the cup of devils."

Quotations Respecting Omnipotence.

Creation.—"In the beginning God created the heavens and the earth." He spake, and it was done. Vastness and variety. —"The heavens declare the glory of God. He spreadeth out the heavens, and treadeth on the waves of the sea; he maketh Arcturus, Orion, and Pleiades, and the chambers of the south; he doeth great things, past finding out: yea, and wonders without number. He stretcheth out the north over the empty place, and hangeth the earth upon nothing. He bindeth up the waters in the thick clouds, and the cloud is not rent under them; he hath compassed the waters with bounds, until the day and night come to an end." The ease with which he works, etc.—"He brake up for the sea a decreed place, and set bars and doors, and said, Hitherto shalt thou come, and no further, etc. He looketh to the end of the earth, and seeth under the whole heaven to make the weight for the winds; to weigh the waters by measure; to make a decree for the rain, and a way for the lightning of the thunder. Who hath mea-

sured the waters in the hollow of his hand, meted out heaven
with a span, comprehended the dust of the earth in a measure,
weighed the mountains in scales, and the hills in a balance?"
His terrible power.—"The pillars of heaven tremble, and
are astonished at his reproof; he divideth the sea by his power.
He removeth the mountains, and they know it not. He over-
turneth them in his anger, he shaketh the earth out of her
place, and the pillars thereof tremble; he commandeth the sun,
and it riseth not, and sealeth up the stars." Subjection of all
creatures.—"He maketh his angels spirits, and his ministers a
flame of fire. They veil their faces before his throne. It is he
that sitteth upon the circle of the earth, and the inhabitants are
as grasshoppers, as the dust of the balance, less than nothing,
and vanity. He bringeth princes to nothing; he setteth up
one and putteth down another; the angels that sinned he cast
down to hell, and delivered them into chains of darkness, to
be reserved unto judgment." The closing scene.—The dead
of all ages shall hear his voice. The sea shall give up the dead
which are in it. "And before him shall be gathered all nations, and he shall separate them one from another. Then
shall the king say unto them on his right hand, Come, ye
blessed of my Father, inherit the kingdom prepared for you
from the foundation of the world. Then shall he say also unto
them on the left hand, Depart from me, ye cursed, into everlasting fire, prepared for the devil and his angels. And these
shall go into everlasting punishment, but the righteous into
life eternal." The power of these amazing views consist in
their truth.

Contrast with heathen or uninspired productions.

Cleanthus, the stoic.—"Hail, O Jupiter, most glorious of
the immortals, invoked under many names, always most powerful, the first ruler of nature, whose laws govern all things.
Hail! for to address thee is permitted to all mortals, for our
race we have from thee; we mortals who creep upon the
ground, receiving only the echo of thy voice. I, therefore, I
will celebrate thee, and will always sing thy power. All this
universe rolling round the earth obeys thee wherever thou
guidest, and willingly is governed by thee. So vehement, so
fiery, so immortal is the thunder which thou holdest in thy un-

shaken hands; for by the stroke of this all nature was rooted;
by this, thou directest the common reason which pervades all
things mixed with the greater and lesser luminaries, so great
a king art thou supreme through all; nor does any work take
place without thee in the earth, nor in the ethereal sky, nor in
the sea, except that the bad perform in their own folly. But
do thou, O Jupiter, ruler of the thunder, defend mortals from
dismal misfortune, which dispel, O Father, from the soul; and
grant it to attain that judgment, trusting to which thou gov-
ernest all things with justice; that being honored, we may repay thee with honor, singing continually thy works, since there
is no greater meed to men nor gods than to celebrate justly
the universal law."

Omnipresence stated in Scripture.—"Whither shall I go
from thy spirit? or whither shall I flee from thy presence?"
etc. "In him we live and move and have our being."

Mark viii, 36: "WHAT SHALL IT PROFIT A MAN IF HE GAIN
THE WHOLE WORLD AND LOSE HIS OWN SOUL.."

The religion of Jesus Christ has one transcendent supe-
riority over all others: it has nothing whatever belonging to
it calculated to make hypocrites. Men may charge this sin
upon the professed friends of Christ, but they cannot charge
the temptation to commit it upon Christ himself. For the prescribed service of Christ is, in the opinion of the world, hard
labor for life; a forfeiture of property, reputation and life itself, without any valuable or substantial reward; the giving up
all we have, and nothing to show for it. The sincerest and
most devoted friends of Christ have never pretended that they
expected any other reward than that, that impenitent persons
consider wholly ideal, "Faith the substance of things hoped
for, and the evidence of things not seen; and hope that is with
patience waited for," and that maketh, as the Christian believes
and trusts, not ashamed.

Dan. vi, 10: "NOW WHEN DANIEL KNEW THAT THE WRIT-
ING WAS SIGNED, HE WENT INTO HIS HOUSE; AND HIS WINDOWS
BEING OPENED IN HIS CHAMBER TOWARD JERUSALEM, HE KNEELED
UPON HIS KNEES THREE TIMES A DAY AND PRAYED, AND GAVE
THANKS BEFORE HIS GOD, AS HE DID AFORETIME."

There are some people who complain that they see no
especial use in the details of the Old Testament histories. They
are so different from the more modern histories. They tell us
so little of the wealth of great kings, of wars, of all that makes
up the splendor of a realm; so little of politics; but the details
are mostly made up of the moral conduct of individuals. The
proper reply to this complaint is that there is no saving importance in the politics of past nations, and the departure of
the Bible in setting forth the whole moral action of people, in
telling us how men stood, how they rose, how they fell, and
how they triumphed in their own souls, is of far greater importance as a record to be read by every tried and tempted
soul in every age. This departure alluded to is a proof that
these writings came from that God who cares for the human
soul. And after all, what is it in novels which interest their readers so? Is it not because there is exhibited to us a true picture
of character? Novels when written well show us models of character which we may safely imitate; and in this they are useful.
Sir Walter Scott's, for instance, give us a type of a nation.

Perhaps no one stands higher than Daniel among the
Scripture writings. He seems entirely faultless, and is mentioned with honor. The point of this discourse will be the
importance of an established character—a moral, resolute
Christian character. Daniel, in his early youth, was taken
captive by the great Babylonian conqueror Nebuchadnezzar,
and instructed in all the thorough scientific knowledge of the
renowned Chaldeans. Daniel became in time superior to
them all; he held high office under seven kings, was a leading statesman, and at the age of eighty years occupied a position corresponding to that of prime minister under the Median
king, Darius. Neither his love of learning, nor the temptations of office, could draw him away from the high religious
principles which he professed. The prophecies of Daniel distinctly pointed out the Saviour.

MISCELLANEOUS.

CIRCULAR LETTER BY REV. S. AARON AT THE CENTRAL UNION ASSOCIATION OF INDEPENDENT BAPTIST CHURCHES, JUNE, 1855.

To the Churches.—Dear Brethren : The subject prescribed for the present communication is " Restricted Communion." The writer appointed prefers to present this topic in the form of a colloquy. Suppose that a pious " Pedobaptist," or rather Pedorantist, or sprinkler of babes and others, be represented by P.; a conscientious Baptist, decidedly Biblical, by B.; and a liberal Christian, not strenuously devoted to ordinances, by L. They are thrown together for an evening, and, with a friendly and confidential temper, engage in the following conference :

L.—What a pity it is that the seamless garment of Christ is rent into so many divisions. The thoughtless, unbelieving world are not without excuse when they ridicule such disunity and confusion in the Christian church.

B.—In my judgment, division on principle is better than union without it. The solidarity of Popery in the twelfth century, when darkness and light, bigotry and piety, virtue and vice, faith and infidelity, were soldered into a mass by inquisitorial fire and fastened together by the clamps of Papal infallibility, was a state of the church less profitable to the world than the abused privileges of Protestant freedom. Our pure standard of truth, with a little phalanx of the faithful gathered around it, is a better instrumentality for saving mankind than the whole babbling mob of Russia or of Rome, driven by the lash of authority or lured by holiday shows.

L.—You are too figurative, Brother B. I want unity, with purity and order too. Is not that possible ?

B.—If it is, it must form around a central truth. Order cannot come out of chaos while confusion is law; chaos may come to order when truth is law. Let men adhere firmly to the Divine Word, and nothing else, and union will be the consequence in God's time and way.

P.—Well, Brother B., you speak plausibly; but, really, you Baptists carry out your principle with too much vigor. You seem to me sternly and even stubbornly exclusive, and verge towards bigotry in your close communion. You refuse acknowledged Christians a place with you when you sit down to eat and drink to the memory of our common Lord. You have no right thus to shorten the Lord's table.

B.—Well said is this last sentence, my worthy brother. But what better right have you to lengthen it? It is the Lord's table, and not ours; he, and not we, must regulate its dimensions, for he assuredly, and not we, provides the feast.

P.—All right, except the hint that we lengthen it.

B.—Pardon me! I inferred from your remarks about Baptists refusing acknowledged Christians, that you admit or at least invite pious Quakers, and in fact every one who has a hope in Christ.

P.—No, sir; we hold that baptism is an essential prerequisite to communion, and that this is the clear and palpable limit of the Lord's table.

B.—Excellent; we are really coming together.

P.—Not so fast, I fear, for you Baptists will not admit the validity of our baptism.

B.—But you fully admit the validity of ours.

P.—Certainly; and therein we display our charity and your exclusiveness.

B.—I am glad of your admissions, and we shall certainly get together. Suppose that some great point of Christian union were proposed to be carried, so that millions of brethren now disunited could be gathered into one visible fold; suppose that this union could be effected by a simple act of the majority, with almost no inconvenience to any one, and without the slightest violation of any man's conscience, would it not be the duty of that majority to effect that union?

P.—Undoubtedly it would, if I understand your hypothesis.

B.—Well, you admit that I am scripturally baptized, and that you would be perfectly satisfied with such a baptism for yourself and your brethren; while I dare not for my life admit that you have been baptized at all, though I love you as a Christian brother.

P.—Be it so. And what then?

B.—Why, then let you and all of your order be baptized as I am, and then we shall form not only a spiritual but a visible union.

P.—What, three-fourths of the church give way to one-fourth? Why, Brother B., are you coming out a bigot in earnest?

B.—Well, my friend, if you will not act in agreement with your conscience for the sake of union, and yet require me to violate mine for the same end, or be deemed a bigot, I leave it to others to decide which is the greater bigot of the two.

P.—I confess my charge of bigotry was rather hasty. But while all our learned teachers admit the validity of your mode as well as ours, still should we not violate conscience in being re-baptized?

B.—Not if you have received the right in unconscious infancy, because your conscience is not bound by another's acts, in which you had not the slightest participation, when that act is neither required nor sanctioned by the Lord. No man pretends that there is in scripture a positive order, a practical example, nor a specific sanction to warrant the baptism of children.

P.—Still my parents dedicated me to the Lord in baptism, and I should wound their conscience or insult their memory in being re-baptized.

B.—They were too fast in the dedication, unless they taught you first. For the Lord's commission is: "Teach all nations, baptizing them," and "He that believeth and is baptized, shall be saved." And besides, if you throw the responsibility off yourself and on your parents, then they are bound by my former proposition, as adults, as you tacitly concede that you are, for the sake of general Christian union, to agree that you should be baptized as I have been, or else admit that their bigotry is greater than mine.

P.—But what if a man has been baptized, as I think, or rantized, as you say, on profession of his faith, and with a good conscience? Is it not sacriligious to repeat the ordinance in that case?

B.—I should be scrupulous about repeating a doubtful baptism; and nothing is more doubted by many, nor more disbelieved by others, than that sprinkling or affusion is baptism; but I should be clear in substituting for it an ordinance whose validity no sane, believing man ever doubted, when by so doing I would aid in effecting a world-wide Christian union. Various modes of baptism are about as plausable as various modes of circumcision.

L.—Come, Brother B., you have been rather too exacting on Brother P., and he has conceded a little too much for his logical comfort. But where is your scripture for making baptism a condition or pre-requisite of communion?

B.—Do you believe that both ordinances are equally positive, that is established and prescribed by the Lord, and real requisites of a true Christian consistency?

L.—I will at least concede it to hear what you have to say.

B.—Well, that is the great point. Baptism and the Lord's Supper have most assuredly been imposed as requisites of an orderly Christian profession. The one, performed once to show our belief in the one great fact of our Lord's death and resurrection; the other, repeated often to show that we live by the offering of his body and blood forever. If both are equally requisites, one must be, with regard to the other, the pre-requisite, and the other, the post-requisite; and scripture practice fully settles the order of sequence. "Teach" or "disciple all nations, baptizing them," said Jesus; and "he took the cup and gave it to his disciples."

L.—I wish you were as liberal as your sentiments, and as tender in your feelings as you are plausible in your arguments; for certainly the children of our father, the brothers and sisters of the same redeemer, ought not to be excluded from the feast of love celebrated in honor of the Saviour's name. It is cruel to shut out one of his humblest or weakest children.

B.—Sentiment and feeling are probably not so good a rule of order as a divine command. But as you seem to be returning to the point at which we started, and are in your turn becoming figurative, I reply in your own style, that I would not permit my own best loved child to sit with me at my own table until his uncleanly face and hands had first been purified. Why then press to the table of my Lord the man who had manifestly neglected a positive duty, the symbolic application of the baptismal waters, and the sublime type of the Christian resurrection.

L.—But how haughty and unkind to say to a fellow-Christian, "Stand off; I am holier than thou!"

B.—It is still more unkind to sanction an error than to reprove it; to believe before God that a brother is wrong, and then do nothing to set him right.

GAMING AND HORSE-RACING.

Resolved, that the practice of wagering on a horse race or on a game of chance, is a violation of the precept, "Thou shalt not steal," as well as a presumptuous appeal to providence for a supposed favor, and that for these reasons, mainly, horse-racing and gaming should be prohibited by law.

We are apt to dwell on the incidental evils;—I would aim here at the root—the unlawful love of money. Incidental mischief is connected with everything. We can lawfully receive for an equivalent or as a free gift. How else can we rightfully get the property of another? Does his consent sanction the acceptance as moral and just? He does not consent. He cannot bestow. The temptation is offered by each to the other to defraud. God is tempted to bestow my neighbor's goods causelessly on me. For these reasons the resorts of horse-racers and gamblers should be broken up.

Civil society is an organization, dictated by nature and inspiration. It distinctly implies and demands the existence of the moral virtues. Civil government is its instrument for certain purposes. Government is not to regulate matters of opinion but to prevent evils in fact.

INFIDELITY.

Norristown, 1854. From reliable sources I learn that Mr. Joseph Barker "undertakes to prove against any clergyman on earth, that there is no evidence of the divine authority of the Bible, and that there can be none." Being a "clergyman on earth," though of the humblest pretentions, I feel disposed to put this extraordinary proposition to the test; for it is truly wonderful if the weakest followers of Jesus can adduce no proof whatever of the divine authority of the Bible, and absolutely amazing if the Supreme Being himself is unable to do it. But as the Bible is to be taken from us and infidelity substituted in its place, it seems fair to give that substitute a thorough examination. If this proposition contemplates a fair and thorough examination and comparison of infidelity and Christianity, and not a mere fencing with phrases and clauses, I feel disposed to assist Mr. Barker in publicly examining and comparing the two systems; and will endeavor to maintain, first, that infidelity has no authority nor tendency to make men good and happy, but the contrary, and is therefore false; second, that Christianity (the religion of our Lord and Saviour Jesus Christ), as fully developed in the New Testament, and foreshadowed in the Old, is adapted to make, and does make, every true believer both good and happy, and is therefore true; third, that the Bible is a revelation from God, and that the objections of infidels against its authority are without any solid foundation.

SAMUEL AARON.

SAMUEL AARON'S CERTIFICATE OF ORDINATION.

To all people to whom these presents shall come, the subscribers send GREETING:

Being convened at New Britain, Bucks county, and State of Pennsylvania, on the 27th day of September, 1828, at the instance of the Baptist church of New Britain, aforesaid, for the purpose of setting apart by solemn ordination the bearer hereof to the sacred office of the ministry; and being, by sufficient testimonials, fully certified of his moral character, real piety, and sound knowledge in divine things, as well as ministerial gifts and abilities, whereof we had otherwise due knowledge: We did, therefore, on the said 27th day of September, in the presence of said church and a full assembly met, solemnly ordain and set apart to the sacred office of the ministry, by imposition of hands and prayer and other rituals among us in that case in use, the said bearer, our worthy and reverend brother, Samuel Aaron, whom we therefore recom mend as such to favor and respect.

THOS. B. MONTANYE, V. D. M.
JOSEPH MATHIAS, V. D. M.
JOHN L. JENKINS, V. D. M.
JOHN L. DAGG, V. D. M.

- ———

The Baptist Church at Norristown, Pennsylvania, to the Central Union Baptist Association of Independent Baptist Churches, GREETING:

Beloved Brethren:—This church, since the last meeting of the Association, have received by baptism 33, by letter 13, dismissed by letter 8, excluded 8, lost by death 2, making the whole number 291, being a net gain to the numbers of the church on earth of 28, and to the denomination of 23.

The delegates appointed to sit with you are Elder Samuel Aaron, Elder David Bernard, Brethren B. F. Hancock, James Ramage, Thomas Shaw, Phinehas Phillips, George

Eve, Thomas Scattergood, Geo. W. Thomas, Samuel D. Phillips, and Joseph Abraham.

The statistics of the Sabbath school is as follows, viz.: Children considered under supervision of the school, 140. Whole number of teachers, 16. Officers—Superintendent and Assistant Superintendent, 2. Librarians, 2. Scholars baptized during the year, 3.

1. Nearly a year since our late pastor, Elder Bernard, who was frequently and unavoidably from home on a highly important religious enterprise, associated with himself in pulpit labors Brother J. N. Hobart, whose services, as well as those of the pastor, were useful, faithful and satisfactory.

2. Brother Bernard, believing that the engagement above alluded to demanded his whole time, advised the church of his determination to decline the pastoral charge at the close of March last; whereupon, after some consideration, they elected as their pastor Elder Samuel Aaron, who entered on the duties of his office on the first Lord's day in the last month. Thus far the congregations have not fallen away; but, as with his predecessors, have been full and very attentive, and there seems to be a reasonable hope that the Lord will bless the connection.

3. The Sabbath school has been a favorite and favored nursery of this church. A number among its worthiest members have devoted themselves to it with a fervid and long-enduring zeal and charity; and the recent determination of the teachers to give away their much worn library, and to raise seventy-five dollars for a new one, is a pleasing proof that their energy is neither dead nor dying. The superintendent, Brother Hancock, says in his late report: "The teachers can all call each other brother and sister in the Lord." Some of the brethren likewise labor in a school several miles from the borough, and are much encouraged with appearances of the divine blessing on their efforts.

4. The church are in principle opposed to the use of intoxicating drinks, and would surely discipline a dram-drinking or dram-selling member, and commend the same rule to their brethren.

5. They believe that the saints are not their own, but bought with a price, and that their silver and gold are the Lord's; therefore, that their personal service and their substance should be unreservedly devoted to the real cause of God, so as to give a translated Bible and the gospel through a pious ministry to every human soul, as well as consolation and aid to saints in affliction, poverty and bondage.

6. They believe in the total and universal depravity of man, which must inevitably produce his everlasting ruin, unless through the influence of the Holy Spirit he becomes reconciled to God by a gospel repentance and by faith in Christ Jesus; and that he only is proved to be a child of grace who perseveres to glory. They therefore approve of the incessant and urgent use of all scriptural efforts for the conversion of sinners and confirmation of believers.

7. They deem the church of Christ no fit asylum for any form of sin. But while immorality, profanity and falsehood are excluded, they mourn that the New Testament idolatry, the worship of Mammon, is not only tolerated in many of our churches but often rules supreme. This covetous spirit rejects the apostle's rules of "equality" in contribution; it often puts a faithful and humble ministry on short allowance; it hardly does so much as say to naked, hungry poverty, "be warmed and filled;" it owes so many debts on accumulating property that it has scarcely a dollar to lend to the Lord; its votaries are found even in the precincts of Zion, who drive a profitable trade in "liquid death and distilled damnation," and thousands indulge in dignified luxurious ease which flows from the church-sanctioned ownership of human sinews, bones and blood. This church are of opinion that the arm of discipline should scourge such money getters from the temple.

8. Finally, we cordially welcome you to our place of worship, to our firesides and our hearts, and may your doings amongst us be such as to prove you not only "the messengers of the churches," but the "glory of Christ"; guided by that wisdom "that is first pure, then peaceable, full of mercy, and without partiality;" not controlled by that caution which is first cowardly, then crafty, and finally treacherous, both to Christ and the brethren.

Adopted Lord's day, May 24, 1841.

AGREEMENT TO UNITE IN A PROTRACTED MEETING BY THE PRESBYTERIANS AND BAPTISTS.

For the purpose of increasing the religious influence of this community, and saving the souls of men, we, with humble reliance upon the blessing of God in the gift of his Holy Spirit, do mutually agree, as the pastors of the Baptist and Presbyterian churches of Norristown, to engage together in a series of religious meetings. And for the purpose of keeping the unity of the spirit in the bonds of peace, and avoiding any evil consequences, we promise to be governed by the following regulations:

1. There shall be preaching alternately each evening in the Baptist and Presbyterian churches.

2. Until the 31st inst., all the preaching shall be done by said pastors.

3. The pastor shall not preach in his own church; but it shall be his duty to exhort after the sermon, and take the general management.

4. No sermon shall be more than forty-five minutes long; no exhortation more than ten minutes at a time, and the prayers short and to the point.

5. If it be found best to have more than one sermon per day, all shall be in the same house.

6. The members shall be exhorted to kindness and good feeling during the meetings, and not dispute about doctrines.

7. Where one is known to be in the habit of attending a particular church of any denomination, or whose family are of a particular persuasion, it shall be considered dishonorable to influence him or her to leave and join elsewhere. But when there are no such connections, it is proper that nothing be done to excite any other than kind feelings in the members.

8. There shall be a collection taken up every evening to defray the expenses of the meetings, an account of which shall be kept by some one appointed for this purpose. Out of this the sexton shall be paid fifty cents per day, for open-

ing and preparing the house. Whatever shall remain after the expenses are paid shall go to the congregations equally, to pay for fuel and light.

9. It will be expected of the members, as well as the ministers, to conduct with Christian courtesy and urbanity towards each other, desiring to increase mutual influence and esteem, "In honor preferring one another."

10. There shall be a prayer meeting each evening at six o'clock, and public exercises at seven.

SAMUEL AARON.
SAMUEL M. GOULD.

Norristown, Dec. 24, 1842.

- —

ESSAY READ BEFORE A DEBATING SOCIETY, 1819.

From amongst the numerous subjects that present themselves for the discussion of critics and philosophers, I (by no means either) have selected the Improvement of the Human Mind. To enter into an analysis of its component parts, or a philosophical disquisition of its properties, I do not wish, or am I able; the utmost in my power will be to offer a few commonplace remarks, and to tell you an old story which you have heard a thousand times, in words perhaps somewhat different.

You are all well aware that where the omnipotent hand has animated any mass of matter with the breath of life, he has also bestowed a love of existence and a dread of annihilation. The meanest insects that crawl on the dust have a kind of instinctive knowledge which impels them to provide for their future wants and those of their offspring with the most faithful labor and tender care. It might be proved, I presume, that there is no such thing as existence without intelligence, nor life without reason. Every creature that lives is happy in its existence and loth to part with it, with one painful exception—creation's exalted lord, unworthy man. This exception,

however, is not general; it is but a few whose heads are
crazed by drunkenness, or whose hearts are broken by disappointed schemes of love or ambition, who repair for an end of
their woes to a pistol or a halter.

But leaving this sad subject, let us pursue our point. The
intelligence of all other animals, when compared with that of
man, loses its effulgence, and is extremely dimmed, if not ex-
tinguished, by the transcendent lustre of his superior understanding; his ideas extend themselves to the remotest bounds
of the universe, and with restless anxiety seek the compre·
hension of all nature's plan. On the proper direction of these
intellectual powers depend his honor and happiness, both in
his temporal and eternal existence.

As it appears then that the improvement of the mind is
of the most momentous importance, it likewise seems almost
equally clear and important that the season of youth should
be devoted to this improvement. "Train up a child in the
way he should go, and when he is old," etc., exclaimed the
wise king of Israel. "Just as the twig is bent, the tree's inclined," is one of the effusions of the eminent poet Pope.
These passages, indeed, have not a very intimate connection
with the subject, yet they clearly shewed the opinion of these
great men (the one, an ancient prophetic king; the other, a
modern and much celebrated poet) to have been that youth is
the proper season for improvement, the era to acquire those
habits that must regulate our after lives, and the time to sow
that good seed from which we shall reap a crop of everlasting
felicity.

Much, indeed, depends on the culture of the mind; if we
trifle away the spring-time of our years in meditating or conversing on light, vulgar and obscene matters, we shall always
grovel in the dust and be the reptiles among men; we shall
most likely become the slaves of passion, or the dupes of in-
trigue; and if we should by chance live to old age, instead of
being honored, our gray hairs will be despised. On the other
hand, if we elevate our thoughts and employ our minds in useful and instructive studies, we shall find it to exalt as much as
the reverse depressed. Instead of wading in the mire of ignorance and smothering in the grossness of human frailties "that

vital spark of heavenly flame that animates our mortal frame,"
it is in the power of man to kindle it into such a clear and
brilliant light as will develop to him the mysteries of science,
and display to his view, what before was dark, the beauties of
philosophy, teach him to reconcile many things before irrecon-
cilable, illumine his way to the temple of truth, and guide
his steps to the sweet vale of contentment. And youth is the
time, the only time, to attain all these noble ends, whilst the
nerves are vigorous and the fire of emulation glows most
warmly in the breast.

A long time used, I fancy you are saying, to prove what
we knew very well before. But, ladies and gentlemen, though
our tongues confess, yet our actions, for the most part, deny
the importance of juvenile improvement.

Let us humbly point out a few things (that ought to be
in some measure dispensed with) operating as hindrances to
mental improvement. Suppose that some of the young gentlemen would employ a part of the time in improving their
minds which they use in paying their addresses to a plurality
of ladies, not one of whom they ever intend to marry (not to
say all), or in planning schemes of love and pleasure which
they have not the most distant hope of realizing; in getting
by rote a collection of witty sayings, polite and love-inspiring
compliments for the purpose of engaging the attention or perhaps beguiling the heart of some fair one whom they never
intend to love. If these hours were devoted to the attainment of some other point than this, it is most likely there
would not be so much complaint for want of time; and it is
possible our president's ears would not be so often assailed
with the well-known address, "I have no remarks to offer, sir,
this evening." And (can my rashness be pardoned?) if a certain portion of the young ladies would curtail a little the time
they spend at the toilet or the glass, preparing to outvie in
finery and beauty all the other belles at some contemplated
party, and to attract the greatest number of admirers, when
their own modesty tells they want but one husband—if a part
of this time were passed at the needle or in the library, there
would no doubt be as many loving and beloved wives, as

many prudent and tender mothers, as there are in the present state of things.

I do not wish to criticise the manners of the age, nor to preach a moral sermon, this evening; but permit me to say that if the youth of both sexes would coolly and impassionately consider how contemptible that mass of mortality we take so much pains to decorate, is, in comparison with the noble intelligence that animates it, which, after it has dropped the burden that clogs it in the grave to dissolve in kindred dust, "will flourish in immortal youth, unhurt amid the war of elements, the wreck of matter, and the crush of worlds"—if these things were duly considered, it would no doubt appear a despicable employment to bend the immortal mind to the pitiful purpose of contriving how to decorate a piece of moving clay, to teach it to put on a number of finical airs, and to utter in soft sounds a few smart things, all which may glitter for a moment like the gay colors of the butterfly, and then be seen no more.

But I am wandering from the subject, in advising those who know, and do much better than myself. The young ladies and gentlemen are well aware that however precious they may be, on account of their beauty or finery, to any one, they cannot be of as much value as the improvement of their minds is to themselves. The fickle and giddy passion of juvenile love, and the boundless desire of being handsome and admired, seem with most young persons, amongst many other things, no trifling hindrance to the improvement of the mind. The young do not consider while so employed that they are planting what will produce the fruit of shame and remorse when they arrive at years which should be employed on the stage of usefulness.

Permit me to name another obstruction which often staggers even the industrious youth. Young persons about entering on the arduous task of learning, think a complete acquisition of science of easy attainment, but upon trial find themselves seriously mistaken. After having a long time pored over some system of grammar or mathematics, which the author gravely calls only an introduction, they find themselves very imperfect in their knowledge of it, and very naturally comparing themselves with some great men, and discovering their own inferiority to be so vast become incredibly disheartened with their ignorance. These considerations, however, are but juvenile, and will give way to more mature age and reflection. Some may allege that they have not the means of becoming well informed; but this is a very frivolous excuse, as nothing hinders but want of inclination. All who have their natural senses may become possessed of much information if they desire it. For in this land of light and liberty the words of the poet, "our needful knowledge, like our needful food, unhedged, lies open in life's common field," are peculiarly applicable here. Not only the useful but the ornamental branches of science; not only the instructive but the polished parts of literature, are diffused with copious profusion.

The fair light of knowledge and instruction does not only come within the scope of popish priests and wealthy lords (for such creatures are scarce here), but is extended to all as freely as the air we breathe, or the liberal principles of our happy government. The farmer and the gentleman stand an equal chance for being advanced to the first honors of the nation. Let there be no complaint for want of means then, at least until the means allowed are made use of and exhausted.

The principal object or summum bonum of mental improvement is, I apprehend, to become intimately acquainted with human nature; not for the purpose of taking advantage of its foibles, so as to lead it captive to headlong passion, or make it the dupe of avarice or wild ambition, but to be able to ameliorate its situation, to strengthen its weaknesses, to soothe its miseries, and to restore it as nearly as possible to its pristine dignity, innocence and happiness.

As the field of intellectual improvement is unbounded, and the species of fruit innumerable, it is neither needful nor becoming for me to point out that which should be gathered; let every one select what pleases him, or, having tested all, keep that which is good. The advantages resulting from virtuous knowledge are incalculable. It may be said, for all to become wise is absurd, inasmuch as there would be no distinction; but we have information that may be relied on,

that "Happy is the man that findeth wisdom, and he that get-
teth understanding," and that the lot of all men should be
peace and happiness, is an event to be fervently desired.

Suffer me to notice one particular advantage that it gives
the ladies. When a sensible young man marries a young
lady of whom he is much enamored, for awhile he thinks of
nothing but her gaiety and beauty, but after the warmth of
passion subsides a little, he begins to look for something
more—her mental qualifications. If he finds her destitute of
information in almost every respect, he shuns her for better
company, in public is ashamed of her, and uses her like hidden
treasure which he is afraid any one should know he possesses;
but if she proves the reverse of this, she becomes his delight
indeed, his solace in adversity, his heaven in prosperity, and
there cannot fail to be enkindled on the embers of expiring
passion a pure and temperate flame of mutual affection, lasting
as existence, quenched only by death.

Literature, however, is not only useful to individuals
abstractly considered, but is also of the highest advantage to
nations and communities. It is not, as is generally thought,
that because the Greeks and Romans excelled all the nations
in warlike and glorious deeds, that they appear so conspicuous
on the page of history, but because they had among them men
of refined and enlightened understandings, whose deep re-
searches into historical and scientific matters enabled them to
transmit to posterity in glowing colors the actions of their
countrymen. In vain might the hero conquer, or the patriot
bleed, their triumphs and their blood would be soon forgotten
but for the faithful pen of the historian. Such precious gifts,
the effects of learning, are indeed inestimable; they unfold to
the eyes of youth the illustrious deeds of ancient patriots and
sages, and kindle the glow of virtuous emulation in the ardent
breast, and nerve the stripling's arm with more than manly
strength.

It is not indeed possible in the nature of things for all to
be great men, or, as the almanac oration said, "to ride the big
horse." It is not the fate of every one to be as was said of
Washington, "the sunbeam in council and the storm in war";
but it is possible for every one to become exemplary in the

class to which he belongs, to enlarge and refine his understanding, and by these means to purify and fortify his heart. It requires more than an ordinary capacity to take up with Milton the angelic lyre and portray in celestial strains the scenes of paradise, to view the vast retrospect of intellectual life, or traverse with fancy like his immeasurable wilds of ether with Satan's banished legions. Seldom do we see understanding like that of Rittenhouse and Newton, whose comprehensive ken embraced all creation; whose unerring judgment, without the assistance of airy fancy, could analyze and harmonize every part of nature's frame; who could follow with undeviating precision the glittering spheres in their meanderings through the heavens; and who were inhabitants as it were of world's immeasurably distant. But to finish a long story with the beautiful language of Grey, "The applause of listening senates to command, and read their history in a nation's eyes," is the fortune of few. Notwithstanding, let all contend for the prize; virtue and perseverance never lose a sufficient reward.

But finally, the most flattering consideration of all is the eternal duration of intellectual improvement; the probability that in a future state the mind will still be approximating towards perfection; and that purged from all alloy of earthly passion, and freed from the incumbrance of a gross load of mortality which enfeebled its power and obstructed its motion, it will be forever investigating still new and nobler principles, and be able to discover that "all discord was harmony not understood; all partial evil universal good;" to trace the connection link by link of the chain of being and reason from beginning to end, both fastening on the throne of omnipotence.

MEMENTO OF AFFECTION.

Dear Aaron: If the remembrance of days that are past, if the retrospect of the scenes of youth can, in riper years, shed a tranquillity over the mind, or gild the last moments of existence with a beam of mental satisfaction, we trust that when raised to that eminence to which your talents entitle you, you will recur with pleasure to those hours which have been spent with us in the attainment of literature, and which have been rendered doubly agreeable by your presence. Your happiness will be our wish through life; but if the chilling blasts of adversity should destroy those hopes we entertain of your advancement in life, we here profess ourselves your warm and unshaken friends. We hope that you will receive this memento of our affection which we offer from the pure and undisguised feelings of our hearts.

Robert Taylor,	Isaiah P. Bonham,
William R. Richardson,	Edmond Morris,
Gustavus Black,	Henry Rogers,
T. H. Yardley,	Job Irick,
Charles Holmes,	William Carpenter,
Thomas I. Newbold,	Walter Browne,
Aaron S. Lippincott,	Joseph T. Price,
Jacob Hewlings,	R. M. Bishop,
Nathl. Sayre Harris,	I. Allen,
Samuel S. Grubb,	J. S. Smith,
John L. Newbold,	W. Shields,
James H. Bennett,	G. Foster,
Samuel B. Tobey,	L. Rodman.
William Kimber,	

Burlington, Feb. 5, 1821.

TEMPERANCE.

PROCEEDINGS OF THE ANNUAL MEETING OF THE "BURLINGTON CITY TEMPERANCE SOCIETY," HELD IN THE METHODIST MEETING-HOUSE IN THAT PLACE, ON THE 7TH OF FIFTH-MONTH, 1834.

The meeting was called to order by Samuel Aaron, President of the Society. Resolutions of a local nature having been presented, were passed unanimously, when the following members were elected viva voce, to serve as a board of managers for the ensuing year, viz.: Samuel Aaron, President; Nathan W. Cole, M. D., Vice President; Joseph R. King, Recording Secretary; William J. Allison, Corresponding Secretary; Charles Atherton, Treasurer; Caleb Gaskill, Thomas Aikman, John Boozer, Luke Reed, Joseph L. Powell, Dubre Knight, Directors.

A report of the proceedings of the Board for the past year was produced and read, as follows:

The Board of Managers of the Burlington Temperance Society, in conformity with the constitution, present to the Society the following report: They will commence with a brief statement of particular facts, and conclude with a few general observations. Soon after the last annual meeting, the Board made exertions to establish an auxiliary society at Coopertown, in the adjoining township of Willingborough, which were successful beyond hope. Several farmers in the neighborhood gathered their harvests for the first time without ardent spirits, the tavern has become comparatively deserted, and though the neighborhood is thinly settled forty numbers of the "Temperance Recorder" are taken, and a society of forty-three members now exists. Efforts of a similar kind, however, in relation to Slabtown, or Jacksonville, have hitherto entirely failed. Though some of the inhabitants are temperate, such scruples are entertained on the subject of temperance societies, that no place, not even the house of divine worship, nor the school-house, could be obtained for the purpose of holding a temperance meeting. The Board of Managers have held meetings through the year, and have collected and expended about twenty dollars for the distribution of valuable temperance papers. One hundred copies of the "Temperance Recorder" are circulated, and two individuals have procured means to circulate thirty copies of the "Temperance Intelligencer."

Two public temperance meetings have been held during the year, one in November last, at which an address was delivered, and one on the 26th of February, when two gentlemen addressed a numerous, respectable and crowded audience, forty-three of whom gave their names to the pledge on the spot. About ninety names have been added to the Society during the past year, and its present number is two hundred and seventy-one. The Board have actively and cordially co-operated with other local societies in happily forming the present society for the county, and they took measures to secure the appointment of delegates to attend the State Temperance Convention, held in Trenton, on the 12th of February last, part of whom were present and active at the deliberations of that important meeting. They are happy to state that a distillery near this place has been discontinued upon principle, and the stills broken up and sold for old copper. They beg leave also to mention to the honor of the individual and for the public good (though the circumstances transpired more than a year since), the conduct of a gentleman of this place, who decided to sacrifice a considerable quantity of costly liquors by letting them waste away in his cellar. They earnestly hope to see all our respectable fellow-citizens, who still furnish ardent spirits to the community, moved by examples like these to give over the work of death; and they tremble in fear of the retribution that awaits the incorrigible.

The Board have been careful to be and to appear free from any political or sectarian motives, and rejoice exceedingly to find the honest scruples of various worthy citizens yielding to the evidence presented before them, that temperance societies are really the means of preserving the unwary and reclaiming the lost. The physicians here, as elsewhere, are mainly and actively with the temperance society, thus showing its great importance, and proving their own desire to preserve men in health not less than to cure the diseased. There are three stores in the place that sell no ardent spirits, except for specified medicinal or manufacturing purposes, thus correctly and wisely furnishing the means of obtaining the article for needful occasions without encouraging its general use. There are some discouragements, of such a nature, however, as to show the need of reformation, and to rouse and exalt the spirit of benevolence. We have to encounter the scoffs and curses of the profane; the song of the drunkard; and, in some cases, the dignified contempt of superior wealth and intelligence, and even the sober opposition of accredited religion. Thus those entirely unlike in themselves, the pious and the profane, the drunk and the sober, the wise and the foolish, are strangely brought together in common array against the temperance society.

A certain amount and kind of public feeling are against the reformation. For instance: Men in our town are notoriously destroying their moral principles, shortening their days, beggaring their families, and thus taxing the public, in consequence of drinking ardent spirits. Youth, mere children, are found drunk about our streets and carried home; individuals have been found dead in the road or in the water, accompanied by a half-emptied jug of whisky. And yet the respectable persons who furnish the means of producing these effects deem themselves wholly irresponsible, and are considered so by many others. It is notorious also that several public houses exist in this place more than are really necessary or strictly lawful, according to the charter of the city of Burlington, Article XI. And yet neither the city corporation nor the community themselves can or dare take any efficient measures to have the number diminished.

The above brief account of particulars must suffice. It is our opinion that those who drink moderately and furnish intoxicating drinks for others, are mainly responsible for the evils of intemperance. The more influence they have, the more responsibility. We believe that temperance consists in partaking moderately of needful sustenance and abstaining totally from all poisons. But the arguments of many of our fellow-citizens would urge the moderate use of opium, and hellebore, and arsenic, and prussic acid, as well as alcohol, when in perfect health, to prove our temperance in the enjoyment of the creatures of a bountiful Providence. The most thoughtful and conscientious of those who furnish rum, deny it to the ruined sot, except it be a few drams to commence a debauch; and only administer it to the man of steady habits, the uncorrupted youth, or the prudent, reflecting tippler. So the genteel debauchee scorns the contact of vulgar prostitution, and finds it more decent and respectable to ensnare innocence and pollute virtue. This is a fatal sophistry; it lays snares for the souls of our youth, inoculates the land with plague, and atones for all the evils it produces by shunning its victims and leaving them to the poor-house and the prison.

We believe the temperance pledge to be, under Providence, the great support and safeguard and the moving power of the temperance reformation. Some object to it as an artificial and arbitrary check upon the natural dictates of conscience. If so, then is conscience improperly checked by the public and solemn engagement in the marriage contract, the oath or affirmation of a witness, juror or public officer, and the written and formal pledge contained in a promissory note, deed or bond? The fact is that fallible beings need fixed and well ascertained points in morals to enable them to shape their course in a world of temptations; as mariners, upon the deceitful and trackless ocean, need the fixed stars for their direction, while subject to the influence of unseen currents and changing winds. This social pledge has been the only thing yet tried, and not found wanting, to arrest the march of drunkenness and its attendant legions of destroyers. The tippling officers of justice had hanged the drunken murderer in vain; the preacher, who had just sipped his moderate dram, had fruitlessly declaimed against a heartier drink; and the boasted common sense of mankind had utterly failed to erect a barrier or even draw a visible and acknowledged line between safe

and ruinous indulgence. But the social pledge to total abstinence has already reclaimed its thousands and preserved its
millions. Like the destroyer it opposes, it has attracted to itself all sorts of persons. Even sects and denominations of
highly repellant properties have been drawn together around
it as a common centre of benevolent attraction; and those of
no profession and no parts, the inert and scattered fragments
from the social compact, have been quickened and concentrated by the same cause. The temperance pledge then, by
its power to unite those that differ in everything else, has amply proved, we think, its claims to general homage. May this
assembly and this whole community subscribe it and maintain it inviolably and forever.

By order of the Board.

SAMUEL AARON, *President.*

The Rev. Stephen H. Tyng, D. D., of Philadelphia, who
was present by particular invitation, then arose, was introduced
to the large assemblage by the chair, and delivered a most
happy and able address, entirely worthy of himself and the
occasion. Immediately after the pledge was read by the President, and upwards of forty new members were added to the
society.

On motion, *Resolved,* That the proceedings of this meeting be published in the Trenton and Mount Holly papers.

The following list contains the names of the various of-
ficers of the Burlington County Temperance Society, as elected
at the annual meeting of the society held at Mount Holly on
April 14, 1834: William Russell, President, Mount Holly,
N. J.; Edward Thomas, Vice President, Medford, N. J.; Thos.
Aikman, Vice President, Burlington, N. J.; Josiah R. Reeve,
Recording Secretary, Medford, N. J.; James H. Sterling, Cor-
responding Secretary, Burlington, N. J. Directors—George
Haines, M. D., Medford, N. J.; John H. Rulon, Yardville,
N. J.; Jos. R. King, Burlington, N. J.; J. L. Stratton, M. D.,
Mount Holly, N. J.; Richard W. Fayre, Mount Holly, N. J.;
John West, Trenton, N. J.; William K. Mason, M. D., Tuck-
erton, N. J.; Hezekiah Cramer, Tuckerton, N. J.; Joseph At-
wood, Tuckerton, N. J.; Conley Plotts, Columbus, N. J.; Paul

Jones, Burlington, N. J.; Thomas Edmunds, Jr., Pemberton,
N. J.; Clarence W. Mulford, Pemberton, N. J.; Samuel Wool-
ston, M. D., Vincenttown, N. J.; John Purdue, M. D., Pemberton, N. J.

---

*The Board of Managers of the Burlington City Temperance
Society do respectfully present the following report:*

The time of holding the annual meeting having been
changed during the past year, a period of only about nine
months has elapsed since making our last report. Since that
time about sixty persons have been added to the list of members, including upwards of forty who joined on that occasion,
and the whole number of members is at present about three
hundred and thirty. Only two or three persons have been so
far overcome by the power of former habits as to render their
permanent reformation hopeless; though somewhat more than
that number have been delinquent more or less. No person
within the bounds of the neighborhood limiting the society is
known to the board to have renounced the traffic from moral
principles during the past year; and while there are four good
stores where spirits are not kept, there are four also, in other
respects, together with five taverns and one distillery, where
ardent spirits are furnished as a common drink. The board
are of opinion, however, that the business has become less
popular and, they trust, less profitable within even the past
year; and they are fully persuaded that fewer individuals and
families than formerly of the more enlightened classes are now
the victims of drunkenness.

The board have acted together very harmoniously, and
most of them have devoted not a little time and reflection to
conscientious and, as they believe, lawful and proper efforts to
promote the cause. What they have done has been done
openly; they have not shunned nor dreaded responsibility.
On the contrary, they earnestly invoke a free and full examination of their actions and their motives. They seriously contemplated holding up to public detestation the scandalous effects of drinking at the great militia training that followed hard

upon our last annual meeting; but concluded finally that the notorious scenes themselves, the courts martial, with the prosecutions for damages that followed that shameful day, would leave them nothing to add. No small exertion was made during the early part of last summer to establish a temperance hotel in this city. And to show that the true friends of temperance are not actuated by niggardly and avaricious feelings, we would state that the board pledged themselves that the friends of the cause would contribute from $150 to $200 for the purpose of having the experiment of keeping a respectable temperance house tried fairly for a single year. This negotiation, however, entirely failed.

The board invited recently the public discussion of some questions touching the character of temperance societies, and several persons freely stated their objections to them. The acknowledged integrity and intellect of these gentlemen afford ample proof that objections among the sincerest and weightiest that can be urged were then presented; and we are happy, therefore, to have such evidence that not a feather's weight of argument can be brought to bear against the grand principles of the temperance reformation.

We will make no invidious comparisons between the members of our society and others; but we must say that the numbers, the experience and the character of those zealously attached to the society, are such as to entitle it to the serious attention and respect of this intelligent community. Not to mention others—that class, not very small, of virtuous, injured and suffering females, whose benedictions attend all our labors —the mothers, wives or widows of men ruined by intemperance, who cry both to God and man for help and pity, present claims to our attention that cannot be innocently or safely disregarded.

In closing with a remark or two, no more plain than they are notoriously and strictly true, we premise the solemn avowal of our good will towards all mankind, and that what we say is from a sense of duty only. We do reiterate, then, as our deliberate and firm belief, the opinion of thousands among the wisest, best and greatest men of this nation—an opinion which they have publicly and formally avowed—that the traffic in ardent spirits with a view to furnishing them to our fellow-men as a common drink, is morally wrong; and that the laws which sanction this traffic are also morally wrong, having no foundation, as all human laws ought to have, in those immutable principles of justice contained in the revealed will of God. We hold it to be self-evident that no man or set of men can have a moral right to do or authorize to be done anything that tends to injure themselves or others. Whatever rights of property a man may have, he can have no right to appropriate his substance in a way that promotes either the voluntary or involuntary ruin of mankind. A man may measure out, with full and honest measure, the gills and quarts that destroy his neighbor's health and character and lay him in a premature and dishonorable grave, and leave his family outcast and penniless. He may balance his book with the last dollar of the drunkard's substance—the voluntary drunkard; he may call it a final settlement, and the law will sanction it as a fair and just transaction. But we believe (the truth, in love, to all) that the settlement is not final, that the transaction is not just, that a Book will appear—a true Book—of entirely different entries on the subject, and that the approving statute made on earth will be pronounced by a Higher Legislator null and void.

Burlington, N. J., February, 1835.

PLAIN TRUTH.

The undersigned presented a remonstrance before the corporation of this city on the 1st inst. against licensing so many persons to keep inns and taverns as have heretofore been permitted to do so. Having, in connection with his late partner, expended from $8000 to $9000 in this city during the eighteen months last past he supposed as usefully to the community as any of the applicants for tavern licenses, and having been deeply aggrieved and injured by permission given to students of only sixteen or seventeen years of age to drink intoxicating liquors in some of the taverns, he hoped to be heard in support of the remonstrance. He could not, however, be heard consistently with the rules of the body, and therefore takes this way of stating a few points that he wished to urge:

1. Some of the tavern-keepers have violated the law by selling without license.—See laws of New Jersey, page 282, Sec. 7; and page 745, Sec. 4.

2. Is not the law violated by licensing more inns and taverns than are necessary?—See page 283, Sec. 9.

3. Has it not been triumphantly and wantonly trampled on by selling to apprentices and school-boys?—Page 285, Sec. 22; and page 532, Sec. 1.

4. The law requires, under a very heavy penalty, a bill of fare certified by the clerk to be exhibited in every tavern. —Page 284, Sec. 17. Is this attended to?

5. The law requires the presiding Justice to call upon the Justices present to make known any facts and objections why such license should not be granted.—Pages 744, 745; Sec. 1. Was that duty performed on the 1st inst.?

6. At one of the taverns an old man, now poor, was allowed to dispose of $15 in three days.

7. At another, a young man, in many respects deserving, was furnished on a Sunday with a pocket bottle filled with spirits, which he carried into the woods, and by which means he was confirmed in a drunken frolic and was permitted at the taverns to drink himself in two or three days out of countenance, out of heart, out of money, out of work, and to leave the place a homeless wanderer on the earth.

8. Very recently a man, who had been drinking for a month, and evidently destroying himself, went home from certain taverns where he had obtained liquor, and was dead two hours after.

9. Groups of men are to be found on Sundays, at some of the taverns at least, drunk, profane and blasphemous, quarreling often, sometimes fighting at or near the tavern, and much disturbing the peaceable citizens. The applicants, however, were all licensed as persons of unimpeachable integrity, and necessary in that capacity for the common good. It was remarkable, however, that of the signers to their petitions, four persons signed each three petitions, making twelve signatures; twelve persons signed each two petitions, making twenty-four

signatures; and twenty-one persons signed each one petition,
making twenty-one signatures. So thirty-seven persons, one
a member of the corporation, furnished fifty-seven signatures.
This fact shows how the one hundred and fifty freeholders (perhaps two hundred) of this city feel towards our taverns. One
petition had been much soiled and handled in procuring twelve
names. On the principle pursued by these petitioners and
signers, twelve freeholders might be the means of licensing
every other man in Burlington; and thirteen might license
every housekeeper, themselves included.

SAMUEL AARON.

Burlington, N. J., April 26, 1835.

THE SEVENTH ANNUAL REPORT OF THE BOARD OF MANAGERS
OF THE BURLINGTON TEMPERANCE SOCIETY.

February, 1836.

Six public meetings have been called by the board during the past year, several of which were numerously attended.
The board themselves have held nine meetings. The net increase of members during the year has been about fifty, composed chiefly of young persons. The number of consistent
members now living is believed to be about five hundred. In
stating this estimate it is proper to say that the Secretary keeps
a list with great care, which is frequently revised and corrected
by the board as circumstances may require.

A sum of $91.56 has been raised by the voluntary con-
tributions of the members and others, and appropriated partly
to the support of the State Agent, partly in aid of the county
society's publications, partly in the purchase and distribution
of the "Temperance Recorder" and "Intelligencer," and in
payment of expenses incidental to public meetings.

The number of taverns within the society's limits is four;
of anti-temperance stores, including one small shop, is three.
The number of stores where ardent spirit is not sold as a beverage is five. To this it may be added, on good authority,

that there is no distillery of any kind in the township, nor any distillery of grain in the county of Burlington.

The deaths occasioned by alcohol within the township during the past year have, it is believed, been fewer than common; though several persons have fallen victims, nameless, dishonored, and too soon forgotten. Its use and influence at the polls still continue, to the scandal of the political parties, the guilt of many zealous politicians, and the degradation of republican institutions.

The board owe it to themselves and their constituents to state that they have expended some money, much valuable time, and faithful and often painful labor of head and heart in support of the cause which you have committed to their management. They have conscientiously labored in discharge of their duty to injure no man, and even to offend no man. Their chief support has been the conviction that you were generally true-hearted adherents to the pledge, and the hope that the righteous and most salutary principles of temperance may ere long generally prevail. Nor is there reason to be wearied with toil or intimidated by opposition. Though fewer names have been added this year than usual, let it be remembered there were fewer to add. The society claims many as its fast friends of those second to none in this community for intelligence or virtue, and rejoices that a number more of the same stamp firmly practice without professing its principles. It is also a source of joyful gratitude that far more children are nursed without the use of whisky baths and alcoholic anodynes, and that very many youth are growing up without the taint of morning bitters and sugared sips from visitors' and parents' unfinished glasses. Thus, a generation born and trained to abstinence are arising to bless and to perpetuate the temperance reformation.

We close with one reflection. To use or to administer poisons, destructive of human life, has always been considered a legal and moral wrong. A general exception, however, has been made in favor of one singular and solitary article, which, to the destruction of the body, adds the eclipse of the mind and the sacrifice of the immortal soul. Why such an exception should secure the currency of opinion and the support of law, we do not stop to inquire, but express our ardent hope and firm confidence that the light and the sound of the temperance reform will rouse the human conscience to consider the question in its application to alcohol. Whether an accountable creature can innocently contribute directly or indirectly to the support of a practice which produces evil, only evil, and that continually. When this question in this application shall have been decided right by the enlightened consciences of our fellow men, the triumph of temperance will have come. It cannot be asked that temperance truths should make all men sober, any more than the divine truth in general should render all men Christians. An obligation will be proved and pointed out, binding man to the throne of infinite authority and justice, and there he must be left instructed, warned and entreated at his own peril. The time is not far distant, we fully believe, when no man can ask or expect the blessing of heaven on the manufacture, sale or use of intoxicating liquors.

NOTES ON THE LICENSE SYSTEM.

The satisfaction I feel in the political arrangements, which allow a hearing before our legislators. The pleasure and confidence I feel in the powers and influence of legislators in our own country. You are the depository dispensers of law.

I. What we ask is not inconsistent with the spirit of our laws on the subject, which are meant to be restrictive. The original mistake of the legislature in letting out this serpent, alcohol. He has not only crawled but flown. He has become a many-headed dragon—wine, ale, beer, brandy, gin, rum, etc. The license system has always been meant to be restrictive. It has meant to make good men—the conservators of the public welfare. The use of alcoholic drinks was deemed needful, and its retail was first restricted to apothecaries. The snake grew, and they confined him to good inn-keepers. He grew still bigger, and they gave him in special charge to formidable statutes. He grew, and they gave him to twelve free-holders.

He grew, and they committed him to the common pleas. Now we ask to give him up to public opinion. Don't hedge him in, but let public opinion at him. Lend the rope and hook of the law, catch him and bind him fast.

II. We believe that the operation of the present laws is oppressive. Could this be properly pressed, I am sure it would have great effect. I shall not dwell on all the oppressions. The pains inflicted on sensibility, idleness, crime, anguish, shame, misery, widowhood and orphanage. Look at our own temptations and those of our children. These awful facts have been poured "on the nation's naked heart," till it is turned to stone. But I would, if I could, expose the oppressiveness of this system in the point of taxation. Taxation, for the most useful purposes, especially when direct, is unpopular. Taxation, without consent, was deemed revolutionary. Taxation, as a bounty on the accursed orgies of Bacchus; what shall we say of it? Ninety taverns in the county of Burlington selling liquors amounting to $40,000, producing a direct tax of $10,000.

III. The remedy we propose is peaceable. What is it? To withhold the privilege to impose taxation, unless a man has the deliberate consent and approbation of the majority of tax-payers. This method avoids the noise and strife of elections. It gives the applicant fair and full access to the understanding and hearts of men, and will quiet the rejected. It gives occasion to every tax-payer calmly to consider his responsibility.

IV. The remedy is republican. This is about self-evident. With due respect to those who say so, it seems to me like quibbling to call this measure an appeal to force. Nor need I dwell upon the moral quibble, nor on the cavils about putting all business on the same footing. Here is a controversy on equal terms. The light of public opinion is hidden under a bushel.

V. It bids fair to be eventually and quietly efficacious. Some will grant, some withhold. The subject will be constantly agitated. In contest and rational discussion, truth will prevail.

TEMPERANCE MEETING.

Resolved, That human society and the proper regulation thereof, called law, are ordained of God.

Resolved, That human law is a "rule of civil conduct, prescribed by the supreme power in a state, commending what is right and prohibiting what is wrong." That "its object is to ascertain what is just, honorable and expedient; and when that is discovered, it is proclaimed as a general ordinance, equally and impartially to all." That its proper tendency is to produce that state of society in which "every man shall do to others as he would that others should do to him."

Resolved, That the legislators of this land are bound by their oath of office to obliterate every statute discordant with the foregoing principles, and to make such enactments, and such only as strictly agree with them.

Resolved, That every judicial and executive officer is bound to explain and enforce such laws according to their true meaning, and to resign his authority rather than sustain unrighteous statutes.

Resolved, That the voters in our country are, under God, the creators of all legal and political functionaries or agents, and are therefore bound by their duty to God, to themselves, to their posterity, and to all the world, to choose such men only to make and administer our laws as have given proof that they fear God, love justice, hate covetousness, and understand and approve the above definition of law.

Resolved, That the statutes and usages which sanction and support the sale and use of alcohol as a beverage, are entirely contradictory of the principles above laid down; that they permit what is wrong, and prevent what is right; that their effects are unjust, dishonorable and inexpedient; that they are unequal and partial in granting privileges to a few; that they allow men to do to others, and to their families, what they themselves would shudder to receive in return.

Therefore, *resolved*, That we will vote for no man for a public office, unless he is known to us to be opposed to the legalizing of the rum traffic, and distinctly pledged to prevent the supply of alcoholic beverages, either by penal laws or by referring the matter to the people at the polls.

Resolved, That there be a committee to ascertain and report to us through the newspapers, or by hand-bills, the views of the candidates for state and county offices, who shall be presented for our suffrages.

Resolved, That said committee call a meeting of the voters, if they deem it necessary, during the present month.

September 4, 1847.

— · —— —

PETITION.

To the Senate and House of Representatives of the Common-wealth of Pennsylvania :

The subscribers, taxables of the county of Montgomery, respectfully represent, that they are much aggrieved by the existing and increasing evils of intemperance, and that they deem it particularly unjust that those opposed to the liquor traffic should be taxed along with those in favor of it, to pay the expenses of the pauperism and crime which flow from intemperance. As they have no share, and desire none, in the profits of the traffic, they wish to be exonerated from all legal obligation to share in the expense it creates.

Further, it has always been the spirit of American legislation to permit no business to impose its cost and losses on those not engaged in it. The subscribers do, therefore, earnestly entreat you to enact a law as explicit and binding as possible, making the liquor dealers, and those who sustain them, personally and pecuniarily responsible for the injuries and expenses now inflicted by the traffic on the public at large. Let the purposed liquor dealer have the written approval of one-half the taxables in his township, borough or ward, before he is licensed to sell. Let him give a bond, with ample sureties, in a sum not less than $1,000, for his strict compliance with the law. Let him and his sureties be suable on said bond, by any competent member or friend of any family injured by liquor supplied by said dealer; let the damages be awarded at the discretion of a jury or arbitrators, and let the dealer always pay costs of suit, if proved to have supplied any liquor as charged. Let the directors of the poor be compelled to sue, as aforesaid, for the support of any person or family becoming a public burden, in consequence, wholly or in part, of using liquor supplied by said dealer; and let the dealer pay costs if proved to have supplied, as aforesaid. Let the defendant, aforesaid, be entitled to maintain a suit, to compel his fellow-dealers to contribute a portion of the damages or fines imposed on him. Let any attempt to collect a liquor debt subject the plaintiff to the loss of the claim and costs. Let every unlicensed dealer be subject to fine and imprisonment. Let no suit for libel be maintained by a liquor dealer when the truth of the charges against him can be proved. Let the coroner in cases of suicide, manslaughter or murder, as the consequence of intemperance, be compelled to ascertain if possible, and publish in his verdict, the name of the furnisher of the liquor. Let such furnisher of liquor be indictable for a misdemeanor, and punishable with fine and imprisonment.

TEMPERANCE COMMITTEE.

Norristown, 1851.

A PLEA FOR TOTAL ABSTINENCE.

Men, Women and Children—Permit one who desires your truest welfare, and that of all the world, to claim your thoughtful and serious attention to a few considerations connected with the temperance reform.

What is the fundamental principle of this reform? Is it not that alcohol is the most insidious and the most destructive of all poisons? "Wine is a mocker," insidious; "strong drink is raging," a fierce destroyer. Such is its description in that most discriminating of all books, the Bible. The experience and inventions of men confirm the testimony. Other drugs and poisons have each some one peculiar effect upon the human system. Opium acts on the nervous structure, perverts the imagination to idle dreams, and destroys the whole man by the indolence and lethargy superinduced through that action. Prussic acid and some of the mercurial poisons seize on the vital fluids—on some more, on others less—and curdle and corrode them through a brief and mortal agony. Arsenic, nux vomica and others act on the stomach in different ways, and produce death or great injury. The poison of the rattle-snake or the slaver of the mad dog may be swallowed with-out harm, but is fatal on the broken skin. Some drugs stimulate the animal propensities to more than brutal excess; some blotch the skin, and others rot the bones. But it is re-served for alcohol to perform at once almost all the functions of other poisons, destroying man as a passive and helpless vic-tim; and last, and worst of all, to make him an active and fear-ful agent in the ruin or misery of all around him. Not only is his own body destroyed, and his own progeny polluted by the bad blood he transmits to them, but his soul is demon-ized, the fountain of natural affections is sealed up, or its pure streams turned into the waves of the burning lake, so that he spurns his loving wife, loathes his sweet children, and curses his weeping mother.

Now what other poison does all this? And when does alcohol fail of such tendencies? And how often do its influen-ces surpass, infinitely surpass, all powers of description? If the foregoing positions are true—if they are but very partially true—should not every moral suasive and every righteous legal power be employed to put away this poison from every human life? How can any sensible man maintain the moder-ate use of such an article on the same ground as he does that of wholesome and needful food? Does the use of food tend at all to make a man a devil? Does the moderate use of it tend infallibly to gluttony? Alcoholic poisons cause intense bodily suffering, infatuate the mind, tickle the nerves, and ex-cite the brain. Our object is definite, most distinctly marked —to put these poisons entirely out of use. The true remedy is voluntary total abstinence.

CORRESPONDENCE.

BURLINGTON, N. J., July 16, 1820.

Esteemed Friend—(Excuse my Quaker introduction; you know where I am.) I confess with no small shame that I have transgressed many of the laws of politeness, and done that which should forfeit much of your esteem and confidence, by neglecting to answer your favor for so long a time. Yet, as you say, "I am selfish enough to hope" that you will not altogether discard me from claims of intimacy, and receiving once in a while a mark of your regard from your hand. You will admit, and so will all my acquaintances, that it was always a foible of mine to disparage or underrate my own abilities, and that among other things I always professed myself unskilled in the art of letter writing; however it might be in other respects, in this I certainly told the truth. And if you till this time doubted it, I may now cry out with Falstaff, " Ecce signum !"

My dear ———, you are now about to become a lawyer, and learn to tell a long story; you will then, of course, not be displeased with a long letter. If there were no other excuse for my delay, this might suffice: that I scrawl enough at once to last a long time. But there are other excuses. I will not enumerate many. One is that I am so crowded with studies at one time, and so beset with boys at another who are too idle to learn themselves and too busy to suffer others, that it is difficult to find an opportunity. Your observation with respect to the value of my correspondence, implying that I could please others when I cannot please myself, I think "savoreth of flattery," which I should expect from almost any one sooner than you. If it could be reduced to a Q. E. D., speaking geometrically, that I do possess the faculty of interesting my friends,

I would certainly, both from vanity and respect, address them more frequently.

I learn both from yourself and others that you are about to "turn over a new leaf." And I am as sincere in telling you, as I am happy in hearing and believing, that your prospects are very fair not only for escaping disgrace but for acquiring honor. Your greatest hindrance was always diffidence; but it is now time to shake off the shackles of boyish modesty and assume the dignity which a conscious sense of manly worth inspires. Do so, my friend; and ever adhere to truth and integrity, and you will find that though mankind are an unco' squad they will pay the respect due to merit and to virtue, and that more than mediocrity will be your fortune. For my own part I would ask no better fortune than a character of unimpeachable honesty, for such I esteem the summum bonum of existence.

With regard to ambition I agree with you, that if it is ever laudable it is when it tends to the acquisition of knowledge. In this case, however, it lays us under some severe restrictions, as you observe; even that, among others, of almost forgetting the existence of the ladies. But so it is: science and a ladies' man are never fond of one another. And since it is probably of more importance to fit yourself for your own emolument and your country's honor than to become the focus of a score of ladies' eyes, when law and love confine you to one, I highly approve of your resolution, arduous as the task is, of forgetting the ladies. Let it be so; at least for a while. Prepare yourself with the good things necessary, and no doubt some tender fair one will partake of your cheer with pleasure.

It would be trifling indeed for me to hint at the importance of acquiring knowledge; it would be an insult to your good sense; it would be a servile repetition of the precept of every one—like other good ones, however, too seldom reduced to practice. I wish I could tell you something that would please you; be good enough, however, to receive the intention for the act. I have never been out of sight of Burlington since I came here, which shows that I have been contented; indeed, with many things I am highly pleased.

I have just commenced learning French; terms, three lessons per week, $5 per quarter. The school is probably as creditable, and as deservedly so, as any in the United States. Our teachers far surpass my expectations, and John Gummere is honored with the correspondence of some of the most scientific men in this country. He performs some philosophical experiments now, but many more in the winter. Some of the students are moral and decent, and some are quite the reverse. Some steal off from their teachers on Sundays and spend their time and money over the flowing goblets of Bacchus, and many of them are as familiar with the awful name of their Creator as with the most intimate of their school-fellows.

The only religious societies in Burlington are the Friends, Episcopalians, Methodists and Baptists, and of these I prefer the Friends, whose meeting I attend, together with most of our scholars, about three times a week.

I will omit a geographical description of Burlington, as there is nothing remarkable in it. It is the residence, however, of some great men, such as the venerable Elias Boudinot, Horace Binney, Gen. Bloomfield, and Lawyers Griffith, Chauncey and McIlvain.

Present my most hearty respects to Mr. H——, and please to tell him that I am as much his friend as if I did write; the only thing that hinders me is a sort of pride that cannot brook the idea of inferiority. There is no one whose correspondence I would more highly value; but feeling unable to give *par pari*, I cannot think of writing. If my friend, however, will wait till I grow a little older and wiser, he will find me most willing to become a Philoctetes to Hercules.

Be particular to remember me to all my friends. Tell James D—— he has immortalized himself by his toast, the 4th of July, and that I am publishing his fame. I am happy to learn your father is restored to health; my sober respects to him (my ever kind friend) and Mrs. ——. The ladies, too —but, stay; you never see them. However, if chance should throw them in your way, you may tell them "I am yet alive." When I go to —— I hope to see you "face to face." Till then and forever you have for your welfare the sincere wishes of   SAMUEL AARON.

BURLINGTON, N. J., January 23, 1821.

My Dear Friend—Without transgressing "truth and justice," I cannot offer any excuse for my negligence. I am generally busied about something or other, to be sure; but none of my engagements are so binding as to justify my neglect of a correspondence so agreeable and so profitable as yours. You mention the probability of my being surprised at your transgression of, etc. I confess your treating me so much better than I deserved did indeed surprise me. You will not think that I rate your natural kindness too meanly, for I would hardly have expected from those who profess to be my very warmest friends such promptness to oblige me where their own interest was so entirely unconcerned. Thrown upon the world as I am, one of the children of necessity, I have more reason than many others who want no assistance to remember with gratitude those that take an interest in my welfare. Memory and gratitude must both desert me before I cease to regard your father as one especially from whom I have received what I had no reason to expect—the most distinguished marks of favor and attention.

But to the point. There are several of my school-fellows who inform me of schools that I can have, but their manner of recommending them loses its effect with me, for they make the number sixty or seventy strong; enough, I think, to craze the clearest brain. A thousand pleasing recollections, which are always connected with a place that has long been our home, the theatre of our favorite pursuits and boyish pleasures, tend to make D—— a situation in my view preferable to any other, and I would rather live there than reign anywhere else. It is absolutely impracticable for me to leave the school here in less than two weeks; but after that time I would cheerfully acquiesce in your father's proposal, provided he could entirely free me from teaching Latin and Greek, which I am positively unfit for. Can he not weather it out until the 7th of February, with R——'s assistance and yours? In two weeks I shall get sufficient knowledge of Fluxions to pursue the study alone, and I am now determined to turn mathematician in my own defence.

Since a complete knowledge of one subject alone requires a life-time, if we wish to excel, we must give a particular subject particular attention. First rate literary acquirements for me are out of the question. Mathematicians are scarce; and those who excel are considered eminent persons. I do not wish to divide my studies, and I believe they must be mathematical. For this reason I must declare "pregnis et calcibus" against teaching the languages. I wish you or Mr. ———— would write me immediately on the receipt of this, so that we may both stand on sure footing and not disappoint or misunderstand each other.

The young men of Burlington, in connection with our students, have formed a society for the encouragement of domestic manufactures. There are about fifty members, some of them very respectable, and some rather the contrary. We admit none above thirty years old but as honorary members. The belongers are generally above eighteen years of age. You will not think me more than usually vain if I tell you that I was president. However, I resigned last Monday night, and one of our Philadelphia boys was elected. Can't you raise up such an association in D————? I forgot to tell you, that if a member was caught with a coat of foreign cloth, he must pay five dollars fine or be expelled.

We have now in our school a debating and recitation society; but I think one will kill the other before long. I am sorry yours has fallen through in D————. It is a very proper place for such a club, and I think you ought to have one.

There is an article in the papers about my brother M———— having killed a wild cat, and I am daily interrogated on the subject. I have seen no account of it myself, but whatever the fact really was, it is here magnified into a great exploit. It is disagreeable to write or compose this morning, January 24th, for the mercury is eleven degrees below zero, and the stove completely barricaded by boys, so that between frost and noise my ideas are all driven away. I am expecting a "feast of reason and a flow of soul" when I see you, which I hope will be shortly. I am glad you went to see and hear Kean; I must ask you a thousand questions about him. To your family, and my friends generally, I would be remembered.

Think of the cold weather and excuse my poorly written epistle. With respect and affection, yours, etc.

SAMUEL AARON.

BURLINGTON, September 19, 1822.

My Dear Friend—Although I promised to write to you soon, partly from a press of business and partly through natural indolence, I have thus long neglected to perform a really pleasing task, and one which, I can truly say, it was not my intention to omit so long. It is evening, and I am writing in the school-room. The boys are not very still, and I have to be calling to "order" pretty often, so that I have not quite a fair opportunity to muster up my thoughts and give you the best of them.

I have often laughed when thinking of the sang froid with which you receive your friends and part from them; and when I lately left you I was better pleased with our parting ceremony than if it had been such as would have taken place between ———— and a friend. Although our words were very few, I was none the less inclined to think you wished me well; nor did I feel any diminution of the warm regard I have long had for you.

Some new things must have taken place in D———— be- . fore this time, and I am all anxiety to have your own curious kind of an account of them. For you must know I think you great at description of this "sort of thing."

I find by the paper just received that "Dennis" has been answered. It is remarked that he "does not deserve a reply"; and it is certainly true that a sorry reply he gets.

You either have, or pretend to have, the advantage of me, in knowing my style, as you call it. I cannot boast this with regard to you, and therefore propose, for mutual amusement, that we make a mutual disclosure of our authorship, if either should scribble anything for the paper, and criticise privately in our own letters each other's faults. These remarks should be delivered in the blunt and candid language of truth and honest friendship.

This is now the fifth week of my being here, and the third of my teaching. I commenced teaching sooner than I expected; but perhaps it is as much to my advantage. I teach all the grammarians and attend to the reading. This takes up two hours and a half. The rest of the time I do whatever wants doing. J. Gummere has been away two days and left to me the charge of the school. The boys are most troublesome after they go to bed. It is rather a temptation for them to cut up when there are twenty or thirty of them near each other at the time of going to bed and getting up, when they are particularly inclined to mischief.

I am reading Telemachus in French; find it pretty easy, and can get ten pages in an hour. I have here a most excellent opportunity to improve in many kinds of knowledge, but not much in general reading.

Remember me to all my friends. I am afraid my letter is not worth a fi'-penny bit; but if you think so, and let me know, I will try and mend in the next.

Yours with all my heart,

SAMUEL AARON.

BURLINGTON, February 10, 1823.

My Dear Friend—I received yours, requiring an answer "right on the reel"; and certainly intended to have one spun sooner, but have been negligent as usual. I had heard of your illness, and was glad to find you in a fair way to recover. I hope you are now enjoying excellent health and your usual good spirits. You have given me a pleasing and humorous account of your debate, and I hope I shall hereafter be obliged to you for similar favors. I have chosen your question for discussion, and taken in my opinion for the best side.

I assert that the spendthrift is a character much more injurious to society than the miser. To do injury in society it is necessary for the man who does it to be a social being. The domestic, private virtues or vices have but little influence; if they spread at all, they are limited by very narrow bounds. I admit that the ruling passions of the miser and the spendthrift are equally corrosive to the soul; perhaps, indeed, those of the miser are more abhorrent to the character of a good citizen, considered within themselves. But the limitation to which they are subjected is what makes them less poisonous to the virtue of the community than the more agreeable, and consequently more prevalent, vices of the prodigal. If, as you observed, "the miser chooses to starve himself, let him do it;" the effect on society, if any is produced, will be slight and transient,—a wretch, despised as far as known, has made room for a better citizen.

Many traits in the character of the spendthrift have their attractions with most persons. His profusion is for a while called liberality; his dissolute manners, a noble independence of mind. The simplicity and fervor of the youthful heart are captivated by these false names, and the companions of the prodigal, who are never few, are often driving in the current of intemperance while they think themselves still on the firm footing of virtue. The miser represents a heap of filth covered up and prevented from doing harm. The corruption of the spendthrift taints the whole moral atmosphere around him. The former is a self destroyer; the latter, like Samson, together with himself, overwhelms many. The miser secretly and silently hoards up wealth, acquired rather by a self deprivation of the comforts of life than by defrauding others, for few will have intercourse with so odious a being; the spendthrift wastes the substance of his fathers in "riotous living." The coveting wretch has no friend; the prodigal, like Altamont, has, and, like Altamont, ruins him. The one defrauds his neighbor of a sum of money, perhaps, if occasion offer; the other allures his associates into habits like his own, and thus effects the sacrifice of their immortal interests. The miser drags on a miserable old age in his own hovel; the spendthrift becomes the tenant of a prison or an alms-house. The former is found dead beside his gold; the other is, sometimes at least, led out before the multitude to a shameful death, a dreadful exhibition of the effects of human depravity; or, perhaps, with a still lofty spirit and outrageous hand he terminates his own existence; or, most likely, he expires among

his equals in wretchedness in the house where common charity just gives enough to misery to support life. You will not
argue that the spendthrift, in the profuseness with which he
lavishes his money, is a supporter of the public prosperity.
You will not say that he enables the indigent to live or the
industrious to thrive by squandering his property.   Alas!
none profit by his profusion but taverns and gamblers. His
good things glut the votaries of vice, and his abundance is
poured into the sink of infamy.   The miser contributes, however unwillingly, his part to the public treasury, and this comprises most of what he gives either for good or evil.

I must speak of the evil resulting to the families of the
wretched subjects of my discussion.   I have seldom known
covetousness to produce the ruin of wife, children, parents,
friends.   In the shipwreck of his character, the avaricious
wretch himself only suffers.   But what I see I believe; and I
have seen, and so have you, the dreadful effects of intemperance and prodigality.   I, myself, have witnessed the tears and
distresses of an amiable and high spirited woman who was tied
to a spendthrift husband.   That woman I saw in the course of
four or five years broken-hearted, and hurried prematurely to
the grave.   I wish to attach no particular importance to this
individual fact.   I only mention it as in point; it has made an
impression which can never be worn away.

To conclude; since we are to judge of evil by its prevalence as well as character, I believe that the spendthrift, who is
an open violator of the precepts of morality and dictates of
reason, is a far more injurious member of the community than
the miser, whose habits are domestic, and vileness not exposed.

You will answer me soon and at good length, I hope.   I
suppose I must reply again to give you an opportunity of
choosing your subject and your side.   I desire you to spare
me a little in your answer, as I dislike in a race to be too far
outrun.   You charge me with flattery; but I cannot for my
life help thinking you far my superior in taste with regard to
writing.   You require an explanation of my remarks respecting your piece.   My criticism would have been "needless,"
because to me there were no obvious faults; "improper," because I certainly could not have improved it.   You must not

be discouraged by my first essay; but try the experiment right fairly, the result may be a mutual if not an equal improvement. Tell me whether this last phrase is correct, "mutual if not equal." I will send R—— a song with regard to the Rencontre of the "Baron Las Cases" with "Sir Hudson Lawe." If you have not seen the "Voice from St. Helena," get it, and read it. Be good enough, if you think of it, and see Mr. Miner, to ask him on what terms he will print an "Almanac adapted to the meridian and latitude of Doylestown, carefully calculated by Samuel Aaron"? Mind, I am in earnest.

Give my love to all my friends. You must tell me more news than I do you, and remember that I am your devoted and most sincere friend,   SAMUEL AARON.

—— Esq. Excuse the Title.

A lady said to the Governor of New Hampshire, "Will your Excellency have a little cream in your Excellency's tea?"

BURLINGTON, April 24, 1824.

My Esteemed Friend—Although, like you, I have nothing to say, I will, nevertheless, attempt to fill up three pages of my sheet. So diametrically opposite are our pursuits in life that anything immediately connected with them would hardly afford matter of correspondence; yet I think our estimates of men and manners, our ideas of honor and principle, of vice and virtue, and perhaps our opinions in politics, are not so dissimilar. But I fear I am a little too fast in thus identifying our political partialities. You are for the Harrisburg ticket, Jackson and Calhoun; I am not. I am for John Quincy Adams and General Jackson (an opinion, of course, of great consequence to the nation), because the former is our most experienced statesman, and the latter a character next in grade, our ablest warrior. Even here we do no doubt really agree in sentiment, only that you, independent as you are, must be somewhat warped by the logic of some of your best and most important friends. I do believe there are very many who have a decided preference for Adams that do not openly declare for him, from some cause which it is difficult to account for in a very rational way, but which arises from the complicate "operation" of party machinery.

Four of us here have subscribed for the "American Monthly Magazine." I suppose you are acquainted with it. We have received four numbers, and I have glanced over them all, but I do not think it to possess much merit. There are sketches of Jackson and Clay that I like pretty well, but there is a great deal of most insipid poetry and a goodly portion of love affairs in the truly vapid style. The editor is said to be the author of the "Star Spangled Banner." He does one thing that is very well—only I fear, like F——'s political exertions, it may produce an effect contrary to his intentions —he reprobates Byron's celebrated writings, and pronounces them entirely undeserving of public patronage, and extremely prejudicial to taste and morals. All this I conceive to be very true, and most heartily wish it to have general effect. I do not read Byron's poetry, but hear enough of it to disgust me.

I sincerely wish it were in my power to tell you news that might gratify you; a difficulty which you do not encounter in writing to me; for what is there connected with D—— that is not most welcome to me? and emphatically so when coming from yourself.

John Gummere has gone a journey which will carry him perhaps to North Carolina, and keep him from home about four weeks. He is accompanying Stephen Grailette (whom you may remember) part of his way on a religious tour, which he is making in the southern and southwestern states. The Quakers in New Orleans are exceedingly despised, and I am afraid poor, old, honest Stephen will fare almost as ill as his venerable namesake in days of old.

Please remember me kindly to all my friends.

Your sincere friend,

SAMUEL AARON.

[ON BOARD A CANAL PACKET ON THE GREAT HUDSON AND ERIE CANAL, NOW LYING IN THE CITY OF SCHENECTADY, STATE OF NEW YORK.]

June 4, 1833.

Dear E.—I have reason to be thankful for the preservation of my life and health, and sincerely hope you may be enjoying the good gifts of a bounteous providence. I staid longer at Philadelphia than I intended, chiefly through the persuasion of Mr. Brantley, who had a protracted meeting in his house in connection with the Central Union Association. I preached there on Wednesday evening. On Thursday afternoon I reached Burlington, where I preached on Friday evening. Many of the hearers were Friends.

The most wonderful of my adventures is now to be told. I conversed with Mr. Gummere and Mr. Atherton on the subject of the school, and have made up my mind to embrace their proposition. Mr. G——, as I told you, proposes to go to Friends' School, West of Philadelphia, and leave his philosophical apparatus and his large library for our use, and proportion the rent to the number of our scholars. Mr. A—— proposes to take the whole charge of the household economy, and that I should reside in a private residence and manage the lectures on natural philosophy. This fall, therefore, you may think of becoming a resident of Burlington, if life and health permit.

I left Burlington Saturday noon, took the railroad at Bordentown, rode on it thirty-five miles to South Amboy at the rate of twelve miles per hour; took steamboat there and arrived in New York about sunset Saturday evening; stayed at New York till Monday morning at seven o'clock. I went to hear Mr. Cone on Sunday morning and to St. Paul's Church in the afternoon, and Dr. McCauley's lecture room in the evening. Took steamboat North America for Albany (the swiftest perhaps in the world) and arrived in Albany before sunset. There is much sublime scenery on the North river, but the land is all barren. Some mountains on the shore rise to a height of about twelve-hundred feet. Albany is a place of great business; has some beautiful buildings and a great number of churches. I went on Monday evening to Mr. Welsh's meeting-house to attend a concert, but as he was sick he was not present. I stayed at the Temperance house in Albany, and left there this morning (Tuesday) for Schenectady, on the rail, in one of nine cars drawn by a steam engine, running part of the way at the rate of twenty miles an hour.

The boat in which I am now sitting has this moment started for Utica, a distance of eighty miles. From there I will go to Erie, Pa.; then to Detroit; and next to Indianapolis. I shall probably be home in five weeks from this time if providence permits; sooner than I expected.

Remember me kindly to all at home, and other friends you may see. May a kind providence protect us both, and permit us to meet again and spend many happy days together.

Your affectionate husband,

SAMUEL AARON.

————

WOODCOCK TOWNSHIP, CRAWFORD CO., PA.,
June 18, 1833.

Dear E.—I write these lines in the house of J—— E——, where I have been permitted, through the goodness of providence, to arrive safely after a disagreeable, if not dangerous, passage over Lake Erie. I have several letters to write, but commence, as is my duty and my pleasure, with you.

After I wrote to you from Schenectady, I went on in the canal packet to Utica (eighty miles) and stayed there two days. Utica is a beautiful town of ten thousand inhabitants, containing many buildings truly elegant, and having a trade and business of great extent. While at Utica I visited a manual labor school called the Oneida Institute, where they have more than one hundred students, and five hundred or more applicants that they cannot admit. From Utica I went on in the canal packet for Rochester (one hundred and sixty miles) where I arrived on Sunday morning before breakfast, June 8th. This is a large thriving town on Genesee river, where the water of that river, one hundred and fifty yards wide, ·

falls at one pitch ninety-six feet, and a mile and a half lower down, eighty feet more. These falls present a sublime spectacle. At the upper one, Sam Patch lost his life by leaping down from a scaffold thirty feet above the brow of the precipice into the abyss below. He had made many such experiments before, but here he took his last leap. I passed Sunday in this place, partly in attending public worship, partly in gazing at the stupendous cataracts, and partly in walking down to Lake Ontario and back, distant seven or eight miles.

Monday morning the 9th, left Rochester in boat, as before, for Tonnewanta, distant eighty miles, on the grand canal, and eleven miles from the Falls of Niagara. Arrived at Tonnewanta at three o'clock on Tuesday morning, whence I sent on my baggage to Buffalo, and immediately set out alone on foot with part of the old moon to light me along the mighty river Niagara, to visit the great cataract, the wonder of the world. I saw it. I gazed upon it with awe. I listened to its tremendous roar, and thought of the voice of Him that is like the voice of many waters, and of the great white throne of Him from whose face the heavens and the earth fled away. I crossed the river just below the falls to the British side, and went to view the battle-grounds at Lundy's lane, Chippewa, and Fort Erie, where thousands of our countrymen and of our country's enemies fell in the fierce strife of battle. I stayed all night on the battle-ground of Chippewa; walked up the next day to the mouth of Lake Erie and crossed over to Buffalo on Wednesday evening. This is a town of nine or ten thousand inhabitants, at the western end of the grand canal, and the eastern end of Lake Erie; a place of prodigious business. I stayed here in consequence of unsettled weather till Friday morning last, when I took passage in the steamboat Ohio, for Erie, Pa. A very strong wind was blowing directly ahead, and the boat had to put in on the Canada side, behind a point of land called Point Ebony, where she cast anchor till dark; then in the teeth of the wind, but little abated, she set out and worked her way against the storm during the whole night. There were probably more than three hundred passengers on board, and among them many women and children, and a great number were sea-sick. The motion of the boat was like that of a galloping horse, interrupted by many a pitch and stumble. After being on the lake twenty-seven hours, we arrived safe at Erie, distant from Buffalo about one hundred miles. I met with no other accident than the loss of my hat, when I was attempting to draw up a bucket of water for one of the women passengers.

I arrived at Erie near one o'clock p. m., then thirty-two miles distant from J—— E——'s. I walked that afternoon on my way fifteen miles; then came the rest of the distance next morning in the stage. They were glad to see me, and gave me a hearty welcome, and say I must not leave them for several days. They are in good health; have a productive piece of land of fifty acres. The country has a very uneven surface; pretty good water; and is as healthy, probably, as about N———, if not more so. I cannot yet say when you may expect me home. I am very anxious to see Indiana and Ohio, though I shall probably not pass through Michigan.

Remember me kindly to relatives and friends.

Your affectionate husband,

SAMUEL AARON.

DOYLESTOWN, May 26, 1821.

Mr. Chairman—The subject I have chosen as the foundation of my remarks on the present occasion, is the use and importance of brevity. Brevity is a rule which I dislike to see transgressed when I am a hearer, and one which I hope ever to pay proper attention to when a speaker. Advocating the cause I do, you will certainly expect me to be concise; and conciseness comports both with my time and capacity. Perspicuity ought to be the chief consideration of every man who is an instructor of youth, a public speaker, or an author. And, I think that, second in importance to perspicuity, we may justly place brevity.

I will first notice the instruction of youth. It is not by a multitude of tedious rules and theorems that the minds of youth are filled with permanent and useful knowledge, but by familiar and brief illustrations and examples. Where is the boy, be his genius what it may, that would understand the most labored description of the nature of that simple and useful proportion called the "rule of three"; and yet, where is the booby, I might ask, that will not directly see its use and application when practically exemplified in a concise and familiar manner? Would you, sir, put into the hands of youth a folio volume of Grammar with which to commence the study? I presume, though the style were masterly and the plan entirely unexceptional, you would prefer a comprehensive and well-arranged manual; and the more concise the better, if general principles were sufficiently attended to. I have ever remarked, in the narrow sphere of my observation, that in instructing youth or explaining to them the nature of any subject susceptible of demonstration, no more steps should be taken in arriving at the end in view than are necessary in order to be clear and lucid. The demonstration should be come at in such a manner that the mind may take in the whole at once, and distinctly see every link in the connecting chain between the premises and inference. Such are the admired theorems of geometry, unequalled for their simplicity, and the incontrovertible certainty and truth with which the conclusion is deduced from the proposition. Truth thus acquired is received with rapture; it bursts upon us with resistless energy: there is no doubt, not the slightest shadow of uncertainty, conviction takes entire possession of the soul, and we are equally pleased with our own and our preceptor's ingenuity. But when the reasoning is clogged with a ponderous load of words, the patience and memory are both exhausted; the object we set out for lost sight of and forgotten; and if we are so fortunate at last as to distinguish the truth at all, we embrace it coldly, and in a manner ill-suited to its value and importance.

In the second place, I notice that brevity is necessary for a public speaker. The great object of every voluntary speaker is to be heard with attention; and the right way to be heard with attention is not to begin till we have something to say, and, continually keeping the end in view, to stop as soon as we have done. We can even bear with the fool in his folly if he makes his story short; yet,

> " We from the wordy torrent fly ;
> Who listens to the chattering pye " ?

The very wisest, greatest, and most eloquent of mankind could not hold our attention enchained long were he to exert every power and energy of his genius and invention. Solomon, who probably never studied the science of modern ethics (or he would not have been so impolite), says, that the "fool is known by a multitude of words"; and a greater than Solomon has denounced the heaviest punishments upon those religious teachers who, for the sake of external show, lengthen out their prayers and speeches beyond proper bounds. The fact is, in attending to specimens of oratory, we shall find that our admiration is not proportioned to the length of the speech, but is regulated by the sublime and elevated sentiments, the clear and conclusive arguments, the tender and unaffected pathos of the speaker. And the properties in their own genuine character do occupy but a small part of every long speech. And most three-hour speeches, I apprehend, might, with advantage to themselves and satisfaction to the audience, be reduced to one-third of their length. It is probably best to ground our arguments on a few clear and fair propositions, to state our reasons with force and candor, and having placed the best of them in their most favorable light, to proceed to the inference, and thus leave the question to its fate. Where such means as these will not gain a cause before an impartial judge, it is not worth defending; where shuffling or evasion must be resorted to, we may with Junius say that the effect will be "to contract the understanding and to corrupt the head." Were these things attended to, we should not see gentlemen of the bar wearying the patience and distracting the minds of a jury with a mass of stuff, the only tendency of which was to convince them of the badness of the cause and the insincerity of the speaker.

Lastly, with regard to authors. How many of those massive volumes that inundate the world are almost entirely neglected, and when read, how little remembered. Every subject must be represented in a striking and pleasing light in order to arrest the attention and impress the mind; and this cannot be done in ponderous folios; the ingenious and inquiring mind must pass with a light and easy step from truth to truth and not crawl lazily and heavily along with an almost imperceptible motion. "Do unto others as you wish them to do unto you," is the concise rule that explains all the duties and obligations in the social intercourse between man and man; and all the refinements of moral philosophy have never made it clearer or more intelligible than it is in its simple state. These fine-spun systems, indeed, have amused the learned, but have never informed or interested the ignorant.

Finally, though subjects may be diffusely treated of for the perusal of the learned, and those who have leisure, yet no work need be carried beyond the extent that is necessary to make it plain and easily understood.

SAMUEL AARON.

BOSTON, Eighth-month 3, 1827.

Dear Friend—Thy very acceptable letter of the 30th we received upon our arrival here yesterday, and as thou mayest feel some curiosity to know a little of our movements in this "land of steady habits," before we reach home, I will scribble a few lines for thy amusement. I think my brother wrote thee from Providence, and probably gave thee a little account of our movements up to that time.

During the second day of our stay at Providence we visited Brown University, and were much pleased with the conversation, manners, etc., of Wayland, their president. We had a letter from J. Griscom to one of the professors, who happened to be from home on a visit, and we in consequence introduced ourselves to the president. He is a young man, a minister in your society, and is said to have made a great revolution in the institution for the better in the course of six or eight months. I mentioned Rush's work to him. He seemed much pleased to hear of it; said he should get it and read it with care, and I think will be able to estimate it properly.

We left Providence yesterday morning about 5.30, took breakfast at Walpole, distant twenty-one miles, and arrived here about one p. m. John and I walked out a little during the afternoon, and took tea and spent a couple of hours very pleasantly with N. Bowditch. This morning we visited the State House, and had a fine bird's eye view of the city from its top. We then went to Faneuil Hall, the cradle of liberty, and afterwards to the Atheneum, etc. This afternoon we went over to Charlestown and Breed's Hill. The situation of the old redoubt is very distinct yet, and, as thou knowest, they have commenced a granite monument on the site where most of the British fell. It is to be two hundred feet in height. Since then we have been to Cambridge and several adjacent places. To-morrow morning we shall set out for Nahant, Lynn and Salem, which will occupy us two days. We shall then return here, and set out by stage for Northampton.

We should like to receive another letter from thee at New Haven, Connecticut, where we shall probably be on Fifth-day next. For further particulars of our movements, I refer thee to S. R. Gummere when he arrives in Burlington. I think one of us will try to write again from Northampton.

Thine respectfully,
SAMUEL R. GUMMERE.

To SAMUEL AARON.

To all people to whom these presents shall come. The Baptist Church at New Britain, in Bucks County, Pa., sendeth greeting :

The bearer hereof, our beloved brother Samuel Aaron, being a man of good moral character, real piety and sound knowledge of divine things, and having been called to the exercise of his ministerial gifts, whereof we have now had considerable trial, both in private and public, we have judged him worthy, and do therefore hereby license and authorize him, to preach the gospel wherever he may have a call, not doubting but that in due time circumstances will lead to a more full investiture of him in the ministerial office by ordination. In the meantime, we recommend him to favor and respect, praying the Lord may be with and abundantly bless him.

Done at our meeting for business the 31st of May, 1828. And signed by order of the church.

ISAIAH JAMES, *Church Clerk.*

BROWN UNIVERSITY, Sept. 5, 1838.

Sir—I have the honor to inform you that at a meeting of the Board of Fellows of Brown University, the honorary degree of Master of Arts was conferred upon you by that authority, and that the act was duly announced on the day of the annual commencement, September 5, 1838.

I have the honor to be, sir, respectfully, your obedient servant, F. WAYLAND.

REV. SAMUEL AARON, Burlington, N. J.

[EXTRACT FROM A LETTER WRITTEN BY JOHN C. TEN EYCK, ESQ., WHO AFTERWARDS BECAME U. S. SENATOR FROM N. J.]

MOUNT HOLLY, Feb. 26, 1841.

Dear Sir—I regret exceedingly to learn your determination to leave Burlington for a residence in Pennsylvania. Thus has it always been in New Jersey, as soon as we begin to take pride in a citizen, either the want of proper encouragement, or a more attractive allurement, is sure to deprive us of the credit which his further residence and usefulness would reflect upon us, and in this way are our proudest possessions made the property of others. I would, as a man and a Jerseyman, it were not so. * * * *

Yours very respectfully,

JOHN C. TEN EYCK.

REV. SAMUEL AARON.

BURLINGTON, Fifth-month 13, 1841.

Dear Friend—At a meeting of the Temperance Union Benef. Society, held this evening, the following preamble and resolution were unanimously adopted, every member promptly rising in token of assent. I was appointed to write to thee.

WHEREAS, Our fellow-member and late fellow-citizen, Samuel Aaron, was intimately connected with the organization of this society, and has rendered important aid by his counsels and services in its subsequent operations; and

WHEREAS, He has been, during his whole residence in Burlington, eminent for his self-sacrificing devotion to the truest welfare of his fellow-men;

Resolved, That we entertain the sincerest affection for him personally, and respect for the enlarged philanthropy and the high moral stand which he has maintained through evil report and good report; and that while we regret the loss of his valuable services among us, we desire that the divine blessing may rest upon him and upon his labors of love in the community among whom he now resides.

James L. Hart and myself were continued a committee to make arrangements for a meeting to be addressed by thee at any time when thou can so favor us.

Thy affectionate friend,

WM. J. ALLINSON.

KENNETT SQUARE P. O. Chester Co., Pa.,
October 11, 1841.

Dear Sir—I have been requested, as Corresponding Secretary of the Chester County Temperance Society, to inform you of our next meeting, and in behalf of the society to invite you to be present and favor us with an address. It would be impossible for me to describe the satisfaction and delight which your speech, delivered in West Chester on the 3d of July last, gave to the members of our society, as well as many others who had the good fortune to be present on that occasion. You remember it was the last day of the week in harvest time, a day when all our farmers were so extremely busy that very many of them were compelled to remain at home who would gladly have been at the meeting. This accounts for the fact that a large portion of the audience were females from different parts of the county, whose zeal induced them to break away from engagements which would have kept them at home had the meeting been of any other kind. On their return to their families they gave (so far as I have had an opportunity of learning) the most glowing accounts of "Samuel Aaron's speech," which has created a•most anxious desire in the minds of hundreds, perhaps I might say thousands, to hear you advocate the noble cause, who were deprived of the opportunity of listening to you then. I, in common with others, do most sincerely hope that you will be able to favor us with your presence and counsel at our next meeting. We want another just such a speech as we had at West Chester, which in my opinion was as luminous as light itself and strong as Pennsylvania iron. Some of the young men of the borough thought it rather harsh; but so long as the truth is deemed harsh, I pray God that your speeches may ever abound with harshness.

We would not call on one who lives so far to leave his home and come to our aid, did we not believe that an effort of yours would do more good at this time, in this county, than that of any man to whom we could apply. We need some one who has power to electrify the people; one whose spirit-stirring voice will strike upon the public ear like the thunders of Otis, of Henry, and of Mirabeau, in former glorious though infinitely less beneficent revolutions; one whose reasoning will break upon the public mind like the sudden light of morning in a tropical clime; one that is able to show the people, in an impressive and effectual manner, the enormous burden of taxation which they are patiently because ignorantly laboring under in consequence of the rum trade; one that can lay a mighty grasp upon the moral sensibilities of his hearers, and shake them until they are thoroughly aroused. Allow me, then, the pleasure of announcing in our county papers your name as one of the speakers, and our next meeting will, I trust, be a mighty gathering of the people.

The society will meet on the first Saturday of November next, at ten o'clock a. m., at Unionville, which is on the State road, about ten miles from West Chester. The friends of temperance, and also the friends of impartial liberty, who are pretty numerous in this section, would be highly gratified if you could make it convenient to yourself to remain in our neighborhood a few days at least. At any rate we cannot but indulge the hope that you will come to Kennett, which is but four miles from Unionville, and spend the night with us after

the society adjourns; and, if it would not be asking too much,
favor us with a lecture on either temperance or equal rights,
as you may choose, the next afternoon at Kennett Square.   I
will say no more until I learn from your own pen whether you
can come or not.   In the meantime I shall continue to hope
until I know the certainty.

> Yours truly,   SUMNER STEBBINS.

To SAMUEL AARON.

[EXTRACT FROM A LETTER FROM JOHN W. HAZLETON, WHO AFTERWARDS BE-
CAME A MEMBER OF CONGRESS.]

> MULLICA HILL, ———, 1841.

My Dear Friend— * * * I believe it is usually
gratifying for persons to hear that they have done some good
in the world; and I think it can be said with justice that your
effort at Woodbury, N. J., had a great effect upon the audience.   Could all the inhabitants of New Jersey heard your
lecture at that time, I have no doubt but that the abominable
practice of horse-racing would be repealed by law; as it is, I
fear the result.   * * * It is with pleasure I inform you
that those persons who objected to your lecturing in the
church at this place, show a disposition to retract their resolutions.   One of the heads of the church wished me to invite
you to come again, and the church, if it is in his power, shall
be at your service.   He was induced to do this by hearing a
part of your discourse at Woodbury on the horse-racing subject.   There is also a person here who wishes to have a private discourse with you upon religious matters, if you should
ever visit us again.   He is, in my opinion, a good man, although he differs from most religious societies; and I think
you will, after conversing with him, come to the conclusion
that he entertains many just notions.   If he does not, then
you will have the pleasure of correcting him, for he is open to
conviction.

But I will not weary your patience longer, but will conclude by inviting you to visit me as soon as practicable.

I am, with respect, your sincere friend, ·

> J. W. H.

REV. SAMUEL AARON.

PHILADELPHIA, First-month 7th, 1843.

My Dear Friend—When I hear of thy labors in the cause of suffering humanity, the relation which formerly subsisted between us of teacher and pupil often calls thee vividly before my mind; and though an opportunity has seldom offered to extend in person the right hand of fellowship, I can assure thee my aspirations have often ascended to our common Father that he would preserve and keep thee, and that thy labors in his vineyard may be blessed. In looking at the present state of the world, and observing the suffering and degradation into which thousands of our race are plunged, the Christian mind cannot fail to be affected with sorrow. While slavery and intemperance are prostrating the physical and spiritual energies of our fellow-beings, it is cause of gratitude to find that a faithful band is raised up out of all the denominations of Christians to bear a testimony to the truth as it is in Jesus.

While many of our brethren are called upon to labor for the suffering bondmen, my attention has often been called, and particularly so of late, to the nominally free among us,—more especially those in large cities. At the last meeting of the Pennsylvania Abolition Society this subject claimed some attention. The school which was formerly taught under their direction, has been laid down in consequence of the free school system, to which all colors and classes are admitted; and this has placed at their disposal some funds which some of the members think cannot be more profitably employed than in an attempt at the improvement and elevation of a portion of the colored population in our city, and it has been thought a home missionary might spend a portion of time among them greatly to their advantage. * * * Let us know thy views respecting this matter. If thy numerous engagements will permit thee to drop a line at any time, be assured it will be very grateful to thy attached friend and old pupil,

DILLWYN PARRISH.

To SAMUEL AARON.

NORRISTOWN, June 21, 1843.

Rev. Samuel Aaron: Dear Sir—I would be doing injustice to my feelings did I not apologize for not calling on you last evening, to express my concern at the outrage committed on your person. My time being fully occupied during the day and evening prevented me from coming. I have never in my life felt as I did when I heard of the outrage. I thought of you as a devoted Christian, a man and a patriot, devoted to the service of thy God, thy country and mankind, and thanked God in my heart that we had just such a man with us. I am not ashamed to acknowledge that my eyes more than once filled with tears of generous indignation, while I trembled with emotion at the treatment you had received in a Christian community. Although comparatively a stranger to me, I have listened to your voice from the pulpit, while my heart was gladdened with the joyful tidings you were proclaiming. I felt that you were my brother, and I have loved you as such, and shall always remain

       Your sincere friend,   THOS. P. KNOX.

P. S.—In the country, as far as I have heard, but one feeling is expressed—that of just indignation at the treatment you have received; and I have seen more than one strong man tremble with emotion while expressing himself.   T. P. K.

————

BURLINGTON, Sixth-month 30, 1843.

My Dear Friend—Samuel Aaron I know will not be unwilling to receive, among the numerous evidences of friendship from other quarters, the expression of deep sympathy on my part (and I may speak in behalf of all our family) with thee in thy late trials and present sufferings; and, I trust, of sincere pity for those misguided men who have so freely lent themselves to do the work of Satan. Probably the greater feeling should be expressed for them. For when a man whose spirit has been long guided by the good Director of Heaven suffers at the hands of the wicked, and suffers patiently, and with a fear of offending his Master only, there is cause to re-

joice that amid the corruptions of the world there are good examples of fidelity and attachment to the laws of truth; but when
those influenced by ungoverned passions, and with their hearts
hardened against the secret impulses of goodness and wisdom,
betray the spirit of violence and rage, there is need to have
compassion for their delusion. Receive, then, this assurance,
that adversity and affliction have not the power to weaken the
attachment and esteem that we have always cherished and will
continue to cultivate for thee and thy services for good among
men.   JOSEPH PARRISH.

WEST CHESTER, PA., July 11, 1843.

Brother Aaron—We have appointed a temperance harvest
home to be held in our borough July 29th on the part of several societies. The meeting will be large. I have been requested to invite you to attend, and give you a special invitation to be the orator of the day. And I will add that it is a
general and ardent desire that you may attend. Your friends
here are numerous, and I hope that you may brush aside every
obstacle to comply with their wishes. It was hoped that your
face would be seen in our midst on the 4th. Let me say, as
one of your friends, that it will be gratifying to me if amid
your numerous calls you will forego any objection or engagement which may be dispensed with, and meet us on that day.
It will be a pleasure to us to hear your voice again in our
town, now that we are grown up to the stature of a man in the
cause. Will you please send me an early reply?

Permit me to express to you my admiration of your bearing in the late conflict and my utter abhorrence of the conduct
of the assailants in their cowardly outrage. If it be agreeable
to the A. General, I should be pleased to have the opportunity of assisting him in the prosecution of the offenders, with
your assent. I suppose they may plead guilty, and avoid a
scathing. However, I may attend your court, and will, if it
is thought a trial will be had and Mr. Fox would permit me to
"put in an oar."

Yours truly,   U. V. PENNYPACKER.

RED LION, NEW CASTLE CO., DEL., August 1, 1843.

My Dear Friend—I am requested by a committee of invitation to solicit the favor of your presence as a speaker at a temperance harvest home to be held at the "Cool Springs," near St. George's, Del., on Tuesday, 22d of August. It is expected that the meeting will be numerously attended; perhaps not less than five thousand persons will be present. I told the committee that I had your promise that you would come down, if it were possible, at any time we had a meeting; so they (the committee) hope strongly for a fulfillment of that promise. Do come, and give your friends in Delaware a sample of your logical reasoning and spirit-moving eloquence.

The good people of Delaware, always remarkable for sympathy and generosity of feeling, sympathize strongly with you on account of your late unfortunate encounter with those friends of tumult and disorder. Allow me to say that the people of this vicinity have a very great desire to hear you speak, and after this invitation expectation will be on tip-toe. Do not disappoint them. I will meet you with a carriage at any time that suits you, at Wilmington or Delaware City.

Please favor me with an immediate answer, and accept the kindest regards of your friend and old student,

JOHN J. HENRY.

To REV. SAMUEL AARON.

KENNETT SQUARE, August 3, 1846.

Samuel Aaron: Respected Friend—I am very desirous of seeing you here at the annual meeting of the State Anti-Slavery Society, which will begin day after to-morrow. Do drop everything and come, if you can. Thomas Earle will be here to defend the invasion of Mexico, and I fear an impression will be made that the non-voters are the only opponents among the Abolitionists of this infamous war. I have been looking for some time to see something from you on the subject. It cannot be possible that you are either in favor of it or indifferent about it. The meeting will be likely to hold three or four days, and if you cannot get here before the evening of the 6th that will do. Your presence would be welcomed more heartily than that of any other man in Pennsylvania by a majority of those who will be present. I speak what I know, not in a spirit of flattery but of frank sincerity. Do come if you can, and oblige your many friends here, and especially yours, etc.,

In haste, SUMNER STEBBINS.

PHILADELPHIA, October 2, 1847.

My Very Dear Sir—As your quondam pupil I have long contemplated a visit to you at Norristown, but the multiplied engagements of a very exacting profession have hitherto denied me that enjoyment. My oldest son, who is on a short visit to a cousin at your place, and who desires to look a little about him there, must for the present serve as my " locum tenens." He will call upon you, and you will have before you, in the size of the lad, a palpable evidence of the flight of time, since I took my first lessons in Greek and Latin under your kind care at Burlington.

I remain, my Dear Sir, very truly yours,

J. PANCOAST.

REV. SAMUEL AARON.

CINCINNATI, OHIO, March 20, 1850.

Dear Brother—Your presence is earnestly solicited at the Christian Anti-Slavery Convention to be held in this city on the 17th of next month. We feel assured that it will greatly enhance the interest and usefulness of the convention to have you with us. We beg you will allow no ordinary difficulty to prevent your coming. Such a demand upon your time and attention does not often occur, and we feel the importance of the present critical time in the American Zion to press all the true friends of freedom and a pure religion to put forth a vigorous effort to deliver the churches from the guilt of slavery. Should Providence imperatively forbid your attendance, please send us your views in writing, and make such suggestions as to the course the convention should take as your deliberate judgment may advise.

Yours affectionately in Christ,

E. GOODMAN,
B. F. AYDELOTTE,
S. H. CHASE,
WM. HENRY BRISBANE.

REV. SAMUEL AARON.

BURLINGTON, Third-month 20, 1851.

My Very Dear Friend—There are very few men on earth, who, in my affection, stand on equality with thee; yet how little we see, hear, or know of each other. The accidents of time do not bring us together. The revolutions of our planet do not jolt thee into Burlington, nor me to Norristown. Our engrossments of business and of sect are not in common, though I trust by no means incongruous in their aims, and so I fail to have the benefit which I assuredly ought to derive from the warm heart which, buttoned up beneath thy vest, pulsates mightily some sixty-five to ninety times per minute with love to mankind, including, among the millions, myself, and many better, and peradventure some worse. I have many times thought of going to Norristown for a renewal of ancient delights, but in scheming such a visit there have always been many things to be accomplished first, which had the imperative claim of duties, and so the months roll on.

Thy removal from New Jersey was a sad affliction to me, and it was a loss to our state. It was just as an appreciation of thee had taken such a hold upon the leading minds of Jersey as would have given thee an increased influence for good. Thy speech on Education, in Trenton, had taken effect. How I needed thee in Trenton recently, when I had to address a meeting on the House of Refuge question. I was one of a committee for the purpose from the New Jersey Prison Reform Association.   *   *   *   *   *

CORRESPONDENCE.

In the ranks of philanthropy, no office is more important to the community than that of a teacher. No one is fit for it who is not a philanthropist, who does not pursue its duties for something more than pecuniary gain; who does not feel to his very heart's core that he is training intellects for eternity. But the sum total of good accomplished, for which the teacher has a right to give God thanks, ascribing to Him all the glory, he may never know. "Each simple effort has its far vibration, working results that work results again." "Therefore," says a British scribbler of the present day,

> " Therefore, though few praise or help or heed us,
> Let us work with head, or heart, or hand,
> For we know the future ages need us ;
> We must help our time to take its stand,
> That the after day may make beginning,
> Where our present labor has its end," etc.

In looking around to think of persons and matters that would specially interest thee, it seems as though a generation had elapsed since thy departure, so changed is ancient Burlington. One item is at least unaltered—the affection for thee of thy friend and quondam fellow-laborer,

WM. J. ALLINSON.

To SAMUEL AARON.

NORRISTOWN, August 15, 1852.

Dear Friend, Samuel Aaron—We have with us to-day our long-imprisoned but now released brother, Daniel Drayton. J—— gave him a special invitation to come up from the city and attend your meeting this afternoon. He is in poor health, and an object of charity. Cannot something be done for him to-day? Pray come this way half an hour before meeting and shake his hand. I am sure it won't check the flow of your inspiration thus to greet a victim from the American Bastile.

Yours truly,

OLIVER JOHNSON.

BOSTON, Nov. 16, 1853.

Dear Sir—The Twentieth Anniversary of the formation of the American Anti-Slavery Society will be celebrated in Philadelphia, on the 3d and 4th of December next. As one of the speakers on that occasion, untrammeled in regard to thought or speech, you are respectfully invited by the Executive Committee to its platform, earnestly desirous as you are for the speedy and eternal overthrow of chattel slavery in our land, which is the specific object of the society, by all rightful instrumentalities and divorced from all other questions. In case your personal attendance should be impracticable, a letter from you, to be read at the meeting, would serve the cause and excite interest.

Yours for universal emancipation,

WM. LLOYD GARRISON,
President of the Society.

WENDELL PHILLIPS,
EDMOND QUINCY,   } *Secretaries.*
S. H. GAY,

————— —

HOUSE OF REPRESENTATIVES, March 2, 1854.

Dear Friend—Mr. ——— has this moment handed me your letter. I am so overwhelmed with my private and official duties that I cannot spare the time necessary to make the examinations you call for, nor to write a notice for Dr. Bailey's paper.   *   *   *   I well remember that Lieutenant Forbes' statements were contradicted. But I never heard that the British Government disgraced him, or were displeased with him. If you can find a file of the African Repository you can learn all you wish to learn respecting the claim of the Colored Society to the extirpation of the slave trade, the extent of their territory, etc., etc. We are greatly excited by the Nebraska matter. What will be the result of this nefarious and bold attempt of slavery on liberty I can hardly conjecture.

Truly yours,

GERRIT SMITH.

REV. SAMUEL AARON.

NORRISTOWN, March 10, 1854.

Mr. Aaron, Dear Sir—At a meeting of the colored population of Norristown, held February 2, 1854, it was unanimously resolved to present you with a trifling "memento" for the handsome manner in which you defend the rights of the colored race and oppose the Rev. Mr. Peace on the subject of African colonization. You will, therefore, confer a favor upon the committee by attending a meeting in the Baptist church on Monday evening, March 13th, at 7.30 o'clock.

Per order of committee.

JOHN WILLIAMS,
GEORGE HENRY,
I. G. JOHNSON,
WILLIAM TAYLOR,
DANIEL ROSS,
HENRY BRATCHER,
JAMES WILSON.

PHILADELPHIA, March 26, 1854.

My Dear Brother—Yours of the 23d is before me. I entirely approve of your plan, and will do all in my power to carry out your noble purpose to fight and whip the devil. You are right when you say that infidelity is making sad havoc among our young men. Barker is a bold and cunning advocate of those doctrines of devils. I still believe you are the man to meet and defeat his vile attacks on God and the Bible. I think Concert Hall, on Chestnut street, between Twelfth and Thirteenth, is the most desirable place in the city. Whether it is best to commence the delivery of the lectures before the Fall or not is a question of some moment, and one that I cannot decide. The evenings are getting short, and soon will be very warm; and, moreover, in the warm weather vast numbers are away from the city. If you determine upon one lecture per week, I would suggest Monday or Tuesday evenings as the most suitable. You may confidently rely on all the aid I can give you.

JOHN CHAMBERS.

REV. SAMUEL AARON.

MOUNT HOLLY, August 16, 1854.

Dear Sir—There being a number of the citizens of Mount Holly very desirous of hearing your views and sentiments promulgated upon the Nebraska Bill, as lately passed by the Senate and House of Representatives, the undersigned therefore humbly solicit your kind attention to the subject, and ask the favor of your indulgence to deliver a public address to the inhabitants of the place and its vicinity, on the evening of the —— inst., leaving the time to suit your own convenience.

> BENJAMIN BUCKMAN,
> JOSEPH CARR, JR.,
> PETER V. COPPUCK,
> EWAN MERRITT,
> ISAAC V. RISDON,
> B. GARWOOD,
> J. M. BROWNE.

TO REV. SAMUEL AARON.

NORRISTOWN, June 15, 1855.

We, the undersigned, remember that Rev. Samuel Aaron, during the warm weather in '42, '43 and '44—that is, from the height of the "Washingtonian excitement" to the presidential contest between Polk and Clay—lectured more frequently in Norristown than ever before or since, especially in the open air, generally standing on "Court-house Hill," and we believe never more than once, if even once, in any street of the town. We are confident that he was never hindered or intimidated by acts or threats.

> JEROME WALNUT,
> GEORGE WRIGHT.

BOSTON, March 21, 1856.

Dear Sir—I am requested, by a unanimous vote of the Executive Committee of the American Anti-Slavery Society, to invite you to be one of the speakers at the Anniversary of the Society, in the city of New York, in May next, 6th. In extending this invitation, they wish you to exercise as much freedom of thought and speech as you would in addressing a meeting of your own in Norristown, and therefore to frame your own resolution and to select your own topic ad libitum. You will be expected to speak as an independent advocate of the slave, not as endorsing the views and measures of the Society itself. They hope that you will see your way clear to give an affirmative answer. Such, also, is the hope of your friend and fellow-laborer,

. WM. LLOYD GARRISON.

REV. SAMUEL AARON.

NEWTOWN, BUCKS Co., August 11, 1856.

My Very Respected Friend—It seems to me a long time since I saw you. I hear of you that you are yet faithful to the corrupt and selfishly wicked. Well, there is a great deal to do. The men and women that feel every fibre within to move from a sense of the many gross and unlicensed doings in the community, must act; they must shower their feelings upon their neighbors' hearts and minds.

What are your prospects? We want you to visit us for a few days; partly socially; a good deal as a preacher in the every day sense. You promised us a visit, you may remember. You may come with what view you please. We want talk to the parents upon the subject of education; education proper, and education considered in a social, moral and religious respect. These seasons are refreshing. We want them to keep returning. The public want Treemount talk. The community needs temperance preaching. Can't you come among us about the beginning of September or near that time; the second week or last of August; though we want time plenty to give notice. We wish to have Dr. Grimshaw, of Wilmington, with us at the same time. He is very happy as a speaker upon the subject of education. A very intelligent gentleman. Can hit the divine institution pretty hard knocks. Write soon. Our regards to you all as ever.

M. B. LINTON.

To SAMUEL AARON.

———

PHILADELPHIA, December 27, 1856.

Dear Sir—After the lapse of several years you have doubtless forgotten the whereabouts, perhaps the name, of your former student. The cares and anxieties, inseparable from your vocation, must necessarily eradicate from your recollection many of those who have received invaluable precepts of truth and morality from your lips. But in the busy,- careless world, they will remember the example that taught them to inscribe over the door of their intellectual sanctuary, integrity, honor and virtue; and that the true aim of learning is to illustrate the glory and goodness of the great Creator of all things. Though one of the humblest among those who then surrounded you, permit me to say the time spent with you has not been lost. I there entered upon a career which, in whatever way it may terminate, that time will occasion no unpleasant reflections.

I am now about entering professional life under perhaps many disadvantages; yet humbly trusting in the honesty of my intentions and blessing of God to become at least a respectable member of that profession and an honorable man if not a brilliant advocate. Full of these hopes and anticipations of success, I send you my best wishes and profound respect.

Yours respectfully,

JOHN A. BURTON.

REV. SAMUEL AARON.

PHILADELPHIA, May 26, 1857.

My Dear Preceptor—For such I do love yet to consider you—I have taken the liberty to send you in the accompanying card a notification of the fact that the mere preparatory studies, of which you laid the foundation more than nine years ago, are now in a measure concluded, and a wider field, a new arena, and a severer struggle, are before me. While I mourn many neglected opportunities, I realize now the wisdom of your teachings, and sincerely hope that their fullest fruition may be but a tithe of the faithful, earnest endeavor with which you did your duty by me.

Desiring to be remembered with sincere affection to your most excellent wife and family, for whose many kindnesses I cherish the liveliest remembrance, and hoping for yourself many long years of usefulness, and that happy satisfaction by you more prized than high honor, permit me to be

Yours ever truly,

JOHN GOFORTH.

REV. SAMUEL AARON.

———— ——

WOODCOCK TOWNSHIP, CRAWFORD CO., PA.,
June 18, 1833.

My Dear Brothers—I arrived safely at J—— E——'s on Sunday morning last, and found them all well. They live, as you have heard, on the great road leading from Meadville to Erie, six miles from the former and thirty-two miles from the latter town. These towns contain about one thousand inhabitants each, and are places of some business; and no doubt when the canal is finished between them, forming a water communication between them and all the most important towns in the United States, their importance will be much increased.

The turnpike is a good road now, though only an earthen one, and divides J——'s place into two equal parts, running very nearly north and south. The soil here is better than I expected to find it; the surface of the ground quite uneven,

more so than in N———, though there are very few steep or
high hills. The water is pretty good, and the country health-
ful. They have found as yet no lime quarries, though they
say that where the creeks cut deep through hills they find
numbers of stones having great resemblance to limestone, and
some say that they afford good lime.

The face of the ground hereabouts is covered with a sort
of shelly gravel like that along the Bristol road. The soil is
not very sure for corn, wheat or rye, though wheat does better than either, and J—— has some that looks well. . Buck-
wheat succeeds very well; J—— had one hundred bushels on
three acres, or somewhat less. The grass here is indeed excellent; white clover is abundant, and that and timothy come
up spontaneously whenever the land is cleared. The cattle
have a remarkably fine healthy appearance, and the cows, of
course, on such sweet pasture, give excellent milk.

I am better pleased with the country here than I expected
to be, but not so well as I still anticipate with the Ohio and
Indiana land. The land of upper Canada, a good deal of
which I have seen, is astonishingly fine for raising wheat, but
they are so perfectly flat that I could never endure to live
there. I passed over from Niagara Falls to view the grounds
where the bloody battles of Bridgewater, Chippewa and Fort
Erie were fought, and stayed all night on the battle-ground
of Chippewa, where the gallant General Scott, at the point of
the bayonet, led his men to victory against the veteran ranks
of Scotch and English chivalry. But if I am spared to see
you, we will talk of these and other matters.

J—— and M—— seem pleased with the country, and
determined to continue here, and earnestly advise that we
should all come here. J—— has now about forty acres of
his land tolerably well cleared. Most of the tracts about him
are still covered in great part with dead girdled trees, which
makes the country look very bad. J—— ploughs chiefly
with oxen, though he keeps two horses. Money here is exceedingly scarce; almost all dealing in an exchange of com-
modities. The store on French Creek, two and one-quarter
miles from J——'s, takes anything in trade that farmers have.

Apples and peaches, when the trees are properly looked after, are produced in abundance.

I will write again from Columbus, according to promise, if I live to get there. That a gracious providence may preserve and bless you and yours, is the sincere wish and prayer of your brother,

SAMUEL AARON.

PAINESVILLE, OHIO, June 30, 1833.

My Dear E.—I stayed much longer at J—— E——'s than I intended, in consequence of their over-persuasion, as they had never before seen any of their relatives there, and have little hopes of ever seeing any again. My stay there was about ten days. Having become weary of travelling by public conveyance, I purchased a good horse near Meadville, and am now travelling on horseback. So far, it has been rather fatiguing, yet much more agreeable than before, and less expensive. I can also stop and start where and when I please. When I last wrote I thought of being home sooner than is my present expectation. I shall hardly get back under six or seven weeks yet, as I wish to see more of Ohio, as well as Michigan, Indiana and Illinois, and shall probably never have another opportunity so suitable. My horse racks, and at this most easy gait will carry me near or quite forty miles a day. During the hottest days I shall not travel in the hottest part of the day, but lie by in the shade and travel morning and evening.

I have met with scarcely any adventures since I wrote worth mentioning. Last night, however, my horse stumbled while I was crossing Grand river, and I narrowly escaped being precipitated into the middle of it, for which I desire to feel truly thankful.

Since I wrote, I have preached three times and delivered one lecture on temperance to respectable and tolerably numerous congregations. I have been to hear two sermons today from a Presbyterian in this place, and they were very good ones. The Presbyterians and Methodists have each a meeting-house here, and they only, though there are twelve hundred or more people in the place. Many of the Baptists hereabout have followed the heresy of Alexander Campbell, who teaches that immersion of the body saves the soul; and many, shame on them, have turned Mormonites, who profess to have received a new revelation, to work miracles, and speak divers tongues by inspiration; and who, in short, rather take the lead of all the fanatics of the day.

The country along here is very sandy; at this place you might fancy yourself among the sand-banks of South Jersey. Fruits of various kinds abound here. Peaches arrive at great perfection. They are so plentiful that they are seldom sold.

As nothing further of any importance occurs to my mind, I close with expressions of kindness towards my friends, and the assurance that I remain your affectionate husband,

SAMUEL AARON.

COLUMBUS, July 11, 1833.

My Dear Brother—According to promise, I am now about to write to you from this place. As I am in a hurry, I must proceed without much attention to order, and will mention the facts seeming to me most likely to gratify you. I have been blessed with good health, and an escape from all serious accidents, for which I desire to be grateful to Divine Providence. Mr. and Mrs. H—— are well, and seem exceedingly cheerful and contented. They have treated me like a brother, and deserve, and shall ever have, my sincere gratitude. This is the third day of my being in Columbus, and I expect to leave them to-morrow. Mr. and Mrs. H—— would rejoice to see you and all their friends established in this country, but very prudently they use no persuasion. As to this place and country they have not been overrated. The town is growing amazingly; at least two-hundred houses are now going up. Money is more plentiful than in D——. The morals and order of the town are good, and the place as healthy as common in any part of our land. The town lies one hundred feet or more above the Scioto river, on a site as well adapted to building as can be conceived. The soil round about upon this higher level is excellent, but that down upon the river bottoms, from three to ten miles wide, is of such strength as far to surpass any that you ever saw, being in many places a black mould for several feet in depth, and resembling a mixture of ashes and moulded manure. This is too strong for wheat; but sixty-five acres of corn that I saw in one tract will no doubt bring about one hundred bushels to the acre. The whole region reposes upon a bed of limestone; and the very pebbles in the street are all, when burned, they tell me, pure lime; and there is no doubt of it.

Wild land of the best quality, from three to ten miles from the town, may be had for five to ten dollars an acre; improved, from ten to twenty-five dollars. The upland produces from fifteen to twenty-five bushels of wheat per acre; and they just sow it among their Indian corn without using the plow at all, and then harrow it over. Better farming, you can tell better than I can, would make a great difference.

There is a cash market, and a very ready one for everything a farmer has to sell. Indeed, no market can be more brisk. Wheat brings from 62½ to 75 cents; wheat flour $2 per cwt.; corn 25; oats 25; cornmeal not sifted, 31 to 37½; butter 8 to 18; eggs 6¼; hams 5 to 8 (hogs are kept on clover during the summer, and some keep $5,000 or $6,000 worth of them and sell them to the pork merchants for cash, who buy them alive and save you the trouble of slaughtering them); beeves 4½ cents; hides 4½; potatoes 25 to 50; wood $1.25 to $2.00; cows $10 to $20; horses in same proportion; teaming with two horses $2 per day. This is unquestionably the place this very day for a man who has a little money to double it very soon. You can loan it at from ten to twelve per cent. Had I my lot sold, I should no doubt buy here before I came home.

I must close. I shall probably go no further, as the weather is getting very warm, and for other reasons I wish to be at home before long. There seems to be a fine opportunity for a school here, but I am engaged to Mr. Gummere. I bought a horse near Meadville, and intend to bring him home with me. Tell my friends I am well, and in particular let my dear little children know that I hope to be at home soon to see them.   May a gracious God bless you and yours in this life and in the life to come.

Your affectionate brother,

SAMUEL AARON.

WOODCOCK TOWNSHIP, Sept. 16, 1836.

My Dear E.—I arrived here yesterday morning at nine o'clock, so tired that I have not yet got rested, feeling so sore and miserable that I have been almost afraid of getting sick. This was the effect of losing a great deal of sleep, and travelling day and night in the stage over some of the roughest roads in the world.   Saturday night overtook me at Hollidaysburg, a town at the head of the canal and foot of the Alleghany Mountains, where a railroad two miles long carries us over the mountains.   Here I spent the Sabbath, and found to my surprise a Baptist protracted meeting going on, at which I spoke three times, preaching one regular sermon with more liberty than common for me.   Monday, before daylight, took the railroad, ascending in ten miles more than thirteen hundred feet, perpendicular, by means of five inclined planes, drawn up by a huge rope moved by a steam engine at the top.   Took the canal again at Johnstown, having descended the mountain to the west by similar planes.   On Monday night, in consequence of the heat, left my berth and passed the night on deck without a wink of sleep.   Arrived at Pittsburg Tuesday afternoon at two o'clock; rose at three o'clock next morning and took the stage and went on one hundred and three miles, day and night, to where I now am.   I do not believe I shall be able to start home before Monday; and at what time you may expect to see me I cannot tell, but I hope before the end of next week.   I find M——'s affairs by no means uncomfortable; fifty acres of the best grass land you ever saw, a good house, and a new barn.   The girls can spin and weave, and they have wool and flax.   I remember with the utmost tenderness my dear children, and please tell them so.   I desire to be remembered with respect and affection to our dear father, and indeed to all the family, as well as to friends and inquirers. When I see you I will tell you all, and now remain your affectionate husband,

SAMUEL AARON.

CLEVELAND, OHIO, Sept. 25, 1851.

Dear E.—We arrived here last evening at six o'clock, after a rough but safe passage on Lake Erie of one hundred and sixty miles from Dunkirk. On the railroad between New York and Dunkirk, we were detained some four hours by something wrong in the locomotive, or other causes, and so lost perhaps twelve hours in starting on the lake. This was well, as the passage might have been unsafe. We left New York at six p. m., Monday, and rode all night in the car, and next day till about five p. m., nearly five hundred miles. I took some cold, but feel quite well this morning, and am in a hurry to get to meeting. Dr. Brisbane, C. M. Clay, Mr. Giddings, Mr. Chase, and many talented men are present. The convention will probably close to-day, and I shall write you again. I shall write soon to Mr. S—— some account of the convention for his paper. Give my love to the family. Tell the children they would have been glad to have been at home if they had got on the lake and heard the winds howling and seen the waves rolling and felt the boat pitching and rocking and staggering to and fro like a drunken man.

Yours truly as ever,

SAMUEL AARON.

NORRISTOWN, PA., August 15, 1857.

My Dear Friend—I understand that it is your settled determination to publish a book on the science and art of elocution, and am heartily glad to learn that such is your purpose. You should have done it long ago; not but that you are better able now, but because intelligent teachers and docile pu-

pils have needed the work; and bad reading and speaking
have been learned and taught by thousands who wished to do
right but knew not how.   Many years ago you taught me,
more earnestly than any other preceptor, to study and endeavor to express the meaning of what I read; and seven
years afterwards we both listened with profit and delight to
Dr. Jonathan Barber, who insisted on adorning the sense by
harmony of tones and variety of modulation, by pitch, slide,
vanish and cadence.   We then studied together Dr. James
Rush's "Human Voice" with a zeal and application not unworthy of success; and I think we understood that original
and profound work; we certainly drew from it more well defined ideas of the uses and powers of the human voice than
from all other sources; and have always rejoiced, like grateful disciples, that Dr. Rush, like other great discoverers, is
worthy of present reward and sure of posthumous fame.   I
recur with fond remembrance to our evening study of the
principles of Rush, and our daily practice in the open air in
training the lungs to give volume of sound and explosive
force, and drilling the other vocal organs in distinctness and
elegance of articulation.   We used to recite to each other at
four hundred yards distance, and sometimes more, in the
open fields, and were distinctly heard without great apparent
effort on your part, and with such success on mine, that I have
often since addressed thousands of people at once, and been
better heard than many others.   With all this mutual study
and practice it is surely natural for me to attribute some importance to our efforts and some merit to our acquirements;
and it has happened to you more than to myself to continue
thinking carefully and pleasantly upon this matter for more
than thirty years.   *   *   *   *   You have my best wishes
for your success, and I hope soon to receive a copy of your
proposed work.

Your sincere friend,

SAMUEL AARON.

MR. SAMUEL R. GUMMERE.

MOUNT HOLLY, N. J. Nov. 11, 1862.

My Dear Friend—Your letter was received on the 3d inst. Its opening gladdened the hearts of us all. * * *

I must notice your four points on state affairs.

1. The thorough abolition of slavery is right, but will never be felicitous (God's existence, and moral and personal character being granted) till the nation, as such, confesses and deplores the wrong done to the enslaved. A nation, to be truly happy, must give moral reasons for its acts and laws; and ours has erred in making no recognition of a Supreme Being in its organic law.

2. Your thoughts on a national system of common schools are excellent. I add, that attendance on the part of sane and healthy children between certain ages should be compulsory, even to the extent of taking the children from worthless or brutal parents. Further; the moral training should be pure and most decided, based without any sectarian bias, on the moral teachings of Jesus Christ. And then, without the least tyrannic spirit, the strictest obedience to orders and subordination to authority should be enforced. I am fully persuaded that the reckless impudence and unrestrainedness of our American youth threaten the nation with as dread a ruin as the struggle now on hand.

3. Your views on "citizenship" are not quite clear to my mind. I agree that the National Legislature would be the best depository of the vote privilege (for this is acknowledged to be a privilege rather than a right), and there would be little or no danger of wronging any one but those of African descent. The open discussion of the suffrage question would probably lead towards justice in regard to black as well as white men, but the "Dred Scott decision," so called, ought not to be quoted, or in any way referred to, so as to act as a hamper on legislative action. You know it was an "obiter dictum," an "out-of-the-way opinion," foisted in by a judicial tyrant, when a totally different question, and that only, was before him.

4. Your ideas on national consolidation are reasonable, and likely to become practical, and your proposed mode of

organizing legislatures and guaranteeing the rights of persons and property, is certainly plausible, in my opinion, good, and very original.

On the subject of choosing representatives, etc., I will suggest a thought for your consideration. Suppose that one member of Congress be apportioned to every 20,000 voters, and that 11,000 or more be required to elect each member; and that on that basis your state would get five members. Let there be no districts, but let every voter in the state vote for whom he pleased, the candidate being an American citizen. Then suppose the "Republican" and "Democratic" parties both corrupt, and that you and 10,999 other men in the state wish purity and reform in the nation, you could, through a small minority of the 100,000 voters, be represented in Congress, and heard by the whole nation. According to our present system, often the best men are not represented for many years, and sometimes not at all. A party commencing with good and pure purposes is tempted to go into collusion with another corrupt minority in order to defeat a still more corrupt plurality. I think this principle is right and wise because it provides, at least in a state having many people, for a respectful hearing of a small minority, and tends to promote the progress of reformatory measures.

You will have learned before you get this that "Democracy" has again a potent voice in our Eastern elections. Still they would have been utterly defeated in every state but New Jersey had the volunteers now in service been permitted to vote. The removal of McClellan gives nearly universal satisfaction. A very few more months of his "strategy" would have crowned the rebels with triumph.

You drop a hint which seems to disparage Fremont. Do you so mean? He has constantly risen in my estimation since the war began. He suggested in Paris in March, 1861, the immediate purchase in Europe of 500,000 small arms and a proportionate quantity of other munitions of war, and sending a corresponding force to use them, and the freeing of every rebel's slave; his subsequent acts have all gone to match that earnest policy; Stonewall Jackson pronounced him his most formidable competitor; and the administration at last, perhaps too late, is adopting his policy.

The school is well patronized this year. I can talk as loud as ever, but am more brief. I hope you will write me when you can and I will generally reply. Nothing but a sense of duty is sufficient to confine me to the drudgery of letter-writing, so little relish have I for copying my thoughts; yet one has but little claim to the favor of receiving letters who is too indolent or too negligent to write to his friends. "Trust in the Lord and do good."

Yours truly,

SAMUEL AARON.

BURLINGTON, N. J., 1837.

WHEREAS, This Association are in the habit of religious correspondence with several Baptist Associations in the slave-holding states; and

WHEREAS, Our Baptist brethren of the South generally do defend and sanction the institution of American slavery as consistent with sound morals and pure Christianity; therefore,

Resolved, That it is the duty of this body to make known to these our correspondents our solemn conviction that American slavery is sinful in the sight of God, directly contrary to the whole spirit of Christianity, and inevitably productive of the worst evils, social, intellectual and spiritual.

Resolved further, That we do hereby admonish and entreat our Baptist brethren of the South and elsewhere to search the Scriptures, and examine all other legitimate evidence in reference to slavery, and if led to adopt our opinion, as above expressed, we conjure them to testify against it as we have done.

ADDRESS OF THE ANTI-SLAVERY SOCIETY OF BURLINGTON, N. J., TO THE COMMUNITY.

Fellow-Citizens—We ask your candid and serious attention to a brief statement of our views in reference to slavery, because we believe the subject to be of the highest importance; because we feel impelled by a sense of duty which we dare not neglect, to labor for the conviction of other minds besides our own; and especially because our principles are, to a great extent, unexamined, misrepresented, or misunderstood.

Anti-slavery principles.

1. In our general principles we expect to agree with you all. That when a man is guilty of no crime against his fellows, it is the prerogative of God alone to take away his life, to impose stupidity and ignorance upon his mind, to inflict disease or wounds upon his body, to prevent or sever the tie of marriage, to deprive him of his offspring, to take from him for private use the earnings of his labor, or the acquisition of his skill. It is self-evident that these principles do not enforce the amalgamation of different races or nations of men, that they do not interfere with the peculiar tastes of individuals or with the gradations of society. They only prohibit encroachment on that free agency of man which the Creator has bestowed. They are the simple elements of justice. The exceptions to some of these principles have been prescribed by the divine law in reference to children; and special license was given to the Jews to enslave certain nations doomed to punishment. But these exceptions only confirm the general rule in the most striking manner, because they are defined and enforced with so great a particularity. And those who maintain slavery on the authority of the law of Moses, should also claim the right to enslave white men, and to extirpate by the sword, as the Jews were bidden to do, the surrounding heathen tribes. To be as explicit as possible, we believe that the only right rule for human intercourse is, "Thou shalt love thy neighbor as thyself"; in other words, "Do unto all men as ye would that they should do unto you." On this precept our Anti-slavery sentiments are founded; by this we intend that

our action shall be limited and restrained; in defence of this, if called to suffer, we hope to be strengthened by its author; and from attempting to propagate this truth we feel that neither public opinion nor human laws have authority to hinder us.

The evils of slavery.

2. The essential evils of slavery, we believe, consist in the violation of the principles above stated; man thus assuming over his fellow man a power which is the sole prerogative of God. The code of slavery substitutes the will of the master for the divine will; and this absurd and sinful beginning, as a cause, produces effects so many and so evil that they can neither be numbered nor described. It must suffice to say that innocent human beings are bought and sold like brutes; that they are tasked, chained, lacerated and maimed as brutes seldom are; that their lives are taken with impunity when the furious passions of their drivers demand the sacrifice; that the marriage relation, ordained by Jehovah, is ridiculed and destroyed; that their minds are kept as dark as possible, on pain of death to him who would enlighten them; and what is, perhaps, worst of all, multitudes of children are reared and held as property, or sold to enrich their own fathers.

The remedies for slavery.

3. Several remedies for the evils of slavery are proposed. The one that is most common and most popular in these parts is to let it alone to work its own cure, assuming that we, of New Jersey, have nothing to do with slavery, and that it is improper, if not criminal, to discuss the subject. But our highest judicial authorities have recently declared from the bench that we are a slaveholding people, and bound by the law to uphold slavery in our own state, for a time at least, and especially in other states, even by the sacrifice of our lives. Recurring then to our first principles, we feel unable to rest tamely under such obligations as these, believing it to be the right and duty of a free people to ask for the repeal or alteration of unjust and oppressive laws; besides that, we believe on such a scheme a crisis of slaughter and devastation

would soon arrive, at which humanity shudders. Some would mitigate slavery, preserving the relation of master and slave, but making it consist of lordly and noble beneficence on the one part, and humble, dependent gratitude on the other. We appeal to our first principles which recognize God only as the bestower of man's inherent rights, and alone entitled to gratitude for their enjoyment. Besides, we refer to all records, divine and human, to prove that a "corrupt tree cannot bring forth good fruit"; that a system founded in error cannot promote truth or happiness.

The complete amalgamation of the white and colored races is another remedy that was proposed with apparent gravity by an eminent Southern statesman some years ago. This process is carried on extensively in the South, with the purpose, however, not to diminish but to increase the number of slaves; and in the North the most violent and practical haters of the abolitionists encourage at the polls and practice individually to some extent a lawless amalgamation, while they inflict all the horrors of the code-lynch on those whom they pretend to think guilty of promoting a lawful intercourse between black and white. Amalgamation, lawful or unlawful, abolitionists wholly disapprove. When lawful and probably innocent, they think it incompatible with a correct taste; practised, as it commonly is, they deem it an enormous sin; in either way, therefore, a doubtful and dangerous expedient for the removal of slavery.

The colonization of the blacks on a foreign shore is much advised by the highest names, and much illustrated and emblazoned by flaming eloquence and zeal throughout the Union; yet the object has been in twenty years most sparingly effected. The most remarkable events connected with the colony abroad have been the wars between it and the neighboring tribes, the forcible acquisition of their lands, and waste of human life by endemic diseases; and at home, the passage by several states of laws, virtually forcing the free blacks from their native land, and the excitement of a public feeling decidedly opposed to their remaining in this country on any terms but that of slavery. Meanwhile, the colonists number about three thousand; and they for the most part are in abject poverty; while the increase of blacks in the United States during the same period has been much above half a million. We can, therefore, see nothing in this scheme, however well meant, that promises, under present circumstances, the freedom or the happiness of the whole colored race.

Finally, we have full confidence in the remedy as applied recently in the British West Indies. Immediate and universal emancipation. We ask our General Government to emancipate first, as far as in their power, and to prohibit the slave trade among the states. We ask the respective slave states to pass acts of universal emancipation, accompanied with ample and wise provisions for the improvement of the minds and morals of the colored race, and for the suppression of indolence and vagrancy. Let those now toiling under the influence of the whip be remunerated with suitable wages, and reason and experience both demonstrate the mutual and happy advantage of the change.

In conclusion, we express the earnest hope that you, to whom we are privileged to appeal, will not strive to cramp the "Genius of Universal Emancipation." Do you doubt the expediency of freeing the enslaved? Examine the evidence in the case of the West Indies and doubt no more. The book of Thome and Kimball has satisfied Dr. Channing, Governor Everett, and many others. Behold, nearly five hundred thousand of the colored race, perhaps ten-fold the number of their masters, emancipated with entire safety in a single day, by those very masters, who, a short time before, predicted havoc and utter ruin as the consequence. With such an example before us and so near us, emancipation in this country almost ceases to deserve the name of a great and hazardous experiment. In the speedy, the quiet and perfectly successful emancipation of the British West Indies, who does not perceive the interposition of Divine Providence in favor of anti-slavery principles. We hope, therefore, that you will not, by your silence or faint condemnation, virtually sustain and encourage (as most of our newspapers have done) that spirit that destroyed Pennsylvania Hall and murdered Lovejoy. That spirit would suppress all discussion of the rights and wrongs of the slave and extirpate his friends by the brand of the mob or the assassin's weapon. We firmly believe there are many thousands of intelligent and conscientious persons in this country who feel it to be their duty to God to publish and peaceably to oppose the enormous sin and the horrid results of slavery. Under this impression they must, of course, surrender life itself rather than cease to do their duty. Shall such persons be sacrificed? Will you give them up as victims to a brutal mob? Or shall they be heard and answered with better reasons than their own? We, in this city, actuated by a peaceable spirit, have asked for several years no public building wherein to make known our righteous principles; we have not, indeed, found here a willing toleration to stand on the bare earth beneath the covering of the free heavens to argue the sin of making merchandise of the image of God. But though the church and the public press and the free air have been consecrated against us, we still have the use of paper, ink and types to ask your attention and invoke your honest and rational judgment.

By order of the Society.

SAMUEL AARON, *President.*

JOHN PARISH, *Secretary.*

August 22, 1838.

The Preamble and Principal Articles of the Constitution of the Burlington Anti-Slavery Society.

PREAMBLE.

We, the subscribers, conscientiously believe that every rational human being comprises within himself a complete system (separate and distinct from every other) of powers and faculties, such as bodily strength, appetites, passions, understanding, will, and conscience, for the lawful use and exercise of which he is alone accountable to the Supreme Being; that man has no right, himself, to destroy, abuse, or surrender these his own powers and faculties; much less can they be destroyed, injured, trafficed in, or controlled by another; that any interference with this divine arrangement is, by the proof of all history, inevitably productive of confusion, crime

and misery, degrading alike the injurer and the injured, be-
getting in the heart of the oppressor a stupid, impotent and
cruel selfishness, and, in that of the oppressed, a spirit of blind
and insatiable revenge, fit elements for the self-destruction of
nations, and for the banishment of knowledge, peace and love
from the minds and hearts of men. Being, therefore, desirous
to promote, in some humble measure, the correct comprehension and universal prevalence of human rights (which we
firmly believe we have a perfect right to do), we form ourselves into a society for that purpose, and adopt for our regulation the following:

CONSTITUTION.

ARTICLE 1. This Society shall be called the Anti-Slavery
Society of the City and County of Burlington and Vicinity,
and shall be auxiliary to the American Anti-Slavery Society.

ARTICLE 2. The object of this Society shall be the use
of all peaceable and moral means to exhibit to public view the
enormous evils of that system of slavery which disturbs, af-
flicts and threatens with destruction this great republic, and
especially to persuade those who hold slaves of their sin in so
doing, and of their duty immediately to emancipate them,
and practice towards them that divine precept which requires
us to love our neighbors as ourselves. The Society shall
also aim to remove public prejudice, and improve the character and condition of the free people of color by encouraging
their intellectual and moral elevation, that thus they may become qualified to share an equality with us in civil and religious privileges.

NORRISTOWN, PA., 1844.

WHEREAS, The Churches of the South do, to a great extent, sanction and sustain the system of American Slavery,
appealing to the Bible for its justification; and

WHEREAS, the great body of the Churches at the North
do regard it as a great moral evil, and very many churches
and associations have declared it to be such a sin against God

and man as to render any individual involved in it unworthy
of a place at the table of the Lord;

Resolved, That with views and practices so at variance
and antagonistical the one to the other, it is in vain to hope
for pleasure or utility from a continued effort to coalesce in
this matter; but on the other hand, that pain to many hearts,
and the crippling of the energies of all concerned, must be the
result; therefore

Resolved, That such a division of the convention as will
leave both of the above parties free to work in the cause on
their own ground and by their own chosen instrumentalities,
unimpeded by conflicting views and feelings, is indispensable
to the success of the cause of missions.

NORRISTOWN, PA., June 15, 1851.

Dear Sir—I have received your very courteous and
friendly letter of the 10th instant and thoughtfully noted its
contents. I will unite with all my heart in the project to procure from the surrounding clergy an expression of their sentiments in reference to slavery. Could they, or any part of
them, be prevailed upon to condemn it, even in the mildest
terms, it would go, perhaps, as far as any one measure to set
the people right. And if the Christian ministry of the whole
country would set their seal of reprobation on this hateful institution, I doubt not it would soon be swept from the land.
Call then the pastors of this town together and let them unite
in an earnest invitation to the neighboring brethren to assem-
ble, consult and resolve. Nothing but good can come of it,
do what they may. I will meet them and advise, if thought
best, but will not even seem to lead in the measures for many
reasons, one only of which is this: I am fully committed,
pledged and resolved, with God's help, to co-operate with all
abolitionists of every shade of opinion in battling against
slavery; and that necessarily creates a prejudice greater or
less against me in the minds of clergymen who attach more
importance than I do to the ministerial profession. I entreat

you to push forward this project without delay and with the utmost energy.

I learn from sources apparently credible, that in your sermon of the 8th instant you made some very disparaging allusions to George Thompson and to his friends here, especially those who were most zealous to get him here. I feel, with others, displeased and aggrieved for the sake of the cause that the force of your eloquence and the weight of your character should be suffered to be thus appropriated by the enemies of human rights. If you would permit me to peruse and copy the notes of the sermon, I would regard it as an act of magnanimity—which a man of your character can well afford to do—as well as of justice, which, I have reason to believe, you are always disposed to do. If the remarks were as represented to me, I wish to reply publicly in defense of Mr. T—— and his friends.

Very sincerely your friend and brother,

SAMUEL AARON.

REV. JOHN M'CRON.

———

NORRISTOWN, March 13, 1844.

Reverend and Dear Sir—If feeling reverence for, or revering goodness, be one of the definitions of the term Reverend, I shall make no apology to Mr. Aaron for addressing him by a title which, in a merely clerical sense, I believe he disapproves. And for addressing him at all, I have no apology to offer other than that I am irresistibly impelled by feelings of earnest gratitude to thank him most sincerely and warmly for his many and excellent teachings since his arrival among us, and to acknowledge the, I hope, lasting benefit I have derived therefrom. The deep regret that Mr. Aaron's contemplated retirement has caused, I cannot so readily express, for I cannot dwell upon it with anything like composure. If I did not know that he was actuated by the most conscientious motives, and had decided, after prayerful and solemn deliberation, I should, judging from my own feelings, beg him to pause ere he resigned a situation of deep usefulness, and where he exercised great influence upon many persons, of whom, perhaps, he never thought and personally never knew. I am, myself, one of that class of persons. Where now shall they look for instruction? Where find the impress of sincerity, without which words fall all powerless upon the heart? God forbid that I should judge any rashly, but when I see men shrink from known duty by refraining, from motives of policy, from denouncing fearlessly and constantly what they know and have acknowledged to be most heinous sins, I think they must have something radically wrong in their hearts; must from the very nature of the case be insincere, and cannot, as a consequence, be respected as conscientious and Christian men, much less have any influence as public teachers, at least upon the hearts of those who are free from sectarian prejudices, and I confess myself one of that class.

And now I would fain give expression to the esteem with which I have long regarded Mr. Aaron's character, were it not that I might be liable to the imputation of flattery. But no! I shall be exonerated from such a charge when I state simply that what I have said, or may say, is in all sincerity. It is said that a knowledge of one's own heart is the only true key by which we can attain to a knowledge of the hearts of others. If true, I abide by Mr. A——'s decision, as the love of truth is one of his most striking characteristics. I have for years, sir, watched your career with trembling anxiety, fearing that you might be induced to swerve from the path of stern duty, from the fear of man, fear of not being "popular," etc. But I forgot, at those moments, that a faithful servant of his master trusted not in his own strength; and he will support those who are faithful and fearless; he has supported. The very persons who are loudest in the cry of "denunciation," "want of charity," "goes too far," are those who envy the courage they dare not imitate; who reverence in their hearts and feel "how awful goodness is." I feel happy Mr. Aaron has not, and I hope will not, notice the slanderous imputations the newspapers have put forth. Methinks, could the pretended friends of temperance "be touched with Ithuriel's spear," we would see exhibited the personification of envy, hatred and malice. It must and will recoil upon themselves.

Ah! how beautiful a thing is faith, firm, unwavering faith in the goodness of at least some of our species; how it repays the possessor a hundred fold. What pity the jewel is so rare. Surely angels must weep that sin will not allow us to retain the bright thing. Sometimes we can do so; would it were oftener. When I have heard Mr. Aaron's motives impugned, his talents deprecated, and even his piety doubted, I have been happy enough never to have had my confidence shaken in him for a moment. I have defended him warmly and fearlessly where I thought there was a possibility of his character being appreciated, but have sometimes found the mist of prejudice so thick that the task was a herculean one. But I have been rewarded in the extorted acknowledgment that perhaps these things were so. I will now relate a case of misrepresentation.

Upon a recent occasion you commented from the pulpit, and that in terms scarcely severe enough, upon the degenerate and vitiated taste of the age with regard to literature. You referred to our own library as a specimen, it being almost filled with light works. Upon the afternoon of that Sabbath the following colloquy took place on the street, the principal speaker being a man who in matters apart from prejudice is clear-headed enough. "Well, B——, were you to hear Mr. Aaron this morning?" "Yes, I was; and, as usual, he was abusing everybody. Why, even poor ——, the librarian, could not escape, and I was so disgusted by hearing him abused that I left the church immediately." That, sir, I consider a pretty fair specimen of the misrepresentations you have been subjected to for the last eighteen months. But the greatest philanthropist that was ever upon the earth, he who went about continually doing good, who lived for others alone—aye, and who died for them also—was hated and despised for his goodness, and had false testimony borne against him. How much more, then, should imperfect man bear with meekness the rebuffs and opposition truth ever meets with at the hands of sinful men! Mr. Aaron loves too well his fellow-man to be deterred from laboring for their good, even if met, as he has been, with the basest ingratitude. Though human nature is so generally perverse, there are many who love and honor him for his efforts to

ameliorate the condition of those around him, and pray often
and fervently that he may be strengthened to plead the cause
of suffering humanity with increased success.   Often and eloquently has he already done so,—may he never falter in the
God-like task.   Great is the strength of an individual soul true
to its high trust.

I will relate an anecdote that I somewhere read, which I
think apropos. "A German whose sense of sound was exceedingly acute, was passing by a church a day or two after
he had landed in this country, and the sound of music attracted
him to enter, though unacquainted with our language.   The
music proved to be a piece of psalmody sung in most discordant fashion, and the sensitive foreigner would fain have covered
his ears.   As this was scarcely civil, and might appear like
rudeness, his next resolve was to rush into the open air and
leave the hated sounds behind him.   But this, too, he feared
to do lest offence might be given, and so he resolved to endure the torture with the best patience he could assume, when
lo! he distinguished amid the din the soft, clear voice of a woman singing in perfect tune.   She made no effort to drown the
voices of her companions, neither was she disturbed by their
noisy discord; but patiently and sweetly she sang in full, rich
tones.   One after another yielded to the gentle influence, and
before the tune was finished all were in perfect harmony.   I
have often thought of this story," adds the writer, "as convey-
ing an instructive lesson for reformers.   The spirit that can
thus sing patiently and sweetly in a world of discord must indeed be of the strongest as well as the gentlest kind.   One
scarce can hear his own soft voice amid the braying of the mul-.
titude, and ever and anon comes the temptation to sing louder,
than they and drown the voices that cannot thus be forced
into perfect tune.   But this were a pitiful experiment; the me-
lodious tones cracked into shrillness would only increase the
tumult.   Stronger, and more frequently, comes the temptation
to stop singing and let discord do its own wild work.   But
blessed are they that endure to the end, singing patiently and
sweetly, till all join in with loving acquiescence, and universal
harmony prevails, without forcing into submission the free discord of a single voice.   This is the hardest and the heaviest

task which a true soul has to perform amid the clashing elements of time. But once done perfectly unto the end, and that voice, so clear in its meekness, is heard above all the din of a tumultuous world; one after another chimes in with its patient sweetness, and through infinite discords the listening soul can perceive that the great tune is slowly coming into harmony."

And now I cannot close this letter without again thanking Mr. Aaron for the kind instruction so often and faithfully given. Often has my heart burned within me when listening to his glowing and fervent pictures of the goodness and love of God towards his fallen creatures; his persuasive invitations to seek a Saviour; and his many incentives to lure his hearers to lead a life of purity and virtue. And I have observed, too, and appreciated his efforts to adapt his language to the comprehension of the more illiterate portion of his congregation, when naturally it would have been more lofty. Such self-denial could not have been practiced by some public speakers, I was going to add, if immortal souls were the price of the indulgence. * * * And now, sir, I think it quite time to close this long epistle. Methinks I see a smile upon your countenance at the Quixotic idea of writing to one not personally known, the more especially as you will see no name given. But I confess I have not the courage to give it, though I should like much so to do. I beg you will not regard it as anonymous communications deservedly are regarded. You know there are exceptions to all general rules. May I hope this will prove one?

And, in conclusion, I pray that the God of all goodness may watch over you and strengthen and support you in the hour of duty. May he prove to you a shield through life and a sure refuge in the hour of death. May he soften your trials, and bless you in all your relations of husband, father, and teacher. And O, may he receive you and yours to his eternal rest. Amen.

JENKINTOWN, PA., July 12, 1886.

During the first of Mr. Aaron's time as teacher at Norristown—probably for a few years—he taught in the old Academy, before building his own residence and school-room, which he named Treemount Seminary. While teaching in the Academy he received the attack and abuse—a fearful whipping with a raw-hide—of which I am about to speak. He had numerous calls to deliver temperance lectures. He addressed a meeting at Spring Mill, some four miles below Norristown, at which time he exposed some of the evils and crimes resulting from the liquor business at the Spring Mill hotel, kept by the McClenaghan brothers. The two brothers came to Norristown some days after with the purpose of taking revenge on Mr. Aaron. William Frick (now Dr. Frick, of Philadelphia) and I were the last students leaving the Academy. As we went down the street we met the two men, who inquired if Mr. Aaron was in the Academy. We answered yes, and went on; but we were soon attracted by the noise of the attack, heard the strokes of the lashes, and returned to the school-room just in time to see the conclusion of the outrage. Mr. Aaron bore it so complacently that the fiend who used the raw-hide did not seem to have satisfaction, as he flourished his weapon in a threatening manner. (Poor satisfaction to whip a post.) The lashes were inflicted on the face and neck and on the back. After the whipping off and breaking of his spectacles, he protected his eyes, I believe, with his hands. One terrible gash on the lower part of his cheek and neck bled very profusely, and was several inches long. He carried the mark while he lived. His back was severely welted. The villains, fool-hardy, gave themselves up, and were bound over to court for trial. They were found to be armed with deadly weapons, which they said they did not intend to use unless it should be necessary. The bully said he understood that Mr. Aaron was an athletic man, and of course expected he would resist. But his principle of non-resistance sustained him wonderfully; or, perhaps better, he sustained his principles. Here he achieved a victory and they defeat.

The trial came off in court before Judge Burnside. I was first witness. A very able and eloquent plea was made by Mr. Aaron's lawyer, David Paul Brown, of Philadelphia. I remember Judge Burnside said in his charge that he was not giving his own decision, or it would have been the utmost extent of the law, for it was the most aggravating case that ever came before him; but he was overruled by two Associate Judges, who were liquor men—I believe, tavern owners. So the penalty was thirty days imprisonment and $30 fine; and it was said, and I believe true, that tavern-keepers furnished them all they wished to eat or drink.

After Mr. Aaron's recovery very enthusiastic temperance meetings were held, and one especially enthusiastic at Spring Mill. Distinguished speakers eloquently defended Mr. Aaron and the cause for which he suffered. JOSIAH PHILLIPS.

———

BYBERRY, Fifth-month 29, 1854.

My Dear Friend—I am astonished to learn that thee is charged with prevarication, in connection with the long past but not soon to be forgotten McClenaghan case. My recollection of the lecture and of the testimony on the trial is more distinct than of most matters of notoriety or public interest occurring before or since. The meeting was appointed and got up by myself, held in my woods, and I was present at the private examination of a large number of witnesses by David Paul Brown, who all, like myself, did not understand Samuel Aaron as having any personal allusion whatever, either to the miserable death of Reese Harry or the McClenaghans.

The lecture was a remarkably pleasant and good-tempered one. Thy nature has always appeared to me entirely above evasion or prevarication. I know no man more entirely candid without regard to consequences. All present at the conclusion of that trial should remember, as I distinctly do, that when Dr. McClenaghan stood up in court, after his conviction of what Judge Burnside called "the most outrageous assault upon a peaceable and unoffending man he had ever known,"

to make his whining plea in abatement of sentence, that he
"regretted the language of Mr. Aaron had been so misrepresented to him," as the testimony of witnesses had convinced
him, and "believed if he had been at the meeting he should
have taken no offence."   J. R. Bowman.

To Samuel Aaron.

Manayunk, February 23, 1856.

My Dear Brother—I feel constrained to send you this little note, that if possible it may, with the interview we have
had, induce you to come forth immediately and take a public
stand against this monstrous evil, spiritualism. Your praise is
in the country as the champion of truth and liberty; the strong
opponent of two great evils, slavery and intemperance. But,
sir, let me tell you that neither slavery nor intemperance has
made such a wreck in the world of mind, and drawn so many
souls to everlasting burnings in so short a time, as spiritualism. I look upon it as one of the best laid schemes of the
devil to destroy mankind. It is the very thing to delude and
destroy the simple mind; the very thing that suits the carnal
heart; the very thing that defiled human nature has been long
looking for. It arose "like a man's hand," but it is now brood-
ing like a dark, gathering cloud over the face of the moral
heavens. I have serious apprehensions of much evil being
accomplished by this fell serpent before its head can be effectually crushed. If otherwise, I will be agreeably disappointed.
I know that sooner or later God will bruise it, but God generally works by the instrumentality of his people.

It has been said that those who have been deluded by this
filthy thing are comparatively worthless. In many respects
this may be true. But, oh! why talk so? Have they not immortal souls capable of being made either happy or wretched
throughout a never ending duration? And is it not the duty
of every Christian man and minister to stand forth to oppose
and expose those wicked delusions by which the souls of their
fellow-mortals are ruined? Did a public abettor of slavery or
intemperance enter your town, I am sure, sir, you would be
with the first to lift up a standard against him. And is it not

evident that the advocates of a system equally as formidable to the truth and ruinous to the souls of men have gone in among you? Are the watchmen on the walls of Zion to look down on such a foe as he does his work of death, and be silent? The Lord hath delivered unto you the weapons of a glorious warfare; and not only so, but endowed you with the power to wield those weapons. And now the giant has stepped up to your door. Arise, in the name of Jesus, and smite him. "Stop his mouth," and "rebuke him sharply." Hear the claims and the teachings of this infernal delusion, and the blasphemy of its victims, and you will be persuaded that it requires but little or no investigation to be denounced.

I am sorry to find that this wicked thing has made such inroads in Norristown. But I do sincerely hope that you will take a decided stand (before the public) against it. I know you are fully able to oppose it, and that your expositions, admonitions, etc., would have a good effect on the community of Norristown, that this woful thing might soon come to its end and have none to help it.

Dear sir, I have written to urge you to assail this "wild-ism." In this it may be I have taken too much liberty; but I wish you to remember I have written as a brother whose heart gushes forth for your welfare and the welfare of mankind. So please excuse this liberty, despise not my youth, and believe me when I say my motive is to establish the blessed gospel and overthrow the kingdom of darkness in the earth.

I am, sir, yours in the bonds of a holy Christianity,

To SAMUEL AARON. W. F——.

April 26, 1862.

Dear Sir—At my request Judge B—— wrote to you the within challenge. I have been some months investigating spiritualism, and have continually found mediums or spiritual speakers advancing arguments destructive of old views of theology. Failing successfully to meet them, I am anxious to hear those better versed than myself pitched in public or private combat against the persons who are with no small influence spreading doctrines which according to Christian belief are dangerous to be propagated in any community. I intended to have seen you to-day, and had a conversation upon the subject; but business preventing, I send you this through mail, hoping to receive an answer at your earliest convenience.

         Yours most truly,   —— ——

To SAMUEL AARON.

MOUNT HOLLY, April 28, 1862.

Dear Sir—I have just received yours of the 26th instant, enclosing Mr. B——'s, and noted the contents of both. To enter into the controversy proposed is entirely incompatible with my taste, my engagements and my sense of duty.

1. My taste forbids me to engage in a mere bootless public or private wrangle with witches, wizards, jugglers or necromancers, as it would seem like casting pearls before swine. Even if that amiable, honest trickster, Signor Blitz, should challenge a preacher to explain his tricks, good taste, I think, would decline the ordeal.

2. My time is so engaged in reading, teaching, preaching, and seeing the sick, that I have not fifty or one hundred hours to spare in hunting to their holes all the itinerant foxes, male and female, that are carrying firebrands through the land.

3. If the Bible is true, this spiritism is a lie. The truth of the Bible is not a question with me nor with any other sane man who has devoutly studied it. Spiritism, like the devil, contradicts the Bible, and mocks and blasphemes both it and its author. I believe that spiritism has skill and power. It has the skill to lie with cunning art, skill to juggle, and the power of fiends to help it out. The demons that Christ sent into the swine gave proofs of greater strength and activity than what has yet appeared in this modern demonology. A sense of duty would permit me to debate with a serious and candid skeptic who consulted only his reason and pretended to nothing supernatural, but I can hold no parley with those who summon the spiritual world to mock and blaspheme its author.

4. The tendency of this spiritism is too loose all the bonds of moral obligation and to give the rein to all lawless appetites and lusts. Therefore, conscience bids me condemn and denounce it as occasion demands, but to hold no intercourse or fellowship with such an "unfruitful work of darkness." You have spent months in investigating spiritism. I have spent years in investigating Christianity. I am settled, satisfied, happy. You appear to be undecided, and want man to do for you by argument what God alone can do by grace. Christ is proposed as the object of our loving faith. God is "well pleased in Him," and only asks man to be so, too, as the passport to a holy heaven.

The terms are easy, and they have never failed the soul that has accepted them. Try them, and may God help you.

Your sincere friend,

SAMUEL AARON.

MOUNT HOLLY, August 4, 1863.

Dear Brother—I have not had time to make an earlier reply to yours of the 12th ult. Be assured, I entreat you, that my good will toward you is not diminished nor can be by the unfortunate difference of opinion between us, which your letter seems to imply. If it were possible, even, for you to decline, not only from what I deem a correct religious faith, but also from a pure, moral life, it would still be my duty, as, I trust, it would be my choice, to pray for you, to advise you, and to love you. Your letter is amiable and christianlike in its language, and doubtless is an honest transcript of your heart, but to my mind it manifests not one single ray of that "reason," to which it lays so strong a claim. Observe, I do not say but that you have reasons for your change of faith, but only that you show none to me. If you have good reasons, they are as good for me as for you (for I, too, am a man), and I need as much as you to know them, to adopt them, and to secure their blessing.

The reasoning faculty enables us to examine evidence, and was manifestly given to be thus employed. The Bible,

composed of the Old and New Testaments, assumes to inform
mankind how they may acceptably worship and serve Almighty God, live a right life here, and secure everlasting purity and happiness hereafter. Is there anything in your "self-
reliant nature" which is authorized to pronounce any of its
requirements to be "useless, outward ordinances?" Is there
anything in "self-reliant nature" or "reason" either, which
can take "one single step" with absolute certainty in the right
direction as to moral conduct, and as to the fact of a future
and eternal existence, without instruction from the Scriptures?
Do you answer, Conscience?   Conscience bids the South Sea
Islanders to kill and eat their neighbors, and, therefore, is not
a certain guide.   It teaches millions of Americans to support
and other millions to condemn slavery, and thus contradicts
itself.   Do you say, Reason?   Reason has made millions of
Greeks (the acutest people that ever lived), Epicureans, or
pleasure lovers, votaries of every brute appetite; other millions, stoics, or pain lovers, glorifying pain as the chief good;
others again materialists, denying all spiritual existence; and
others immaterialists, denying the existence of matter. Remember these people were the masters of reason, hitherto unequalled, at least unsurpassed, among men.

What then of this humbug of "self-reliance," or "reason,"
or even "conscience?" And how did you find out that the
"teachings delivered by a messenger from heaven inculcated
by all Christendom," and which you still "reverence as holy
teachings," are merely "of the past," and "have fulfilled their
destiny as far as they were intended for yourself?" Such vast
knowledge as this on your part requires a revelation from
heaven, contradicting a former revelation from the same source.
And when heaven contradicts itself, what shall a man believe?
As to your hypothesis that some "principles" (I suppose you
mean moral and religious principles) are safe for me, and other
different principles safe for you, the proposition is absurd, unless you first show that you and I are beings of different na-
tures, under different obligations, or that there are two equally
powerful Gods, who are pledged to each other to remain at
peace.   In fact your supposition is infinitely more absurd, as

it supposes a different God for every different man, or else a Divine Almighty Being who has no uniform rule of action.

You use the phrase, in reference to yourself, "deluded enthusiast." The phrase is absurd, as it means "enthusiastic enthusiast"; like saying "wet water." I therefore do not apply it to you. But in all sincerity and affection, I believe you to be a deluded man, as the tenor of your letter and of my reply most amply prove. And I infer from your letter and from remarks of our mutual friends that you have been deluded by attending on the teachings of "spiritism," that shallowest and vilest of modern impostures. I am satisfied that it is indeed a dealing, as the Bible says, with "unclean spirits," for its legitimate tendency has been to promote immorality and contempt for all truth in testimony. The "spirits" contradict one another, and therefore lie, disparage divine revelation, and therefore blaspheme God, and in a word present the boldest public display of rogues on pretended supernatural authority that Christendom has ever seen. These harsh conclusions are derived partly from the confessions and recantations of some of the most eminent professors of its revelations, and partly from the unchanged lives of vile men and women who remain eminent among its votaries.

Reason has no power apart from evidence. On that it can act and on nothing else. Those vast intellects among the Greeks, etc., above referred to, had facts in nature, mathematics and rhetoric, and reasoned safely and profoundly; on spiritual and divine principles, having no revelation from God, even their reason was impotent. Bacon, Newton, Locke, Butler, Saurin, Cuvier, Chalmers, Edwards, and many others of similar powers, examined the authority of Scripture as a revelation from the Most High, by applying reverently the mighty energies of their reason to the light of testimony, intrinsic and extrinsic, and reached the same conclusion, viz.: "That Jesus Christ is the only name given under heaven and among men whereby we can be saved."

That a set of flippant blasphemers should be able to turn a soul as candid and as strong as yours away from your duties towards the Lord Jesus Christ, and from your interest in his redeeming blood, and set you to talking about "my followers," is indeed as gall and wormwood to every feeling of my heart. And again, on the other hand, if you mean to set up the powers of your own "reason" in opposition to that of the men named above, and that too without examining the case as thoroughly as they did, and so on the spur of impulse fix on conclusions involving your eternal destiny, I declare that such conduct appears to me the most unreasonable as well as the most perilous within the limits of the human will.

I shall always think of you with amazement and with sorrow, and pray for your recovery till I learn that you walk in the revealed commandments of the Lord.

Very truly your friend,

SAMUEL AARON.

UNITED STATES CONSULATE,
CARDIFF, ENGLAND, April 16, 1862.

My Dear Friend—I can hardly tell you how sad and vexed I have felt within the past week to see by our papers that Wendell Phillips had been disturbed while lecturing in Cincinnati, and that you had met with some opposition at Burlington, N. J. This makes me feel more disheartened than anything else. I fear not the powder, the bullets, the guns, the Merrimacs of the traitors, one-tenth part as much as I do a corrupt and consequently a divided public sentiment of the North. If all our people felt in their own hearts the iniquity of slavery; if they felt that they had sinned and done wickedly in the sight of God and man for the past half century for apologizing for slavery and sustaining it, then I should have no fears for the traitors, however great their number or formidable their power. "If God be for us, who can be against us?" But what I fear is that the virus, the poison of slavery, has so infused itself into our very veins and bones and marrow that we are hopelessly corrupt; that there will be more vile and unprincipled "compromises" made with the slaveholding power to bring them into the Union. God grant that I may not be right in my fears.

You will be glad to learn that since I have been here my health has improved very much. My thirty-four years of constant teaching from the time I left college had completely broken me down, and I required an entire change. The climate here is remarkably mild for its high latitude. I have not been obliged to wear an overcoat to my office six times the whole winter. I have seen nothing that deserved to be called ice or snow; once a little sprinkling of snow, that did not cover the ground.

My duties are generally very pleasant and not laborious, though this is, I think, the third Consulate in Great Britain. I cannot help, now and then, thinking of the time when I must return home, and where I shall go. My family say I shall never teach again, and I want to get some small place, in a good country town, of from two to six acres. I shall not wish to be at a great distance from Philadelphia, for what little material interests I have are there. May I ask a few questions about Mount Holly? Is it an expensive place of living? Is there good society there? How high does the anti-slavery thermometer range,—at 32°, temperate, 56°, or blood heat? Have you any good public libraries? I know it is looking rather far ahead; but it will do no harm, if we are not "anxious about the things of to-morrow."

Most truly and cordially yours,

CHARLES D. CLEVELAND.

REV. SAMUEL AARON.

July 20, 1862.

Dear Sir—I was glad to see (for the first time) the writing of one whom though personally unknown to me I felt so intimate with from the report of those we both love. It would give me real pleasure to oblige you in any way. At present I am not able to leave home, and whether I shall be able to do so next winter I cannot now say. All that I can promise is that I will try to plan so as to accommodate you. If you should hear of my being engaged to speak in your neighborhood please write and remind me, and I will do all I can.

Truly yours, WENDELL PHILLIPS.

REV. SAMUEL AARON.

CAMP ——, January 19, 1864.

My Christian Friend and Brother—This is a dismal, rainy morning, and I thought I could spend a few moments with pleasure in penciling a few lines to a friend I hold most dear. I have sufficient reason for loving you: for the good I have received from you, in the Christian instruction you have imparted unto me, the kindness I have received, and, best of all, your daily walk and conversation. You have erected the Christian standard so high that your image is so indelibly stamped upon my heart that eternity can never obliterate it. The teaching I have received from you has led me nearer to the loving Saviour. I fear I shall very much miss you when I cannot hear your voice. But, thanks be unto God, I have "a friend who sticketh closer than a brother," and I will put my trust in him, in the camp, upon the battle-field, and in the hour of death.

A soldier's life is a hard one for a Christian. I have found but a very few who love the Saviour. A few of Christ's disciples met on last Sabbath and had a very good season of exhortation and prayer. It grieves me to hear the curses, the wicked songs and jests, the foolish talk, and, worse than all, the making fun of Christ and his religion.

It is most astonishing to me to see so many drink rum and lager beer. There is a great deal of card-playing going on around me. A young man who slept with me, from the "pines," spent on Sabbath day nine dollars; another said he spent four hundred in a few days. One man lost the night before ninety-four dollars; still another, one hundred and ten; and I cannot enumerate the cases.

I have learned that we will not leave here until the old regiment comes back. I would be pleased to receive any word from you. Give my respects to Mrs. Aaron and family.

Yours affectionately,   L—— S——

REV. SAMUEL AARON.

WASHINGTON, D. C., June 2, 1864.

Dear Sir—Mr. Charles S. Bates has called upon me with the request that you should be invited to preach in the Hall of Representatives some Sunday during the present session of Congress. I requested him at once to write to you, and in my name to extend to you a general invitation without assigning a day. I now write to say that it will give me great pleasure to place the Hall of Representatives at the service of one so distinguished for earnest advocacy of the cause of freedom on the second or third Sunday in June. There is some hope and expectation that the highly honored Dr. R. J. Breckinridge, of Kentucky, may be able to stop and preach here on the Sunday after next, when returning from the Baltimore convention. But if he cannot come I trust that you will be free to accept my invitation. Will you then have the kindness to make your arrangements contingently for the 12th or 19th of June, so as to ensure your being able to visit Washington on one of those Sundays.

As an additional motive for your coming, I would state that no Baptist minister has thus far preached in the Hall this season, and it is desirable to have each leading denomination represented there in the people's church. Hoping to receive a favorable answer by an early mail, I remain,

Very respectfully yours,

WILLIAM HENRY CHANNING,

Chaplain of the House of Representatives.

REV. SAMUEL AARON.

———

MOUNT HOLLY, N. J., June 4, 1864.

My Dear Friend—Your favor of a day or two ago was followed by one from Dr. Channing, dated June 2, 1864, both inviting me to preach in the Hall of Representatives. This is indeed a most unexpected distinction, and the acceptance of it has cost me a mental struggle which I need not describe. I have, however, concluded, if God please, to make the experiment on the 19th inst., if that day will suit. Dr. C. writes that

Dr. R. J. Breckinridge may or may not occupy the 12th, and, as I understand him, leaves the 12th contingently between Dr. B. and myself, but leaves the 19th positively open to me. Please, therefore, my dear friend, to inform me certainly whether I can have that day or the 26th, if Congress sit till then. About the 26th our school will close.

I am ashamed of not writing to you, but truly grateful for your kind promptness in scouring the friendly chain; and be assured it is not tarnished. I really have not time to write as I ought. You have never happened to say whether you saw Dr. Elder. A response from Dr. Solger implied that you handed E. my letter.

Your views of men and policies accord with my own, but I have been very careful to keep them in my own breast; at least such as the unfriendly could use to your disadvantage. I should be glad to know the drift of any powerful under-current before I come to Washington, that I may expose it, or warn against it, as I shall speak very boldly, though not abusively, of men, measures and theories.

Fremont is nominated. What then? Our conservatives here are alarmed and offended. I tell them to take it patiently and thankfully; the people as well as the politicasters have a right to declare their preference, and it has long been needed that those who pay and earn the public expenditures should dictate who should use and disburse them. Fremont's pro-gressive platform and vast popularity will compel the adoption of an advanced position at Baltimore, and convince Mr. L. that "Kentucky pets" are not much longer to be the Jugger-naut of this great Republic. I suppose Mr. L. will be nomi-nated at Baltimore, and unless utter madness and stupidity, even the Weed-iest, rule the hour, I think that a platform richer in promise at least than even that of 1856 will ask the support of the people. If they give us one as good as that of Cleveland, I will for unity's sake support it; if they falter, I will vote for Fremont, as I think him brave and true. Grant, so far as we know here, is doing grandly, and Lee seems over-matched. Write soon.

                    Yours truly,   SAMUEL AARON.
MR. CHARLES S. BATES.

MOUNT HOLLY, June 10, 1864.

My Dear Friend—I wrote to you a week ago, enclosing a reply to a letter from Dr. Channing promising to come to Washington and preach on the 19th or 26th inst., if either of those days would suit. Your note, delayed on the way, informs me that mine has not been received, and meanwhile I have concluded that as the session has so nearly closed, and adjournment may take place in a week or less, I will request that my coming shall be postponed till December next, when, if permitted, I will comply with the invitation if Dr. Channing and you think proper to continue it. I am truly grateful for the good opinion of both of you, and that you have both desired for me the opportunity of giving so eminent publicity to views so long and so honestly entertained; but my ambition of notoriety has nearly passed away. Still I will, more to please you than myself, cheerfully tell Congress what I think on public affairs, next session.

My mind is not clear as to what I shall do in the coming Presidential election. Both platforms ignore the franchise of the negro, and I firmly believe that we can neither deserve nor possess true and permanent prosperity till we render equal and impartial justice to all honest men. On the whole, I know not what to do yet; if Grant is repulsed, Lincoln will be disgraced and forsaken, and Fremont will probably become the nation's hope whether nominated by the Democrats or not. If in the divisions likely to occur the Copperheads get the reins, then look out for national dishonor and destruction, for the triumph of blackguardism such as the city of New York has maintained and exhibited for some years past. I firmly believe that a civil and social war would ensue if Christians and moralists did not conclude to yield to extermination, in which men of the nerve of Fremont would have to rally the true-hearted and fight even the forms of government for the realities of civil and religious rights. A dark day is approaching if Copperheads are to rule,—dark as that foreshadowed by the good Quaker's vision. But I feel sad to-day; let us all be cheerful and trust in God.

Your friend as ever,   SAMUEL AARON.

MR. CHARLES S. BATES.

MOUNT HOLLY, June 16, 1864.

My Dear Friend—My coming *must* be deferred till December. Your last note fails to say what date was fixed for my visit. I left to Dr. Channing the choice of the 19th or 26th inst., and much correspondence would be needed to reach a right understanding. But this is not the cause of my declining to come. The uncertainty before, and the need, if I came in June, of making a disjointed harangue, deterred me. Every moment of my time is used up by daily teaching and frequent attempts to preach.

I see your children frequently; the two little girls spent the afternoon of Monday last with my little grand-daughter, and had a jovial time.

I have not a moment more, and remain

   Truly your friend,   SAMUEL AARON.

MR. CHARLES S. BATES.

MOUNT HOLLY, December 19, 1864.

My Dear Friend—Your letter was received, and I attended to the business matter you wrote about. I have not made a special visit to your children for some time, but see some of them every few days and know of their welfare.

Mount Holly is in *statu quo*, so that I can think of nothing worth telling you. My discourse on the evening of Thanksgiving day pleased many loyal people well, but gave great, almost unpardonable, offence to a few skin-deep Democrats, some of whom thought of having me cashiered from the pulpit. My reply to them was that I could not help thanking a good God for the overthrow of rebellion in the South and murderous treason in the North; that on all subjects within the scope of moral and religious instruction I should say just what Scripture and my own conscience dictated; that mean, ungodly factions in churches often made out to drive off honest preachers, and so control the churches and corrupt both them and the ministry, making cowards of the one and hypocrites of the other; and that I had determined to stand by the upright and progressive part of the church, and let the others leave or be excluded, as the case required. This position seems to have calmed the surface; but the dregs of hate and prejudice lie deep.

I am sorry that my friend ——— has been imposed upon by sharpers. I see nothing immoral in his risk. But is it not better for those who take a high moral stand to have almost nothing at all to do with men of reputation in the slightest degree uncertain? Perhaps he did not know they were "disloyal" when he trusted them, though I understood he found them so. We are compelled in the daily current of affairs to float alongside of the base, but we ought never to trust ourselves in their hands nor touch them except to do them good. I do not censure a want of principle in ———, but of prudence.

The President has taken a manly stand in his late message, and I am especially pleased by his nomination of Mr. Chase to the office of supreme expounder of the Constitution and the laws. Chase has been weighed in the balances for twenty-five years by many hands, and never found wanting. No other man capable, except Sumner, has been so thoroughly proved, nor he for so long a time. I would have preferred Sumner, because he is ten years younger, a greater legal scholar, and equally a friend of universal justice and humanity. But, thank God, one of the noblest men on earth has now the highest seat for life among the judges and expositors of human law.

I see that Ashley, of Ohio, has the floor whenever he chooses to call up the question of advising the states to amend the Constitution so as to prohibit slavery forever. I wish you would ascertain and inform me whether petitioning would do any good, as I have a petition here but have thought its circulation needless.

Chandler, I believe, is proposing to prepare and present a bill to the government of Great Britain, demanding indemnity for the three or four hundred millions' worth of property destroyed by vessels built and manned by British hands; and perhaps for further damages to our commerce by the preventing of thousands of our ships from venturing to sea. It strikes me as the profoundest stupidity among the acts of nations that Great Britain should permit these, and like insults and wrongs, to be perpetrated by her people against a nation so mighty and so chivalrous as ours. It will be easy to show that our people are $1,000,000,000 poorer on account of the wanton intermeddling of British avarice and pride in the current of our civil war; and I shall not wonder if sooner or later her people compel the government to pay us half that sum rather than go to war with us and lose Ireland, most of her colonies, and all her navy and commerce. She will reflect, probably, that we have a compact territory forty times her island in extent and one hundred times at least as rich in natural resources—perhaps five hundred times—with a people equal in number, incomparably more enterprising and intelligent, and many of them, alas! hating her most heartily not without cause. Britain seems mad to her own ruin, and false to her boasted love of human rights.

The prospect of victory, even of the extermination of the rebel armies, looks brighter now than ever before. We were alarmed by the successful audacity of Hood, whose every stroke was exaggerated by rebel falsehood and our own fears; but now it appears that Grant, Sherman and Thomas understood the force of his temerity, and lured him to ruin. The march of Sherman for three hundred miles through the best, the very garden of the rebellious country, not only unimpeded, but strengthened and enriched as he proceeded, is among the military wonders of the age, and confirms the soundness of the views of himself and Fremont at the beginning, who both advised to pierce the very heart of the rebellion with an adequate force. For such advice Sherman was ignored as a madman by "Little Mac," and sent to command an obscure fortress I know not where; and Fremont ostracised by the Blair-Weed dynasty. I begin now to think that Fremont ought to have pursued the policy of Butler and Sherman,—pocketed all snubs and gone wherever ordered, and so have become the foremost "Roman of them all." But I don't know. It seems almost inevitable that Savannah, Charleston and Wilmington will soon be ours. The Rebel order already given to economize arms and missiles proves the supply to be scanty. What then when British aid is utterly prevented? Sherman has, no doubt, collected an army of able-bodied negroes, and our multiplied stations on the highland and the ocean frontier of the remaining rebel territory will speedily draw the rest. It is now desirable that Davis and his confreres should be thoroughly stubborn to the last, so that their banishment or death may result in spite of Presidential or Congressional amnesty; and then, with God's blessing, we shall have a just and glorious peace.

Keep thinking now and then whether there is a place in some department, Freedmen's Bureau, &c., wherein I could be useful. Allow something for a bad pen, and think me

Your good friend,   SAMUEL AARON.

MR. CHARLES S. BATES.

———

WASHINGTON, D. C., February 9, 1865.

My Dear Friend—I called to see Mr. Sumner, and spent a good part of the evening of the 2d of January with him, and was advised to write you to come on here, or get Dr. Channing to invite you to come, which I have been endeavoring to do. But before I got to see Dr. Channing, he had made arrangements for all the Sundays of this short session, which have thus far been occupied by himself, he having closed the church for the session. Another reason has been that the Grand Division resolved to have a great celebration in the capitol on the evening of the 15th, which has now been interfered with by their evening sessions. Still, we intend to have one after the adjournment. In the meantime I am advised by the officers of the Grand Division, who have charge of the subject, to invite you to come on at your earliest convenience. I am particularly desirous to see you here, as Mr. Sumner told me the bill before Congress to establish a Freedman's Bureau would become a law, and that you are the very kind of man that must be put at the head of it, and I am satisfied he will have a large say in the appointments under its provisions. I know also that Mr. Stevens and ——— would be glad to aid in having you appointed. There is a great field here for you to operate in, and I hope soon to see you here.

This evening I shall introduce the subject of having a public meeting held by our division in one of the large churches, and will leave this until to-morrow. It was decided at our meeting last night to hold a public meeting on Thursday night the 26th inst., at my instance, and a committee appointed to procure one of the large churches and speakers for the occasion, and make all necessary arrangements. I, therefore, as chairman of the committee, take this early opportunity of inviting you, my dear brother, to come and take part with us; chief part, in fact the only part, save what our G. W. P. may have to say. I trust you will make arrangements to come and spend at least a week; I hope until after the 4th of March. Your travelling expenses will be borne and all other expenses. I have enough boys in the division from our department who would be glad to contribute to bear all your expenses. I have consulted G. W. P. Bradley with regard to your coming, and have his approbation; in fact, the intention was to invite you for the 15th (by the officers appointed at the session of the Grand Division), had it not been delayed. I hope you will be able to stay with us for some time.

My daughters informed me that you gave them an address at the Methodist church on Sunday afternoon. They also told me that you had been quite ill, but are now convalescent. May I not hope that you will call and see my little flock soon?

Yours truly,   C. S. BATES.

REV. SAMUEL AARON.

NORRISTOWN, February 11, 1865.

Dear Sir—I hope you will not think me very importunate if, notwithstanding your refusal, I beseech you to come and give us a lecture, and when I tell you my reasons you will not be surprised at my persistence. George Francis Train lectured here last night, and came out in a most shameful tirade against England, urging war with her; and what is much worse, spoke in the most degrading manner of the poor down-trodden Africans, making them little better than monkeys, and only fit to be the bearer of burdens. He said he had always found them so in their own country and everywhere he had seen them. My indignation would hardly allow me to keep my seat; and when he had done speaking, I went to him, and told him he had done more harm than he could undo for a long time. His reply was: "I never was on their side"; and yet, a short time before, he had said he was always on the side of the weak. He is a very amusing lecturer, and there was a large audience, and he pandered to their prejudices, and no doubt one-half of them thought him right, and many more were glad of an excuse to be of the same opinion. And now, unless you, sir, or some one equally true to the good and right, will come, and before the same people, will vindicate the cause of the poor African, and show how un-Christian the desire for a war with any people, except for a great cause, like the one we are now engaged in, is for an enlightened people, such as we are, to indulge in, I shall feel that our Saviour's teachings have been trampled under foot by an infidel, and no one has thought it worth while to speak against him. In addition to what I have already said as a reason for your coming, we still need money for the poor, and I know of no one who would fill the house as well as you, as both your friends and enemies will go to hear you. I wish Mrs. Aaron would accompany you, and let us have the pleasure of a visit from you both. I will mention the 10th of March, if that time will meet your convenience, as that will give you time to refresh your memory on all the points in history of the intellect and strength relating to the African character. I know I am asking a great favor. Please remember me kindly to all your family.

Sincerely your friend,   —— ——.

Rev. Samuel Aaron.

—— ——

Mount Holly, February 15, 1865.

My Dear Friend—I feel most grateful to you for your unfaltering kindness to me, and almost flatter myself that some great advantage must grow out of it. But it is absolutely impossible for me to leave home even for three days at this season of the year. I teach the largest classes, and there is no substitute to be found in my place.

I enclose herewith a letter to Senator ————, in which I have requested him to urge the claims of Governor Andrew to a place in the new Cabinet; and have also asked him to think of me for a place in the Freedmen's Bureau, and to speak to Senators Harris (who is a Baptist), Sumner and Wilson, and to Thaddeus Stevens. Whatever you can do through Senator ———— and otherwise, I will be unspeakably obliged to you to do; though I earnestly request that it may all be done as quietly as possible. I have scarcely the slightest expectation of a favorable result, and deprecate the effect of disappointment at home. I rejoice at the promotion of Mr. ————, and still more at his integrity and courage in effecting the removal of immoral public servants. May heaven preserve and strengthen him in all such noble efforts, and may the American people and their representatives soon accept the same views on this point which he and I have so long cherished.

And now a word about our public affairs. Thanks be to God for the vote in Congress proposing to the states the great amendment. I think three-fourths of the loyal states have the power to ratify that vote and make it valid. Mr. Sumner urges this view; and it is absurd to call on those who have tried to murder the constitution for their help in giving it a new vitality. It is likely, however, that this absurdity will be insisted on, and possibly the determination of the question may come before the Supreme Court. There can be no doubt that three-fourths of the loyal states will assent to the amendment. It is really amusing to find the Rebel oracles who determined to crush the Union because, as they said, the North would discuss the "negro question," engaged themselves in discussing that and nothing else; discussing it, too, much more radically than was ever done in the old Congress, whether the negroes shall be made soldiers to secure Rebel independence, and whether all or how many shall be emancipated. How amazingly clear in these things is the interference of Divine Providence, in forcing to the lips and throats of reluctant tyrants the very dregs of that cup to avoid which they rushed into the blackest treason and the bloodiest war.

I predicted rightly the course of Sherman in his career through Georgia, viz., that he was aiming at a sea base. And now I venture to prognosticate that he is pushing forward to co-operate with Grant for the great purpose of crushing Lee, the Rebel military genius, in whose hand alone the sinews of their war-power meet, and whose heart and brain give plan and spirit to their treason and rebellion. Sherman is now about three hundred and fifty miles from Richmond and one hundred from those parts of North Carolina where he will find more friends than Lee can. In thirty days of far more moderate marching than he made in Georgia he can reach the Appomattox. I cannot conceive that any formidable force can be concentrated to impede his progress; and the nature of the season, though unfavorable to rapid marching, is well adapted to connect him with the sea, because the rivers will be full for the next two months, and the Santee, Wateree, two Pedees, Cape Fear, Neuse, Tar, Roanoke and Ohowan, all large winter streams, can surely be controlled by our mighty navy and Sherman's army abundantly supplied with men and munitions at intervals averaging forty miles. These suggestions may be practically blank, but the natural basis stands as I have stated; and if I were as great a General as Sherman, I should try to realize the plan. The Rebels will hardly carry out the arming of the blacks, and will fail in the attempt if our people will only have the sense and magnanimity to give the franchise to the bravest and most intelligent among them; and especially if military honors and posts are given to the capable and true. The massacre resulting from the act of Jeff. C. Davis at one of the Georgia rivers should be the subject of investigation by the War Committee, and whoever is responsible for it should be signally punished and forever disgraced. Wendell Phillips blames Sherman; but I hope so brave and wise a man will escape that stain.

I do not heartily approve Mr. Lincoln's condescension to those artful Rebels whom he met at Fort Monroe; but still it seems to have impressed some of the conciliators that traitors' hearts are not so soft as they regarded them, and the *Tribune* of to-day thinks it stimulates desertion from the Rebel ranks. I rejoice with all my soul that Lincoln and Seward did not lower their terms. I feared that Seward might do so, and that he would influence Lincoln. But all seems well. Honor to

Stanton and Dana for the ground they take about the clerks.

I have had various invitations this winter to lecture here and there, and have now an urgent one to answer George Francis Train at Norristown. Perhaps I may go. Give my respects to Senator ———, Mr. Stevens, Dr. Elder, and others that you know I esteem, and regard me as ever,

Your sincere friend,   SAMUEL AARON.

MR. CHARLES S. BATES.

———

MARTINSBURG, VA., November 2, 1864.

My Friend and Brother—During the past month I have written to a number of my correspondents, and thought your turn had come to-day. I am here alone, and have been for several days in a house (and a very poor one; my former one a few days ago burned to the ground, and some things with it) about five by six feet, with plenty of ventilation, and the weather here has been very cold.   *   *   *   It affords me much pleasure and consolation when I learn from my wife that you and your family are so kind and sociable to my little trio company while I am far, far away from them in this land of blood and carnage.

Last summer while I was at Cold Harbor I volunteered my services in our hospital. Amongst a large number of poor wounded soldiers (Union) were two rebels, one not dangerously and the other the surgeons did not touch, thinking the wound mortal, and left the poor fellow there to die. He laid there weltering in his blood for some time, and I thought I must try and do something for him. I put forth all the skill I had and nursed him faithfully for a number of days, and had the satisfaction of hearing the surgeons say that they thought he would recover, and I helped move him into a wagon to come North. Did I do right or did I not? My conscience answers, yes. If that poor rebel gets well I shall feel that I was the humble instrument of saving his life. My motto is, use our enemies well when we have them wounded or prisoners.   *   *   *

There is much profanity and most intolerable drunken-ness in the army. How I do hate rum; if I had no other name to call it, I would call it devil. I think your skirts will not be covered with blood in the great judgment day because you have not testified against this monster; but I believe that many who call themselves the ministers of Christ will have a most dreadful account to give. I venerate Brother ——— for the noble stand he takes in testifying against rum and slavery.

While I think of it, I would say that Lieutenant ———, a former pupil of yours at Norristown (now in the hands of the rebels since the battle of the Wilderness), wished me to give you and your family his respects. He told me many things to tell you that I have forgotten, not having seen him since early last Spring. He thinks there are few such women as Mrs. Aaron. He spoke about being sick while at school, and of her great care for his comfort. I liked him myself, and he drank no rum. He and Captain ——— came very near fighting a duel last winter, with rifles, only five yards apart. I think he was writing and arranging his business all the night before the conflict was to take place. Some of the superior officers heard of it and placed them under arrest, thereby, I suppose, saving the life of one of them. Captain ——— was shot by a rebel; the bullet entered his chin and passed out through his left ear. I helped carry him about a mile and a half to the hospital, while solid shot fell thick and fast around us and very near.

I have many things to tell you, but cannot write more now. I trust I shall see you before many weary months pass away and speak face to face. I have a great love for the Bap-tist church at Mount Holly, and have been hoping and pray-ing for a great outpouring of the Holy Spirit there. I hope the Lord will give you the power of breaking many a hard and sinful heart. My respects to all of good will. My kind regards to all your family.

Yours in Christian bonds,

L.—— S——.

To REV. SAMUEL AARON.

PHILADELPHIA, April 13, 1865.

Dear Brother—Your kind favor of yesterday is just received. I am truly sorry that I am unable to attend the funeral of precious Brother Aaron, but I am quite ill and under the doctor's hands. For no man living had I more respect than for Samuel Aaron. One of nature's noblemen, he grew in my love and admiration at every interview. Brilliant talents, sound learning, unfailing industry and symmetrical piety, distinguished him on all occasions. Few have his courage, and still fewer his strong common sense. Oh, what a loss he is to the militant church. I rejoice that he lived to see the opinions as to justice to the black man, for which he suffered ignominy and reproach, become the sentiments of the nation. He suffered the fate of all who are in advance of their age; but his God has crowned him with honor and eternal life. I hope the family will send to the Historical Society his likeness, and any manuscripts or other mementoes, to be preserved in its archives. I hope, too, that his pamphlets will not go to the paper mill, at least not until such as should be treasured up, where they will be useful, are gathered out.

Yours in the great bond,

HOWARD MALCOM.

To MR. C. E. A.

———

[EXTRACT FROM A LETTER FROM REV. WILLIAM SCOTT.]

April 14, 1865.

When I heard of Brother Aaron's death, I felt that I had lost a personal friend, one to whose instructions, counsels and prayers, I was greatly indebted during the hazardous period of youth. The cause of truth has lost one of her most faithful, earnest and eloquent advocates. Though "the good which men do is oft interred with their bones," it will not be so with our highly esteemed brother. His works will live after him. The freedmen of to-day are under lasting obligations to one who was the staunch advocate of the rights of man; the bitter foe of oppression in all its forms. Many, no doubt, were delivered from the curse of intemperance through his efforts or taught to shun the intoxicating cup. His influence upon the young men who enjoyed his instruction was, I believe, of the most salutary character.

-- ------- -

PHILADELPHIA, April 29, 1865.

Yours of the 27th inst. has just come to hand, and I hasten to reply. When I left you the day of the funeral of your venerable and honored father, I did fully expect to write to you soon, but other duties have put this out of the question. Yesterday I received a letter from Dr. Nathan Brown of the *American Baptist*, New York, requesting me to prepare a memoir of your dear father. I replied to Dr. B—— that I was incapable of doing anything like justice to such a man; such a Christian; such a Christian reformer; for I did not think we had the like of him in our denomination. The man, the scholar, his spirit, principles, labors and triumphs, demanded something more than I was competent to prepare. I therefore suggested that the Board of the American Baptist Free Mission Society, at their meeting on the 8th of May, would appoint a committee of three, Rev. A. L. Post, C. E. Aaron and myself, to prepare or provide such a notice of your father's life and character as was due to the cause he served. I shall in all probability go on to attend the meeting of the Board to further this object. Rev. J. Hyatt Smith, and others, suggest that we should publish a small volume, as hundreds would want it. If you have anything to suggest in this matter, I should be pleased to hear from you next week. There was no man on earth that I loved and tried to honor as I did your father. He made me a better man and a better Christian, and more determined to live, suffer and die, if need be, for our principles.

To MR. C. E. A.

FREE MISSION ANNIVERSARY—ADDRESS OF THE PRESIDENT.

May 8, 1865.

* * * Our song is still "of mercy and judgment." The rebellion which has for four years afflicted our country, the most gigantic in history, is virtually crushed, and slavery, "the sum of all villainies," its cause, in its organic iniquity, is virtually dead. * * * All loyal hearts must rejoice with exceeding joy. And yet, too, we mourn. * * * Among the many thousands who have fallen victims to the slave power, or have been offered as martyrs upon the altar of country and freedom, Abraham Lincoln, our late President, honored as no other man in this country has been honored, stands most conspicuous. * * * He died a martyr to liberty; and well may the nation mourn. We, as a society, mourn, and well we may, one not so honored in obsequies, not having so world-wide a fame as the lamented President of the United States, and yet, in many respects, greater than he. Our beloved brother, Samuel Aaron, one of our oldest members, brightest and most cultivated intellects, noblest hearts, and most eloquent advocates, has finished his work on earth; and after seeing the dawning of triumph for the cause in which he had so long and devotedly labored and sacrificed, has gone to rest with other kindred spirits in the bosom of him whom they had served and loved. He died, true, not by the hand of violence, but disease took him in the quietness of home, and he passed away in the conscious triumph of the Christian's hope. While rejoicing in this, we bow and weep over our loss, and in deepest sympathy with the loss of his bereaved family. Let due honor be given to his memory. When our giant republic was held in the slimy folds of slavery, and our government bowed to its behest; when it was a signal for political proscription and impunity for mob violence to speak of liberty and the rights of humanity, with the few, he stood up in his noble manhood, and thundered God's anathemas against the national guilt. When the churches were made to bow in silence to the slave power, and D. D.s even to quote texts of Scripture for its encouragement and support, he, in the face of proscription and denun-

ciation as a fanatic, lifted up his voice like a trumpet, and showed the people their transgressions and the churches their sins. With a power of argument and eloquence of language and pathos unsurpassed, he swept away the cobweb of pro-slavery sophistry, and in the light of an unperverted Bible and a pure Christianity, raised the humblest and most degraded slave to the dignity of an equal manhood and Christian brotherhood. When the tide of intemperance was deluging the country, and drunkard-makers were made honorable by public opinion and public law, he stemmed the current, gave a helping hand to the poor inebriate, and at the expense of stripes many, poured burning truth and stern rebuke upon the consciences of those who had made him such. Beloved by the poor and oppressed for his deep sympathy and liberal-ity in the hearts of all who loved purity, truth and moral cou-rage; admired by even those who, in their time serving, feared him, and hated only by the vile, he lived. Among the world's noble men, her educators, her patriots, her preachers of the Gospel, and Christian philanthropists, he stood and labored in the front rank. He rests now from his labors, and his works do follow him. It will be ours, individually, sooner or later, to follow; and heaven grant that our work, accord-ing to our several capacities, may be as well done, and our death as triumphant as his.

NEW LONDON, PENNA., April 18, 1865.

My Dear Niece—On my return from the meeting of our Presbytery last week, I received letters from my brothers William and Louis, giving me the unexpected and startling tidings of the death of your father, who was also my own dear friend and brother. I also received on Saturday, at noon, an invitation to myself and family to attend his funeral. It was a matter of much regret to me that I could not see my way clear to be with you on that mournful occasion. Though sad in itself, there would have been a kind of sorrowful satisfaction in thus witnessing the last on earth of one whom I so highly esteemed. But as it was on Saturday, and I could not return the same day, I did not feel at liberty to disappoint the people by leaving my pulpit vacant. I have since received a letter from Louis, giving me an account of the funeral and of the exercises connected with it, and was gratified to hear of the very large and serious assembly that came together to pay their last tribute of respect and affection to the memory of their departed friend and pastor.

Your late father and I were once closely and intimately connected in business, and otherwise, for five or six years. During that period, and often at other times, I had frequent opportunities of observing his character as a teacher, a minister of Christ, a citizen, a moral reformer, a husband and father and friend, and a Christian man. He was certainly a very able, talented and faithful instructor of youth. His former pupils are scattered by hundreds all over this land; and whatever of good they may do, he has helped to prepare them to do it. As a preacher, he possessed a rare and a stirring eloquence. He loved his country, and stood by it in its darkest hours. How manfully he battled for temperance and for freedom every one knows. I have seen him in some of the most trying scenes of domestic life, when bereavements touched his heart, but he bowed his head to the storm, and could say, "Thy will be done!" What he was as a father you very well know; and what he was as a friend I have reason to know. He was true and faithful to me; helped me in my difficulties; and though we have been much separated for many years, I have reason to believe that he never forgot the friendship of our earlier life. But what was better than all these, he loved Jesus, trusted in him, followed him, and served him. That blessed Saviour has at last released him from his labors on earth, and said to him, "Friend, come up higher!" You, and all his family, his people and his friends mourn, but he is rejoicing. We have lost for a season one that we loved; he has gone to his rest and entered the kingdom of glory.

When I met him last month at brother Charles's funeral, he was talking about his good health; said that he had not yet begun to feel that he was growing old; "but this event," said he, referring to your uncle's death, "has impressed it more powerfully upon me than anything that has ever occurred, for we were very nearly of the same age." Little did I then think that in one short month he too would be numbered with the dead. But such is life. We are here to-day; to-morrow we are in eternity. Oh, how important that we should ever be found waiting and watching for the coming of the son of man.

I trust that a kind Providence will watch over you all, your mother, your sisters and yourself. Please give our kind regards to your mother, your sisters, and your brother and his family. May our Heavenly Father sustain and bless you all.

Your affectionate uncle,

ROBERT P. DU BOIS.

MRS. M. D. WIEGAND.

———————

NEW YORK, June 6, 1865.

My Dear Friend—I view Brother Aaron's death as a great national and denominational calamity. I loved him as I love only a few, though I had not the pleasure of knowing him intimately. He was one of the few who are what God intended to make when he created Adam—a man. He strove to be what a man ought to be, what God requires. For his honest, lofty, godly manliness, his generous and religious benevolence, his unsullied purity and unselfishness, I loved him, and do mourn his loss as a dear personal friend. God had gifted him as only a few are endowed, with a mind of the first and highest order; for this I admired him. Oh, how it does seem as if we could not spare him. He was greatly missed at our anniversary in everything. But God knows what is best. You must all be deeply grieved. You better and only know what a vacuum is made by his removal. I seem to realize almost how I should feel if I had been daily accustomed to listen to his wisdom and look upon his unsurpassed loveliness. I need not repeat to you what you realize too keenly. I am not trying to write you a letter to express something that will please you. What I have said is purely accidental, and I hope you will excuse it, but allow me to say

for my own relief what wells up in my mind almost every day
as I think of him.   It is pleasurable and painful in equal degrees to have had so loved a friend.   We never shall see his
like again, I fear.   Would we might.   Will you please express my regard and sympathy to your mother.

Yours truly,   John Duer.

—— ——— —

Bordentown, October 10, 1865.

My Dear Sister in Christ—At the last meeting of the
West New Jersey Baptist Association, with which your husband was connected at the time of his decease, by virtue of
being pastor of the Mount Holly Baptist Church, it was voted
a letter of condolence to you should be forwarded from me,
expressive of our deep sense of your loss, and the high esteem
in which your companion was held by us all.   It has always
seemed to me that flattery of the living deserves reprehension;
but when death has divided us from the loved, the good and
the true, it is not only well, but wise, to call up in remember-
ance their virtues, and make mention of them to others, that
they may escape the grave's oblivion, and stimulate the living
to emulate them.

Your dear husband was one to whom nature was prodigal
in her best gifts; and assiduous application to study, and a
long course of teaching, had enlarged the original bounty,
while the workings of divine grace had carried him quite well
along towards the point of a perfectly ripe Christian manhood.
He was born to be no idler in whatever field his lot might be
cast; and his native humanity, largely improved by the spirit
of that Gospel which he preached, made him see the two common wrongs, under which the poor and weak suffer and groan;
and it would have been a violation of all that was good and
noble in him to have kept silent.   You know he always took
the part of such; hence his life could not have been expected
to be free from turbulence.   But all grows quiet when the
turf lies on his breast; and even the oppressor, called back to
a better consciousness, has tears for his memory and words of

praise for his broad humanity and Christian fidelity. Few men have been followed to the grave by truer friends or more tender recollections. Our Association, in which he was long known, and which had honored him with its highest gifts, did not refrain from tears at the mention of his name in its last meeting. He was largely what he was in those things which endeared him to us most, by the influence and effects of the Gospel on him and in him, a humble, conscientious Christian man.

All we can say to you is, that the loss of such a husband is to sustain a loss for which there is no earthly measure; and in such a deprivation only one can come near enough to comfort and support, and that is Christ the Lord. But the period of separation from the departed cannot be long, for the distance of travel is shortened by every setting sun, and the end of Christian journey is in "our Father's house on high." Certainly, to you, sister, the boundary stream that divides the wilderness from the promised land is not far away; perhaps, sometimes it seems almost in sight; and the beautiful words of another may not be inappropriate to you in your longings and loneliness.

> "Now I sit and think when the sunset's gold
>   Is flushing river and hill and shore,
> I shall one day stand by the water cold,
>   And list for the sound of the boatman's oar;
> I shall watch for a gleam of the flapping sail,
>   I shall hear the boat as it gains the strand,
> I shall pass from sight with the boatman pale
>   To the better shore of the spirit land.
> I shall know the loved who have gone before,
>   And joyfully sweet will the meeting be
> When over the river, the peaceful river,
>   The angel of Death shall carry me."

In behalf of the Association, as well as with feelings of respect and deep sympathy,

I am truly yours,   A. P. BUEL.

MRS. E. G. AARON.

WASHINGTON, D. C., October 25, 1889.

My Dear Miss Aaron—I received your letter of the 8th
inst., and was very glad to learn that something was about to
be done to commemorate the life and work of your dear, distinguished father, whom I loved and venerated above all men
I ever knew. After he came to Mount Holly I had the grati-
fication of being much in his company and learning more of
his excellence than I had ever before had opportunity. Prior
to that time I had only seen and heard him occasionally when
he came there to preach and lecture on temperance. The first
time I ever heard him was about 1847 or 1848, during the war
with Mexico, when he came to attend a Baptist Association
and addressed it at a night session upon the war with Mexico,
which he denounced with all the energy he possessed as a war
for the extension and perpetuation of human slavery. Few men
at that time, of any profession, would have dared to speak as
did he; but his courage never failed him in warring against
wrong. I regret that I have not been able to find all his letters, as I have always prized them so highly and shown them
with so much satisfaction to my friends, which will explain
their worn condition. My estimate of your father during our
long intimacy was and is that he was not only the best man I
ever knew but the most eloquent, and in that I was fully sustained by two friends whose good judgment was acknowledged
by all who knew them, and they knew him well.

One morning on the cars from Burlington to Philadelphia
I met William R. Allen, ex-Mayor and ex-State Senator, and
John C. Deacon, a well known Quaker. On the way they
spoke of Mr. Aaron, who had decided to come to Mount
Holly, and expressed their regret that he did not decide in
favor of Burlington, as they had always listened to his addresses with so much delight while in Burlington, where he
had spent several years in connection with the Gummeres in
their large school, and where he preached for several years. In
the course of conversation Mr. Allen said, in his very sober
and deliberate way, "I have heard many of the most eminent
preachers and statesmen, and am free to say that Samuel Aaron
is the most eloquent man I have ever heard"; when Friend

Deacon said, "I agree with thee in that opinion fully, and regret that he did not cast his lot with us in Burlington."

Nor is that the only evidence of the correctness of my judgment in that respect, as upon another occasion when I accompanied him to New York in September, 1860, to attend the annual meeting of the American Bible Union, at which Prof. Hackett's revision of Paul's Epistle to Philemon was to be considered. Mr. Aaron took serious exception to it because of his making Onesimus in a lengthy argument in his accompanying notes a slave of Philemon, while in the Epistle he termed him a servant. The convention was held in a Baptist church and presided over by Dr. ———. The body of the church was filled largely by delegates, ministerial and lay, Mr. Aaron and myself sitting in the front pew at the right of the platform, on which was seated the committee of final revision, composed of nine Doctors of Divinity, all of whom took occasion to speak in defence of their report and complimentary of the work of Prof. Hackett, and the Secretary read from a number of leading newspapers complimentary notices of Prof. Hackett's work. When Dr. ——— arose to put the question on the adoption of the report of the committee, Mr. Aaron arose and made the most eloquent speech I ever listened to against it, the effect of which exceeded anything I ever witnessed or ever expect to. For some time not a word was spoken; the convention seemed to have been paralyzed by his anti-slavery utterances, and after a long and painful pause a lay delegate from Philadelphia moved that the report be referred back to the committee with instructions to report in accordance with the sentiments expressed by Brother Aaron, which was done without a word of objection by the committee who had commended it so highly. The conservative spirit was then so potent that not one of the daily papers reported the speech; and the only paper that gave any report of it was the *American Baptist*, which was but a brief one, as they had but brief notes.

In the summer of 1864, soon after I came to Washington, Mr. Aaron requested me in one of his letters to call on his old friend, Thaddeus Stevens, and sent me a note of introduction, that I presented one evening soon after, and was heartily welcomed. Mr. Stevens expressed himself very glad to hear from him, and speaking in a very solemn tone said, "Samuel Aaron is of the salt of the earth; no better man than he has lived, in my opinion, since St. Paul." He told me much of their long intimate intercourse as co-workers in Pennsylvania in behalf of education, temperance and abolition of human slavery, and invited me to call and see him often, saying he should always be glad to hear from his old friend.

In June, 1864, and again in the spring of 1865, as you will see by the letters, I made arrangements with Dr. Channing, then Chaplain to Congress, for Mr. Aaron to preach in the hall of the House of Representatives, a notice of which Mr. Stevens was to write, to be published in the newspapers in advance of his coming; but in consequence of delay from miscarriage of letters, and the near approach of the close of the session, he decided to defer it, partly on account of the many daily duties devolving upon him. I was very sorry he declined coming, and so also was Dr. Channing.

Until receiving your letter I was not aware that anything emanating from him had ever been published, or anything relating to him, and should be glad to have a copy of the pamphlet, as I prize highly everything connected with his name. I send you what letters I have, to make use of as you propose, and hope you may be successful, with the promised aid, to present a creditable sketch of your deceased father, who was so much loved by all who knew him.

Sincerely your friend,   CHARLES S. BATES.

Mount Holly, April 12, 1865.

My Dear Friends—I hasten to express the deep sympathy I feel for you in your great bereavement, and shall be thankful to serve you in any way I can. We must all feel that a good and useful soul has left this world to commence in a higher state of existence a life still more useful and active because unimpeded by a feeble and suffering body. Our dear friend was retained here long enough to see the fulfillment of his most earnest wishes, for which he labored so faithfully. Truly we can say of him, he dared to do right. Who would wish a more noble epitaph. I pray that you may be supported in your affliction.

Believe me very sincerely your friend,

C. L. R.

Mrs. E. G. Aaron.

[Extract of Letter from J. W. Loch, Ph. D.]

Norristown, January 21, 1889.

Miss Aaron—The memory of your father is dear to many Norristown people, and he has left his impress upon this community more fully than any other man who has lived here; and while many differed from him then, all now agree that he was the pioneer of many righteous reforms.

Plainfield N. J., November 25, 1889.

My Dear Miss Aaron—I am glad that you are about to write a sketch of your father's life, and am glad of the opportunity given me to subscribe for it. The memory of so great and good a man ought to be preserved so as to be an inspiration to those who are to come after those of us who knew and loved him. A generation has grown up that scarcely knows that there was among us so recently a man who, in some respects, stood among the men of his own gen-

eration almost without a peer.   My brother, the late Judge
Yerkes of Philadelphia, was one of your father's pupils, and
his admiration of your father was unbounded.   That was the
feeling of all his pupils whom I have ever met.

Most truly,

D. J. YERKES.

AMESBURY, MASS., First-month 3, 1889.

Dear Friend—I knew thy father very well in the years
1838, '39 and '40.   He was one of the truest and bravest of
my anti-slavery friends—a Christian gentleman.   I have always remembered him with affectionate interest.

Thy friend,

JOHN G. WHITTIER.

To L. C. AARON.

[EXTRACT OF LETTER FROM HON. THOS. ADAMSON, U. S. CONSULATE GENERAL.]

PANAMA, January 10, 1890.

Dear Miss Aaron—I have just received your letter of the
23d ult. on the subject of the book you are about to have published, which is to contain a sketch of the life of your father,
with some of his sermons, lectures, etc.

I am very glad to learn that there is a prospect that we
may soon have such a memorial of one of the best and one of
the *most truly great* men our country has ever produced.   To
those who never had the privilege of knowing the Reverend
Samuel Aaron, my admiration for him might seem to be almost
idolatrous; but to you, his daughter, who know so well his
greatness of mind, the nobility of his nature, and the tenderness
and warmth of his affections—to you I need not explain *why*
I loved him.

I cannot claim to have been one of his "good boys," for
I often incurred his displeasure and no doubt gave him cause

for anxiety as to my future. Like others of his pupils, I sometimes had to have interviews with him in a private room—interviews that were not of my seeking; but I always left his
presence with the feeling that he had tried to be thoroughly
just, and that a reasonable explanation of seeming misconduct
would always receive his full consideration. The only things
of which he was altogether intolerant were deceit and plain
falsehood.

If our national politics had ever been sufficiently pure to
enable him to have secured a seat in the Congress of the nation, he would have shown himself to be a head and shoulders
above the average of the men around him and the peer of the
greatest of them. I have heard some of the greatest orators
of the last fifty years, but I never heard such a thrilling speech,
such words of burning eloquence, as when during the old
anti-slavery days he addressed a great audience in Norristown
on the subject of the attempt of the slave-hunters to capture
the runaway slave "Bill" at Wilkesbarre. I see him now as
if it were yesterday, the tears coursing down his cheeks as he
described the poor hunted slave plunging into the icy torrent
of the river to escape the human bloodhounds. There were
many in that audience who were unused to the melting mood,
but there were few if any whose tears of sympathy failed to
flow then. Even now, after a lapse of almost forty years, my
cheeks are wet as I recall the incident and the impressive manner in which it was described.

With the memory of my good, loving and strictly conscientious parents I shall always associate that of my dearly
beloved teacher, the truly Reverend Samuel Aaron, and of
that most excellent woman, your beloved mother.

Boys are irreverent creatures and often apply appellatives
to those they love which may sound disrespectful. You, however, will not misunderstand me when I say that more than
any diploma of the greatest of our universities do I prize the
distinction of having been "one of Sammy Aaron's boys."
You will hardly need to be told, then, how glad I shall be to
have you put my name on your list of subscribers. * * *

Sincerely your friend,

Thomas Adamson.

MOUNT HOLLY, N. J., September 15, 1862.

Dear Sir—Learning within a day or two, on supposed good authority, that you regard American slavery to be an institution compatible with the teachings of the Old and New Testaments, and believing, myself, exactly the contrary, I thought it best not to attend the prayer-meeting without further consideration. I should be afraid of disturbing the harmony of the meeting, as conscience would demand, that God would lead the whole nation to repent of slave-holding as our greatest national sin. I should feel compelled to name that and other sins, and should feel a sort of devout indignation rather than brotherly union at hearing the vague phrases, "sin," "transgression," "iniquity," "unholiness," etc., repeated for an hour. In the deepest convictions of my heart, I feel that in this matter of slave-holding, my country has made, or tried to make, a "covenant with death and a league with hell;" and I expect no rest for the people, North or South, till the nation confesses its sin in oppressing the poor and the innocent, and does the work meet for repentance, by proclaiming "liberty throughout the land to all its inhabitants." If it is thought that such feelings, earnestly uttered, would profit the prayer-meeting, I shall be glad to attend.

Yours truly for the oppressed,

SAMUEL AARON.

TO REV. —— ——.

ANTI-COLONIZATION.

REVIEW OF REV. MR. PEASE,

ODD FELLOWS' HALL, March 10, 1854.

Ladies and Gentlemen—I appear before you this evening with the most sincere and earnest purpose to vindicate what I believe to be truth and benevolence, and to oppose, with all the might that God has given me, falsehood, injustice and oppression. I intend to make my appeal to reason, to facts and to justice, and to them alone. There is no occasion for me, nor those that I represent, to invoke the applause of the people; and I sincerely hope that there may be no disposition in this assembly, or the part of it who sympathize with me, to give me any applause except that which may consist in a quiet and patient hearing, nor to express opposition in that manner against those who may differ from us in their views, though they differ even rudely. Let us show, my friends, that we stand upon the merit of the principles which we advocate, that we ask no favors, that we grant all justice, that we even grant more—that we are willing to be abused, injured and misrepresented. I hope, then, that we shall be quiet. I hope it may please all to be quiet. If there is anybody that does not want to be quiet, let him take the responsibility of his position. We need not take any appeal to the mob—the mob in satin and in broadcloth, nor the mob in rags and tatters, for these two extremes of society are very apt to come very close together. There are many men in all communities, and especially in this, who have manly thoughts and manly purposes, whether in broadcloth or in cassinet. To them I appeal; and for everybody else I don't care much, I tell you, and you know it. [Laughter.] I work for nothing and find myself, and the person who does this it is pretty hard to stop.

This is a question that is to be settled by evidence, and that evidence I intend, as far as time will allow me, to present before you this evening. It has been said very lately, if you will permit me to be so personal for a moment, that I was never before put down. It has been recorded in a most respectable paper of this town that the other evening I was put down. A reverend reporter for that paper, as I am very credibly informed he is, states that I was stamped down, that I was hissed down. Well, now, it is true that while I was down I was kept down by that kind of operation, whether to my own glory or to the glory of those who used the means it is not for me to say. I was stamped down, I was hissed down; but I can truly say that neither myself nor my friends, at any time, in this community, have resorted to stamping down or hissing down. We have always been perfectly willing to listen with respect. We have not stamped; we have not groaned; we have not hooted, nor whistled, nor hissed, to stop any sort of man, drunk or sober, from expressing an idea, or a fragment of an idea, if he happened to have any such about him. For myself, I never was put down before; and I have met, in this very place, the drunken mob, the profane mob, the street mob, the "old court-house" mob, the political mob, furious mobs of every description. With these I have always got along with tolerable satisfaction.

It then must be taken for granted that this was a very different mob, and so it was. Why this, my friends, was not a profane mob, nor a street mob, nor a political mob, nor a court-house mob, nor a brutal mob; this was a colonization mob. This was not a sacrilegious mob; this was a holy mob, this was a dignified mob [laughter], this was a colonization mob. [Applause and laughter.] I do not want anybody to stamp but a deacon. [Continued laughter.] I say in the distinguished opposition sat an eminent clergyman with heels, hands and head going; at a little distance off, a little further from the platform, sat the starry lights of the colonization dignitaries, Olympian Jove in the centre, and all the lesser divinities around about him. There they sat in dignity while groans and hisses, and whistling, and squealing, and other such noises, were going on around them. A little further along there were

the ruling elders, the leaders of the pious societies and com-
panies,—there they were, stamping and clapping; and a little
further from them were the boys and young men. These were
lifting up the benches and letting them fall again, to keep up
the noise; and at the very tail end was the poor ragged rab-
ble, that were in unison with the rest, head, neck, heart and
body. These were the sanctified ones of the colonization society. There I, poor man, was down on the broad of my back,
it is true. I had to be still, for the most part, and the further
I went the worse it got. The question I was particularly desirous to ask was, Who is authorized to explain the doctrines
and principles of colonization? There stood the reverend orator; he gave me no quarter, he would answer not my question, Who is the person to expound the principles of colonization? We are told that Henry Clay was not, and I, in the
sincerity of my soul, wanted to know. I have asked again
and again who is prepared and authorized to answer this question; to tell us what colonization is; what its principles are.
Who? I ask, Who? Echo answers, Who? And I presume
we never shall know who is to tell us the meaning of colonization. It is a matter of testimony, and we want to know before we can be decided. You may ask what my religion is,
and I can tell you; but you do not go to Matthew, Mark,
Luke, John, Peter and Paul, in this matter. [Laughter.]
There is no such mark that has been revealed yet, but the
thing is good; it is unexceptionably right, and there can be
no mistake. And this is all we know about it.

I am now going to examine very briefly the testimony of
Bishop Scott. I suppose most of you have read it; and it was
said in that testimony that "all positions taken by those in opposition to me were right, and those positions taken by me
were wrong." Now, for the Bishop. I have no doubt at all
that he was an upright and truthful man. If I am not sincere,
he will tell you; you will find it out. But these Bishops are
very ecclesiastical men, and those that are the most devoted
among them are the most ecclesiastical. There are some exceptions, however. There is the Right Reverend Alonzo Potter, a man remarkable for his general knowledge and liberal
principles, and for piety. And there is my good friend, Bishop

Paine, with his poor little flock about him, against which the
wolves howl and yell terribly. Bishop Scott acknowledges, at
least, his incompetence to speak in this matter. And now
just hear him. [The speaker here reads from the testimony
referred to, at the same time making remarks on certain passages.] Haven't I got him here, hooped up? You do not
suppose I'm blaming the Bishop, do you? I know but little
about him. He tells us he never was ashore but once.
He went there and came away, and I guess that was two
days. That was the only time that he was ashore. I say put
on a Bishop's ecclesiastical dress, and send him here to Norristown upon an ecclesiastical errand, and I say he can't find
out much. He ought to come here to-night to learn human
nature. But he is among the good men, the good clergy, the
good ladies; among the pious people. What does he know
about Tom, Dick and Harry, and all those who make up the
bone and muscle of society? It is not in him to know. [Reads
again.] Well, now, the Bishop does not believe that domestic
slavery exists there. Why, you might go down, as a Bishop,
into the Southern states, and come to the sage conclusion that
Mississippi and Alabama were the very seventh heaven of
negro bliss—they would use you there so well. "My dear
sir, how have you been? I am extremely glad to see you.
It does my soul good to see a man of God among us, and I
have great satisfaction and great comfort in your society."
They don't go out to see what is going on among the poor
blacks. It would ruffle their robes, it would hurt their feelings, it would distress them, if they were to come in contact
with such things as these. [Reads again, and speaks of the
blacks in connection with schools and churches.] It is not,
after all, the law or the rule that makes the objection; it is the
prejudice, it is the feeling, it is the contempt.

There are churches even here where they cannot go, they
are so holy; the men in them so holy; in the churches where
the colored man cannot come. They have a hatred against
this poor people, whom they regard as a caste, a down-trodden
race, and whom they think it true glory to trample upon.
Friendless, alone, oppressed, injured by our government; all
its power at work, particularly at this time, to outrage them;

therefore they are not allowed to come into their churches.
[Reads.]

He tells us in another report that there is not a single
public school in the whole colony of Liberia, yet they are
better of, have better advantages, than in this country. Have
not we got a public school in this town, a respectable colored
school here, where they may be instructed in the branches of
useful knowledge, and where they may even learn the Latin
language. Yet the Bishop tells us they are better provided
for in that country, there where there are no public schools,
than they are in these very states, here where they are among
schools. And in these very states there are colleges, too,
where colored women and colored men may go and get an
education, bad as we are. And yet the Bishop tells us they
are too poor to obtain their own schooling; and if there is any
school at all, it is kept by Methodist missionaries who are sent
there. Yet they are better off there.

I might have said a word about the post-offices. A man
may go there and write a letter, and it may not be interfered
with in the post-office; it may come safely through. Do you
think that letter written for the ignorant black man, who sits
by, not knowing what its contents are, think you that the
authorities of Liberia would undertake to stop that letter?
Oh, no; it is the poor people; these are the ones that feel
that pressure. The Bishop's letters go free; and that is a
proof, as strong as holy writ, that there is no overbearing
power poured upon the wronged and the unhappy.

It is no proof for me. [Refers again to the testimony.]
He could not go ashore one single night for fear he would be
taken sick and his mission should not be carried out. He
says "I cannot answer as to the provision." This, one of our
worthy ladies certified, that "the officers of the government
did use surreptitiously the good provisions and give them bad
and damaged food." He says, "I cannot answer as to the
provision; officers may sometimes look after their own interests, just as they do in this country." Maybe they do; don't
know; let that pass. [Quotes further.] "There is no ab-
straction that I know of." Poor soul! I will just leave him
in your hands, but do not take him about your heels, take

him to your brains and use him well. [Reads.] The custom
is to bribe these poor people, and give them a pretty good
share of rum, and then they will listen, and then they say, "he
good man; he fine man." [Testimony concerning the doctrines inculcated.] There is the testimony of the Bishop, and
I leave it for reasonable men to consider and say whether it is
at all calculated to promote the religion of the meek and lowly
Jesus; a religion which I love; in which my hope and joy
are based.

I am now going to turn to some more testimony. Remember, my friends, this is only testimony, and it is my business to show that it is an invalid testimony. [Here he speaks
of the testimony of Thomas Morris Chester.] Cheap servants
there; nothing to wear; don't have to put anything on them,
you know [laughter]; very cheap. Now I thought that this
young man told such a beautiful and rose-colored story that
I would like to hear further about him, so I wrote to a gentleman in Harrisburg. A brave and fearless, upright, noble
man. Oh, I must not praise him too much or else I will catch
the infection. I wrote to them to tell me something about
this Thomas Morris Chester. [He here read the letter that
was received in answer to his inquiries.] It is almost two
sides to the story, isn't it? Well, now we are told that that
gentleman is soon to appear here on this platform to enlighten
us. I learn further from Mr. James Miller McKim, whose
veracity no man dare impeach. I spoke to him about this
famous Thomas Morris Chester; he went away and got his
"Ledger"; his "Pennsylvania Freeman" ledger; he opened
it and showed me that he had sent for the paper, and had received it two years, and had not paid one cent of his subscrip-
tion. This is the gentleman that is to be here to enlighten
you.

The next subject we come to is a remarkable man. My
friend was scolding me for having so many documents here.
We have had a great deal without documents; we now must
make free use of them. There has been something said about
me being a "bumping buck." [Laughter.] Now, you know,
I am as gentle as a lamb; I never yet delivered a "colonization" lecture. We have had here a most distinguished orator

(counts the lectures delivered); he has given nine bumps to my one; and if there is any "bumping buck," I think somebody else had better take it on his horns besides me. [Laughter.] My head must be very hard and my horns very sharp to resist them. [Slight confusion and attempted applause.] No! no! none but the ruling elders. Don't want common people to stamp. [Laughter.] If there are any clergy among you, you may stamp. There are two constables here. [Laughter.] [Here he reads a document on colonization.]

We are told on still higher authority than this, gentlemen, that "the slave trade had been exterminated for three thousand miles upon the African coast." This had been accomplished by this "Liberian Colony"; not quite so big, and certainly not so rich, as Norristown. This gentleman says, "if the American squadron should be taken away"—remember he is the commander of it—"then the slave trade would be renewed and extended." These don't exactly agree; but great men differ. I desired the name of this gentleman. I civilly asked, Will the speaker be so kind as to tell me the name of the gentleman? I was referred to the Secretary of the Navy; and by writing to him I could probably find out. Well, that brought down a roar, a hissing and stamping, while every man in that assembly, poor soul, could say "pease." I still insisted upon my question being answered. At length it came out, "Isaac Mayho." Yes, Isaac Mayho. Now we have him. The business he follows is rearing slaves and selling them off to the highest bidder. This man might'well say that he wished to suppress the foreign slave trade, because he is the most interested in the domestic slave trade. This is the man, as I learned from gentlemen in Philadelphia, who is a drunken, brutal rowdy and a ruffian. This Isaac Mayho But you need not wonder that such men are employed by the government. Mrs. Stowe, that excellent authority that was quoted and dwelt upon here so eloquently, declares that "this domestic slave breeding" (she calls it breeding) amounts to eighty thousand slaves that are bred for market every year. Then talk about the slave trade on the African coast. Now, hiss! the own shame and love of your country.

I love my country. I tell my country of her wrongs. I do not first throw myself into the hands of the North, and then into the hands of the South. I love the truth, and will stand on it and die by it, to the end. [He now refers to a letter from C. Morris.] He is a first-rate man, kind of Quaker Episcopalian; was bred a Quaker, and became an Episcopal minister. Such a man can't be beat, I take it. [Laughter.] He married a slaveholder's daughter, and to his infinite credit be it spoken, as soon as his father-in-law died, the will favored Dr. Morris, and the whole family agreed that they would set free all their slaves. The slaves of Mr. Justin, of Maryland, were then set free; he was a near neighbor of Mayho. [Speaks of Richard Neal. Gives an account of an affair in which Neal and his family were the sufferers.]

Now, let us have Robert Cushman. He says, "As to the slave trade being completely extirpated by the Republic of Liberia, there is no man under the heaven that believes it; that thing is impossible. Is there a man among us here who believes that that little colony can drive off the slave trade from the coast of Africa? The power of England could not do it. Where is the reverend gentleman to-night? Does he believe it? No! no! no! It can't be done. The whole naval force of the Republic consists of one man-of-war—a schooner, and that was presented by Queen Victoria. Now, Queen Victoria recognizes this government. She also recognizes the mosquito government, Guatemala. It is said there are two sloops, of two guns each. No one of these vessels would be capable of contending with a slaver as ordinarily equipped. Do you believe this squadron capable of extirpating the trade from a coast three thousand miles in extent? You can't believe; you dare not say it. The slave trade is carried on there.

Lieutenant Forbes talked about that. Dr. Bacon talked about that, and he published it in his own paper; and he published it when Governor Roberts was in New York, and he did it because they were about, and he said to them, "Contradict, if you dare." They didn't do it. [He referred to a letter from Lewis Tappan.] This gentleman says that slaves can be purchased from the natives for articles of goods worth

four or five dollars. Now, you may call them slaves, or something else. I say slavery is this: Suppose you catch me, and
put me in the power of my friend Hooven—and, by the way,
he is about as good a master as I would wish to have—you
put me in his power; then I am his. You may give me a
gold watch and chain, if you like; but they don't do that there.
Put a few clothes on them and sell them for five dollars each.
[He here quotes Cushman.] He says the slaves are cruelly
treated. The instrument of torture is a whip containing a
number of large lashes with knots on the ends. With these
the slaves are scourged on their bare backs, until, in some
places, the flesh is laid open in large gashes. Now, you may
call them slaves or not; I don't care what you call them. The
slaves, it is said, are in a degraded condition. They go to
church and are made to sit outside of the door; and if they
go inside to sit on the floor. [Refers to Cushman.] It is a
slaughter house; it is a place of skulls. [The speaker here
called upon a gentleman present, Mr. Robert Purvis, to bear
witness to a certain fact.] He said, "My friend has called
upon me, and I have to say that John B. Russell, who was
President of the Colony after the auspices of the American
Colonization Society, said, that the once colonial Secretary of
Liberia, the editor of the 'Dingy Sheet,' stood convicted in
the court for having facilitated the trade in slaves in that
colony." [Mr. A. continues.] To throw such masses of
ignorance and barbarity upon a foreign shore is both cruel
and wicked. Who are these men? These people are said to
be so degraded. We are told that they are the worst race on
the earth. One of the worst races upon the earth. That they
are incapable of being reached by Christianity. Will salt
water purify them? Make a heaven out of Liberia. Now, I
do not believe that they are a worse race than some of the
rest of us. They are my brethren; I hold them as such; I
mean to treat them as such if these colonizationists will let
me. [Reads from another document in reference to a Presbyterian Board of Missionaries sent out to Liberia.] "I have
heard it said here that there have been slaves shipped out of
this colony for the last year, and many emancipated slaves
have died from the force of the climate," etc.

I think I have cut out a little more work than I can sew up to-night, and it is now nine o'clock. [Cries of Go on! go on!] Now I do not know, but you may be in a pretty good humor to-night; it is not often that I please people. I always had politicians on my back, but I have generally succeeded in getting along somehow. Now, when I heard of the colony of Liberia emancipating eight hundred thousand slaves; when I heard all that, I felt a little wicked. I did. I went to Mr. S—— and said that was not true. Said he, "It is. I will take my oath upon it." "I will too." "Your oath isn't good for much." "It's as good as yours." [Laughter and confusion.] Well, it went on. I went up to Mr. J——. Said I, Mr. J——, that is an infernal falsehood. I said it in a whisper. It was an ugly word for me. Paul spoke more dignified. Paul said, "O full of all subtlety and all mischief, thou child of the devil, thou enemy of all righteousness, wilt thou not cease to pervert the right ways of the Lord." That is what Paul said. I went the other way. [Laughter.] Now, I hope you will forgive me; it was an ugly expression, and was not made in public.

Now I come to the notes of the reverend reporter in a neighboring paper. He states that "the closing scene, on a certain occasion, was one of great excitement." He says, "Such was the decided victory achieved by the champion of colonization, and so fully convinced were the people, that Mr. A. was not allowed to say one single word, but was stamped and hissed down." Stamped and hissed down! "Whenever he arose to speak," he continues, "nine cheers were given to the side that he favored and three groans were given to me." "That was a defeat," he declared, "that he never had in Norristown before." That is true. I got it. It is a wonder I survived it. We will pass on. The reverend gentleman gives me a little tickle because I would not continue the debate. He says I was scared. Evidently, and in fact, I was. When I heard about the three thousand miles of coast, and that eight hundred thousand people had been emancipated in three years, —that had been emancipated by the Liberian colony; and when I heard other things, I declare I was scared. Like Randolph with his history. A fight occurred in the street; on making inquiry about it he was told so many different stories that he said, "If that is the history, I am done with it; I am done writing history." Well, this was a signal defeat. My dear friends, it was very much like the defeat of the Apostle Paul at the city of Ephesus. He went to make a speech, and the people gathered in a great multitude to hear him. He tried to push his way into the theatre. Great man! great man! And when the people heard him they were full of wrath, and cried out, saying, Great is Diana of the Ephesians. Paul was defeated, hissed, hooted, and stamped down. [Laughter.] [Reads further from the report.]

Now we come to another point. "Mr. A. denied that the British government imposed the slaves upon the colonists of this country." I will tell you what Mr. A. did. He attempted to ridicule the expression that the British government forced the slaves upon the colonists. [He here spoke of the "tea" and of the "stamp" act.] He remarked that he brought forward the two best histories of the United States to show that a Dutch ship in 1620 brought slaves to the port of Jamestown; and also admitted that other ships brought them in, and that the settlers brought those slaves because they were too lazy to work themselves, and they were not forced. That is what I said, and who dares deny it? Not a soul of you! [Reads a clause in the Constitution of the United States.] [Judge Story.] Now, what is this movement for,—all this about the British forcing slaves upon us, and our government being the first to drive down the African slave trade? What does this mean? It means, my friends and fellow-citizens, a contemptible apology. Our fathers did right and nobly in some respects; and their sons are trampling upon every right of man, every claim of God, and every principle of benevolence and reason. These people, what are they doing? They are now coming upon us of the North and trampling upon us, sweeping away the solemn contracts like the cobweb, breaking in upon the "old thirteen," and determined to plant slavery all over the country. These are to be apologized to, not for what they have done but for what their fathers have done. That is the argument, this the object. Colonization began with slaveholders and their apologists. Amer. Enc., Vol. III, 328.—

"A caste (composed of the free blacks) is formed in the state, below the salutary influence of public opinion, cut off from all hope of improving their condition, degraded, ignorant, and vicious themselves, and leaving the same legacy of humiliation and shame to their children. A common descent and color unite them to the slaves, and render them the fit agents for fomenting insurrection among them. On this account they have become objects of suspicion and alarm in the slave-hold-ing states, and the owners of slaves consider it impolitic and dangerous to emancipate their negroes, since they contribute to increase the strength of a dangerous class." This state of things gave rise to the colonization society.

"So early as 1777 the plan was proposed by Jefferson in the Legislature of Virginia."—Judge Jay. December 23, 1816, the Legislature of Virginia passed a resolution request-ing the Governor to correspond with the President of the United States for the purpose of obtaining a territory on the coast of Africa to serve as an asylum for such persons of color as are now free and may desire the same, and for those who may hereafter be emancipated. Henry Clay said: "This cause proposes to rid our own country of a useless and pernicious if not a dangerous population, and contemplates the spreading of the arts of civilized life and the possible redemption from ignorance and barbarism of a benighted quarter of the globe." Dr. Finley, according to Mr. P., urged three great objects: First, to rid ourselves of the free blacks; second, to benefit them; third, to benefit Africa. Mr. P. showed that the dispo-sition to emancipate is not so great as it was a few years ago. He said: "The Legislature of Virginia a few years ago came very near abolishing slavery altogether from the state, and would have done it long since had it not been for the radico-politico Abolitionists who entered the state, and with their fiery speeches and incendiary documents excited the slaves to thoughts of blood and murder, and to a fearful extent were in-strumental in bringing about the Southampton massacre. And who has not heard of that fearful tragedy? Mr. P. showed that the matter could not be denied; there it stood in charac-ters of blood, and all might read. Colonization was there as an angel of mercy, spreading out her balmy wings to shelter and protect the poor negro, and was well nigh bringing about his liberty. But the dark-winged demon of rabid abolitionism came and dashed from his hand the cup of liberty he was about to sip, and riveted upon him much more tightly the chains of his bondage. Colonization has many characters. It makes love to the great ones of the earth, and tramples and crushes the weak. But abolition is plain, straightforward and fearless.

Mr. Aaron left notes only of the preceding speech. The above was written out by a reporter.

COLONIZATION.

To a Local Journal.

Mr. Editor—The Rev. R. R. Gurley, the most eminent advocate of African colonization for more than thirty years, and the Rev. Mr. Quay, the present agent of the Pennsylvania branch of the American Colonization Society, addressed a public meeting in the largest church in Norristown on Monday evening, the 16th inst., after public notice given in the churches the day before. I attended, expecting a house full of listeners as earnest as myself. From fifty to sixty persons were present, and many of them were Abolitionists of the various stripes of that original and unmanageable portion of society. I heard the conclusion of a prayer, delivered in cadences so deadly deep and dull as are seldom used when a man wants anything. It was stated, not prayed, that "God had made of one blood all nations of men to dwell on all the face of the earth, and had appointed the bounds of their habitation," etc. This last clause with some emphasis, as if to show that the American Colonization Society had to help fix the localities for fear of mistake.

SAMUEL AARON.

AN ADDRESS

DELIVERED BY MR. AARON ON SUNDAY, JULY 8, 1855.

AMERICAN INDEPENDENCE AND INSTITUTIONS.

Righteousness exalteth a nation, but sin is a reproach to any people.—*Solomon.*

American Independence, its antecedent causes and subsequent effects, must remain to the orator and the sage, not merely a flowery but a fruitful theme for ages to come. The waking up, three hundred years ago, of the human intellect to catch a glimpse of that Heavenly vision, the vision of personal and rational freedom, freedom for the body and freedom for the soul—a vision which the human heart had for thousands of years panted to realize, but which mistaken priests and tyrant kings had taught to be impossible on earth—was the dawn, the earliest gleam of that glorious liberty which crowns this Western World.

The loud shout of the nations that answered to the battle cry of Luther, was the morning song of freedom; the whirlwinds of revolution and war that swept over all civilized lands for two centuries, were like the breath of God to cleanse the seed of righteous principles and waft it hither to be planted in this Western wilderness.

The harrowing power of British pride and tyranny, which meant to tear out the roots of human hope, that had been watered with Pilgrim tears along our Western Atlantic border, only served to give them a deeper, healthier grasp of Freedom's chosen soil.

But, to speak without a figure of the great preliminaries which prepared mankind for the vast experiment now making on this Western Continent by the mingled tribes of men, to urge on human progress and develop human destiny.

Three hundred and thirty years ago, Martin Luther said, "We will believe in and worship God alone; we will look for His justifying favor, and the eternal joys of His salvation to the merits of Jesus Christ; His Bible shall remain no longer in an unknown language, chained to the rostrum of a Popish Bishop, with its lids padlocked together; it shall be written in the mother tongue of every nation, spread open before every eye; aye, and every man and every woman shall in the light of conscience and of reason be the sole, exclusive judge of the doctrines which it teaches, and the duties it imposes, accountable to God alone for mistakes and disobedience." "Amen! Amen!!" shouted the sturdy toilers of Germany, the yeomanry of England, and the lively artisans of France! "No," growled the Pope; " I will sooner burn you all with the timber of your forests, or beneath the thatches of your own hovels. I will burn you in a transient, present blaze, and then hurl you into a future, everlasting fire! My voice is the voice of God. I hold the keys of earth and heaven. All, from the prince on the throne to the beggar in the straw, shall put their souls into my hand, and cleanse their consciences by my absolution." "Even so," responded the Emperor of Germany; "my sword of steel shall bring all under the staff of Peter, or cut them in pieces." " Not the people of my dominions," said Frederick of Saxony; "they are growing intelligent and fit to think for themselves in religion, and may do so, provided they obey my laws." " But," rejoined the people themselves, at last, "if Luther be right as to the divine beneficence providing food for each individual soul, we think it follows that he meant a little more for our starving bodies than we get, and that you kings and princes should make a fairer distribution." " Be quiet," said the Rulers; "the people must obey the laws; the powers that be are ordained of God! He that resists the king, resists the deity." " But," said the common mass, "the Ruler is only legitimate when he is the minister of God for the good of all; a terror to evil workers, and the praise of them that do well."

Luther, great as he was, now inconsistent with his own first principles, began to hush into a slavish apathy the people whom he had roused. " Be still," he said; "rest satisfied with the bread of life, and mind not that which perishes." "But," replied the outraged, "Godliness is profitable unto all things, having the promise of the life that now is, and also of that which is to come! You have taught us our rights spiritual; we will improve on your suggestive lessons, and look after our rights natural." Thus loud and fierce discussion came, then civil and bloody war. The spirit of liberty, defeated in Germany, but not slain, escaped into France, wounded and bleeding, and roused the Huguenots to contend in a bloody struggle with a power beyond their strength. They triumphed, however, in argument, eloquence and wisdom; and driven from their native land, the remnant of an almost universal slaughter, they carried their principles to foreign homes, and a few found a refuge on these wild shores.

But liberty kindled her warmest fire in the Anglo-Saxon soul. Her sons in England said, "Let us limit our king; let us teach him that he is only our minister; a magistrate under the people, for them, rather than over them." Henry the VIII. thundered in reply, "I will be both Pope and King; the fountain of law and gospel, too." He was fierce and persevering. The people quailed; they saw the light at a distance, but only gazed and waited. The King, however, had snapped the chains of Popery, and thus had taught that monarchy, too, a weaker power, might fall by a bold and persevering hand. He died furious, though broken-hearted, that mortals should resist his will. Then Edward, the thoughtful boy, wept for seven years over the havoc of slaughtered martyrs, which his father's fury had entailed upon him; and died, too tender to endure that iron age. Then came the bloody Mary. A bigot herself, she must needs obtain, by her own courtship, a Spanish bigot for a husband, and the sanguinary pair determined to carry all England back to Rome. She would weld in the fires that roasted three hundred Protestants the chain which Henry, her father, had broken, and which had bound her people to the Pope. But she made the flame too hot, and the fetters she intended to fasten were only melted in the blaze. She perished, stricken of God, and cursed by mankind. Men thanked heaven that she was gone, and took courage for the young tree of liberty, when even she could not utterly blast it. Then followed the haughty and talented Elizabeth in a reign of forty-five years. She clearly demonstrated that an imperious Protestant English woman could with impunity defy the Pope, the assumed vice-gerent of the Almighty; and by thus trampling on the tradition of Divine Right, she taught mankind to follow her bold example.

Next came the Stewarts of Scotland. The first proved that kings are not always born with brains, and lived and died an object of contempt. The second used badly, falsely and rashly what brains he had, and lost his head, a royal martyr, in a civilized Christian nation, to the cause of perjury and despotism. The men who doomed him to die were mostly true lovers of freedom, and cherished her growth in the new world of America. At this crisis rose Oliver Cromwell, the best single embodiment of a sturdy Englishman; honest in principle, vigorous in mind, steady in purpose, unwearied in toil, and fearless in execution. He proved to his countrymen and all the world, that a man may be born to rule, to make laws and to enforce them, without having a queen for his mother; an invaluable lesson, by which our great Republic has, in many instances, vastly profited.

Then, in the reaction, in contrast with Cromwell, the Puritan, came the third Stuart, the laughing, revelling, wasteful, lying Charles II., as if to show mankind how inferior is gay folly to serious wisdom.

Last of this race was James the II., a monster of perfidy and cruelty. For three years and nine months he swam, on the back of Jeffreys, in the blood of Englishmen, determined to torture his Protestant subjects back to Popery, and to substitute blind submission for free enquiry. But then the land vomited him out, and from that day forth, Great Britain, with all her faults, has been a progressive, reformatory nation. Let us ever remember that she is our mother, a surly, ungenial parent to be sure; but still the mother of our nature and our principles, if not the kind nurse of our weakness and infirmity. The bravest and most generous of her sons and daughters have been the actual ancestors of our noblest men and women; and every throe and convulsive agony of that most wonderful of all the nations brought forth children of liberty to be reared in this nursery of political and moral freedom. The warlike, fervent Puritan, who sung the loud praises of Jehovah, God of Hosts, and the quiet, unresisting Quaker, who worshipped in silence, Immanual, the Prince of Peace, all sought a refuge here from that impudence of power which invaded their private thoughts; and learned, through Roger Williams, and afterwards through William Penn, to be tolerant of mere opinions, to regulate the social relations of life by human laws, and to leave religious persuasions and conscientious scruples to God alone. So every party planted its own peculiar tree; the Quaker, his Quaker tree; the Presbyterian, his Presbyterian tree; the Baptist and Methodist, each his tree; even the Episcopalian brought over a seedling quite different from the parent stem, and it took root and bloomed in the wilderness. But every one was a tree of liberty and brought forth the sweet fruits of freedom; and every man sat down with his wife and children under his own, rejoicing; none daring to molest him or make him afraid.

Such is a hasty and most imperfect sketch of the preliminary process employed by Divine Providence to furnish material of which to construct the Temple of Liberty. The timber was hewn, like Solomon's cedar beams, in the far off forests of Lebanon, and brought by ships on sea to the place of construction. The marble was shaped for the walls by many a careful blow in the distant quarries, then borne to the spot and laid in silence. God would not have His temple where the Heathen would profane it, but bore His people and their principles to this chosen land. That men needed preparation by the sifting process of mental and moral conflict carried on for centuries in Protestant countries of the old world, is evident from the utter blindness and inaptitude for freedom of the Spanish and Portugese colonies on this continent. It is not by a hasty, bloody war, kindled up in a spasm of excitement, like those in Mexico and South America, thirty years ago, that a nation wins its liberty. Our own revolution was not so much a cause as an effect of freedom. People may shake off a foreign yoke, and fasten upon themselves one of tenfold weight. They must think and pray and struggle with heart and soul, and seek light from God above, and study well

His works and ways below, before they can bring forth new order, beauty and truth, from old confusion, grim abuse and hoary falsehood.

It was, then, after a vast and almost infinite series of human events, that our national freedom became ready to be born. Men had to examine long and reason much before they could see that "all men are created equal" in their claims to justice before God and especially before man; that government is made for the people, and not the people for the government; that all magistrates from high to low are only the people's instruments, and that a man or woman, even the poorest, is infinitely greater than the highest magistrate as such; that natural rights are so much a man's own, that no power on earth can take them from him, and inhere so strongly in his person that he cannot himself give them away. It took time to reach these conclusions; but at last our fathers reached them. They proclaimed them in the thrilling tones which rung out among the nations like the trump of jubilee. Multitudes of men politically dead and buried under despotisms, started in mental resurrection; and from that time to this the political earth has been quivering and heaving with the life that has been struggling for birth in its bosom.

But what have we been doing here, freed by a bloody struggle from British power, and cut off by vast oceans from fear and danger? Some noble things, which should be ever sacredly and thankfully commemorated. The sublimest written theory of human rights which had been up to that time put forth in form, the Declaration of American Independence, was the work of fifty-six brave and upright men, whom, I trust, we shall never forget. It expressed not only bright and generous thoughts, but it required almost superhuman courage and resolution. One of those heroes said at signing, with equal wit and firmness, "Now, gentlemen, we must all hang together by our own consent, or hang apart by British authority." You are acquainted with the terms of this great paper; I need not repeat them. It placed society on the broad, level platform of justice; denied all inherent authority, except that of inborn rights; and asserted that from these all government must spring. This writing and signing was noble in those delegates; and the support of it was noble in the people. That support involved a struggle; not so much a bloody agony of war as a trial of long patience and painful endurance, requiring far more faith and firmness than the burning of gunpowder and the braving of cannon balls. When the British saw that our fathers, like the good Washington, were governed by a principle rather than maddened by revengeful, murderous passions, they knew that such a people were invincible, and would be free. Our feeling was the love of liberty and not the lust for power; and that, when intelligent and pure, will conquer all opposition. These acts and sentiments were sublime and worthy of a great people.

Our fathers told God and all the world that they believed in and relied on his providence, and invoked his protection and his sanction upon the pledge of their lives, their fortunes, and their sacred honor. Their prayer was, "Let us be free; commit to us the grand experiment to make our laws, to choose our magistrates, and work out our destiny, exempt from the selfish interference of lords and kings; and we will remember thee, Almighty Father, imitate thy justice and copy thy benevolence." This aspiration and responsibility was sublime.

When the pressure of war which bound them in one—*E Pluribus Unum*—was over, and repellant local interests threatened to divide them, they determined to form a general constitution, and this was its basis: "We, the people of the United States, in order to form a more perfect union, establish justice, ensure domestic tranquillity, provide for the common defence, promote the general welfare, and secure the blessings of liberty to ourselves and our posterity, do ordain and establish this constitution for the United States of America." These propositions are grand and Godlike. They cover, not a favored portion, a class or a clique, but "the people," every human being, male and female. Under them must be no discord, but perfect union; no oppression, but unyielding, established justice; tranquillity is ensured by cherishing impartially the rights of all; all men in common shall be defended from injury; general and universal, not merely a selfish or local welfare, shall be promoted; and last, and best of all, these almost heavenly blessings shall be secured forever to ourselves and our posterity.

This bright theory resembles the millennial glory; and what have been its fruits? Why, really, the mightiest nation on earth has been born in a day; mightiest in its power of defence, the only violent power that a nation needs, a wall of freeborn hearts; mightiest in its moral example, to prove that intelligent and virtuous men need no other king than the Majesty on high; mightiest in its utilities and locomotion, making the wilderness rejoice and blossom as the rose, and casting up highways among the nations both by land and sea, so that many may run to and fro, and knowledge may increase. Our nation has been mighty in its attractions, so that crushed outcasts have flocked hither from many lands and found plenty, peace and home. Here woman has found, or is finding, her highest, noblest career; the acknowledged equal of man in education, talents and rights, she becomes the intelligent, high-souled mother of a generation still more progressive and enlightened than our own; and there begins, in this land, to be seen, what ought to have been plain before, that her capacity to perform is the best index of her duty; and that the radius of her own intellect is the best measure wherewith to describe her sphere.

Further still, the strife between labor and capital, that terrible element of discord and suffering among the older nations, is not here, on one side, an imperious cry, "Drudge or starve!" nor on the other a hungry tiger's growl for "bread or blood." I cannot say, with a flowery orator, on a late occasion, in a contiguous grove, that this and nearly every other possible social and moral problem has been solved, and that American legislation has nothing more to do. But I do rejoice to feel that this question of work and wages is becoming every day more and more a question of mutual, calm, deliberate, determined, intelligent discussion; and, trusting in the kind wisdom of God to guide the honest efforts of men, I cherish the hope that the day is near when moral laws, laws of benevolence and equity, shall regulate production and distribution as harmoniously as physical laws control the planetary forces. I trust that soon every family shall have its little

spot of ground, its own pure, beautiful home, inalienable like
the inheritance of the Hebrews, to be invaded by no cunning
speculator, nor torn away by the greedy creditor's relentless
hand. May the time come when pensions shall be given, if
need be, to the faithful, worn-out laborer in the arts of peace,
even more than they are now to the transient and often worthless straggler in the bloody acts of war; when every virtuous
young man and woman who need it shall receive a premium
at marriage, as men now get patents for useful inventions;
when the floating currency of banks shall be taxed in the
hands of those who hold it, upon the institution that issues it;
when the hoarded bonds of covetous wealth shall be reported
by the debtors who must pay them, and taxed upon them who
hold them; and when the rich shall be assessed beyond the
poor, not as now in an arithmetical, but in a geometrical proportion.

Last of all, it is to the glory of our country, that a moral,
reformatory spirit is more and more pervading its legislation,
preventive rather than punitive. As every good parent en-
deavors to prevent the seeds of vice from taking root in the
hearts of his offspring, so a wise and virtuous commonwealth
will look after her children, and see that their souls are not
corrupted by those selfish foes of the human race that are
found in every community. It is therefore matter of devout
thanksgiving to behold our various states, one after another,
crushing the eggs and tearing up the nests of the crocodiles
which give being to drunkards and gamblers and licentious
ruffians. The smiles of heaven must grow more bright when
its inmates look down on the messengers of love and peace
below, who, like the Hebrew prophet, have struck with devout
hand the barren rock of legislation and caused the healing
waters of a nation's benificence to flow for the satisfying of the
fainting heart and the cleansing of the neglected, degraded
soul. The proud monarchies and fierce republics of old, and
the refined and heartless civilization of our modern era, have
always poured the public treasures into the vortex of war, or
employed them to gild the monuments of victory, or at best
lavished them on works of mere national utility and glory.
The wail of the God-stricken, of the lame, the deaf and the

blind, was unheard or disregarded by the public ear of Greece and Rome; and modern nations give millions to destroy, but little to save, mankind. Not so here. In our land free discussion and a free press are like the harp of Orpheus; and the genius of eloquent Philanthropy plays upon its strings. The stubborn trees and hard rocks of public indifference are moved; the greedy, voracious beasts of party politics are softened and charmed. The heart of the nation grows tender when the good Miss Dix and her loving fellow laborers make their appeal; its coffers are opened; the palace-asylum springs from the ground, a garden-like Eden blooms around it; "the eyes of the blind are opened, and the ears of the deaf unstopped; the lame man leaps as a harp, and the tongue of the dumb sings." The flickering ray of intellect is cherished even in the idiot's soul; drop after drop of the oil of gentleness and love, applied for many years to that dim spark, is found to kindle it to a flame of happy consciousness and heavenly hope. The poorest man's child, whose birth in many a land is a great sorrow to his mother, and whose life is a burden to himself, is here invited, a welcome guest, to the common "feast of reason," and lured to the race of intellect and honor by the side of the rich man's son. The commonwealth says to every one, "I am thy impartial mother, and will feed thee with the sweets of wisdom."

Such is a feeble sketch of the daylight of America. Now, behold her darkness, her shame and her dishonor! Oh, my country! art thou at once the greatest and the meanest of nations? Truly, our institutions present to the world a paradox, which must, by turns, delight and terrify the good and the wicked, and at all times puzzle the wise. It is a crime against our statute and organic laws, to deprive one individual of a single privilege; but it is the glory of those who control the land to rob four million human beings of every right, and of themselves besides, their children, their bodies and their minds. Our national theory says we must "establish justice and secure liberty to ourselves and our posterity"; our national practice aims to build up wrong and outrage and make slavery universal and eternal. "Hide the outcast, and betray not him that wandereth," said the oldest law-giver; and "no man shall be deprived of life, liberty or property without due process of law," is the language of our own Constitution. "But, thou shalt surely seize the friendless stranger and deliver him to the man-thief who claims him as a slave," is the most strenuous command of our Federal Government since 1850, to a free people. Its surest protection and highest rewards are bestowed on him who is most zealous in that cause; but the man who scorns to be a bloodhound incurs its bitterest fury. The pettiest federal appointment is conditioned on a zeal for slavery; and men without intellect or standing are fit for national service, if they have yelled fiercely on the track of a hunted man. But, should Washington return to earth, invested as he is with sacred memories and crowned with world-wide and undying fame, he would be unfit, because he hated slavery, to command a regiment or collect the revenue at Charlestown; and Jefferson, the Solon of Democracy, and writer of the great Declaration, could not be appointed Librarian to Congress, nor Minister to St. Domingo.

The most popular feature of American Christianity is a bitter hatred to the practical lovers of impartial freedom; and no man is hired to say one prayer for Congress, unless he believes that Paul sent back the slave Onesimus. The Protestant Bible and religious books and tracts are scattered broadcast over all the earth, and are declared to be the leaves of the tree of life for the healing of the nations, while the voice of the living preacher rings out in every tongue. In carrying on this great mission, the various governments are conciliated, deceived or defied, on the plea that God has sent a message which every man must hear. But, lo! the Southern half of this great republic quashes this plea, with the entire approval of those who urge it, shuts out from four millions of its people the message and the messenger; sells women at high prices into prostitution to send the Gospel to China; gashes the flesh of the slave at home who would spell the name of Jesus; tortures or murders the man that would teach him. Meanwhile it claims to possess the purest religion and the warmest piety to be found on earth; and, by the churches of the North, that claim is widely conceded. All sins in our land are discussed and denounced in sermons, books and tracts, from the crime of murder down to the gaiety of the ball-room, and the love of show which sets a feather on a matron's bonnet or a ring on a maiden's finger; but the act of tearing infants from their mother's bosoms, or of selling one's beautiful daughter into nameless infamy, or of scourging men and women to deathly toil, is not once named in the catalogue of transgressions, nor does the word "slavery" appear in the millions of pious volumes which are diffused throughout the community. The phrases, "peculiar institutions," "pious masters," and "happy servants," dwell, to be sure, on many a consecrated lip, where logic, eloquence and "piety" combine to save our Union and the "church"; but contempt and starvation in the North from persons of "standing," and curses, hemp and faggots, in the South, await the man who preaches equal liberty and justice to a l throughout the land.

To maintain the harmony of such a brotherhood, and cherish and extend the spirit of such a patriotism, in willing subordination to the two hundred thousand voting dealers in human flesh, is the way, the only way, according to the teachings of Church and State, to preserve "this glorious Union;" and such an agreement of North and South and East and West —"is the Union," the salvation of which, our orator of the Fourth assured us, would be cheaply bought by the life-blood of every soul in this great commonwealth. "*Credat Judæus Apella!*" On the contrary, if this be our Union, and these its purposes, the curse of Heaven and the scorn of earth shall fall upon it; the irrepressible instincts of nature, controlled by the fury of revenge, shall wake up massacre; civil and servile strife shall ripen to anarchy, and our boasted institutions rot into despotism.

But let our "Union" be made a means to the glorious end of impartial justice and equal liberty; let it be a safe asylum for every fugitive from oppression and outrage; let it be an hospital, where the wounded and the broken hearted, the sinful and the sorrowing, may find healing, purity and peace; let it be a sacred temple, wide as the continent, high as heaven and free as air, in which every human being may keep his own conscience here below, and worship, at its dictates, his God above; then shall our "Union" be the light and the glory of all nations. It shall attract the hearts and win the confidence of men, and pay back their tribute with peace and freedom. It shall point out to rational princes a higher elevation than their thrones; and make an injured peasantry more noble than their former kings.

> For this our prayers shall rise,
> To this our hearts shall cling;
> 'Till earth become a paradise,
> And God our only King!

SELECTIONS.

ODE TO SIMPLICITY.

Artless Simplicity, wilt thou inspire me
    To sing of thy beauties in strains of thy own?
O, breathe through my lines, and with energy fire me,
    To paint thy soft charms to the pompous unknown.

Thy mien how engaging, how graceful each feature,
    Thy form has the semblance of beauty above;
The first and the favorite offspring of Nature,
    The sister to Virtue, companion of Love.

How modest, how humble the train that surround thee;
    How sweet are thy pleasures, how often denied,
How seldom beheld as the prophet first found thee
    With Adam in Eden and Eve his fair bride.

Adorn'd with thy beauties and clad with thy graces,
    They needed no tinsel to heighten their charms;
In bow'rs breathing odors, in halcyon embraces
    They felt divine raptures enclos'd by thy arms.

Yet, mournful delusion! these scenes so endearing
    Were doom'd to be blasted and render'd forlorn;
The specious dissembler, the tempter appearing,
    Pluck'd up the fair primrose and planted the thorn.

He ting'd false enjoyments with colors deceiving,
    He painted the wisdom that thou couldst attain;
Simplicity heard, and, too fondly believing,
    Partook of the pleasure,—but, ah! it was pain.

With shame thou wast cover'd, thy loveliness vanish'd,
    The groves odorif'rous beheld thee no more;
From Paradise quickly thy train were all banish'd,
    And its children left naked thy loss to deplore.

Thy charms now forgotten, unseen, undesired,
    No longer man woos thee to make thee his own;
Parade, pomp and splendor are only admired,
    Whilst thou art forsaken, despis'd or unknown.

Remote from the concourse of follies and fashions,
    Inspiring the notes of the songsters of spring,
The woodland inhabitants, breathing thy passions,
    Thy beauties instinctively, artlessly sing.

Oh! if thou art found in the dwellings of mortals,
  Where, where shall I seek thee, Simplicity? say.
Thou art not enclos'd by magnificent portals,
  Where tyrants command and where menials obey.

Perchance with the school-boy thou climbest the mountain
  To see the wild cuckoo or nest of the dove;
Perchance thou art found at the crystalline fountain
  Where young men and maidens are dreaming of love.

Perhaps with the shepherd thy footsteps are wand'ring,
  Whilst tuning his lute to some wild rural strain;
Whilst thro' the green pastures his flocks are meand'ring,
  And cropping the daisies that tincture the plain.

That household contains thee whose members united
  Are paying their vows to their sov'reign above;
Thou bearest, sweet maiden, the tribute, delighted,
  On angelic wings to the mansions of love.

And the era approaches, unspeakably glorious,
  When mankind in concert shall socially join
To give thee kind welcome, o'er fashion victorious,
  And bury their pomp at the base of thy shrine.

Then vice, fraud and calumny, envy and slander,
  Shall sink to the regions of darkness again;
And virtue, simplicity, truth, love and candor,
  Take up their abode with the children of men.

1819.

LINES

Written on the death of a young girl, aged 15 years.

Life triumphed in the blooming girl,
  The parents' hope, the brother's joy;
Death, envious Death, beheld the scene,
  And hastened, ruthless, to destroy.

Death triumphed in the fell disease,
  Made the young form a lifeless clod;
But Life, unconquer'd, kept the soul
  And bore it to the throne of God.

Death grimly closed the stony vault,
  And locked the portals of the grave;
But Life, triumphant, grasped the key,
  Constant in love and strong to save.

And, lo! the resurrection voice
  Which woke the dead of Palestine,
Shall call to Rachel's sleeping dust,
  And raise it to a life divine.   S. AARON.

A PLATFORM SCENE.

On the 22d of February, 1862, Colonel James W. Wall was invited by the Common Council of Burlington to deliver an address on the "Compromises of the Constitution." Colonel Wall, it will be remembered, had been arrested as a rebel sympathizer, incarcerated in Fort Lafayette, and was subsequently released without parole. In his address, he took the ground that the Constitution was a compromise. The hall was crowded, many Republicans who opposed his views being present. There was no disturbance.

Rev. Samuel Aaron was invited to answer Colonel Wall. The following is a copy of the notice published in the Burlington papers:

The Rev. Samuel Aaron is to give a lecture, admittance free, at the City Hall, Thursday evening, the 27th instant, at 7.30 o'clock. Subject: "Our Constitution." He means to elaborate the idea that the Constitution of the United States is not a compromise between right and wrong, but a covenant between the whole nation and all its parts to establish justice and secure and cherish liberty; to protect patriotism and punish traitors.

The invitation was extended to the Mayor of Burlington and other prominent citizens of the place, and it was understood Mr. Aaron's remarks would be a reply to the arguments of Colonel Wall. When the lecturer commenced his discourse the hall was crowded, two-thirds of the congregation being ladies. There were no indications of a disturbance. Mr. Aaron proceeded, and among his first declamatory remarks was an assault upon General McClellan, who, he said, had been frightened by wooden guns.

A voice demanded, "What have you to say against General McClellan?"

The speaker said he was only commenting upon facts.

"Yes," replied his interrogator, "If McClellan had a black stripe down his back he would suit you better."

Mr. Aaron proceeded again for some ten minutes. He spoke of John Brown as being a martyr to principle—as a meek, heavenly-minded man, who went down south with peaceful intentions; whose sole object was to free the bondman from his shackles; and the bloody assassins murdered him. He went on to say that Colonel Wall had recently delivered a lecture in the same hall, in which he had charged the abolitionists with denouncing the Constitution as a "covenant with death and a league with hell." He did not believe this, unless the declaration of Judge Taney was correct—that the negro was not a citizen. If that decision were true, then he (the Rev. Mr. Aaron) did not hesitate to declare that the Constitution was a "league with the devil and a covenant with hell"; and the sooner it was abolished the better.

Here there was a volley of eggs aimed at the speaker, but none of which touched him. The confusion which followed was almost indescribable. Ladies became frantic with alarm, and some jumped from the hall windows, about eight feet from the ground. None were, however, seriously injured—a sprained ankle being about the most serious damage. The lecturer stopped during the occurrence, but subsequently resumed his remarks.

He dwelt with severity upon the last Administration, denouncing with particular vehemence President Buchanan. He spoke of William Lloyd Garrison as a very much abused man, and described him as a great defender of liberty. He declared that the men who abused Wendell Phillips were unworthy to tie his shoe latches, and said that he (Mr. Aaron) had been for years laboring to bring the public mind to a right way of thinking on this subject, and that the people of the North, he was proud to say, were flocking to the platform he had stood upon for so many years.

Here there was another volley of eggs and intense excitement. The Mayor, who was on the platform with the speaker, left it for the purpose of suppressing the disturbance. As he proceeded to the entrance of the hall he found it blocked up by exasperated people, and a city constable was found in the condition of being throttled by one of the rioters. * * *

BANKS AND FINANCIERS AND CURRENCY.

Mr. Aaron in "Truth," February 10, 1842.

The utmost efforts have been used for a number of years past, by the keen-witted and glib-tongued idlers of our land, to convince the great body of the people, the producing mass, that the prime object of legislation should be to aid the aforesaid idle schemers in getting rich, and the wealthy in increasing their abundance, so that these two classes might, of the fullness of their bounty, deal out enough and to spare to the sweaty-browed laborer and care-worn toiler for daily bread. Their language, meant if not spoken, has been, "Help the gifted financier and protect the moneyed class, and they will make money plentiful and good, and take care of all the rest." This experiment has been tried in Pennsylvania on a magnificent scale, by the agency of mammoth banks and financiering on public works, and has resulted in bestowing unearned and sometimes princely wealth on a few persons, and saddling a public debt of forty millions on the Commonwealth, and a much greater loss than forty millions on private individuals, many of them widows and orphans, reduced from an easy competence to actual destitution.

This wretched state of things has resulted in a great measure from the arrogant assumption that the honest laboring people are incompetent to ascertain and promote their own best interests, and that, therefore, men of talents must manufacture for them wealth and happiness. These brilliant financiers and active guardians of the public weal have given the people plenty of promissory rags instead of their hard cash. This seeming plenty of money has made us all luxurious; and while foreign nations have shut out our produce our financiers have sent them our specie to pay in part for what we should have done without. And so we have European luxuries and irredeemable bank notes, and a foreign debt of two hundred millions, instead of hard money and homespun independence.

Now, when the people at large shall be really satisfied that their own common sense and home-bred honesty are as

essential to public as to private welfare, they will insist on less
legislation, and on none at all of a partial character; they will
see that a free people should have no laws to help one man
up by putting another down; that they need none to aid them
in getting rich; but solely to protect them in the sacred
rights of property and person; to protect them effectually in
doing what they please, while they do no harm to themselves
or others.   The desire and the right of an honest man are to
be let alone and have a chance to reach that standing to which
his real worth entitles him.   Away with the idea of giving
some men power and authority by law on the pretext that
they will use them for the good of others.

And what gives any useful article of exchange its real
value?   The amount of human labor bestowed upon it, is the
answer of honest common sense.   Why is a bushel of potatoes
worth fifty cents?   Because it requires as much labor to raise
the bushel of potatoes as it does to find, and dig, and melt,
and refine, and shape, and coin the silver ore in half a dollar.
A favorable season will produce more potatoes for the same
labor, and then they will be cheaper.   But does a slip of bank
paper take its value from the labor expended on it?   No.
It is, then, good for nothing, unless it represents the specie it
promises to pay.